M000226628

The Way I Hate Him

USA TODAY BESTSELLING AUTHOR

MEGHAN QUINN

Prologue

HAYES

"How good are you at giving head?"

The girl straddling my lap, tits bouncing in my face, a G-string being the only thing on her body, leans in with a smirk. "I've never had any complaints."

I wet my lips and rest my head against the back of the couch. "Show me."

A half-empty tequila bottle is on the coffee table in front of us, salt is sprinkled all over, and her tits are still wet from where I was licking the salt off. Lime wedges are scattered along the floor with her clothes and my shirt.

And . . . I'm not really feeling it.

Fuck, what's her name again?

I know she told me . . .

Kendall?

Kinsey?

Kaliope?

She scoots off my lap and kneels between my legs. Before she can undo my pants, I ask, "What's your name again?"

Her big blue eyes stare up at me, and she seductively says, "Tara."

Tara?

Oh fuck, I was way off.

A snort pops out of me because, Jesus, I couldn't have been more wrong.

"Is there something wrong with my name?" she asks, sitting back on her heels.

"No." I shake my head.

"Then why are you laughing?"

Yeah, dickhead, why are you laughing?

"Your hands tickled my dick," I say because hell, I'm drunk and can barely hold it together. Her brow rises, and yeah, I realize the truth is probably better. "I thought your name was Kendall. I wasn't close to guessing it correctly."

Her brow pulls together with disdain. "Who the hell is Kendall?"

"You got me," I say just as a knock sounds on my door, and my agent pops his head in. "Dude," I say, gesturing to Kendall . . . I mean, Tara. Jesus Christ.

Ruben winces. "I have to talk to you."

"It's fine," Tara says as she grabs her dress and stands. "I was leaving."

My dick wants me to protest, but I don't have it in me, so I watch as she slips her dress over her head, shimmying it over her large tits. Such a shame. I would have had fun with her.

But I'll tell you one thing—I'm never fucking desperate for pussy. Ever.

I'm not the begging kind.

So if she wants to leave, I won't stop her.

And from the pause at the door and the glance over her shoulder at me, I know she wants me to stop her, to beg her to stay. Sorry, not going to fucking happen.

I lift two fingers to my forehead and offer a salute, causing her brows to turn down.

"You're an ass," she says as she pushes past Ruben and leaves.

Yeah, tell me something I don't know.

I lean forward with my elbows on my thighs as Ruben shuts the door to my dressing room and straightens his tie. The man is a killer in negotiations and the smartest man I know, but he's a goddamn dweeb. It's not the first time he's walked in on me with a girl, and it won't be the last, yet he still has the same nauseous and uncomfortable look.

I pour myself another shot of tequila but then lift the bottle to inspect it. We didn't drink that much. "Fuck." I sigh. "I think Matt's stealing from me."

Ruben steps closer and picks my shirt up off the ground. He folds it and gently sets it on the coffee table. "Your assistant?"

"Yeah," I answer. "Things keep going missing, and he's the only one besides you allowed in my private space." I lift an eyebrow. "Unless you're stealing from me?"

Utter shock and disgust cross Ruben's face. "You . . . you can't be serious." He tugs on the cuffs of his paisley button-up shirt. "I would never—"

"I'm kidding, Ruben." I toss the shot back and then lean against the couch again. "What's up?"

"Two things," he says, holding his fingers up. "Carlton called and wants to know when to expect the next album." I roll my eyes.

"Jesus Christ, I told him he'll get it when he gets it. I'm just finishing up his goddamn tour."

"That's what I told him, but since you've recently gone viral again, he wants to capitalize on that."

"I'm sure he does," I say. "Well, I have nothing, so he'll be waiting a while."

"Not even a single?"

3

"Ruben." I stand from the couch and snag the shirt he folded. "You know me better than anyone, do you think I have a single up my sleeve I can just release?"

"Didn't think so, but I thought I'd check." I slip my shirt on. "What would you like me to tell Carlton?"

"I'm working on it."

"Are you?" he asks.

"Nope," I answer, picking up my faded gray baseball hat. "But I will." After slipping it on backward, I grab my phone and place it in my pocket. "What's the second thing?"

Ruben hesitates. "Abel called."

That makes me pause and turn toward Ruben. "Why?"

"Your grandma fell again, fractured her hip. She's been asking for you. She thinks this is the end."

"She thinks every day is the end," I say.

Ruben keeps me from moving toward the door when he says, "Abel thinks she really misses you and will say anything to get you home." Ruben sighs. "I think you need to go back to Almond Bay."

Ahh . . . fuck.

Chapter One

HATTIE

"This is humiliating," I say as I closely approach the place I grew up.

"Listen, no one knows that you failed your last semester. We went over this. You're taking some time off," my best friend Maggie says through the car speakers. "Earning a master's degree isn't easy."

"Says who? It's just like earning your bachelor's."

"I'm trying to help you out. Why won't you let me do that?"

"Because you're bullshitting me," I say with a sigh. "God, Maggie, I don't want to be here."

"I told you, you could stay with me."

"In your San Francisco studio apartment where you sleep on a futon because you'd rather have space for your thriving business?"

Yup, my best friend, Maggie, has a thriving wedding planning business. She's been featured in many bridal magazines and is fully booked until next year. She's been interviewed by a few key celebrities in the Bay Area who might just throw her business into the big leagues.

And she's only twenty-three.

And then there's me. Not that we should compare ourselves, but it's hard not to when I see her living her dream, and I'm still trying to obtain a master's in business management but flunking out.

What am I going to do with that degree? I have no idea . . . manage a business?

God, I'm so fucked.

"The futon is my friend," Maggie says. "And I told you it folds out. There's nothing like a good snuggle at night."

"Not happening. Anyway, I haven't seen Matt in a while. He's returning from tour, and it would be good to rekindle our love."

"Rekindle your love . . . You know, I'm in the business of love, and even hearing you say that is making me gag."

"What do you want me to say? Fuck on every surface?"

"Ew, is that what you're going to do?"

"Ew? Why did you say ew?" I ask.

"Because Matt gives me the ick. You could do so much better than him."

"So you've said," I say with a sigh as I turn onto Almond Ave, aka the main street of Almond Bay, California.

Population 3,239, Almond Bay is on the Northern Californian coast, right above the not-so-famous bay in the shape of an almond. With one whole stoplight in town, we're best known as the birthplace and hometown of the great Ethel O'Donnell-Kerr. Haven't heard of her? Shame on you. Once a bright Broadway star notorious for her renowned leading role in *Annie Get Your Gun*, she spent over thirty-five years on stage and is now the proud owner of our town inn, Five Six Seven Eight. The unofficial town mayor, she makes it her business to know everyone else's business and then selectively spreads the news according to what the news is. Not to mention, she's the community event coordinator, therefore constantly puts on plays, dances, and activities to keep the town together. She's exhausting.

But most importantly, Ethel O'Donnell-Kerr is the matron of the Peach Society.

If you look at Almond Bay from above, the roads connect like an A and have four corners on each end of town. Members of the Peach Society own these four corners. Let me break it down for you:

As you know, Ethel O'Donnell-Kerr owns Five Six Seven Eight. Located in the southeast part of town next to the cliffs that overlook the ocean. Beautiful location.

Second is Dr. Elizabeth Gomez's veterinary clinic. She's the loving, kindhearted lady who you'll find rolling around in the town's park with any animal that approaches her. The nicest of the four, her clinic is situated in the southwest part of town, right next to the post office and the pharmacy/doctor's office.

Third is Coleman's General Store, owned by Dee Dee Coleman in the northeast part of town. The general store has been passed down from generation to generation, and with every generation, it's been given a makeover. It currently has immaculate hardwood floors and beautiful shelving stock-piled with everything you might need. Dee Dee sets the gold standard of what's to be expected from the store owners in town.

And last, By the Slice in the town's northwest, next to the drive-in theater—which is subsequently owned by all four members of the Peach Society. Keesha Johnson is the owner of By the Slice, the pizza shop here in town. Known best for the dip varieties offered for her crisp crust, they range from ranch to honey to something a touch spicier. She has brought in multiple Food Network shows to try her pizza, which has put Almond Bay on the map as a food destination. We don't say that around Ethel, though, because as you know . . . Ethel is the main attraction.

These four cornerstones are the holy grail of Almond Bay as well as their owners. They decide what's allowed in town, hold every business to a high standard, and keep the residents in check.

And why are they called the Peach Society when clearly our town has gone all in on almonds? Because the cornerstones of our town, the holy grail of women, are all lesbians, and that's what they decided to call themselves.

I'm here for it.

"You're seriously going to stay with him?" Maggie asks, clearly disgusted with me.

Matt isn't *that* bad.

Sure, he's had his quirks, and it would be nice if he acknowledged me more when he's on tour. And maybe he forgot about my birthday once, but people get busy. I once forgot to tell him how much I liked his new Nikes when he sent me a picture, and according to him, I committed a sin. So we all apparently make mistakes.

"He's my boyfriend, so . . . yeah, I'll stay with him."

"Or, hear me out. You go to his place, break up with him, and seek refuge somewhere else, like . . . oh, I don't know . . . Hayes Farrow's house?"

"Maggie," I groan, fiercely annoyed with the mention of Hayes. The moment she found out I lived in the same town as the one . . . the only . . . Hayes Farrow—breaker of hearts and delicious musician—she's been clawing at me to go see him. "How many times do I have to tell you? We hate the man, according to my brother, and if anything, I'm a well-trusted sibling who will hate the people my sibling hates. Plus, Hayes Farrow is a giant dick."

"Oooo, I bet he has a giant dick." She never gives up. "And tell me this, if you're supposed to hate him, how come I hear you listening to his music all the time?"

All the time is a bit of a stretch, but . . . *raises hand* guilty.

I might not like the guy. He might be one of the biggest assholes I know, and even though he was born and raised in Almond Bay as well, I refuse to acknowledge he's more famous than Ethel O'Donnell-Kerr—even though he is—because where she has class and pizzazz, he has a backward hat and a grumpy scowl.

But with all that said, I can't help but like his music. He has this sultry, seventies rock vibe which is my favorite genre of all time. He did a cover of Heart's "Barracuda" that made my nipples hard. And thanks to the fact that he likes to wear these low V-cut shirts during his concerts showcasing the apparent muscles he's grown over the past few years, he's become a total heartthrob, filling up every social media platform with videos, pictures, interviews . . . and thirst traps. Even Maggie was drooling over a few collages she found on Instagram. To my dismay, she even reposted them on her stories.

You can't escape him. He's everywhere.

Clearing my throat, I say, "I barely listen to his stuff." Lies, I have a secret Spotify playlist of his songs. "He's overhyped. Not to mention, my boyfriend works for him as his assistant. Did you happen to forget that? If anything, I listen to his music to support my boyfriend."

"I like that you've rationalized all of this in your head."

"I haven't rationalized anything," I say, taking a right on Nutshell Drive toward Matt's apartment. "I'm just stating the facts."

"Whatever makes you feel better, Hattie."

"Well, I'm getting close, so I should go."

"Okay. I miss you already, and if you need anything, you know where to find me. I plan on coming up in a few weeks. I'll reserve a room at the inn because there's no way in hell I'm staying with you and Matt."

There wouldn't be enough room anyway.

"Sounds good."

"Love you."

"Love you too, girl," I say before hanging up and pulling into the back parking lot of Matt's apartment building—if that's what you want to call it. It's two houses broken up into apartments. Matt makes really good money, but he's been wisely saving it rather than paying expensive rent or a mortgage.

He's always been smart like that. We met back in high school. He's a year older than me, and when he graduated and shipped off to San Francisco for school, I followed him. I've been waiting for him to pop the question, and I'm pretty sure he's been waiting for me to finish school, which . . . well, I think we know how that's going. He's been traveling with Hayes anyway, so it's not like a proposal was coming anytime soon.

I can still remember when he got the job with Hayes. He told me to my face he didn't care that there was bad blood between my family and Hayes, but he was taking the job. My brother, Ryland, went on and on about the lack of loyalty, my sister Aubree told me I needed to dump his ass immediately, and Cassidy . . . well, I can't stomach thinking about her right now.

And with all that, I stayed with Matt because . . . because he's my high school sweetheart. And you can't fault the guy for getting a great job with a musician who, I hate to admit . . . is going somewhere. Well, I guess at this point, he's already *gone somewhere*, made a splash, and is living in the glory of his fame.

I turn off my car and head toward the back door of his apartment. I called him ahead of time to let him know I was coming. No one likes a surprise visitor. Also, I wanted to make sure he had time to clean up and shower. He's rabid when he sees me.

I knock on the back door, and as I wait for him to answer, I glance around the back of the building. Even for an apartment/townhome, it's pristine thanks to the Peach Society. I've seen Dee Dee walk around the town early on the weekends before the general store opens, taking notes in her notebook of who's not holding up their end of the town's beautification.

It might be frustrating for proprietors, but then again, the town is immaculate.

The door opens, pulling me out of my thoughts. Matt stands on the other side in a plain blue T-shirt and cargo shorts. His hair is longer than normal, and his face is freshly shaved, something I've never cared for.

"Hey," I say, smiling up at him.

He nods at me. "Good to see you, Hattie."

Good to see me? Uh, kind of formal, don't you think?

I move in for a hug, but to my horror, he palms my forehead, keeping me at a distance.

Excuse me, sir!

We don't stiff-arm each other.

I swat for him to pull me in closer, but he braces his arm, not allowing me an inch closer.

"What are you doing?" I ask him.

"Hattie, we have to talk."

I straighten up so he's no longer palming my head. "Why does that sound like you're going to break up with me?"

He sighs heavily. "Maybe you should come in."

"Matt," I say, confused. "Are you breaking up with me?"

"Unless you want the entire town to hear this, you might want to come inside."

Lips pursed together, my heart hammering in my chest, I reluctantly follow him inside. After we walk up the back steps to his second-floor apartment and enter his living room, he turns toward me.

"I've waited to tell you this long enough." He pauses for

dramatic effect—because that's the kind of man he is. "I don't want to be with you anymore."

Well . . . God, that's a harsh way of putting it.

Couldn't he have sugarcoated it a bit?

And where is this coming from? Last I checked, we were . . . content. Sure, we haven't seen each other in a long time—he's been on tour, and I've been in school—but we've made long distance work.

"Is this because I live in San Francisco? I . . . I only have one semester left. I mean, I might have to do an extra one because of this last semester, but—"

"It's because I don't like you anymore."

Well, Jesus.

"You . . . you don't like me?" I ask, confused and caught off guard. Where's the consideration for my feelings?

He shakes his head. "No, I don't. I haven't found you entertaining for the past couple of months."

Uh . . . what's that?

Did he just say entertaining? Pardon me, but I wasn't aware that was part of my responsibilities as a girlfriend.

"Entertaining?" I ask in a low, steady voice. My hurt quickly subsides as anger rears its ugly head. "Oh, I wasn't aware that, as your girlfriend, my main duty was to entertain you."

"Don't do this," Matt says with an irritated sigh as he turns away.

"Do what?" I ask, tugging on his hand so he's forced to face me.

"Be dramatic about this. Okay? Let's be mature adults."

"Mature adults? Matt, you're breaking up with me because I haven't entertained you enough. That's not being a mature adult. That's being a fuck wad who expects his girlfriend to dance like a monkey when he demands it."

"That's not what I meant."

12

I put my hands on my hips. "Then what exactly did you mean?"

"You've just been . . . lackluster. Mopey. And it hasn't been fun to be around you. Or on the phone with you."

My eyes nearly pop out of my head. Mopey? Is he fucking kidding me?

"That's because my fucking sister died!" I yell.

To his credit, he keeps his voice steady. "I understand that, but you were mopey before your sister died, and to be honest, I did the right thing and waited to break up with you after a couple of months. I wanted to break up with you before your sister died but waited."

I sit back on my heels, raise my hands, and offer him the slowest clap known to man. "Well, pin a fucking rose on your nose, Matt. You are truly a hero."

"See, I knew you were going to be like this," Matt says as he moves toward the couch and flops down. "I knew you were going to be dramatic about it."

"I'm not being dramatic." I point at my chest. "This is a normal reaction for someone finding out their boyfriend of nearly eight years is breaking up with them . . . because he finds her boring."

"I didn't say boring," he says, pointing his finger at me. "We had some good times, but just lately, you haven't been fun, and now that we're older, I'm afraid you're settling, and I don't want to settle. I want to be free. I want to be with someone who wants to do fun things, travel the country, get in trouble."

"I've been in school," I yell. "What did you want me to do? Skip class to go steal something from your boss?"

"See, that's the kind of fun I'm talking about," Matt says. "Remember the night we stole one of Hayes's Grammys? That was a night to remember."

"And so fucking illegal. You're lucky we didn't get in trouble."

"But that's what I'm talking about, that kind of fun."

"Felon fun?" I ask. "Is that what you want? To be a felon? Because if that's the case, have a good life, Matt. Not interested."

He rolls his eyes. "You've become such a square, Hattie."

"I'm not a goddamn square. You're going through some sort of pre-midlife crisis. I'm sorry if I've been mopey and not fun, but that happens when your closest sister has stage four breast cancer, and you have to watch her slowly die. So yeah, maybe I wasn't fucking fun."

"Thank you for admitting it." He throws his hands up in the air as if he just won the battle and is relieved.

And for a second, I have this out-of-body experience as I stare at Matt, the man I thought I'd marry one day. Yeah, we've had our ups and downs, and we might have been drifting apart lately, but I still loved him . . . but this man standing in front of me, this is a different man. This isn't the man I fell in love with.

He's cruel.

He's rude.

He's inconsiderate.

He's . . . as Maggie put it so eloquently, he's the ick.

And I can't believe I'm finally seeing it. Talk about rose-colored glasses. Cassidy never liked Matt. Maggie has never liked him. Ryland tolerated him, and Aubree told me to dump him back in high school. It's taken me this long to realize what kind of character he has, so what the hell does that say about me?

After a bout of silence, he stands from the couch, presses his hands into a triangle, and says, "Anyway, I'm moving out, so you're going to have to grab your stuff and get it out of here."

"You're moving? You didn't plan on telling me?"

"I did. I'm telling you now."

Nearly growling with frustration over my stupidity for

liking this man, I push past him, stiff-arming my hand into his shoulder to get him out of the way, and grab an empty box on the couch.

"Hey," he bemoans as he rubs his shoulder. "You don't need to get physical."

"That was barely on the blip of what I could do to you, Matt, and unless you want to find out the full extent of my physicality, I suggest you give me ten minutes to myself to grab my shit and leave."

He slowly nods, eyes on me. "So I'm guessing you won't want to be friends with me after this?"

Add moron to the list of things that Matt is.

Moronic ick.

Yup, couldn't have said it better.

"Friends?" I scoff. "Matt, I'll be spending the next year of my life manifesting the shit out of you losing your testicles by an inmate you meet on your first day in jail after committing one of your felonies you seem to find joy in."

His face falls flat. "Don't you fucking dare."

I press my fingers to my temples and squeeze my eyes tight like a child. "Thank you, universe, for introducing Matt to Homer, the inmate with the vise grip, and popping Matt's testicles right off his body."

"Stop that," Matt yells, pulling my hands from my head.

"It's out there, beware." I twiddle my fingers at him.

"You know, I'm glad I broke up with you. You're all kinds of fucked up."

"Ha, pot calling the kettle black, Matt."

With my box back in my hand, I move toward the bedroom, and before entering, I look over my shoulder. "Ten minutes. Get out of my face, or I'll call my brother, and he'll take care of you for me."

Knowing Matt is absolutely terrified of Ryland, he descends the stairs in a hurry, shutting the door behind him.

What a fuckwit.

I'm not entertaining enough . . . who says that to another human being? Let alone someone they're supposed to love. The standards these days, sheesh.

I sigh and lean against the doorway of the meager bedroom, staring into the nearly empty room, with just a few of my things on the unmade bed as well as a box full of his possessions. He's been planning this all along and couldn't have even given me a heads-up as I drove here. My biggest concern in seeing him was that he showered, and now . . . this is what I'm dealing with.

You're better off.

You didn't even love him that much either. The past couple of months, he's shown his true colors. He wasn't there for me like a boyfriend should have been while I dealt with losing Cassidy. I blamed it on his work schedule, when in reality, I should have blamed it on his lack of concern.

As much as my pride might be hurting at the moment, I know deep down this is probably for the best.

Doesn't make me any less bitter, though. Nope . . . I'm going to ride that bitter train for as long as I can.

I move into the bedroom, set my box on the bed, and start piling my items in it.

Oh, how nice of him, giving me all the pictures he has of us together, as if I'd want the reminder of his idiotic face.

No, thank you.

I toss the pictures in the trash and then sift through the rest of the junk he assumed was mine.

Some cosmetics.

A book I bought for him that he never read because heaven forbid, he does something other than look at his phone.

A broken iPhone charger. Pleasant.

A few pens from different hotels he's stayed at. What on earth? Toss.

A pair of his boxers. *Is he for real?*

And two of my shirts that I will in fact be keeping because they're vintage rock band shirts, and I've been looking for these. But the rest, mainly the boxers and the pens, can be shoved into his box.

Speaking of his box . . .

Curious as to what he considers his, I thumb through the box that he has marked as his. Let's see what he has in here . . . . Oh . . . oh my, would you look at that. These aren't his things. These aren't my things, no . . . these are his boss's things.

A signed Hayes Farrow album, his first. A hat that looks like his. Some T-shirts. I move aside the shirts and find a few bottles of tequila—unfortunately, a drink I know Hayes likes to consume. What is this? Some sort of fanboy box? *What the hell is Matt doing with all these things?*

I paw through it a little bit more, and then a flash of gold . . . the Grammy.

Holy crap.

I pull it out of the box and examine it.

Best New Artist: Hayes Farrow.

I remember seeing him accept this on stage. He was wearing a black suit with a white button-up shirt, the first three buttons undone, showing off the leather necklace with a silver pendant he wears everywhere. He combed his hand through his hair in disbelief as he stared down at it and thanked his grandma for buying him his first guitar.

And then . . . Matt and I stole it.

Well, I didn't really steal it. I was an accomplice. I held the door open for Matt. I wasn't sure what he was doing until we were in the car, and he pulled it out of his suit jacket.

I've felt bad knowing Matt has had it even though Hayes Farrow is the scum of the earth.

Even the scum of the earth deserves their *well-earned* trophies.

Eyeing the box of my things and the fanboy box, I make

the executive decision. I toss my shirts in the fanboy box along with the Grammy, and as I clutch it close to my chest, I head toward the staircase.

There can't possibly be anything in this apartment that I care about—oh wait, my puzzles.

I pause in the living room and set the box down. Confused by the liquor bottles Matt collected, I pull them out of the box, making some room, and put them in the box on the bed I left behind. I then open the cabinets under the TV and spot three of my puzzles stacked neatly together.

Oh noooo, I'm not leaving my puzzles with Matt. Grant him hours of entertainment? No fucking way.

And he said I wasn't entertaining. Clearly, he forgot about these purchases.

I slip my puzzles into my box, then head back down the stairs and open the door to the outside. Matt stares down at his phone—shocker—while sitting on the stone wall that encases the parking lot behind the buildings. He glances up. "That was quick."

"It smelled like you in there, and it was sickening. The quicker I could leave, the better."

"You used to like the way I smell," he says, for God knows what reason. Maybe he's starting to have regrets.

"Well, things change. Just like you changed your feelings about me, your signature scent has also changed. Quite musky smelling if you ask me, like an old bottled-up fart."

His expression melts into irritation. "Once again, very mature, Hattie."

"Glad I could be of service," I say as I stick my box in my car and open the driver's side door. "And for the record," I say loud enough in case anyone wants to listen. "You're terrible at giving oral, you couldn't find my clit if it knocked you on the nose, and your penis is crooked, and not in a good way. It felt more like trying to wrangle a bent pencil in my vagina than getting pounded by a beefy salami."

"Oh, fuck off." He points his finger at me. "I made you come every goddamn time."

"It's called faking it, Matt." And with that, I turn my car on and drive off, his steaming face in my rearview mirror.

Task number one of making him feel inferior, done.

Now, task number two . . . get him fired.

Chapter Two

HAYES

I forgot how quiet it was here.

I've been on the go for the last goddamn year with the tour, interviews, and promotions with all my sponsors that I forgot what it meant to sit in a quiet spot and listen to nature around me.

I arrived back in Almond Bay yesterday and stopped by to see my grandma first thing. As expected, she was as happy as she ever is. Just as I thought, she'd lured me back to Almond Bay, knowing damn well I was done with my tour. I probably would have come back anyway. I enjoy the calm, and I need calm right now with my label breathing down my neck.

When I arrived, she gave me her signature hug and kiss, and then we sat down on her balcony that overlooks the town while her aide brought us tea. I offered to grab it, but she told me to sit down—and I listened to Gran bitch to me about the Peach Society for two solid hours.

Gran has NEVER gotten along with Ethel O'Donnell-

Kerr. Something about stealing her man back in the day. She won't go into it because it makes her too upset, and Gran makes it a point not to rage—she says it brings on too many wrinkles. She also doesn't like how Ethel claims the top celebrity card in Almond Bay because, as Gran says, I'm more of a household name than Ethel could ever dream.

I made sure Gran was comfortable, spoke to her aide, Roseanne, and then headed back to my place, about ten minutes up the coast. Just far enough away from Almond Bay to offer me my sought-after privacy.

I purchased the coastal home a few years ago and reno-vated the entire thing, swapping out the bright white palette for deep grays, blacks, and greens, along with concrete floors and sophisticated leather furniture. I designed the entire reno-vation, focusing on bringing darkness to the tall windows and nature inside with fresh plants that I pay my buddy Abel once a week to water. At first, he wouldn't take payment, but after a month of heading to my place, he changed his mind. Not like the man needs money as the doctor and owner of the phar-macy in town. He's sitting pretty. But he's not a fool. He's not going to perform a task for free for over a year.

He also keeps a close eye on my grandma while I'm gone and makes biweekly checkups to make sure she's doing okay.

A light wind blows through the tall bushes surrounding my porch as I lean against my black Adirondack chair. It feels good to take a break for a second, step away from the tour, and be back in Almond Bay, even though more tragic than good things have happened here. My childhood wasn't anything a child should experience.

Yelling.

Emotional abuse.

Abandonment.

I had to grow up sooner than any child should, and I truly believe I'm where I am today because of the one person who wouldn't give up on me, my gran. It's why I bought a house here, so when I was taking a break from the fast life, I could come back, visit with her, and have a place just outside of Almond Bay to relax. *So why did I need to be persuaded to return this time?*

Probably because I'm so fucking lost, I don't even know what I need in my life to be happy—but let's not get into that.

Even though I'm here to write some songs, there's a household full of boxes and mailings that have to be sifted through, organized, and dealt with. A task my assistant would have taken care of, but unfortunately for me, I fired him this morning for stealing. He tried to claim I needed to keep him on because he had to support his girlfriend, who had just failed out of school and didn't have a job, but I told him to take his sob story somewhere else.

Which has put me in a tough situation.

My phone chimes, and I glance down at the screen. *Ruben.*

Fucking hell, I can't escape it. Not even for a morning.

"Hello?" I answer.

"Hayes, I just received a complaint from Matt that you fired him. Is this true?"

"He did not fucking call you." The balls on that guy.

"He did. Begged me to put in a good word for you. Claims he has to support his girlfriend or something? What's going on?"

"Said the same bullshit to me," I say. "And the answer is no. The fuck was stealing from me."

"Do you know that for sure?"

"Ninety-nine percent positive," I say. "I have camera footage of him and a girl leaving my house one night. I noticed my Grammy was missing after that. I didn't want to assume it was Matt, but he was the only one with access to my house. I decided to watch him carefully, and that's when I noticed things going missing. Tequila, shirts, hats. Pretty sure he was collecting the shit to sell and make more money."

"Do you want me to press charges?" Ruben asks.

"No, but tell the fuck that I will if he keeps bothering us. Tell him he's fucking lucky it's me he's dealing with and not someone else."

"I'll take care of this, don't worry." Ruben clears his throat. "Are you in Almond Bay now?"

"Yeah, saw Gran yesterday. She's looking good. Plan on catching up with Abel later."

"And maybe there's some writing going on as well?" Ruben not so nonchalantly presses.

"Dude, I'm going to fire you if you keep pressuring me."

"We just need something. A scrap of something. Anything to hold over the label."

"I know." I drag my hand over my face as a red car pulls into my driveway. "I'll work on it. Hey, someone is here. I have to go."

"Okay, keep me updated, and I'll take care of Matt. Want me to look for his replacement?"

"No," I answer right before hanging up.

I set my phone down on the armrest and remain seated as I watch the car door open. Because of the bushes lining my sidewalk, I can't get a good look at who it is until a box is hoisted in front of the person, and they start walking toward me.

Her tan, toned legs come into view first.

Pristinely white sneakers.

Olive-green spandex shorts.

An oversized sweatshirt.

Her face is blocked, but I do notice a long, honey-blond ponytail swishing back and forth.

I stay seated, observing as she sets the box in front of my door . . . and that's when I get the first look at her.

Holy shit.

Fucking Hattie Rowley.

What the hell is she doing here?

Pretty sure her brother would have a goddamn heart attack if he knew she was at my doorstep.

Can't remember the last time I saw her, but hell, she's grown up, that's for damn sure. Filled out in all the right places, her hair slicked back into a tight ponytail, an effortless glow to her cheeks, and long, black lashes framing what I know are intense green eyes. All the Rowley kids have them.

She reaches into the box and pulls up a piece of paper and a pen. She faces away from me, giving me the perfect view of her ass as she writes something on the paper. Wasn't she going to school in San Francisco?

Wonder if she still is or if she moved back here after Cassidy passed?

She was dearly loved by the town and by her siblings, and her passing rocked the town. From what Gran told me in one of our weekly talks, Ryland was given custody of Cassidy's four-year-old daughter, MacKenzie, and Aubree, their sister, took over The Almond Store and Cassidy's farm. Both of them have been struggling with the new responsibilities.

Maybe Hattie's back here to help.

When she's done writing, she sticks the paper in the box, and I take that moment to ask, "What did you write?"

She leaps about a foot in the air before falling to the right, up against the house, hand clutching her chest.

"Jesus fucking Christ," she breathes out, her shoulders nearly kissing her ears from shock. When she spots me in my chair, she says, "Have you been sitting there the whole time?"

"Yup," I answer as I stand. Her eyes fall to my bare chest for a moment before they pop back up to my face.

"You've just been sitting there, watching me?"

"Wanted to know what you were doing before I made you aware of my presence."

"That's some freaky shit," she says, pointing her finger at me.

24

Tilting my head to the side and studying her, I say, "It's Hailey, right?"

I know damn well it's Hattie, but I pretend I don't know to hold the upper hand, especially against a Rowley.

Her eyes narrow as she corrects me. "Hattie."

"That's right, Ryland's sister." I give her a quick once-over. "Does your brother know you've crossed over into enemy territory?"

"He doesn't, not that I'd need his permission." She sticks her chin up. *I get it. You're not intimidated. Never have been.*

"What's with the box?" I ask, nodding toward it.

"Some things I thought you might want. My ex-boyfriend, Matt, your assistant, stole them from you."

Matt was dating Hattie Rowley? How the hell did he manage that? Sorry to say, but she's way out of his league. And why didn't I know they were dating? *Probably because the tool has never spoken about her or even let on that he had a girlfriend.*

Wait . . . was she the one he was talking about? Failed out of college, doesn't have a job? Is that why she's back here in Almond Bay? I thought it was because of her sister, but this is a new development. And the fucker lied to me, saying they were still together when clearly, they're not.

Lying and stealing. Thank God I fired him.

I glance at the box, taking in the contents. "I never owned puzzles."

"Oh, those are mine." She snags the boxes and holds them close to her chest. "So anyway, if you want to fire him, I highly suggest it."

I glance down at the box and then back up at her. Almond Bay was a weird place to grow up. There were always odd things happening around town. Like one day, a naked man rode down Almond Ave on a unicycle, and no one blinked an eye. Or the time The Talkies—our drive-in theater—showed a porn film for precisely one minute and thirteen seconds. Everyone just laughed about it. It wouldn't be abnormal for someone to drop off a box of stuff and request their boyfriend be fired. I'm just surprised it's coming from a Rowley, the least eccentric family in town.

Then again, from what I've observed, Hattie has always been different.

"Why would I fire him over a few T-shirts?"

Her eyes fall to the box. "Shit, those are mine too." She picks them up, and what I see underneath makes my teeth clench.

My Grammy.

I knew the fucker stole it.

Keeping it cool, I bring my attention back to her. "How long have you dated Matt?"

"Since high school, and if you're going to judge me about being with him, he wasn't an anus back then. He took over that title just recently."

"I see." I glance back at the box. "You know, I have video footage of the night my Grammy was stolen." I bring my gaze back to her and catch the widening of her eyes and the clench of her mouth. Just what I thought. Fucking guilty. "And Matt wasn't alone."

"It wasn't me. Whatever you're thinking, I had nothing to do with it." Hell, is she bad at lying.

"Funny, my cameras tell me differently." They actually don't, but I love watching her squirm.

Her mouth falls open, appalled, but she quickly closes it. Her eyes study me, gauging her next move. A few seconds go by, silence falling between us, and then in a flash, she turns on her heel and bolts to her car.

She's not going to get away that easily. Not on my fucking watch.

"Run all you want, but the sheriff will know where to find you."

That makes her pause and slowly turn back toward me. "You wouldn't."

"Wouldn't I?" I ask. "You're a Rowley. Pretty sure we're supposed to hate each other. What would stop me from calling the police and reporting this? I have cameras all over this goddamn house currently recording this conversation. You're caught."

The color drains from her face, and the bravado she had only a few minutes ago has vanished. "Don't call the sheriff," she says, looking scared for a moment. "My family has been through a lot lately, and I don't think my brother could take well, needing to bail me out of anything."

I don't think he could, either. Does he even know about her school—if it's even true? I know Ryland well enough to understand he wouldn't take failing out of school lightly, especially one of his sisters.

I nod toward the house. "Why don't you come in, and we can discuss our options?"

"Options?" she asks, her eyebrow raised.

"Yeah, options." I bend down and pick up the box of stolen items and then open the front door. "I suggest you follow me. I'm not opposed to calling the sheriff. He's a huge fan." I smile broadly, which makes her lips flatten in disgust.

Grumbling under her breath, she follows me into my house, puzzles and shirts in hand, and I kick the door shut when she's fully in. I set the box of contraband on the entryway floor and head toward my kitchen, but when she doesn't move, I say, "Come in. I won't bite . . . at least not yet."

"What the hell is that supposed to mean?" She's about to approach me when she stops and adds, "If that's some sexual innuendo, I'm going to tell you right now, I don't even like to be bit when having sex. I think it's weird, also . . . if you think I'm going to be some concubine for you, you better think of something else."

I turn on my coffee machine and say, "You clearly haven't been bitten by the right person. That much is true when we think about who you just dated." I choose a coffee pod—donut shop—and I put it in the machine and start it up. I lean against the counter and face her. "And I could do better when it comes to concubines."

That makes her anger rear up, her mouth twitching with irritation. "You would be so lucky to have me in your bed."

I give her a smooth once-over, my hand running along my jaw, and reply, "Debatable."

"Ugh, you're such an asshole. No wonder no one likes you."

"Interesting. I have a fan club of over three million people who would challenge you on that statement."

"They're fans. They don't count."

I take in my home and then say, "I'm pretty sure they do, since they're the ones who funded this house you're standing in and helped me earn the Grammy you stole."

"Matt stole it, not me. I was just . . . there."

"Is that the story you're going to tell the cops?"

"I thought you weren't going to tell the cops," she says.

"Never promised that. Said we had to talk about options."

"Well, what are these stupid options you speak of?" she impatiently replies.

"Why don't you come in farther, set your shirts and puzzles down, and take a seat? Want some coffee?"

"No," she answers. "You might poison it."

"With you watching me make it?"

"I don't know what you have in those coffee pods. They could be pre-poisoned."

"I see that we're acting rational. Good to know," I reply, full of sarcasm. I pick up my coffee and grab some almond creamer from the fridge—yeah, I live in Almond Bay and drink almond creamer. It's good.

"Never would have seen you as a creamer kind of guy."

"Oh, I cream a lot," I say as she takes a seat on an island chair right across from me.

She sets her puzzles and T-shirts down and rolls her eyes. "You're disgusting."

"Or honest?"

"Disgusting." She folds her arms and says, "Now tell me these options so I can get the hell out of here and never return. My skin is starting to feel itchy."

Can we say dramatic?

But despite that, what are the options? Because right now, I have no idea what I'm doing other than not letting her slip away just yet. Call it the feud with her brother, but having one of Ryland's sisters in my clutches feels nice . . . like I have a momentary upper hand over this battle I've been unwillingly fighting for over a decade. Not to mention, given my lack of an assistant, I feel like I could use her. I have a room full of boxes and letters from fans that need to be answered. It might work out perfectly.

"You want options?" I ask.

"Yes, Jesus, that's why I'm sitting here."

Short-tempered. I like it.

I also like the light freckles that dot around her button nose and naturally blushed cheeks.

"Your options are as follows." I hold up one finger. "I can call the police and turn you in, press full charges, thanks to your confession . . ."

"Going with the scare tactic first. Great. What's the second option I'll clearly have to take?"

I hold up a second finger. "You work for me."

She snorts loud enough for it to echo through my kitchen. "Work for you? Okay. Yeah, that's going to happen." She shakes her head. "What's option three?"

I set my coffee on the counter and place my hands on the marble, my eyes matching up with hers. "There is no option three. That's it. You get turned in, or you work for me. Take your pick."

"You can't do that," she protests. "I have . . . I have school."

"Do you? Because last I heard, you failed out this semester, and I was also informed you don't have a job."

Her expression falls flat. "Who told you that? Was it Matt?" Muttering to herself, she says, "I'm going to kill him."

"That's the reason you're here, in Almond Bay. No school. No job. No money . . . *according to Matt.* Seems like you're in a tough spot." I take a sip of my coffee before setting it back on the counter, playing the cocky asshole, a role I know very well.

"Yeah, and being the antihero you are, you're taking full advantage of it."

"I wouldn't be in a feud with the Rowleys if I didn't, would I?" I smile at her, a smile made from sins and tequila.

Her lips twist to the side as she glances away. "What exactly do you want me to do for you? If you say sexual favors, the answer is no. I'd rather bury my head in the jail toilet bowl than get inches within your crotch."

"Nice visual, but like I said, I could do better. Your pussy is not worth my time."

"I have a great pussy," she defends. "You're not worth my pussy's time."

I stare at her, unmoving. She is hot, I'll give her that. Like I thought earlier, she is way out of Matt's league. But between her being a Rowley *and* mouthier than I could be bothered with, it's a no from me. "Glad you got that off your chest? Are you cheering for yourself on the inside for sticking up for yourself?"

"You're an asshole."

"I know," I reply, then move away from the island and down the hall.

"Where are you going?" she calls after me.

"Showing you what I need help with. Follow me if you don't want to go to jail."

I feel her hesitate before she grumbles again and traipses

30

down the hallway after me. When I reach my office, I turn toward her, grip the doorknob, and then fling the door open, revealing the disaster.

"What the hell is this?" she asks, taking it all in. Boxes upon boxes are piled up as high as the ceiling while several large, protruding blue mailbags have been dumped along the floor. Files, manila folders, and binders are stacked as tall as me on my desk that all need to be copied, saved to my cloud, and filed. New merchandise is scattered across the floor, waiting for approval. Pictures framing my platinum records lean against the wall, and handwritten lyrics are stacked on my chair, waiting to be copied and saved as well. Not to mention, the computer and printer I purchased that haven't been opened yet.

"This is just half of it. There's more in the garage."

"Jesus," she mutters, moving forward but stepping on an empty protein wrapper, the crunch causing her to lift her foot to see what she stepped on. "Are you a hoarder?"

"Does the rest of my house look like this?"

"There's always the one room people don't know about." She picks up a red lace bra with her finger and raises her brow at me. I just smirk.

"This happens when you've been on tour for a year. Things stack up. Matt was supposed to tackle it all after the tour but was fired before getting his sticky hands on it. Best he didn't, given the box you brought me."

"Which, by the way, I don't think I'm getting enough credit for. I could have stolen those items from Matt and sold them on the black market."

"Do you even know what the black market is?"

"No . . ." She pauses and flicks the bra to the ground. "But a healthy search on Google would probably help steer me in the right direction."

"Yeah, that Google search wouldn't be flagged," I sarcastically reply. "Also, I am giving you credit for bringing back the Grammy. I gave you two options."

"You gave me one option, knowing damn well I wasn't going to turn myself in to the police."

"Doesn't mean I didn't give you options."

Arms crossed at her chest, she turns toward me, irritation on her face. "So what, you want me to clear this out for you, and you'll pay me?"

"That's usually how a job works."

"For how long? Because, you know, I have better things to do than clean up *your* mess."

"Do you?" I ask as I lean against the doorframe. "Please enlighten me."

Her lips purse as she narrows her eyes. "Uh, like . . ." She pauses as she tries to come up with something more important, but I think we both know at this point, she's mine for the taking. "You know what? It's none of your business."

"That's what I thought." I push off the doorframe and head down the hallway back to the kitchen. "I'll pay you one thousand dollars a week in cash."

"One thousand dollars?" she shouts after me. "Matt was making way more than that, and he was the one who stole the Grammy."

I pick up my coffee and take a sip. "Matt was doing a lot more than just cleaning up my shit as you like to put it, so unless you want to field the pussy that comes knocking on my door, take my phone calls, schedule my life, and deal with all my brands, you'll take one thousand dollars a week and be happy with it, or else I can just call it community service and leave it at that."

"Is this how you're going to be the entire time? An unrelenting ass?"

I turn toward her as she approaches, her young face both irritated and scared at the same time. I can't remember the age difference between her and Ryland, but I do know she's the youngest in her family, and there's a big gap. It's evident in her naive eyes.

I sip my coffee and meet her gaze. "Yes."

"Great." She tosses her hands as if she gives up.

"You can start tomorrow. Seven in the morning, sharp."

"Seven?" Her eyes nearly bug out. "Have you lost your mind? I'm not arriving at seven."

"If you arrive at seven, you can make my morning coffee for me."

She glances at the mug in my hand and then back at me. "You can fuck off with that. Make your own damn coffee. Unless you want to pay me fifteen hundred dollars, then sure, I'll be here at seven."

"That's a one-hundred-dollar cup of coffee a day."

"That's what I'm worth."

"Fine," I say, calling her bluff. "Fifteen hundred a week, you're here at seven making me my coffee . . . and protein shake." I hold my hand out to her. "Deal?"

Chapter Three

HATTIE

What the hell am I actually doing, and how did returning a box of items to someone turn into a job with the devil?

Oh, I'll tell you how.

Hayes Farrow.

That's how he works. There's always an angle with him, and this angle seems to have taken me down within a matter of seconds. Do I truly believe he'd report me to the police so I'd get into a shit ton of trouble? Yes, absolutely. The feud between him and Ryland runs deep, so for Hayes to consider throwing another Rowley under the bus to spite Ryland, yup, I one hundred percent believe that could happen.

"I asked you if it was a deal," he says, still holding his hand out.

His large, calloused hand.

I glance up into his light-gray eyes. There's barely a drop of color in his irises, yet they're rimmed in black, a unique color that only adds to the obsession people have with him. Little do they know the devil that rests behind them.

And that devil has me by the uterus.

What option do I really have?

Create more trouble in my family that doesn't need it right now? It's not like I have something to offer, even showing up at their doorstep. He's right. I failed out of this semester. I have no job, no money—no place to crash while I try to figure out what to do—meaning, I'm out of luck, and shaking hands with the devil himself might be my only option.

I also don't want to admit it, but fifteen hundred a week is more than I could get somewhere else, and I could desperately use the money.

I must reek of desperation because as I stare into his cold, dead eyes, I know he knows this. I know he can see my moment of despair.

Because of that, I take a deep breath and hold my hand out to him, connecting our palms with a shake.

"Deal," I say, a shiver passing through me.

That shiver . . . that's the telltale sign of hell burning up through me.

A slow, maniacal smile creeps over his mouth from my concession, and I know I just made a deal with Satan himself.

When he releases my hand, he brings his mug up to his lips, eyes set on me, and he sips. I hate to admit it, because I can genuinely say I despise this man, but he's ungodly attractive. His tanned skin makes his eyes seem endlessly light, framed by long dark lashes. His morning scruff is dark, deliciously coating his strong jaw, and his backward hat covers up his nearly black hair that women have a conniption over when he styles it—which is rare. And then there's his body. He's easily six foot three or taller, with long limbs and a toned torso, which only seems attainable for those who spend forty hours in the gym—yet here he is, standing in front of me with a six-pack that I could lose my finger in. His pecs are the main feature of his body, lined with sinew that connects in the middle of his chest. It's probably the most famous part of his body besides his eyes because he shows it off during his concerts. The many collages I've seen of just that part of his chest is frankly disturbing—yet I've watched every one of them. Even though I think he's a horrible human, I can't deny the fact that he's the hottest man I've ever laid eyes on.

"Do you need a place to stay?" he asks, pulling me out of my thoughts.

"What?"

"Weren't you going to stay with Matt?"

"Oh, yeah," I say.

"So do you need a place to stay? It'll knock a few hundred off your payment, but I have a few guest rooms to choose from."

"Ew, you think I'd stay here? No, thank you."

"Why ew?" He glances around his house. "It's pretty nice here."

"Yes, your house is nice. You, on the other hand, just popped out of Satan's asshole, and I'd rather not share a living space with a fiery anus. Thank you very much."

"That's a lot of ass talk." He smirks. "Have a fixation with that? Because I can show you a good time if you do."

The fucking audacity of this man.

"In your dreams, Hayes," I say even though I bet he could show me a good time. A time to remember. I grab my puzzles and shirts and hold them close to my chest. "Now, if you'll excuse me, I need to go scream into a pillow while I come to terms with the deal I just shook on."

He smirks, the corner of his mouth pulling to the side, and it's both hideously annoying . . . and seductively attractive. "Happy screaming. See you bright and early tomorrow morning."

"Fuck off," I mumble as I push through the door to his house and out to my car.

I toss my items on the passenger side and grip my steering wheel. Looking up toward his house, I see him standing on his porch, mug of coffee in hand, watching over me.

Ugh, he's infuriating.

I start my car and drive away. I'm not going to give him the satisfaction of seeing me distressed over my current predicament, no way—he'll just take pleasure in it, the sadist.

When I'm driving down the road, I reach for my phone and call Maggie. When the Bluetooth connects to my car, her voice sounds through the speakers.

"Why are you calling me? Shouldn't you be with Matt? Oh my God, did he cheat on you? Did you go there and find him with someone else?"

"Why would you assume that?" I ask, leaning my head back against the headrest while still keeping my eyes trained on the road.

"Because, I told you, he gives me the ick."

"Well, he didn't cheat on me, but he did break up with me for being boring."

"What?" she yells.

I give her the entire rundown from what he said to telling me to grab my things, and then how I found the Grammy and decided to be a good freaking Samaritan and drop it off at Hayes's house.

"So you went to his house to give him his Grammy back? You're a saint."

"Thank you, that's what I thought until he decided to pin me for the crime and threaten to call the cops on me."

"Nooooo," Maggie growls. "He did not do that."

"Oh yes, he did. Which then led to me going inside his house to save my ass, and guess what, Mags?"

"Tell me."

"I'm now working for him."

There's a pause. "Wait . . . what?"

Yeah, I'm still trying to process it all too.

"Apparently, the man has no sense of organization because his office and garage are trashed. Matt was supposed to clean it up, but because he fired him for stealing—shocking —he now needs the help and told me I could take the job or he would call the police."

"That's blackmail." Her outrage is just what I need at this moment. Find yourself a friend like Maggie. She's the absolute best.

"Are you surprised? The guy has no moral compass."

"I can't believe that," she says as I make my way toward The Almond Store. "Is he going to at least pay you?"

"Yes, thank God, and I hate to admit it, but given my circumstances, I could really use the money."

"True, but it's Hayes Farrow . . . your brother hates him."

"That's why Ryland is not going to find out."

"And how do you plan on keeping your new employment a secret? What are you even going to tell them about being in town?" Maggie asks.

"I thought about that, and since I'm returning midsemester, I'm going to tell them I spoke with my professors, and we all agreed that I need to take some time off because of Cassidy's death. They don't need to know that time off is because I failed every one of my midterms. I came back here to gather myself and found an internship to help tide me over."

"Internship. That's believable."

"I'll say one of my professors hooked me up with it. And thankfully, since Hayes lives outside of town and far away from any family members or townspeople, it won't be a problem."

"Okay, and what about the whole he's the sexiest man ever to walk the planet thing?"

"What about it?" I ask.

"Uh, are you going to be able to control yourself?"

"Maggie," I say on a huff as I drive down Almond Ave.

"Unlike Hayes, I have standards, convictions. He might be hot, but there's no way I'd touch that man with a ten-foot pole. Also, he's twelve years older than I am. He's the same age as Ryland."

"That's hot."

"Wait, so Matt gives you the ick, but a twelve-year age difference doesn't?"

"Age gap is in."

"Something is seriously wrong with you."

"Come on, the thought of being with an experienced man doesn't make your body tingle with anticipation?"

"No," I say even though that's slightly a lie. Sex with Matt was . . . okay. I did fake it a lot, but there were some good times . . . maybe like a few. Not many actually. Either way, who's to say Hayes would even be good at sex? He probably has a gaggle of women lined up and ready to fake it as well.

"I don't believe you."

I sigh. "Can we just agree that I'm in hell?"

"If hell is being able to smell and stare at Hayes Farrow daily, tell me where to sign up."

"You need help."

"I know." We both laugh.

"Hey, I'm at The Almond Store, and I need to present myself to my sister, see if I can find a place to stay."

"Good luck. Let me know how it goes."

"I will."

I hang up the phone and turn off my car, but don't exit right away.

I need to take a second.

The last time I was in The Almond Store, Cassidy's pride and joy besides her daughter, I was picking up some almond butter to take back to school. Cassidy teased me about taking advantage of the family discount—free—and then gave me one of her signature hugs.

Warm and full of love.

Cassidy was my best friend growing up. Nine years older than me, she took me under her wing and kept me close. She played with me, even when she was too old to be playing with dolls. She colored with me. She spent countless hours making up dances to our favorite songs with me. I idolized her and when Mom passed, she was so . . . present. In some ways, she became my mom.

When she was diagnosed with breast cancer, just like our mom, it felt like I was living in some sort of dream, like it wasn't happening in real life but in some sick nightmare.

And when I got the call that she died, I broke down. For days, Maggie held me as I cried. She never said anything, just sat there with me like the best friend that she is.

I came back for the funeral, and we released her ashes in the bay.

And when her will was read to us, I felt . . . let down.

Ryland was assigned the challenging task of taking custody of MacKenzie, an assignment I can understand. He has a solid job, he has no plans of leaving Almond Bay, he's situated in his life, and can offer stability to a four-year-old after losing her mother.

But The Almond Store? *Our* dream? It went to Aubree. The store and the farm.

And sure, Aubree helped out at the store, she knows how to run things, but it doesn't negate the hurt. The Almond Store is my baby with Cassidy. I helped her design and come up with the concept. Aubree could have taken the farm, but the store . . . Cassidy should have left that to me to carry on the legacy we created.

I've never expressed my feelings about it because I didn't want to sound jealous or bring up bad feelings in a moment when we should be coming together to support each other and MacKenzie, but fuck does it make me sick to my stomach.

And I know walking in there will bring up all of those feelings.

The feeling of loss, not seeing Cassidy behind the counter, not feeling her sunny hug, not seeing her joyful smile.

I take a deep breath, willing back the tears. Don't cry.

Crying will do nothing.

You're in a predicament, and crying will not help the situation, especially with Aubree. She's not one who deals with crying very well. Or emotions in general.

I lock my car, then move around to the front of the store. One of the reasons we loved this building so much in town—it used to be a salon—is because it's in the shape of a triangle, and the entrance is at the tip, giving it a unique and cute storefront.

We whitewashed the outside that used to be a deep red brick, added a pale blue and white-striped awning, tore out the old linoleum floors, and replaced them with white oak. It was a hell of a job, but I helped her one summer, and nothing felt more satisfying when it was all done. We kept the theme of open white shelving held up by iron brackets, with white oak islands in the middle of the store in the shape of triangles to go with the flow of the floor plan, and filled the empty spots with black-and-white photos of the farm as well as eucalyptus branches. It's my favorite place to be not just because of the memories but the smell as well.

The door rings as I walk through, and Aubree, who is hunched over the counter, looking through her iPad with a serious expression pulling on her brow, glances up. When she recognizes me, she stands taller.

"Hattie, what are you doing here?"

"That's how you're going to greet me?" I ask as I walk up to her.

Aubree, not much of a hugger, offers me her one arm and taps me on the back, almost as if we're sharing a bro hug. "Good to see you. Now what are you doing here? Shouldn't you be in school?"

Can you tell education is important in my family? It's why I don't want to tell them what happened.

"I'm actually going to be home for a little bit."

"What do you mean?" she asks.

"Well, I spoke to my professors, and we all agreed that after losing Cassidy, it would be best to take a semester off." Aubree's eyes narrow. "But they hooked me up with an internship." I swallow back the nausea that's boiling in my stomach from the lie. "It's just up the coast, so I can gain some experience while I take time off."

"What's the internship?" she asks, hand on her hip.

"With a media mogul," I say, sort of telling the truth. Yeah, I'm stretching it a lot, but at least it's something.

"Is that what you want to do when you graduate? Work in media?" she asks.

"Not really, but any experience is a good experience. At least that's what my professor said. Plus, it's close to home so I can help you guys out when I don't have to work."

"I love you, Hattie, but we don't need your help. We need you to focus on school." She moves around me and goes to the front of the store, where she bangs on the window, drawing someone's attention.

When I see who it is, I inwardly groan.

Ethel O'Donnell-Kerr.

"What on earth are you banging on the window for?" Ethel asks when she walks in. She glances around, spots me, and clasps her hands together. "Well, Hattie dear, the town wasn't expecting you to be here."

The town.

As if she collectively took a poll about my presence.

"Took some time off from school," I say.

She frowns. "Oh dear, too hard for you?"

"No," Aubree snaps. "Hattie is the smartest out of all of us. Nothing about school is hard for her. She got an internship and will be working on that for the rest of the semester."

"What kind of internship?" Ethel asks.

"Nothing the town needs to know about," Aubree says, putting a bee in Ethel's bonnet.

"Well, I don't seem to care for the tone you're using with me, Miss Aubree."

Aubree's shoulders tense, and I can tell something is bothering her, but lord knows she won't say anything. She never talks about her feelings . . . ever.

"I'm sorry," Aubree says. "But I was wondering about that shipment of bottles. You said your bottle guy would get them to me by Monday. It's Tuesday, and there are no bottles. I need them, Ethel, and I went with your guy because you recommended him."

"Ah, I see." Ethel pats Aubree on the shoulder. "You're stressed. Well, let me call the man, and we can see where they are. You just had to ask, dear. You don't need to take that tone with me."

Aubree's shoulders relax, and she says in a calmer voice, "I'm sorry."

"Quite all right. I understand you're going through a lot. I'll update you once I hear from him. Would you like me to bring the Peach Society over later to help stock the store?"

What? Aubree has the Peach Society helping out?

"That's okay. I have it handled. But thank you."

"Of course, anything you need. You're doing a beautiful job, dear. Your sister would be proud." Ethel glances up at me. "And we're so happy to have you back, Hattie. Interesting that we have two out-of-towners come back in the same week."

"Who is the other one?" Aubree asks.

"Well, Hayes Farrow, of course," Ethel says with disdain. "Did you not see the red carpet rolled out for him?"

Can you tell how much Ethel loves Hayes? Pretty sure the only people who like Hayes in this town are his grandma, Abel, and Rodney, who owns the Model Railroad Museum up the street, and I think that's only because he's always had a thing for Hayes's grandma.

"Hayes is back?" Aubree says.

"Apparently, his tour is over, and his grandma took a nasty fall, so he's here to care for her."

"Well, that should be fun," Aubree says sarcastically.

Ethel leans in. "Word on the street is he fired Matt." Ethel glances up at me. "Did you know this?"

Aubree whips around to look at me. "Did you?"

"Uh . . . yes," I answer. "He was the first one I saw. He told me."

"That's right, Yahnoosh said he heard you two fighting in his apartment," Ethel says.

Of course he did. Because nothing is ever freaking sacred in this town.

"That's because he broke up with me," I say because I might as well just put it out there.

"He did?" Aubree asks. "Why?"

"Said I was too boring," I answer, wanting to throw him under the bus because, why not? "Said I was moping."

Ethel clutches her heart in shock. "Your sister just passed. Of course you would be mopey."

"That's what I told him." I shrug, glad he broke up with me because who says that to someone? Maggie was right. He is the ick.

"Well, that just won't do. I shall have a conversation with his mother."

"Uh, that's all right, Ethel. I'm sure he heard enough from me."

"Still, you poor dear." Ethel walks up to me in all of her redheaded glory and pulls me into the type of hug where her bosom greets me first and then her arms. Her signature scent of Chanel N°5 fills up my nostrils. "I'm so sorry you're experiencing so much pain lately. And now, with dropping out of school."

"Uh, hold up, she's not dropping out of school," Aubree corrects quickly. "She's doing an internship. Please, Ethel, please don't get the two mixed up."

Ethel lets go of me but holds me close as she looks me in the eyes. "My apologies."

And I swear on my right boob, the look she gives me, it's almost as if she knows the real reason I left school. But how? Does she have someone keeping tabs on me in San Francisco? Some secret teleportation where she can be in multiple places in minutes? Has she tapped my phone?

I wouldn't be surprised if she did. This is Ethel O'Donnell-Kerr, after all.

"Well, I best be on my way," she sing-songs. "The lunch hour is coming up, and you know my guests love a good reprise while they eat." She clears her throat and starts singing octaves on her way out. With a twiddle of her fingers, she's gone.

Aubree returns to the counter and starts looking at her iPad again.

"So," I say awkwardly as silence falls between us. "Do you need some help around here?"

"No," Aubree says without looking up. "I just had one stressful night, and the Peach Society caught me. Everything is fine."

"Okay, because if you need my help, I know this store in and out. I'd be more than happy—"

"I need you to focus on school and graduating," Aubree snaps. "That's what I need you to do. So if this internship will do that, then focus on that."

Caught off guard by her irritated tone, I take a step forward. "Aubree, if you want to talk . . ."

"I don't," she says and then takes a deep breath. When her eyes connect with mine, she says, "I don't need to talk, okay? I'm fine. Everything is fine."

"Okay," I reply, not believing her for a second.

"Now, I have to get back to work, but first, where are you staying while you're here?"

"Oh, right. Well, Ryland sold his house, right?" I ask.

Aubree nods. "Yes."

Dammit.

"Is there room with him and MacKenzie?"

Aubree shakes her head. "Ryland sleeps on the couch because he won't consider sleeping in Cassidy's room." Oh God, he's been sleeping on the couch this whole time? For two months? How is he doing it? "I'm taking up the guest house on the farm." Damn, that was my second option, and the guest house is one room with a bed and a bathroom. That's it.

"Shit," I say as my mind flashes to Hayes's offer. *No, don't even think about it because it won't happen.* It's one thing to work for the man for a short period, but it's another thing to live with him. If I combined those two, Ryland would for sure disown me. I run my hand over my forehead. "I wonder if Ethel will give me a room at the inn for cheap?"

"She says it's a community here, and we help each other out, but never in her life has she discounted one of her rooms. Don't even bother. But if you want, you can take the room upstairs here in the store."

"The storage room?" I ask in disbelief.

Aubree nods. "Cassidy turned it into a small studio about six months ago for whenever she stayed at the store too late and didn't want to make the drive back to the farm with Mac. It has a double bed, a full bathroom, and a mini fridge." Aubree shrugs. "It should work for what you need."

"Oh, I didn't know she did that."

"It's not glamorous, but Cassidy always treated it as a wilderness-type thing with Mac. They would make shadow puppets on the wall under a tent of blankets. Mac loved it."

Yeah, that's something Cassidy would do because she was the best mom ever.

"Okay, yeah, I'll go up there. You don't mind?"

Aubree shrugs. "You're not going to bother me being up there. As long as you're not stomping around during shop hours, I don't care."

"Well, thanks. I appreciate it."

An awkward silence falls between us. We've never been super close, at least not like me and Cassidy. She was the glue that held us all together, and now that she's gone, it almost feels like we don't know how to interact.

It also doesn't help that Aubree is holding something back.

"I guess I should take my stuff upstairs then."

"Have at it." Aubree waves me off as her attention turns back to her iPad.

"Thanks." I move toward the door to grab my suitcase but then think better of it. I might as well check out the space first. "Is it right up the back stairs?"

"Yup."

I move around the counter and head toward the back of the shop when I pause at the doorframe. Glancing over my shoulder, I ask again, "Aubree, are you okay?"

"Fine," she answers, but I know she's not telling the truth. Not with how tense her shoulders are, her voice is terse, and the demand for bottles earlier with Ethel, but I'm not one to push her. She doesn't like it, so the last thing I want to do is start a fight with her.

"Okay, well, you know where to find me."

She doesn't respond, so I retreat to the back, past all the boxes of product, and straight to the stairs covered up by a blue and white-gingham curtain. I move through it and take the wooden stairs up to a closed door. I test the handle, and finding it unlocked, I open it to reveal a tiny room, no bigger than my dorm room in San Francisco. Angled ceilings close the sides of the room and come to a point in the middle. A full bed is pressed up against the left of the room, the angled ceiling not offering that much headspace, but it's perfect for shadow puppets. Dressed in whites and light blues, the room is airy with one window that overlooks the parking lot but offers enough natural light not to cast a shadow of darkness in the room. To the right is a dresser, mini fridge, and the door to the full bathroom. Cassidy would have hated the dead flower in a pot on the dresser. She cared so much about every living thing, even her plants.

A beige area rug is spread across the floor, probably so Mac can play on the hardwood comfortably. And even though the space is sparse, it still feels homey because that was the type of person Cassidy was. She made the light shine in any room she was in.

Sighing, I lean against the doorframe and take a deep breath.

God . . . I miss her so much.

Why did she have to leave this earth so early? Too early. The world needs more people like her, and now . . . now it feels like everything is out of sorts.

I FINISH UNPACKING my clothes and setting my puzzles on the dresser—because those are important—just as my phone dings with a message. I check the screen to see my brother's name.

He's been informed of my presence.

Ryland: *Not going to tell me you're in town? I have to hear it through the grapevine?*

I sit on the bed and text him back.

Hattie: *I was going to make my way over there. Had to find a place to live first.*

Ryland: *Live? Why aren't you in school?*

Hattie: *Surprised that wasn't relayed to you. Professors thought taking a break after Cassidy's death would be good. Working an internship up here. Aubree said I could stay in the bedroom above the shop.*

Ryland: You're taking a break? Is the internship at least for credits?

God, I hate this, having to answer to my brother, who stood up for us when we were little, who took Dad's spot when Dad wouldn't bother parenting. The one who I've looked up to my whole life. And my answer is going to be a lie. But how could I possibly tell him that I failed this semester? He would be so disappointed in me, and right now, a lie outweighs the disappointment I know I'd face if I told him the truth.

I'm just hoping this job with Hayes will get me through the rest of the semester, and then I can figure out what to do during the summer. Maybe I could take a job with Ethel, making beds and cleaning rooms. Or I can help Dee Dee Coleman stock the shelves at her grocery store.

Or perhaps . . . Aubree will let me help her.

Hattie: Yes, this internship is for credit.

Ryland: At least there's that. Wish you were still in school, though.

Hattie: I know, but this is a great opportunity.

Yeah, a great opportunity with your enemy, sorting through boxes and organizing said enemy. Maybe I can stick it on my résumé as something fancy like . . . executive business associate. Some crap like that. I should have worked a title into the deal with him.

Ryland: Well, Mac knows you're here. She wants to see you.

Hattie: Let's plan for tomorrow. I'm exhausted.

Ryland: Okay.

I stare at my phone, the worry of my siblings floating through my mind. I feel so out of touch with them, like an outsider trying to weasel my way back in.

Hattie: Hey, is everything okay with Aubree? She seemed short with me.

Ryland: She's fine. Nothing you need to worry about.

His answer frustrates me. I'm not blind. I can see she's not in a good headspace, and she's stressed. Why isn't she saying anything to me? Why are they both passing it off as if every-thing is just fine?

Hattie: *Let me guess, I just need to worry about school.*

Ryland: *Exactly. See you tomorrow, kid.*

I shake my head and toss my phone to the side before leaning back on the bed. School, that's all they care about. I had a short time back home after Cassidy passed before they rushed me back to school, telling me it would be best to get back into my routine.

But the last thing I wanted was to get back into a routine. I wanted to be with them. I wanted to be with Mac. I wanted to feel Cassidy surround me.

I didn't get that. Instead, I was greeted with a cold apart-ment with no family to help me through the pain. They pushed me away then, just like they're pushing me away now, and I have no idea why.

What am I supposed to do, Cassidy?

Why did you leave us?

Chapter Four

HAYES

She's late.

Granted, it's only one minute, but she's still late.

I don't know what came over me yesterday, but the moment I knew I could force Hattie Rowley into helping me, I made it happen. Sure, I could find someone else to assist me with my office, maybe someone less temperamental, but I also saw this look of desperation in Hattie's eyes, and I felt that deep in my soul.

Desperation will get the best of us. You either rise from it or you sink, and I've experienced both. Desperation to prove myself, to make something of the person my parents both abandoned, to show them that I have value. And I sank before I rose.

I don't know Hattie that well, but I do know something about the Rowleys. They'd rather sink before asking for help, especially from me.

So why even bother? Because at that moment, as fear

crossed her eyes when I pointed out she didn't have a job, and she didn't have school, I saw myself in her, and I felt this instinctual need to toss her a bone.

Well, not really tossing her a bone but rather offering her a very unfair ultimatum.

At least that's what I'm convincing myself of this morning —that I saw a little piece of myself inside those pools of green as she stared up at me.

It has nothing to do with the fact that if her brother found out about her new job opportunity, he'd probably murder me. Pissing off Ryland Rowley has its charms.

Or the fact that she looked incredibly hot in those spandex shorts. I hate to admit it, but I checked her ass out more than I should have.

Or the bright green of her eyes that seemed to cut to my very core. A color so green that I thought about them the moment I woke up this morning.

Nope, none of that. It was the desperation *and* paying her debts because she did participate in the night my Grammy was stolen.

I rest my head against the Adirondack chair on my porch, my hand devoid of my morning coffee. Coffee that I could use right about now after a semi-sleepless night.

I'm about to check the time again when I hear the sound of a car flying down the road. I glance up over the hedges just in time to see a flash of red pull into the driveway. At least she knows she's late.

The car turns off, her door slams, and she jogs up to the door, not noticing me once again. When she reaches the door, she takes a second to straighten her T-shirt and pat down her hair before she rings the doorbell.

She rests her hands in front of her, waiting, and that's when I say, "You're late."

She flies to the side, startled to her very core. "Jesus fuck, Hayes."

I smile and stand from the chair. In a pair of jeans and a black shirt, I stuff my phone in my pocket and move past her to open the door.

"I'll give you the passcode to get into the house so you don't have to ring the doorbell. I hate answering the door."

"You just enjoy scaring the ever-living shit out of people, instead."

"Precisely," I say as I move toward the kitchen. "When you arrive, I expect you to come straight to the coffee maker and make my morning coffee."

"So we're just going to get right down to work, no pleasantries. Like a hello, how are you?"

I raise a contemplative brow. "If you expect pleasantries, you're working for the wrong person."

"That much is obvious," she mutters.

I show her where the coffee pods are stashed in the drawer. "This is where I keep my coffee."

She examines the coffee pods that are all the same flavor. The only flavor I bother drinking. "Wow, don't care for a variety, do you?" she asks with sarcasm.

"I know what I like," I answer. "Why change it?"

"I don't know . . . to live life? It's not going to kill you to try a different coffee."

I turn toward her and lean one hand against the counter. Looking her in the eyes, I say, "Like I said . . . I know what I like"—I pause to drag my eyes down her body and back up—"and I know what I don't like. Don't change that."

Her eyes narrow. "You don't have to be rude."

"Not being rude, just telling you how it is. If you want me to be rude, I can be fucking rude." I turn back to the pods and pick one up. "Drop this in the coffee maker, make sure there's a mug underneath, and then—"

"Oh my God, I'm not an idiot. I know how to make a cup of Keurig coffee."

"Are you sure? Because you did date Matt for a long

fucking time. Anyone who lets that man stick around for that long seems to have a screw loose."

"Yeah, so what does that say about you for hiring him?"

"The man was good at masking himself professionally, but he was inside you, so you knew him more intimately."

"Ew, don't say inside me." She grimaces.

"Would you rather me say you let him come inside you?"

Her eyes shoot open as her jaw drops. Stunned, she says, "First of all, that is completely out of line when it comes to a professional atmosphere. I very well might sue you for sexual harassment."

"Go ahead. Bring it up with HR . . . oh wait, you're being paid under the table."

That makes her lips twist together in annoyance. "Second," she says slowly, "he never came inside me. I wouldn't let him. He was always covered."

Interesting.

"Not that you need to know that," she continues and then turns back to the coffee machine. "We're off topic. Anything else you want to show me about your coffee, my prince?"

"King," I say.

"Huh?" she asks.

"I'm anything but a prince. If you want to address me, you can address me as king . . . or daddy. Never prince."

A snort pops out of her mouth. "Oh, okay, let me just go around calling you daddy. Sure, that's going to happen. You're delusional."

I knew she was going to be mouthy, challenging . . . defiant, but hell, I didn't know I was going to get so much joy out of her attitude, at least not this quickly. It's tempting to fuck with her every chance I get.

I move past her and grab my almond milk from the fridge. I hand it to her and say, "Two splashes and then stir."

"You know, if you put the almond milk in first, there's no need to stir."

Is this how this is going to go? Is she going to argue every goddamn thing?

Of course it is. She's a Rowley, and just because she's here doesn't mean she'll make it easy on me.

"Two splashes, and then stir," I repeat to let her know I'm not interested in her doing it any other way. I then pull down the recipe for my protein smoothie. "This is for my protein drink in the morning. I want both served at the same time."

"Served?" Her brows shoot up. "Wasn't aware I'd be serving you."

"In my bedroom."

"You can't be serious." Her shoulders sag in disbelief.

"One thing you can count on when it comes to me is that I'm always serious."

"Clearly." She rolls her eyes. "Your house is the no-fun zone. Got it. Now, will you want me to serve this in a maid's outfit since that's how you see me?"

"What you wear is up to you. If you want to be sarcastic about it, by all means, wear a maid's outfit. Just keep your tits out of my drink."

"Oh damn." She snaps her finger in irritation. "And here I was about to stir your coffee with my nipple. What is a girl to do now?"

Let me lick the excess off . . .

"Follow me," I say. I take her down the opposite hallway from my office toward my bedroom.

"Are you taking me to your dungeon for mouthing off? Because any torture you might have in mind will never match having to sit through a night of Matt trying to figure out where my clit was."

That pauses me.

I glance over my shoulder and catch the way she's worrying her lip. Before I can say anything, she says, "I don't know why I said that. I'm feeling a little unhinged at the moment from this hostile environment. You bring it out in me, but if you must know, which I know you didn't ask, but I will tell you anyway because of that look on your face, I think I'm bitter about the whole situation with Matt. I mean, if it weren't for him, I wouldn't be standing here, paying his dues for something he did, and of course you wouldn't realize that because all you see is someone to blame for what happened to you, but in reality, I was just doing a good deed." Her eyes line up with mine. "But you know how it is. Karma never comes back to bite the right person in the ass. It always seems to side-step and grab the innocent. It's just like when I found a twenty-dollar bill on the ground at the grocery store. Instead of keeping it for myself, I paid it forward and stuck it on someone else's windshield to brighten their day, and then do you know what happened to me five minutes later? A cop pulls me over. If that wasn't karma slapping me in the face, then this surely is because all I wanted was to—"

"Get your boyfriend who broke up with you fired," I say before she can finish her tirade. She stares at me blankly. Got her. I know exactly what she was doing coming here. Sure, she returned my Grammy, but there was a motive behind it. "Looks like karma chose the right person." I continue to move down the hall, and reluctantly, she does too.

"He deserved to be fired," she whispers, not sure why. "He was stealing from you."

"But you purposely tried to mess with someone's life, and the universe didn't like that."

"What about you?" she fires back. "You're messing with my life. Where's your slap in the face by the universe?"

"Am I messing with your life?" I ask as I turn around and lean against the doorframe that leads to my bedroom. "Or am I giving you an opportunity to hide from school, hide from the truth, and earn some cash while doing it?"

"Ohhhh, no." She shakes her head. "Do not play the saint card with me. I know enough about you to know you're anything but a saint."

56

"Is that right?" I ask. "Tell me, what do you know about me?"

She goes to open her mouth and then closes it as she takes a second to think.

"That's what I thought," I say as I push my bedroom door open.

"You're an ass," she says quickly. "A jerk. You take what you want without any thought of the people around you."

"Do you know that firsthand, or are you just hearing stories from your brother?"

"Given my current predicament, I know that firsthand." She raises her chin, as if she got me. Little does she know, her assumption is the furthest thing from the truth, but she doesn't need to know that.

Ignoring her, I push the door to my room open and walk in.

"This is my bedroom," I say. She peeks inside, and I watch her carefully as she observes the dark, almost midnight room —concrete floors, nearly black walls and molding, and a black-framed bed with gray velvet bedding. The only light in the room comes from the floor-to-ceiling windows overlooking the ocean.

"Uh . . . why are you showing me your bedroom? Because if you expect me to—"

"So you know where to bring my drinks," I say, exasperated. "Jesus, are you paying attention?"

"Oh, that's right." She nervously smiles. "You just get my feathers all ruffled. And I know you have a reputation, so—"

"If there is one thing I can guarantee, it's that you're not here as a fuck toy. I have no interest in taking your clothes off, so whatever reputation you think I have, it doesn't apply to you."

"Well." She crosses her arms. "Can't hear that enough."

I raise a brow. "Really? Angry that I won't fuck you?"

"No . . . I mean . . . no." She shakes her head. "But you

don't have to make me feel like a troll."

"You're a child," I say as I move past her. "I prefer women with more experience."

She chases after me. "Twenty-four is not a child, and I have experience."

I turn on her and say, "Not five minutes ago, you told me Matt had a hard time finding your clit. Do you really consider that experience?"

"Experience in patience, yes."

"So you want me to fuck you then?"

"No!" she shouts. "I just . . ."

"You want the satisfaction of knowing that you're desirable, right? You want to know that Hayes Farrow finds you attractive. You're barking up the wrong tree."

Best to put her in her place now because even though I do find her attractive, and I could easily get lost in her eyes, I won't allow myself to explore those internal desires. She has a job to do, and that's it.

From her expression, I can see she probably wants to murder me right about now, but I don't care. She's not here to be my friend. I need help with my office, and she happened to be in the right place at the right time—not to mention, she possibly needs even more help than I do.

So I continue down the hallway toward the other side of the house, and she silently follows. When I reach the kitchen, I snag my cup of coffee and move toward the office.

"Don't you want me to make your smoothie, your majesty?" she asks.

"I'd rather you get started on the office. We've already wasted enough time with your late arrival."

"By one minute, not sure that makes a difference."

"Makes a difference on the opinion I have of you," I reply when we reach my office.

"Well, good thing HR isn't involved, right? Can't get reprimanded if there's no official employment."

Such a smart-ass.

I push the office door open and gesture for her to enter. She glances up at me, and I catch the irritation in her eyes before she moves past me and into the room.

"Leave it to men to make a woman clean up the mess they created." She toes a few boxes. "Seriously, how does someone accumulate this much crap and do nothing with it?"

"Someone who is never home."

"Clearly." She turns toward me, hands on her hips. "How do you want me to handle this? I'm not into trashing things. Our landfills are full enough."

"I wouldn't want you to trash anything either," I reply before taking a sip of my coffee. "I need you to go through every piece of mail and set aside the most important letters I need to respond to."

"Wouldn't you think every letter is important? I mean, your fans are the reason you are where you are as stated by you yesterday."

"I don't have time to respond to every letter."

"Then what would you qualify as important?"

"Like if a kid wrote to me, or if someone was going through a rough time while listening to my music, something like that."

"I see." She reaches down and picks up a partially opened envelope. She pulls out a piece of paper, and her eyes widen before she turns it toward me. "And these naked selfies, what should I do with those?"

I glance at the picture of a woman in front of a mirror, completely naked.

"Is there a scrapbook you have of these, a little collection?"

"Shred it," I say, unamused.

"Are you sure? I'm pretty good at scrapbooking."

"The shredder is in the corner. Shred anything that's not important. Keep the clippings, I drop them off at the composting center. But if the picture is photo material, keep that separate from the paper clippings, as those can't go to the compost."

"Do you really drop clippings off at the compost center?" she asks, surprised.

"Yes. Now start with the mail. There are more bags in the garage. I can carry them in here when you're ready for them."

"Okay," she answers. "Can I grab some water or something to drink, or am I imprisoned in this room?"

Dramatic much?

"You're not restricted to this room," I answer. "If you want to move into the living room to spread out, have at it. Just don't go in the room across from my bedroom. Other than that, you have free range."

"Ooo, is that like a west wing type of thing?"

My brows pull together in confusion. "What's that?"

"You know, how the beast from *Beauty and the Beast* is like don't go in the west wing?"

Understanding falls over me. "No, it's my studio and I'm trying to work. I don't need you needling me with your smart-ass questions and comments."

"Oh . . . studio, huh? Writing some new music?"

"What's it to you?"

"Nothing." She glances away. "But according to my friend, who is a fan, you haven't released anything new in a while."

Yeah, because my mind has been an empty vessel for the past year.

Touring.

Drinking.

Partying.

Loneliness . . .

It will do that . . . squash any creative flow.

"I've been touring. Hard to release new music when you're traveling the world nonstop."

"I'm sure." She moves past me and heads down the

hallway to the kitchen. This time, I follow her. "So let's say I was hungry, could I pop open this cabinet and grab a . . ." Her voice falls off as she notices there's nothing in my cabinet. She moves to the pantry and discovers nothing really in there as well. When she turns around to face me, she asks, "Where are your snacks?"

"Don't have any."

"What? How can you not have snacks? You have almond creamer, but not snacks?"

"Don't really need them," I answer.

"Uh, everyone needs snacks." She shakes her head. "I can't work under these conditions. I need snacks."

"Are you telling me you can't get anything done if there aren't snacks in the house?"

"Exactly."

Sighing, I grab my wallet from the counter and pull out a few hundred dollars. I hand them over to her and say, "Grab snacks, some fruit and veggies, as well as hummus from the general store."

"Pardon me, but that's not part of the job description."

"If you want snacks, it is now. Your choice." I then pull my phone out of my pocket and hand it to her. "Plug your number in there."

She takes my phone. "Is this so you can call me at all hours of the night and make more requests that don't fall under the job description?"

"You know, I could hire someone else and just report you to the police. Is that what you want?"

As she types away, she glances up at me. "You know that's not what I want."

"Then enough with the smart-ass comments. Jesus."

"Can't take a little sarcasm. Noted." She hands me back my phone. "I'm in your phone under *Wench*."

"Charming," I reply and pocket my phone. "Last, were you able to find a place to stay?"

Her head tilts to the side. "Man, with a comment like that, it almost seems like you care about me."

"I care about you getting to work on time, and if you're sleeping in your car, that might be a setback."

Her expression falls flat. "Yes, I'm staying in a small studio above The Almond Store. You know, in case you need to fetch me . . . errrr, actually, don't fetch me."

That makes me inwardly smile. "Why? Don't want your family finding out who you're working with?"

"Exactly. They think I have an internship up the coast, and why the hell did I just tell you that?" She looks up at the ceiling in frustration. "Ugh, now you're just going to use that against me. More fodder for you."

"So you told your family that you're here for an internship, not because you failed out this semester? Wow, digging yourself a hole, don't you think?"

"How about this," she says, looking me dead in the eyes. "I'll mind my business, and you mind yours."

"Fine by me," I answer as I turn away from her. "I have no problem staying out of your way."

"Good," she replies. A second later, she asks, "So would it be cool if I went to grab those snacks now?"

Jesus Christ.

"Yes," I groan as I move toward my studio.

———

I'M in the middle of strumming my guitar when there is a loud crash in the kitchen followed by a "Noooooo."

Hattie just got back—an hour later—from getting snacks, and I caught sight of her bringing more paper bags into the house than I expected. I thought she was just grabbing snacks. I didn't think she was grabbing a week's worth of groceries.

I set my guitar down because, frankly, I've done nothing productive for the past hour other than play the same three chords over and over again, and I head out into the open living space that connects with the kitchen, where I find Hattie kneeling on the floor, looking completely distressed.

"What happened?" I ask.

She glances to the side and says, "I dropped my pickles."

"What?" I peer over the counter and see a broken jar of pickles on the floor. "You got pickles for a snack?"

"Yes, if you must know. I love them, and when I tried to open the lid, the jar slipped out of my hand and broke. Now my life is over."

Okay . . .

"Do you need my help cleaning them up?"

"No," she says as she stands. "Just tell me where your cleaning stuff is."

"Under the sink." Clearly upset, she walks over to the sink and pulls out paper towels as well as cleaner. "You can put the broken glass in a bag as well as the pickles. I'll toss them in the trash later," I say.

"Fine," she says as she sniffs.

Wait . . . is she . . . is she crying?

I bend at the waist, trying to get a good look at her, but I can't quite catch her eyes.

"What are you doing?" she asks, head down. "I can feel you staring at me."

"Are you really that upset over pickles?"

"Just leave me alone." She starts picking up the broken jar's large shards and putting them in a plastic bag.

I think she's upset, and for some fucking reason, I feel bad for her.

Annoyingly bad.

They're pickles. Why is she so upset over fucking pickles?

Maybe she likes snacks that much. Who fucking knows. I shouldn't care.

But . . .

A small piece of my black soul flickers alive for a brief

moment.

"Were they special pickles?"

"I said just leave me alone, Hayes." She swipes at her nose and continues to clean up.

Okay . . .

"Are you sure you don't need help?" I ask, because frankly, I don't know how to leave this situation.

"Positive," she answers but doesn't look my way, just continues to pick the pickles up one at a time and deposit them into the bag.

I guess that's that.

Confused and feeling a slight tightness in my chest, I return to my studio and sit on my couch. Instead of picking up my guitar, I stare out the window, Hattie's sad expression imprinted on my brain.

Her sniffles echo through my head.

Her reluctance to look up at me is annoying.

I shouldn't care. She broke her pickle jar. Who fucking cares?

I really should just let it go, but . . . hell, I feel fucking bad.

And why?

Why do I feel bad?

Maybe because no matter how hard I try to deny it, I really do have a heart.

Even though I like to paint myself as the asshole and ride that persona to the grave, a part of me is trying to break through that tough exterior and make himself known.

Fuck.

And for some annoying reason, he's trying to break through when it involves Hattie.

Once again, it's the desperation in her eyes.

The sadness.

I lift from the couch and head out toward the kitchen again. I snag my wallet from the counter and move toward the garage. "I'll be back," I say, climbing into my car.

I HATE MYSELF.

Truly . . . truly hate myself.

For one, I should be working in my studio, trying to come up with lyrics that might make my studio execs happy. Instead, I spent forty-two dollars and ninety-two cents on pickles at the general store, as well as half an hour in the pickle section, racking my brain to remember what the godforsaken jar that she dropped looked like.

The entire time, I was inwardly chastising myself for even caring. This is Hattie Rowley. I have no ties and no connections to her. I technically forgot she even existed until she tried to secretly deposit that box on my front porch, yet here I am, caring that she dropped fucking pickles on my concrete floor. That's a smell I'm sure will live there forever, no matter how many times I clean it.

There's no reason for me to do this.

Therefore, I'm blaming my erratic actions on procrastination. I'd apparently rather spend my time in the pickle aisle with Dee Dee Coleman staring me down with a sneer on her lips than on my studio couch with my guitar across my lap and a pen in my hand.

Someone, please explain to me how this makes sense.

Irritated with myself, I exit my car with a reusable bag full of pickles, and I head into the house and straight to my office, only to stop halfway in the hallway when I hear the telltale sounds of music, but not just any music . . . *The Mamas & the Papas*.

Holy shit.

Color me shocked.

I wouldn't have expected Hattie even to know who The Mamas & the Papas are, let alone softly sing to their music. And hell, her voice isn't too bad at all.

Not to mention, it's one of my favorite songs: *Dedicated to the One I Love.*

I can't remember the last time I listened to The Mamas & the Papas, but their flawless harmonies always captured me. John Phillips's songwriting mirrored that of The Beatles, while Denny Doherty led the group with his pure voice. Michelle and Mama Cass, fucking perfect together, their voices harmonizing so well that it almost felt like they were one human, one powerhouse staking claim to the song.

Hell, hearing them again makes me want to search for the record I have of theirs and play it on my Crosley record player.

Hmm . . .

Maybe that's not a bad idea. I could possibly use them as some inspiration.

Although they were better known for their sunshine pop, I'm more suited for a dark folky vibe. Nonetheless, any inspiration is good inspiration.

Pickles in hand, I make my way to the office and knock on the door. Not sure why. It's my house, my office, after all, but just out of respect.

The music stops, and Hattie says, "Come in."

I open the door and spot her sitting cross-legged on the ground, piles of letters and empty envelopes scattered across the floor.

When she sees me, she immediately says, "There's an order to this madness. So don't judge me."

"Didn't come here to judge," I reply, feeling awkward because this is so outside of my comfort zone. I'm truly having an out-of-body experience. "Just came to drop this off." I set the bag in front of her, not even handing it to her. That's how uncomfortable I am.

With a confused look, she peers into the bag and then back up at me. "You got me pickles?"

That look of surprise and the lack of disdain for me in her

eyes makes me very uneasy. See, this is why I shouldn't do nice things because it confuses everyone . . . even me.

I pull on the back of my neck. "I didn't know what kind you were crying over—"

"I wasn't crying over them. I was just . . . upset."

It seemed like she was crying, but I won't push it.

"Either way, I didn't know what kind, so I just got one of each."

Her eyes stay fixed on me, studying, trying to see into the depths of my dark soul.

I don't like it.

I don't like how exposed it makes me feel.

Like I'm naked and raw, ripe for the picking.

After a few seconds, she asks in disbelief, "You got me pickles?"

She's softening toward me, I can see it in the way she slowly lowers her defenses, and I don't like it. I want her annoyed with me. Angry. Irritated. So irate with frustration over being my assistant that she contemplates spilling my morning coffee on me.

Note to self, don't do fucking nice things.

"Can you not make a big deal out of this?"

"But this is nice. You're not nice to me or my family, so why would you do this?"

Precisely what I'm trying to figure out.

"I don't know, you got me," I say, tossing my hands up in the air. "Probably lost my goddamn mind." I adjust the hat that rests on my head. "Just eat the fucking pickles, okay?"

"Okay," she replies. "Thank you."

I cringe. No . . . no, she can't be grateful. That's too much.

"No thanks needed. Forget it even happened." And with that, I head out of the room and back to my studio, where I sit down on the couch and groan.

Fuck, why did I do that?

Chapter Five

HATTIE

"How was your first day?" Maggie asks into the phone as I drive from Hayes's house to the farm to visit with Mac and Ryland.

"Weird," I reply.

"Weird, how?"

"Well, once again, he was sitting outside on his porch, this time waiting for me. I was a minute late, and he made a big deal about it."

"The man needs his coffee, what are you doing being late?"

"Shut your pretty mouth." We both laugh. "And then he showed me how to make his coffee, gave me a quick tour of his bedroom, and took me to his office. When I say this man receives fan mail, I'm not kidding. I spent eight hours working today and got halfway through one bag. And Maggie, oh my God, the naked pictures he gets."

"Really?" Maggie asks, her voice full of humor.

"Yes, like . . . so many naked pictures, and these girls are gorgeous. Some of their boobs . . . I'm really jealous."

"You're jealous of anyone with boobs since you don't have any yourself."

"Facts, but seriously, like even their nipples are perfect, not the slightest bit wonky. Although, I guess if you take a picture of yourself naked and send it to a popular singer, you wouldn't have wonky nipples."

"What is a wonky nipple?" Maggie asks.

"You know, like if one is a hamburger and the other is a hot dog."

"What?" Maggie laughs.

"Like . . . if one nipple is longer horizontally and the other is longer vertically."

"You think that's wonky? I call that exciting. My right nipple is longer than my left, and I always tell myself it's because that nipple was trying harder when growing. And you know what, I'd totally send a naked picture to Hayes Farrow if I weren't worried that picture would somehow resurface and come back to bite my wedding business in the ass. Or else Hayes would be staring down the barrel of two non-wonky yet exciting and puzzling nipples."

I let out a light laugh. "Puzzling nipples, now you know that's something I could get on board with. And if I think about it, my nips are a touch wonky too."

"I bet if you looked closely, the pictured nipples have a wonkiness to them too. That or the ladies facetuned them."

"Can you facetune a nipple?"

"I think you can facetune anything at this point. Technology is freaky," she says.

"I guess so, but yeah, lots of nipples."

"What are you going to do with the nipples? Make them into a collage? Turn them into a puzzle? Oooo, imagine a puzzle of just nipples."

"I'd do it," I say.

"I know you would, and you would take it seriously."

"I would. No matter the picture, every puzzle deserves the same amount of time and attention."

"You are so . . . perfect," Maggie says with a laugh. She's always thought my puzzling was, as she put it, cute. "So what do you do with the pictures?"

"He told me to shred them, but I feel bad just shredding the pictures. These women took their time to pose and print a picture for him, so before I send them down the shredder, I offer the lady in said picture a silent compliment."

"Stop, no you don't." She chuckles.

"I do!" I say. "I tell them how I liked the angle they chose, or wow, good job shaving everything, or lovely piercings."

"Only you, Hattie."

"They deserve the praise. It takes guts to send those and worry why you don't get a response. So a silent praise, I think, is good. But I have to say, a few of them have made me consider a nipple piercing."

"We've gone over this, the minute they clamp your nipple, you're going to be kicking anyone in sight to get away from you. You could never do it."

"I know, but these ladies make me dream that I could."

"Don't let them convince you." Maggie laughs.

"I won't. But anyway, the naked pictures weren't the weird part."

"That's a plot twist. Color me intrigued. What was the weird part?"

"Well, I noticed he didn't have snacks or any food for that matter. It was eerily weird. Not even a bottle of ketchup. So I told him I needed snacks."

"Naturally. You can't function without at least a granola bar in hand. I hope he understood that."

"He got the hint real quick. He gave me money to go get snacks and asked for some healthy shit, which annoyed me—"

"Like what? Vegetable crudités?"

"Uh, yeah."

"Ugh, that makes me hate him. Try a donut, Hayes. It won't break the finally stacked abs you've created."

"Tell me about it," I agree with her. "Anyway, I returned with everything you would expect in my grocery bags. Chips, cookies, candy . . . some fruits and veggies for him. Some of those pretzel peanut butter things I love and my coveted pickles."

"The ones that you and Cassidy would snack on every summer?"

"The exact ones." Maggie gets it. She knows all about my pickle obsession with Cassidy. One summer, when she came to visit, Maggie was drawn into the pickle eating. She went home with a few jars. "I was so happy to see them that I nearly cried in the store. So I bought them, obviously, brought them back to his place, and when I was trying to open them, I dropped them."

"Nooo," she replies in distress. "Not the pickles."

"Yup," I say. "And guess who has concrete floors?"

"Hayes fucking Farrow."

"Oh yes," I answer, still mourning the illicit drop of the jar.

"What a disaster. And who has concrete floors? You don't see that choice in houses often."

"Yeah, and since the man is so minimalistic with his decorating, there was not an area rug in sight to save the glass from breaking. I was so distraught I almost started crying. Thank God I didn't because he came to check to see what the ruckus was. And then do you know what he did?"

"Kick you in the ear and demand you clean it up?"

"What?" I ask with a laugh.

"Just trying to keep the conversation lively."

"Take it down a notch." I chuckle. "He didn't kick me in the ear, but he did leave the house for almost an hour, and when he came back, he had a bag full of pickles. All for me."

There's a pause on the other end and I'm about to ask her if she heard me, but then she says, "Wait, he got you pickles?"

"Yup, every flavor the general store had."

"Oh my God," she whispers.

"Yeah, I know, weird. He dropped the bag off and left. I didn't know what to do when he left, so I just sat there, staring at them for probably ten minutes. I'm still confused. The conversation we had before that was tense and irritable. We were both going at each other and then . . . pickles."

"Pickles," she says softly.

"Yeah . . . pickles," I mutter, still utterly confused about the action.

This is Hayes Farrow we're talking about. He has been nothing but rude and obnoxious to the town and to us as a family. He doesn't care who he hurts, he just takes what he wants. The only people he's nice to are his grandma, Abel, and Rodney. That's it.

He couldn't care less about the town he grew up in.

Doesn't participate in any fundraisers.

And will walk all over you to get what he wants, hence my current situation.

So the pickles . . . yeah, that was very confusing.

"What if . . ." Maggie pauses for a moment. "What if he likes you?"

Oh Maggie, how did I know she would jump to that conclusion?

"Please, Maggie, please don't start with that. I know your little romantic heart always thinks the best of everyone and every situation—*except icky Matt*—but Hayes Farrow liking me is completely off the table. So off the table that he actually made it a point to tell me, straight to my face, that he had no desire to take my clothes off."

"Oh God, he said that to you?"

"Yup, made it quite clear he's not attracted to me in the

slightest. So the pickles have nothing to do with any attraction."

"Maybe he was masking—"

"He said it several times. Even looked me up and down a few times. It was . . . it was rude. Trust me, I think he'd rather make love to the broken jar of pickles than even consider peeling my bra off me."

"Huh, well that's disappointing, but also confusing, because he's never been nice to you, so why would he give you pickles?"

"The question of the day. I told you, it was weird." I see the farm up ahead and inwardly sigh as I spot the split-rail fence I helped Cassidy build. We started it with the best of intentions, dreaming up how beautiful it will make the farm, but very quickly got sick of putting it together and never finished because mentally, we couldn't do it anymore. However, the portion we did build still stands.

And it stands beautifully.

I can still hear her frustrated laughter as we'd slip one end in, only for the other end to pop out.

God, this will be hard. Memories are already flooding me.

"Not sure how to take this pickle delivery, but I'm going to think on it because . . . how weird."

"Yup," I sigh into the phone. "Okay, I'm here. I should go."

"Have fun and if you need someone to talk to after, I'm here for you."

"Thank you," I say, knowing damn well I have the best friend ever. I hang up the phone and pull down the dirt road leading to Cassidy's farmhouse. It's quaint with two bedrooms and one bath and has everything she needs for her and Mac. *Needed. It's everything Cassidy and Mac needed.*

The potato fields are scattered all around it, giving the whole place a very earthy scent.

And yes, I said potato, not almond.

I know what you're probably thinking—why would she have a potato farm when she has an almond store?

It was a question we all asked too, until she unveiled her master plan.

You see, she harvests the potatoes and makes vodka with them. A special vodka she sells around the town, as well as in her store, even almond flavored. *She did. She made . . .*

It's still so hard to believe she's gone. *And that everything about her is now past tense.*

This was also where she excelled. At business. She sold the leftover potatoes to the local restaurants to use for fresh-cut fries. Provisions, the burger place in town, is best known for their fries and has even started a fry bar so people can load up on whatever toppings they want.

With the vodka, she bottled it and sold it but also made almond extract with it.

Famous almond extract.

The best almond extract in the state. California is known for producing the most almonds in the country, and Cassidy took advantage of that. Homemade vodka turned into almond extract that she then sold to some of the top pastry chefs in the state. It's what Aubree continues to do now.

And the reason Aubree was probably freaking out about the bottles was because the extract is in high demand.

It's an odd, eccentric business model, but boy, did it work. Now, The Almond Store is a main stop for anyone traveling up the Pacific Coast Highway or in Northern California in general. They come for the almond vodka, the almond extract, and the toasted, roasted almonds. They come for the almond butter, the creamer, the milk. They come for the pastries, the candles, the illustrated almond cards. It's easily the sweetest store I've ever walked into, perfectly executed, and it kills me knowing that she's no longer here to see her hard work pay off.

I park the car in front of the white farmhouse and

unbuckle my seat belt just as Mac flies out of the screen door and down the porch.

A head of bouncy brown curls and freckles just like mine, but blue eyes like her father, she is the spitting image of Cassidy. And with a horse stuffy named Chewy Charles tucked under her arm, she bounds over to my car door and knocks on the window, a bright smile on her face.

Jesus, seeing the joy on her face nearly breaks me in half because this girl has been through more than any person should go through, and she's only four. Yet look at that smile. Look at her excitement. If I were her, I'm not sure I'd exude such joy.

I open the door, and she leaps into my arms. "Aunt Hattie," she squeals while giving me a large hug. "You're here. You're here. You're here."

"Hey, baby girl," I say as I return the hug just in time to see Ryland walk out the door as well and lean against one of the poles on the porch, arms crossed.

Just from one look, I can tell he's been run ragged.

And he probably has.

I don't think it was ever in his plans to have kids, yet here he is, a single dad to a little girl who just lost her mother a few months ago. Not to mention living in his dead sister's house while being a full-time math teacher and varsity baseball coach for one of the most prestigious high schools in the state, specifically known for its athletics program despite the town's size.

Friday night lights mean something completely different here. Instead of hitting up the gridiron, the town rallies around the fences of the baseball diamond.

"Chewy Charles is so excited to see you," she says as she makes a licking sound and mimics her horse licking my face.

"Hi, Chewy Charles," I say. "I've missed you too."

"He says you taste like broccoli."

"Oh, I don't know if that's a compliment or not."

She curls her nose. "He says it does not taste good."

"Soooo not a compliment."

"What's a complent?"

"Compliment." I chuckle softly while correcting her. "It's when someone says something nice about you."

"Oh." She brings Chewy Charles to her ear and listens as he "speaks" to her. The whole time, she nods.

"What's he saying?" I ask.

Her eyes narrow at me. "That's private, Aunt Hattie. And we respect privacy."

I nod. "That we do."

She hops off my lap, and with Chewy Charles under her arm, she says, "But between you and me, he doesn't want to lick you again."

And then she takes off.

Insulted by a goddamn stuffy. I can't imagine what Chewy Charles says about Ryland.

She runs back into the house, and Ryland waits for me as I get out of my car and walk up to him. He pulls me into a hug, tighter than Aubree but not as tight as Cassidy. A solid medium between the two.

"Hey, brother."

"Hey, sis," he says before opening the door to the house for me. "How are you?"

"Good," I say even though I've definitely been better. I don't want to tip anything off.

"Handling the breakup okay?"

"What breakup?" Mac asks as she jumps on the recliner chair beside the window that overlooks the potato fields.

"Mac, I said no jumping on the chair," Ryland says in an authoritative voice I heard many times growing up. He's raised me just as much as Cassidy. Tag-teaming me whenever we were home together.

She flops down on her bottom and asks again, "What breakup?"

"Matt and I are no longer dating," I answer.

"Oh . . ." She looks to the side and then brings Chewy Charles to her ear. She nods and says, "We didn't like him. He poked my shoulder, and I didn't like that."

"I can understand that." I mutter, "He tried poking me but always seemed to miss."

"Hattie," Ryland says under his breath.

"What?" I whisper, "She didn't hear me."

Ryland whispers back, "She hears everything."

"Uncle Ry Ry, what's for dinner?"

"Hot dogs and beans," Ryland answers as he moves toward the kitchen. "Go potty and wash up. It should be ready soon."

She flings Chewy Charles in the air and then bolts upstairs as I follow Ryland into the kitchen, taking in the house and how nothing has changed. Not one picture is out of place, not one piece of furniture. The only thing missing is Cassidy's warm presence and superior cooking.

"Hot dogs and beans, huh?" I ask as I sit on the counter in the corner of the kitchen like I did many times when Cassidy was cooking.

Ryland lights up the stove and pours a can of opened beans into the pot. "It's the best I've got right now." He goes to the fridge and pulls out a pack of hot dogs. "I want to take some cooking lessons but haven't had any fucking time. Trust me when I say I feel like shit serving this to her. I know Cassidy would be pissed."

"I didn't mean to make you feel bad. I know you're doing the best you can, Ryland."

"I could be doing better." He pulls out a knife and then looks over at me. "Did you know they have spirit days in preschool? Apparently, all last week was spirit week, and I had no goddamn idea. I picked her up from day care, and she was crying hysterically because she didn't have crazy hair like everyone else." He shakes his head and starts cutting the hot

77

dogs straight into the pot, not bothering to use a cutting board. "The girl has crazy hair every day because I don't know how to fucking do it. You would think she'd fit right in."

"You're being too hard on yourself," I say.

His eyes fall to mine. "I'm not. Cassidy would expect more." He shakes his head and blows out a heavy breath. "Tell me about the internship."

"Ryland," I say softly. "Don't change the subject like that. If you're struggling, it's okay to admit. I can help—"

"You need to focus on school."

"Jesus," I say. "What is with you and Aubree? You know there's more to me than school, right?"

"There shouldn't be," he says. "That's what you should focus on. That's what you should be figuring out. Hell . . . you should be graduating this semester, but you took an internship instead."

My brows pull together. "It was a smart move." We all know I'm in defense mode, so ignore the lying on my end. Thanks.

"Better than graduating?" he asks. "I don't see how that's possible."

"Can we not talk about it?" I ask. "I didn't come over here to get lectured, Ryland."

"You're right," he concedes. "Sorry. It's just been . . . stressful."

"If it's so stressful, why won't you and Aubree ask for help?"

He finishes cutting the hot dogs and picks up a wooden spoon to stir his concoction. "Because you're in school. And there's a transition stage. We're just trying to figure that out. It will take us a second."

I nod. "I can understand that, but I can help." He grunts in disapproval. I won't get anywhere with that narrative, so I switch things up. I look around the open space, noticing the stack of blankets in the corner as well as the pillow. That must be Ryland's bed, pushed out of the way so Mac doesn't notice. "Are you sleeping on the couch?"

"Yeah." He sets the spoon down and then turns toward me, leaning his hip against the counter. My eyes roam over him, noticing how his eyes are sunken with dark circles under them. He's always been extremely fit, but he's lost weight, and not in a good way. Now it's almost like his skin sits on top of muscle. And the smile he used to carry as a fun-loving guy is nowhere to be found. In its place seems like a ball of stress rests directly on his chest.

"I can't convince myself to sleep in Cassidy's room. I barely go in there."

"Does Mac?"

He shakes his head. "Not really. She said it makes her sad to go in there. She doesn't like to remember the place where her mommy passed away."

"God," I say as my throat chokes up. "That's heart-breaking."

"Tell me about it." He crosses his arms. "I try to talk to her about Cassidy, but she just shakes her head and tells me Mommy will be back. She's just gone for now, but she'll be back."

Well, fuck me.

Tears cloud my eyes, and I take a few deep breaths because I don't want Mac to walk in and see me crying.

"What do you tell her?"

"Nothing," Ryland says. "I don't have it in me to tell her any differently."

Just then, Mac comes barreling down the stairs, her feet pitter-pattering across the hardwood floors. When she flies into the kitchen, she has her pants on backward and one side of her hair tied up into a ponytail.

"Oh yeah!" she says, shaking her bottom. "I went potty."

Ryland smiles softly at her. "Good job, Mac." He reaches into the cabinet and says, "Can you set the table for us?"

"Can I use the fancy napkins?"

"Always," he says as he pulls out the cloth napkins Cassidy made from a drawer.

"I'm going to make cats out of them."

"Can't wait," Ryland says and turns back to me.

"Can she make animals out of the napkins?"

He subtly shakes his head. "No, it's just a balled-up mess on the plate, but I act impressed every time."

"Now that's a good uncle."

Just then, Aubree pushes through the door. "I could smell your beans all the way from outside." Mac runs up to her and hugs her. "Hey Mackie, where's Chewy?"

"Chewy Charles." Mac stomps her foot. "You have to use his whole name."

Aubree winces. "Sorry, where's Chewy Charles?"

"Outer space," Mac says casually. "Don't worry, he won't be late for dinner. You know he loves the dogs."

That makes me chuckle.

"Hey, sis," Aubree says, walking into the kitchen and taking a seat at the island. "Telling Ryland all about how his nemesis is back in town?"

Did I mention Aubree has also been known as the pot stirrer? Yeah, she holds the title, and I think she holds it with pride.

And the mention of Hayes, or rather the suggestion of him, makes me internally sweat. They might not know about my new arrangement, but it still doesn't negate the fact that I know the implications if they find out.

Ryland flips off the stove burner and turns toward us. "Abel told me."

Here's the thing.

Back in high school, Ryland, Hayes, and Abel were the three musketeers and the best of friends. They all played baseball together, partied together, and even helped each other cheat on tests. And then something happened, a truth I still don't know to this day, and it drove them apart. Hayes went one way, Ryland went the other, and Abel stayed in the middle, not wanting to choose sides. He's remained a good friend to both, being able to keep them separate. Honestly, it takes a strong man to be friends with two rivals, but Abel has always been the sweet one of the group, the caring one. No wonder he's a doctor now, and he's handled the challenge gracefully.

"You knew Hayes was here, and you didn't burst into flames? I'm shocked," Aubree says.

"It's not like our paths will cross," Ryland says. "Whenever he's around, he usually sticks to his place and doesn't venture into town."

"He came into town today," Aubree says. "Dee Dee told Ethel, who told me that he went into the general store, bought every pickle jar in the place, and then left. That was it, just pickles."

Sweat creeps down my neck as I remember how talkative this town is. Did Dee Dee think it was weird that I was in the store only moments before buying a jar of pickles as well? Did she make the connection? Did she notice that he bought the same pickles that Cassidy and I used to buy? Am I over-thinking this?

Can they see my sweat?

God, why did he have to buy the pickles?

He's making this more complicated than it should be.

"He doesn't even like pickles," Ryland says.

Great!

He doesn't like pickles. Information I didn't know, but do you know who does? Me. That's who likes pickles. They're probably connecting the dots as I sit here, palms sweaty, back sweaty . . . ass sweaty.

"You know, people can change within the eighteen years since you last spoke to them. He might have an acquired taste for pickles . . ." Aubree suggests.

"Yeah," I chime in, my voice cracking. "Or maybe they were for his grandma." There, maybe that will help them steer clear of me.

"True, they could be for his grandma," Aubree says, and I inwardly heave a sigh of relief. "Or maybe he brought a girl home. Dee Dee said she saw a car driving up toward his house."

Oh, sweet Jesus Christ.

Yup, sweat just rolled down my ass crack.

This godforsaken town and their inane nosiness.

"Either way, I'm not interested," Ryland says. "He can fuck off."

"Ooo, Uncle Ry Ry, that's a bad word," Mac says from the table where she's sitting cross-legged on top, bunching napkins together.

"Sorry," Ryland says just as my phone buzzes in my hand. I glance down at the screen and see a strange number. Speak of the devil—literally.

I hop off the counter. "Be right back. My new boss."

Happy to pull myself away from that conversation—I don't need them seeing my sweat mark—I move out of the kitchen and to the back den where Mac has her playroom. Full of stuffed animals, beds for her stuffed animals, and clothing for her stuffed animals, I unlock my phone and stare at the text.

Hayes: *The code to get into my house is 6935. Don't be late.*

I text him back quickly.

Hattie: *About that. People are already starting to notice a car driving up to your place, and since my car is bright red and all, it's not looking good on my end.*

Hayes: *If you're trying to get out of this, you're not going to.*

Hattie: *I'm not. I'm just . . . trying to figure out a way I can serve my time without getting caught.*

Hayes: *Serving your time, that's how you see it?*

Hattie: *Uh yeah, when you say things like you're not getting out of* *it, I'm serving time, so a little help on how I can be inconspicuous would be appreciated.*

Hayes: *What do you have to hide?*

Hattie: *Uh, the fact that I'm working for the Antichrist.*

Hayes: *According to your brother.*

Hattie: *And a lot of people in town.*

Hayes: *Because they have their head so far up your brother's ass that they'll take his side.*

Hattie: *None of that matters. What matters is if I'm seen with you, it will be the talk of the town, and my brother very well might disown me. I've already lost a sister. I don't need to lose a brother too. So what the hell should I do?*

I stare down at my phone, waiting for a solution from Hayes, so when I find Mac standing right in front of me, I nearly scream.

"Christ," I say, bringing my hand to my chest. "MacKenzie."

"Who are you talking to?" she asks, swinging Chewy Charles around in a circle.

"My . . . my boss," I answer.

"Uncle Ryland told me to tell you the dogs are ready, and it's rude to make everyone wait for you."

"Sorry," I say. She holds her hand out to me. I take it, and she pulls me back toward the kitchen just as my phone buzzes in my hand. I glance at the screen as I'm dragged by a four-year-old.

Hayes: *You know where the old barn is outside of town? I'll leave my car behind it so you can swap and drive that to my house. There are enough bushes and trees to hide yours. Be here at seven.*

⸻

"WHAT THE HELL kind of car is this?" I ask, staring at the SUV I've never seen before in my entire life. "And how the hell am I supposed to drive this?"

Of course he'd have some fancy vehicle no one has heard of. What is a Rivian anyway?

I pull up my phone and type the brand into Google.

Your electric adventure awaits.

Oh . . . an EV. I've never driven one of these.

I thumb through the website, locating his SUV, and then my eyes nearly bug out of my head.

"Oh my GOD!" I shout. "Over one hundred thousand dollars for a used one? Who spends that much money on a used vehicle? I thought when buying used, you're trying to save money. Ridiculous," I mutter and then set the phone down.

What I could do with one hundred thousand dollars.

Not take this job, that's for sure.

Skip another semester of school.

Build an extension on the farmhouse so Ryland doesn't have to sleep on a freaking couch!

But nope . . . I'm driving one hundred thousand dollars instead.

"Okay, how do we start this?" I look in the console for a key, but don't see anything. So I look in the glove box. Nothing. I search the car, now becoming frantic as I see the time staring me in the face. Two minutes until he's going to bitch about me being late again.

Well, how the hell am I supposed to be on time if he doesn't leave me a key to drive the damn thing?

What an idiot.

I grab my phone again, but this time, I call him.

It rings twice, and then he answers.

"You're going to be late."

"Yeah, because you're a moron," I say. "You didn't leave me a key to start this spaceship."

"You don't start it. And yes, I did leave a key."

"What do you mean you don't start it?"

"You just activate it."

"That makes no sense."

"Jesus, Hattie," he groans. "Do you see the key card in the middle console?"

I look down and see a white key card with a yellow symbol in the middle. I pick it up and say, "This is what starts your car? Like you're opening a hotel room?"

"Yes. Hold it against the driver's side door and that will activate it, then put the car in drive and press down on the pedal."

"So there's like . . . no engine you have to start?"

"It doesn't have an engine, it's an electric vehicle."

Huh . . . interesting.

"Leave it to you to have some nonsensical car."

"It's not nonsensical. It's just not what you're used to. Now stop jabbering and get here."

With that, he hangs up.

God, he's cranky in the morning . . . or every hour for that matter.

Looks like the momentary lapse of pickle niceness has subsided, and I'm entirely okay with that.

Okay, so we just hold the key card up to the door because that makes sense. Doors drive cars after all . . . right.

I press the key card up to the door and the screen lights up.

Would you look at that?

Fascinating. I put the car into drive and press down on the pedal to go, only to fly forward at a speed I wasn't expecting, shooting me nearly across the small ravine in front of me.

With a death grip on the steering wheel, the hair on the back of my neck standing to attention, I breathe out heavily, "Good fucking God."

That . . . that could have been very bad. If I drove Hayes's car into a ravine, I could only imagine the caustic mood that would put him in.

Not the pickle-buying mood, that's for damn sure.

Okay, let's try this again. I reverse the SUV and then slowly—and I mean slowly—pull away from the ravine and then put it back into drive where I maneuver my way out onto the road.

Ah, there we go, just takes a second to get used to. And even though I feel this vehicle could take me to another planet if I press on the pedal hard enough, I have to admit, it drives smoothly. I feel fancy driving something that isn't rumbling beneath me, on its last leg, coughing and sputtering down the road.

I smooth my hand over the steering wheel. Oh yeah, a girl could get used to this.

The drive to his house is too short. I've just started getting used to the car when I pull into his driveway, but since I'm three minutes late, I hop out of the car quickly, type in the code to his house, and let myself in.

I decide to make his coffee first and skip the protein shake for after the first delivery. Maybe he'll be grateful for the coffee first.

Because I like to do things my way, I pour the creamer in the mug first, stick it under the coffee maker, and press start once I load it with one of his pods. I smile to myself as I watch the brown liquid mix with the creamer, stirring itself. See, genius and I'm not dirtying a spoon.

Satisfied, I pick up the mug and carefully walk it down to his bedroom. Such a lazy ass that he makes me do this. Just his way of holding control over the situation. When I reach his bedroom door, I part it open and stick my head in.

"Coffee delivery." I push the door all the way in just as Hayes walks into the bedroom from the bathroom, wearing nothing but a low-slung towel around his waist.

Dear.

Mother.

Of.

God.

I feel my jaw slack as my eyes fall on his wet, toned body. Still wearing the necklace he doesn't seem to ever take off, my eyes scan over his thick pecs, his toned, sinew-covered shoulders and biceps, and his stack of abs covered in droplets of water. Water that slides down each curve and bump of his fit stomach, all the way to the light patch of hair just below his belly button that extends to . . .

Oh God.

There's a bulge.

My eyes snap up to his, and my mouth goes dry as his wet hair falls over his forehead and a light smirk plays on his lips.

Damn him.

Damn him and his sexy, mouthwatering body.

And damn that knowing smirk.

Yup, he's not going to let that once-over slip by.

I can only imagine what he's conjuring in his head.

Chapter Six

HAYES

Her curious and impressed eyes snap up to mine, and I watch as she visibly gulps, her throat contracting.

Now this is what satisfaction is, knowing damn well I caught her staring when she said she'd rather bury herself in a jail toilet than admit she finds me attractive—well, something along those lines. I can't remember verbatim what she said. The point is, she just had no problem looking me up and down.

"Get a good look?" I ask as her cheeks stain with pink.

"What?" she asks, her eyes wide. "I wasn't looking. I mean, I looked, but I wasn't *looking*. I was taking in my surroundings. There was no leering or ogling, if that's what you're implying. Because honestly, there's nothing to look at."

"You're staring at my crotch right now."

Her eyes snap up. "I was looking at the coffee. I didn't want to spill it."

"You were looking at my dick."

"I was not . . ." She shakes her head, her eyes falling to my crotch, and when she realizes what she's doing, she looks back up again. She clears her throat. "I was not looking at your dick. Also, don't you think being in a towel in front of your employee is inappropriate?"

"My house. I can do what I want."

"Ah, I see." She nods. "So if you walk around the house naked in front of me, that will be okay since we're under your roof?"

"I wouldn't do that because clearly, you wouldn't get any work done with your staring problem."

Her eyes narrow. "I don't have a staring problem. I was just caught off guard is all." She closes the distance between us and holds out my mug of coffee. "Your majesty, your coffee."

She bows her head and curtsies before lifting up and pushing the mug toward me.

I clasp my hand around hers around the mug, holding her in place. I take a step closer and watch as she inhales deeply and her eyes slowly move up from my chest to my face. She swallows again, clearly affected by me in a towel, which I find far too gratifying.

"You keep checking me out."

"No, I don't," she says, her voice shaky as I hold her in place and move an inch closer.

"Then why are your eyes telling me a different story?"

"Don't flatter yourself. You're in a towel, and I wasn't expecting that."

"If that were the case, it would almost seem like you would want to avert your eyes. But that hasn't happened, has it?"

Her lips twist to the side and she says, "If we're done here, I'd like my hand back."

"Where's my protein drink?"

"I thought you might want your coffee first."

"I want both at the same time," I say as my thumb grazes the back of her hand.

Her eyes widen, but I pull away with the mug before she can say anything.

"You can leave now." I turn away from her, grip my towel just as it starts to fall, and head back into the bathroom, completely satisfied.

"FUCK," I mutter as I drag my hands over my face and stare down at where I've scribbled the start of a song in my notebook. I immediately reject the lyrics the minute I read them.

Trash.

It's all trash.

It's never been this goddamn hard for me. I can usually come up with something, but it's almost as if my life has been at a standstill for the past year, and nothing significant has happened to warrant a song.

Maybe I'll write about how I feel like a goddamn empty sack of skin.

Nothing sounds more poetic in a song than sack of skin.

Fucking hell . . .

I lift from the couch and toss my pen on the coffee table in front of me. This is pointless.

Leaving my studio, I head out to the main living space only to find piles of letters surrounding Hattie as she listens to Blondie.

Another solid choice.

Instead of making my presence known right away, I pause for a moment, watching her.

She's tied her hair up into a high ponytail and bobs her head around with the music, totally immersed in her sorting. Instead of wearing her crewneck sweatshirt, she's now wearing a sports bra and her spandex shorts in a matching set of bright red. It's hard to miss her today . . . or any day for that matter. She owns her presence and makes herself known despite her smaller stature. If I were interested in pursuing her, it wouldn't be hard, not when she shows her true colors so unconsciously, something I really like. Being in the spotlight, I'm surrounded by people who aren't always real and will do anything to appease me, so having Hattie around is refreshing. And her music choices, hell, that's hot as well.

She stands from where she's sitting and stares down at her piles, counting them with her finger. That's when I take in her long, toned legs. For her height, it's surprising to see long legs, but they extend a good portion of her body, leading up to a pair of grippable hips made for finger indents. Her narrow waist is accentuated by her hips and perky ass, and when my eyes work their way up to her tits, I notice just how small they are. Barely a palm full. Her athletic build means she has a great fucking body, but it's those eyes—the ones staring at me right now—that I could see myself getting lost in.

"Can I help you?" A knowing smirk plays on her lips because she just caught me staring like I caught her staring at me this morning. Unlike her, I'll own it. "Get a good look?" she mimics.

"Good is a stretch. Decent, sure."

Her expression falls, hands now on her hips from the insult. "Did you come out here to snub me or is there a purpose for disrupting my peace?"

"You realize this is my house, and I can do what I want, right? I don't need to tiptoe around you."

"I'm aware." She raises her arms above her head and stretches from side to side. My eyes fall to her stomach again, and I wonder if she's ever pierced her belly button because there's a small scar above it, but rather than ask—or get caught again for staring—I turn away and head into the kitchen.

I know I told her I have no interest in taking her clothes

off, but hell, that doesn't negate the fact that she's hot. Under different circumstances, I could easily see myself making a move on her. I probably wouldn't let her leave my sight without doing so, but I'll never cross that line for many reasons.

One being she's Ryland Rowley's little sister.

Also, she's far too innocent for someone like me. Hell, Matt had a hard time finding her clit. I'd not only locate it in a second, but I'd destroy it.

And last, she seems like the type who clings, who enjoys a relationship, and I'm not that guy. Not even close. I'm a loner, and I do my own thing.

Not to mention, I'm a complete and utter asshole, something drilled into me from a young age. She deserves more than someone who will take what he wants and leave her with nothing but the dust of him driving away.

I grab a glass from the cabinet and fill it with water before pulling out my drink drawer and grabbing an electrolyte tablet.

"What are those?" she asks from my side, startling me.

Jesus fuck. So lost in my thoughts, I didn't even notice her step up.

"Electrolyte tablets," I answer.

"Oh, I thought you were popping an Alka-Seltzer or something. Didn't know if it was something you had to do because of your old age."

I look her in the eyes. "Cute."

She smiles. "I'm here to charm." She moves over to the fridge and pulls out a jar of pickles. She pops the top off, leans against the counter, and picks a pickle, only to chomp down on it with a snapping crunch. She holds the jar out to me. "Want one?"

I shake my head. "No. I'm good."

"Not a pickle fan?"

"Not really."

"Snob," she says as she takes another bite.

"Have you always loved pickles that much?" I lean against the opposite counter, my drink fizzing in its cup. I shouldn't engage in conversation with her, but procrastination makes you do stupid things, like flirting with the line of getting to know someone and ignoring them for your sanity.

She glances up at me, skepticism in her eyes. "Are you asking me a personal question?"

See . . . exactly what I'm talking about. I'm just as surprised as she is.

"Is there a problem with that?"

"I didn't think we did that. Then again, I didn't think we bought pickles for each other, and you did that yesterday, so . . ." She pauses, thinking. "You're not trying to pull me over to the dark side, are you?"

"The dark side being the enemy?" I ask.

"Yes, of course."

"I have better things to do with my life than convince you that your brother is in the wrong with our feud, not me. I was just trying to be polite." I push off the counter and start to move away when she shifts in front of me, pickle jar held close to her chest.

"What do you mean Ryland is in the wrong?"

I look down at her, her green eyes piercing. "Maybe something you should talk to him about."

Her curious eyes study me. I can practically see hundreds of questions forming, but I move away before she pins me with a lengthy interlude of inquiries about the past.

I'm halfway to my hallway when she calls out, "Cassidy and I used to eat pickles together." I pause and listen. "This brand, actually. It was our favorite. I haven't had them in a while, and when I saw them yesterday at Coleman's, I knew I had to get them. When I dropped them on the floor, I was devastated. So you bringing these to me, it was . . . it was nice. Unexpected."

I rub my lips together. I knew she was so upset for a reason. I didn't know it had anything to do with Cassidy, though. And now that I know why, I regret what I did because now . . . now, there's an unspoken bond between us, and the last thing I want to do is bond with Ryland Rowley's sister.

"Don't look into it," I say as I push my hand through my hair and glance at her. "If I knew it meant something to you, I never would have purchased them."

Her expression drops. "Of course, because you obviously don't want me thinking you have a heart in that black soul of yours, right?"

"Exactly," I reply. "When I say there's nothing in this chest but skeletons that still haunt me to this day, I mean it. It will be best for everyone if you stay the fuck away from me."

———

ABEL: *Want to meet at By the Slice for dinner?*

Hayes: *Sure, what time?*

Abel: *I'm starving. Twenty?*

Hayes: *See you there.*

I check the time and notice it's almost six, so I flip my empty notebook shut—another wasted day with nothing to show. I exit my studio, where I find Hattie lying on the floor. Her mess extends to the dining room table. What the hell is she doing?

She hasn't organized one damn thing. She just made it worse.

It was simple instructions.

Open the letters, sift through them, keep the important ones, and shred the rest. Now there are at least two dozen piles and no shredding. Is she keeping everything?

"What are you doing?" I ask as she lies with a letter on her stomach.

She pops her head up. "Resting my eyes. They're burning from all of the reading."

"You're reading all of the letters?"

"Yes," she says, exasperated. "How else am I supposed to know if they're important?"

"A quick scan would work."

She shakes her head. "I'm not much of a scanner, and some of these letters have me invested. Like this one." She waves a pink letter in the air like a white flag as she lays her head back down. "It's all about how your song, *The Reason*, helped her realize that she needed to divorce her husband because he wasn't treating her right. And how she got the courage to divorce him, and do you know what that bastard did? He took her dog in the divorce. She was the one who brought the dog to the relationship, and he went and took it. The freaking gall of that man. Anyway, she sent you a bracelet she made, and I thought I owed it to her to pass it along after everything that happened to her. She put her dog's name on it." She shakes her head. "Mitzy, poor, poor Mitzy, is with that motherfucker." She flings the bracelet at me, and I catch it one-handed. I look at the homemade bracelet and back down at Hattie, who clutches the letter to her chest.

"You're becoming too invested. You need to be more cutthroat because at this pace, you're going to be working for me for the rest of the year."

"I wouldn't mind," she says dreamily. "Reading letters in a nice house, stock full of pickles? You're making it too comfortable for me. Frankly, this is on you."

Shaking my head, I say, "You need to leave."

She sits up. "Wait, like . . . you're firing me?"

"No, but I like to see that worry. Maybe you're not as comfortable as you think."

"Ass," she mutters.

"I have dinner plans, and it's nearly six. So time for you to leave."

She stands from the floor and lays her letter gently on a pile before picking up her crewneck that was draped over the couch. "Who are the plans with? A hot date?"

"None of your business," I answer as I move toward my garage.

"Oh, it is a girl. I'm sure someone who you have interest in taking their clothes off, unlike present company?"

I turn toward her and say, "I'd rather stab myself in the eye than take off Abel's clothes."

Surprise falls across her face. "You're going out with Abel? I haven't seen him in a while."

"If you're fishing for an invitation, the answer is no."

"Uh, I have to drive your car here to hide mine. Do you think I'm going to dinner with you and my brother's best friend?"

I pocket my wallet. "You never know with you."

"The answer is no. But please explain how I'm supposed to get back to my car if you're leaving?"

"I'm taking my bike."

"Aw," she says. "You're going to ride your bike there? That's funny."

I exhale sharply. "My motorcycle."

"Oh." She chuckles. "Sort of wish it was a bicycle. I'd pay money to watch you ride down the road on a cruiser, basket attached to the front, trying to gain speed to get to town."

"You need to figure out a better way to spend your money," I say. "Don't worry about locking up. It will lock on its own."

"Okay."

"See you tomorrow." I look over my shoulder at her. "Don't be late."

"Lighten up, Farrow," she replies before leaving the front door and heading to my car.

I move into the garage and open the door. I hop onto my bike, situate my helmet, and then start it up. Pulling out, I speed past Hattie as she tries to figure out how to put my car in drive.

She is something else.

I speed down the coast, the ocean and cliffs to my right. One thing I missed while on tour was the feel of the ocean below me. I've always found solace in the waves crashing onto the beach. Maybe I should head out to the beach tomorrow. Perhaps that will clear my head so I can finally start getting something down on paper.

It doesn't take long to get into town and since By the Slice is one of the first restaurants I pass, I pull in just as Abel gets out of his car. I park next to him, and the first thing he says to me as I remove my helmet is, "Thank fuck, dude. If you weren't here when I arrived, I was going to start eating without you."

I tuck my helmet under my arm and move toward him, giving him a brief hug. Just a dude pat on the back since I haven't seen him in a while. "Not eat anything today?" I ask.

"Just a protein bar. I haven't had time to breathe. It's been patient after patient."

"Then let's get you some food," I say as I open the door for him.

By the Slice is easily the best pizza I've ever had. I know everyone says that about the pizza joints in their hometowns, but I'm not kidding. The crust is crisp on the bottom and the sides, the cheese is perfectly matched with the sauce, and they have the cooking time down to a science, eliminating any possibility of overbaking. Not to mention, the pepperoni they use is out of this world.

We walk up to the register to order, and the girl behind it does a double take when she sees me, but thankfully doesn't fangirl. Instead, she pushes her hair behind her ear and straightens. "What can I get you?"

"Three slices of mushroom pizza," Abel says, "with some honey for dipping and a water."

She places a cup in front of Abel, and then she directs her attention to me. "And for you?"

"Three slices of pepperoni. No dips for me. And a water as well."

"Not a problem."

I reach for my wallet, but Abel stops me. "My treat, dude. I asked you to dinner."

Even though I make more money than Abel, he's still a pretty rich bastard. Since he's sitting pretty, I allow him to pay.

We're handed a number, and then we grab our waters. "Want to sit out on the deck?" he asks.

"Sure," I answer. As we work our way through the restaurant, a few heads turn in our direction, but thankfully, no one bothers us. We head out to the back deck, and Abel finds a table in the corner, secluded from everyone else.

When we take a seat, he says, "You look old."

"Wow." I chuckle. "Way to fucking open the conversation."

"You do. Like you've been pushing yourself too hard, and it's catching up with you."

"It is," I say. "I'm fucking exhausted from the tour, and of course, my label now wants a new album, so I've been trying to work on that."

"Don't you want to take a break?"

"Yes, but I don't have time."

He lifts his water to his lips. "Haven't I told you time and time again that you need breaks every once in a while to recharge?"

"You have," I say. "Not sure I know how to do that."

"Maybe just sit back and relax for a second. Hell, I saw you for what, a minute? And I knew you needed a break. Why can't you look at yourself in the mirror and think the same thing?"

My brows lift in surprise. "Man, this conversation got deep real quick."

He laughs. "Sorry, it's the doctor in me. I assess and give my opinion."

"Well, shut it off for a second." I laugh. "Tell me, what's been going on with you?"

"Nothing much," Abel answers as he leans back in his chair. "You know what it's like in a small town. The Peach Society argues about pretty much everything, the news spreads like wildfire, and the moment anyone tries to come into this town and make a ruckus, we all join forces and push them out."

"So no girls in your life or anything like that?"

Abel raises his brow. "When have you ever cared about that?"

I shrug. "We're getting older. I assumed that maybe you would settle down at some point."

"With whom?" Abel asks. "Meghan down at the drive-in theater with a very unhealthy addiction to Harry Styles? She came into the office the other day because her thumb was hurting, and it's because she's been scrolling so much for her next fix of Harry in a glittery vest—her words, not mine— that she's strained the muscles. And don't worry, I'm not telling you anything the world doesn't already know. She's blasted it all over social media, making it seem like a trophy to rest on her shelf. *Harry thumb* is what she called it."

I chuckle. "Meghan's a good time."

Abel shakes his head. "She's changed, man. Trust me . . . she's changed."

"What about Aubree?" I ask.

"Aubree Rowley?" Abel lets out a large guffaw. "Yeah, and risk the chance of getting my dick chopped off by Ryland? No thanks. Also, she's going through a rough time right now with having to take care of the store and the farm simultaneously. I also heard from Ryland that Cassidy's brother-in-law is trying to come back into the picture with the farm, but that isn't public knowledge."

"What do you mean?" I ask just as the server delivers our pizza. We thank the server, and Abel picks up a slice and takes a huge bite before his eyes roll to the back of his head, and he moans. "Dude, can you not do that? You sound like you're fucking coming."

He chuckles. "Sorry, but fuck, I should have ordered four pieces." He wipes his mouth with a napkin and says, "Half the farm was left to Wyatt, and they didn't think he was interested, but all of a sudden, he sent an email saying he's coming into town and wants to talk about his rights to the farm."

"Oh shit," I say, wondering if Hattie knows that, and then I realize what we're doing. "Hell, we're no better than the Peach Society with our gossiping."

"It's in our blood, dude. Nothing we can do about it." He shrugs it off, and he's right. Gossiping has been ingrained in us.

"True." We both take a bite of our pizza, and when I wipe my mouth, I sense Abel studying me. "What?" I ask.

"There's something you want to tell me, isn't there?"

"What?" I shake my head. "No. Why would you say that?"

"For one, you don't ever take your motorcycle out anymore because it requires gas. For another, you seem tense and uncomfortable, as if you're hiding something."

What the hell? Does he have a backstage pass to the inside business of my life that I don't know about? How can he see that just from my outward appearance?

"Jesus, you're annoying," I say.

He chuckles. "I told you, I observe. Now what is it?"

I contemplate whether to tell him or not. The thing about Abel is that he's the most trustworthy guy you'll ever meet. Ryland and I can be best friends with him because, when everything went down, Abel said he wouldn't take sides. He would be friends with both of us, and if either tried to sway him differently, our friendship was done. Ryland and I have both respected that. It's why I'm even considering telling him what's been going on.

"Must be good if you're this silent," Abel says.

Yeah, he's not going to drop it. He never does.

I wipe my mouth again and say, "This has to be locked up between you and me, Abel. If this gets out, it won't be pretty."

"Dude, like you even have to say that."

"I know, but I'm serious. This is . . . this could be damaging."

He nods. "You have my word. What's going on?"

I pull on the back of my neck, wondering why I'm going to say this out loud, but then again, I need to get it off my chest. Maybe it will help clear my mind.

I glance around the restaurant to make sure no one is listening in, and then, in a low voice, I say, "The other day, Hattie came to my house to drop off some shit her ex-boyfriend stole from me when he was working for me."

Abel winces. "I don't like this secret already."

"Then tell me to stop if you don't want to hear it."

He shakes his head. "Nah, I can handle it."

"Well, I knew she failed her semester, and that's why she was back in town. I don't know what came over me, but I basically blackmailed her into working for me."

"Jesus Christ," he says, leaning back, hands on the table, looking up to the sky. "Yup, I didn't want to hear it."

"I'm paying her under the table. She's helping organize all my fan mail and a year's worth of shit accumulated in my office. Ryland doesn't know the real reason she's in town. She told him she was doing some internship. But yeah, she's coming to my house daily to work."

"Ryland is going to lose his shit." Abel presses his fingers into his forehead. "Are you trying to blow up the town? Because you know that's what will happen when Ryland finds out."

"I don't know, man. She looked desperate, sad . . . and for

some reason, I took pity on her. I mean, the feud has always been between me and Ryland. She's just an innocent bystander, but for the life of me, I couldn't stop myself."

"Tell me this," he says, leveling with me. "Are you fucking her?"

"No," I reply. "It's nothing like that."

"Good." He pinches his brow now. "I don't think I could handle that kind of news." He looks me dead in the eyes. "It's just a job?"

"Yeah, just a job." I fail to mention how I might have checked her out a few times, made mental notes about how I could twist and turn her body into submission, and fully thought about how her breasts would fit into my palms and into my mouth easily. "And for the record, she needed the help. Badly."

"Are you trying to paint yourself as a saint?"

"Is it working?"

He laughs and shakes his head. "I mean, if I didn't know about the other half, I wouldn't see anything wrong with it, but given Ryland is my other best friend, my dick is quivering in fear as to what he might do if he finds out."

"You think he'd be mad?"

"Are you kidding?" Abel asks, dumbfounded. "Dude, if he finds out about this, it won't end pretty, guaranteed. Not only will he probably end your life for even talking to his baby sister, but his relationship with Hattie will suffer greatly. This is . . . this would be the ultimate betrayal in his eyes. I don't think they'd recover."

Fuck, he's so right.

This isn't just some simple agreement between me and Hattie. This is so much bigger than that. This is bad blood, and testing the strength and power of that bad blood can only lead to more trouble.

Trouble Hattie can't afford. Trouble Ryland can't either. The man is so fucking proud and a damn good big brother.

He always stepped up more than I thought necessary when his mom died—looking after his little sisters with ferocity—but now . . . having Cassidy's kid too?

I could take anything that comes my way, even if it's a barrage of Ryland's fists. I have no stake in the game. I have nothing to lose.

But Hattie, she has everything to lose. As much as I want to pretend I don't care about anyone, a small piece of me does care. I was once very close with the Rowleys. With Ryland. With Cassidy. I know the bond they have, a bond I so desperately wanted to be a part of . . . that I was a part of before everything went down. I know what it feels like to be shunned by the Rowleys.

I wouldn't want Hattie to have to go through that too.

"Don't worry." I pick up my water and take a sip. "We don't plan on him finding out."

"You better hope not. Your chances are slim, though. You know you can trust me, but one slip-up and the town will put the pieces together. You're treading dangerous waters."

"It's not like I'm doing anything wrong," I defend.

"Other than blackmailing Ryland's sister into working for you?"

"That's a minor detail."

"Let's hope it stays that way."

Chapter Seven

HATTIE

"Do you need help closing up?" I ask Aubree as I step into the main part of the shop.

"Nope, I'm all set," she says as she shuts down her laptop.

"Okay." I stand awkwardly, unsure how to bridge this uncomfortable gap between me and my sister. Granted, we've never held super close, best friend status, but with the death of Cassidy, it feels like there's a Grand Canyon worth of space between us. "What are you doing for dinner?"

"Probably eating whatever leftovers I have in the fridge," she answers while packing her backpack.

"Well, I don't have any plans if you want to get something."

She glances up at me, a lift in her brow. "You want to grab dinner together?"

As if her sister asking her to dinner is the most insane thing she's ever heard. See, Grand Canyon-sized space.

"I mean . . . it would be cool to catch up, spend some time

with you." When she looks away, I can tell she's trying to come up with an excuse why she can't do dinner, so instead of letting her, I say, "Come on, Aubree. It's been a while."

After a few seconds of contemplation, she says, "Yeah, sure. Okay." She slings her backpack over her shoulder. "How about we grab pizza? I've been craving the pineapple pizza with hot honey dip."

"Sounds perfect," I say, letting out a pent-up breath. Sheesh, she's my sister. I shouldn't be so nervous about asking if she wants to grab something to eat. Then again, a lot has changed, and with change comes challenges.

For me, it seems like the challenges keep piling on.

"Want to walk?" she asks.

"Yeah, that would be great. I need to stretch my legs out. I swear they've been crossed for the whole day."

"At your internship?" She looks me over. "Is that what you wore?"

"Uh, yeah," I answer. "It's a casual internship. Thankfully, I can wear what's comfortable. Currently filing at the moment and sifting through papers."

Her brow knits together. "That's what you left school for? To file?"

Crap, probably should have left her alone instead of pushing her to go to dinner with me. I ramble too much, and that gets me in trouble.

"No," I say. "I mean . . . yes, but it's a great experience."

"For someone earning their bachelor's, that might be a good experience," she says. "But not their master's."

"Trust me, it's all good. I promise."

"Okay," she says, slightly skeptical but drops it as she heads out of the shop with me behind her. She flips the welcome sign to closed and then locks up before pocketing the key. She grips her backpack straps and crosses the road to the left side of town.

One of the things I love about Almond Bay is how clean it

is. It has that unspoiled yet cute, small-town vibe. Every building is Victorian designed but freshly painted so they beam brightly along the boardwalk-style sidewalks. Iron light posts line the sidewalks as well as wooden planters, all the way through town with bustling bushes, and in the summer, they're full of flowers. And every place of business has a cute sign outside their designated building, advertising what this town has to offer. From an antique store to restaurants to a book and puzzle store to an emporium of freshly made soaps, Almond Bay has it all.

Even a model railroad museum for those who enjoy a good train.

"Oh, hello, girls," Ethel says as she pokes her head out of her inn. I swear she looks out the window, waiting for someone to pass who she can talk to. She pops up all over the place and at the right time.

"Hi, Ethel," I say with a wave. Aubree waves as well.

"Thanks for the bottles," she says. "They came in perfect condition."

Ethel winks. "Told you I knew a guy. Glad they worked out for you."

"Yeah, they were great. Filled them today. Was able to get the extract out on the shelves again."

"Thank goodness," Ethel says, hand to her heart. "Before the weekend, good work. I know my guests will be asking about it. Are you off to dinner?"

"We are," Aubree says. "Pizza is calling us."

"Enjoy, ladies," she says with a smirk and then sits on one of the many rockers that line the inn's porch.

Once we're a good distance away, I say, "You know, I can help you if you need it, especially this weekend."

Aubree shakes her head. "I've got it covered. Marlene and Fran are coming to take some shifts this weekend, so we're good."

"Okay," I reply, trying not to be hurt by the rejection again.

In silence, we walk the rest of the way to By the Slice, and when we enter, I take in a big whiff of the gooey, crusty, delicious pizza smell. So good. Easily the best pizza I've ever had.

"What do you want?" Aubree asks.

"I can get it," I say, but she shakes her head.

"Tell me what you want, and you go grab us a table outside."

"Okay," I say. "Uh, two slices of the pepperoni and pineapple with honey on the side. And a Sprite."

"Sure. Meet you outside."

I work my way through the restaurant, waving to a few people, and then reach the deck that overlooks the ocean. A table is open near the corner, so I head over there, only to stop in my tracks when I see Abel and Hayes talking at a table with empty plates in front of them.

Uh . . . yeah, we won't be sitting outside.

I go to turn just as Abel spots me. "Hattie, hey."

Dammit.

Why does Abel have to be so friendly?

"Oh, Abel, hey." I glance at Hayes, and because I'm immensely awkward, I continue, "And, Hayes, wow, it's you, the man my brother hates. Didn't see you there for a second since your soul is so black, you fit in with the chairs." A single brow of his raises. "Anyhoo, you're back in town. That's unfortunate for everyone." His face falls flat. "You know, I knew I smelled something weird when I came into town. I couldn't put my finger on it, but now that I know you're here, it must have been your overpowering aftershave."

His lips thin. "I don't use aftershave. It must be your breath you're smelling." He leans back in his chair. "Might want to get that checked."

Hands on my hips, I say, "I'll have you know, I just went to the dentist, and I have the cleanest mouth he's ever seen."

"Then you're not hanging out with the right people. Someone needs to dirty that mouth up for you."

"Not all of us can be sluts like you."

"Especially when your boyfriend can't find your clit."

"Hey," I snap at him and point my finger. "Sometimes men don't understand a woman's anatomy."

"Not that hard to google."

"Something I'm sure you've done plenty of." I pretend to type on a computer. "Dear Google, please tell me where the clit is so I can be a horny madman while singing my low-key, swill-like songs and pick up ladies with my stupid tongue ring."

"Trust me, you wouldn't think it's stupid if you had a chance to sit on it."

"Ew." I shiver. "I'd rather stick a fork in my ear."

Abel glances back and forth between us, his body language hesitant but his eyes interested. "Is this what it's like working together?" I snap my head at Hayes, fury erupting through my veins, and he gives Abel a death stare.

I step in closer and whisper, "What the actual fuck, Hayes? I thought we weren't telling anyone."

"Abel's my best friend who I trust. I didn't think he was going to open his damn mouth."

"It's just us," Abel says. "I wouldn't have said anything if anyone else was here."

"Well, you better not say anything to my brother. I can't afford to be associated with Hayes. I don't know how you do it."

"Lots of Valium," Hayes says while downing the rest of his water.

"Did you grab us a table?" Aubree asks, causing every hair on my body to stand to attention. "Oh, hey, Abel . . ." Her voice dies off, and I'm assuming that's the moment she sees Hayes.

"Hey to you too, Aubree." Hayes lifts his hand in greeting. "Good to see you."

Aubree tugs on my hand. "Come on, we can sit inside."

"Oh, don't let us deter you from enjoying the evening outside," Hayes says. "Why don't you join us?" He gestures to the empty seats at their table.

"Fuck off, Hayes," Aubree says, dragging me away and back into the restaurant, where we find a seat off to the right. "Why were you talking to them?" Aubree asks as we both sit down.

"I didn't see them at first, and then Abel said hi. I thought it would be rude if I didn't say hi back."

Aubree shakes her head. "I don't know how Abel does it, be friends with Hayes and Ryland. I wouldn't be able to keep the two relationships separate. I can barely look at Abel."

"That's because you always had a crush on him," I say, causing Aubree to shoot a death stare at me. *Geez, they're common tonight.*

"Not with that shit, Hattie. You know that's not true. There has never been anything between us."

"I know, but it's fun to tease you. Abel is like a brother."

"Exactly." She pauses. "Cassidy was the one with a crush on Abel."

I pause while opening my straw. "Wait, what?"

Aubree nods. "I think they actually kissed once."

"Are you serious?" My shoulders droop because I feel like Cassidy should have told me that. We told each other everything.

"Yeah, they liked each other, but Abel was too good of a friend to risk messing anything up with Ryland, so he never made a move. Cassidy was devastated."

"How . . . how come she never told me?"

"Probably too young when it happened. She was really upset, though. There could have been something great between them, but they never explored it. I truly believe it's one of the reasons Abel was so involved in her cancer diagnosis. Not just because he's close to the family, but because a part of him wanted to try to save her."

"Oh God," I say, my throat growing tight from the thought of them never being able to explore a deeper connection. "Do you think that's why he never goes out with anyone?"

Aubree shrugs. "Probably."

"That's so sad."

Just then, the server delivers our pizza, but now, I don't feel as hungry. My stomach churns from the thought of Cassidy being denied a bigger love than what she had with her husband. Don't get me wrong, they loved each other, but Clarke got her pregnant, and that was why they got married. They made a life together, but he was gone a lot on Peace Corp missions down in Costa Rica while she was left to tend to her business and Mac. It wasn't the kind of love affair you write stories about. It was average. And then, when he passed in a bus accident, Cassidy never looked for anyone else. Was it because she was saving herself for Abel, waiting for a time when he thought it would be okay to ask her out?

"Why aren't you eating?" Aubree asks.

"Because I'm struggling with the thought of Cassidy missing out on love."

"She had Clarke. She loved him," Aubree says coldly.

"But there could have been so much more for her," I say.

"You don't know that. Sure, Abel is a good guy, but they could have just been friends. I don't think you can look too much into it, there's no use. You're just going to drive yourself nuts."

I know she's right, but it will still bother me.

There's so much about Cassidy that bothers me, so much that I'm still trying to work through.

"Do you miss her?" I ask.

Aubree takes a bite of her pizza, chews, and once she

swallows, she quietly says, "Every damn day." Her eyes meet mine. "Every day, I try to make her proud. I try to carry on her legacy. And every day it feels like an uphill climb with no rest in sight."

"Why don't you talk about it?" I ask.

"Because there's nothing to talk about. It will come across as complaining, and I'm not going to complain about anything. Not when I have a niece without parents who needs to see strong adult figures in her life working to keep her mom's memory alive."

"Aubree," I say softly and reach for her hand, but she moves out of the way.

"It's fine." She takes a deep breath. "You know, I might take my pizza to go. I have to go through the books and write some checks."

"I didn't mean to upset you. You don't have to leave," I say.

"I never should have agreed to this in the first place. I have too much going on."

"But it's me," I say. "Your sister. Don't you think it's important to have dinner together?"

"You're supposed to be in school, not having pizza dates with me," she says harshly before rising from the table and walking over to the takeout part of the restaurant. *What the hell? Why did you push, Hattie? Why?*

My shoulders sag as I stare down at my pizza. Well, there goes my attempt to get closer to my sister.

NOT WANTING to go back to my small studio above The Almond Store, I decide to take the Almond Staircase to the beach. Located behind the drive-in theater, they're quite steep and sometimes rickety. The Peach Society has discussed tearing them down and not letting anyone down to the beach, but so far, they haven't implemented those plans. But a giant caution sign next to the stairs says to use at your own risk.

I have no problem risking it.

I sit on the last stair and pull off my shoes and socks. I put them on a rock next to the stairs, something I've done too many times to count, and with my phone in hand, I let my toes sink into the sand as I walk along the beach toward the water.

About five minutes into my walk, someone says, "Out here by yourself?"

Startled—again—I look to my right to find Hayes sitting on a rock, staring out at the ocean.

"What the hell are you doing there?" I ask.

"Waiting to scare you."

"I wouldn't put it past you." His hair has been tugged on, almost as if he's been sitting there, trying to come up with a solution. "Seriously, why are you here by yourself?"

"Probably the same reason you're here by yourself," he says.

"I don't think we should be comparing ourselves. Our lives are completely different." I don't stick around but keep walking on my way. The last thing I need is some sarcastic ramble with Hayes Farrow.

"Don't want to walk with me?" he asks, not letting me find my peace. I should have known.

"I'm surprised you'd even make the suggestion, given how my breath curls your toes."

"Not what I said." He hops off the rock and joins me, his strides falling in line with mine, his shoes and socks are off as well. Weird, I didn't see them over by the stairs. "You were the one who implied I was rolling into town with a stench. I was following your lead."

"Well, congratulations. Job well done."

"Not in a good mood, I see."

It's so easy to gauge this man. He has two versions of

himself—asshole and sarcastic asshole. The sarcastic asshole usually comes out when he's trying to shield himself from any feelings. So he projects his assholery to others.

"And that mood is getting better with you here now," I reply.

"It's funny how much disdain you have for me when I've done absolutely nothing to you."

"Blackmailing me to work for you . . . umm, I'd consider that something."

"You were rude before that," he says.

"Family loyalty rises above all," I say.

"I can see that. It wouldn't hurt you to chill for a second, though, because no one is around us. They won't see that you're being civil around me."

I glance over at him. "Chill? What is that supposed to mean? You're not trying to be my friend or something, are you?"

"I have enough friends," he answers. "I don't need another. But Jesus, you don't have to have your guard up all the time."

"Says the guy who has his guard up twenty-four seven."

"You don't know enough about me to make that assumption."

"Don't I? You've been an ass to me ever since I walked up to your house."

He shakes his head as he turns toward me. "You have no idea the kind of man I am."

"Then tell me something about you. If you're not so guarded, tell me one thing that isn't sarcastic or made up, or some stupid way to impress someone with everything you've accomplished."

"You want something?" he asks. "Okay. Take a seat." When I don't join him on the sand, he tugs on my hand, forcing me to sink to the sand and pebbles with him. Facing the ocean with his legs pulled in, he says, "You want something? Well, here's something. I can't write a song to save my goddamn life right now. Everyone thinks I'm this amazing songwriter, brimming with ideas, but in reality, I'm a guy with a guitar and an empty notebook."

"Is that supposed to make me feel bad for you?" I ask.

He looks over at me. "No, but it's real."

"Is it, though? The rich musician can't think of a song to write?"

His eyes narrow. "Music is the one thing that helped me escape everything awful in my life. It helped me breathe air into my lungs. It allowed me to get out of the place I was in and never look back. And the fact that I can't feel that same feeling, I can't taste the melodies or tap out a rhyme, a thought, anything . . . eats away at me. You might not think it's a big deal, but to me, it's as if a small piece of me is dying."

Oh, huh . . . that does seem like a big deal when he puts it like that.

I feel that. I understand what it's like to have a piece of you die.

I know the guttural feeling of not being able to breathe, like you can't get enough air into your body because of the outlying factors around you, controlling your life.

And I don't like that.

I don't like that I can relate to him. I don't want to relate to him.

I don't want him buying me pickles, sitting down with me on the sand after my sister pretty much abandoned me, and I definitely don't want to be able to share the same sort of feeling as he does.

And why? Because he's supposed to be awful. That's what I've been told nearly my whole life. And if he's not awful, then that opens the door for other things . . .

Things I shouldn't even be thinking about.

Like how his deep, sultry voice captures my attention every time he speaks.

Or how he looks hot with a backward hat on, but how I love it when he wears no hat at all.

Or the automatic curl in his large hands when he walks around, almost like he's walking around with the neck of an imaginary guitar in his palm at all times.

No, I can't think about that at all.

"Yeah, that's what I thought. You don't understand." He shakes his head.

"No, I do," I say, breaking out of my thought. "Is that what you've been trying to do while I sort through your mail? You're trying to write a song?"

"Yes," he answers. "And before you ask, I've come up with nothing."

"Maybe it's because you're forcing it," I say. "You can't force creativity."

"You can when you have studio execs breathing down your neck."

"Do you?" I ask.

He nods. "Yeah, they wanted something new months ago."

"Seems like a them problem to me. Not that I'm coming to your defense, because that would pretty much make me burn up on the spot, but you just came off a big tour. Don't they know you need some time to breathe, some time to recuperate? You have to recharge before you can jump headfirst into a mentally and physically demanding job."

"Not defending me, huh?" he asks. "Sounded like you were defending me, and look at that . . . you didn't burn up like you thought you would."

"Must have been a lucky moment," I answer.

And crap . . . the tension in his brow has eased, and the expression on his face is more favorable. I warmed him up and chilled like he asked, leading to . . . dare I say . . . a bonding moment?

"Tell me something real about you," he replies.

See, Hattie, this is exactly why you don't bond with people, because when they start to open up, they expect you to do the same.

And I know that's a dangerous thing because ultimately, everyone I've ever loved has left me. Not that I'll ever love this man. *So I deflect.*

"Are we really sharing?" I ask, trying to get back to maybe a more volatile state with him.

"Do you have something better to do?"

"No." I'm just scared that maybe I'm opening up to someone I shouldn't be opening up to. But if I think about it, other than Maggie, who do I really have? Aubree practically kicked me away today. At least Hayes is listening. Oh dear God, what is happening to my life that Hayes Farrow is the second-best person to talk to at the moment?

"Well . . ." he presses.

Looks like he's not going to back down, so . . . "I think my family hates me."

He turns to look me in the eyes, and the lightest smirk passes over his lips. "Would you look at that," he says. "We do have something in common."

"Come on." I nudge his shoulder with mine.

"I'm serious. Commonality might make the workplace relationship better."

"Yeah, I might have to join the dark side with you, especially after tonight."

"It's fun over here. I live in a land where I don't give a shit. One where I enjoy watching those who hate me go into a tizzy whenever I'm around."

"Sounds like fun."

"It is," he says in a deep tone. "So why do you think your family hates you?"

"They don't tell me anything. Getting Aubree to go out to

dinner with me was like pulling teeth, and she ended up leaving me at the restaurant to finish my pizza by myself. They're preoccupied with their new responsibilities, which I understand, but they won't talk to me about them. They won't even let me help. All they're concerned about is me going to school and making sure I graduate, and you and I both know how that's going. There's such a big disconnect between us that I don't know how to bridge the gap."

He pulls on the back of his neck. "Working for me won't do it, that's for damn sure."

"Working for you is the only thing I've got at this point." And that's the scary truth. "God, what the hell am I doing with my life?" I turn toward him so I'm sitting cross-legged and facing him. "Cassidy never liked Matt. She told me several times how much she didn't like him and thought I was too good for him, but I didn't listen. I wasted my time with him only for him to tell me I was boring in the end."

"You're anything but boring," Hayes replies.

"And now that I failed all my classes this semester . . . like what am I doing? All I had to do was pass these classes, and I was good to graduate. Am I self-sabotaging? I mean . . . I took a freaking job with Hayes Farrow, my brother's least favorite human in the world. I'm asking for trouble. Is this a pre-midlife crisis?"

"Are you asking me?"

"I don't know what I'm doing." I lean back on my hands.

We're both silent for a second, and then he says, "I don't think you're self-sabotaging. I think you're lost. Not that I know much about your family life, but I do know that Cassidy was a bright light in your lives, and that light has dimmed. Of course you're lost. You don't have anyone guiding you like when she was around."

That is . . . annoyingly insightful. *"Cassidy was a bright light in your lives, and that light has dimmed. Of course you're lost. You don't have anyone guiding you like when she was around."* Why can't my siblings see this? Why can't my siblings talk about this? *Why don't they even want me around?*

"You're probably right," I say quietly. "I honestly don't know what I'm doing, and it doesn't help that the only family I have left is occupied with their own issues."

"So then, maybe you try to find yourself again."

I glance over at him. "Don't you think that's something you should be doing?"

"Probably." He shrugs and looks out toward the ocean.

After a few minutes, I say, "You know, you're not as bad as you seem."

"Should I take that as a compliment?"

"Probably. I don't hand them out often."

He stands and lends his hand out to me. "You should get back. The sun will set soon, and you shouldn't be out here alone."

"I'm not alone. You're weirdly here."

"Yeah, that's not good either," he says and then helps pull me to my feet.

We head back toward the Almond Staircase. "I don't want you to think this changes anything," I say. "I still hate you from the tips of my toes."

"Good," he replies. "Wouldn't want it any other way."

HATTIE: *When do you think you can come visit?*

I stare at the slanted ceiling in my studio apartment that feels more like a walk-in closet. It's lost its luster. I don't feel my sister in this space like when I first arrived, and I know it's because of my strained relationship with my family. Therefore, the relationship I had with Cassidy is strained.

Talking to Hayes on the beach felt nice, like someone was listening to me. Someone cared to listen to me. And I know when I say that in my head, it sounds bratty because Jesus,

Ryland and Aubree are going through a lot right now, but why block me out? It's almost like being in school has isolated me from everything, and I don't understand why.

So now I'm talking to Hayes Farrow, probably the last person on earth I ever would have considered someone I told my feelings to. And oddly, it felt sort of right. He's easy to talk to, which freaks me out because I don't want him to be easy to talk to. I don't want him to be nice to me. I want him to be an asshole. I want him to insult me, blackmail me.

NOT buy me pickles and walk alongside me on the beach when I felt so utterly alone.

My phone dings with a text.

Maggie: *Why do I have a feeling that you want me to come earlier?*

Hattie: *I need you, Mags.*

Maggie: *Say no more. I'm there for you. Want me to come this weekend?*

Hattie: *Can you?*

Maggie: *I can make it work. But I require an almond extravaganza, including my favorite almond cherry cookies that you make.*

Hattie: *Done and done.*

Maggie: *Care to tell me what's going on so I can prepare myself?*

Hattie: *Things are rocky with my family, and I'm resorting to leaning on Hayes Farrow for emotional support. That can't happen.*

Maggie: *So basically DEFCON 1.*

Hattie: *Precisely.*

Maggie: *Got it. Manning my bosom now.*

Chapter Eight

HAYES

I let out a large sigh as I stare down at my phone.

Five minutes late so far.

I swear she's doing this intentionally to drive me nuts.

If she is, it's fucking working.

Instead of sitting on the porch, I'm sitting on my island, staring at the front door, waiting. That's when I see her fly into my driveway, in my car, putting it in park and sprinting to the front door with her backpack in hand. Funnily, she glances at the Adirondack chair I've scared her twice in, and then she puts the code in my front door and pushes through, only to come to a screaming halt when she sees me sitting on the counter.

"Dear God, don't you have better things to do than wait around to startle me?"

"You're late," I say.

She pushes her wet hair out of her face. "The commute was a real bitch."

"It's fifteen minutes."

"A stressful fifteen minutes at that, can't even fit in a solid playlist." She sets her bag on the couch, near her bundles of papers, and then scans me. "Did you seriously not make yourself coffee?"

"That's your job. I'm paying you extra for it, which seems like I'm getting the short end of the bargain with that deal."

"The minute you hired me, you were getting the short end of the bargain."

She moves past me, the sweet scent of her shampoo wafting by me. She grabs a mug from the cabinet and pulls out the creamer. I watch in dismay as she pours the creamer into the mug, sets it under the coffee maker, then fills it with a pod and turns it on.

"I thought I told you creamer after."

"You did, but I've done this for the last two days, and you didn't notice, so suck it, Hayes."

She then pulls out the things needed for my protein shake. I watch her work around my kitchen as if she belongs here, and it oddly feels right. Don't think I've ever had someone familiar with my home before, other than Abel.

"You know, you should switch it up every once in a while with these smoothies. Don't you get tired of the same thing over and over again?"

"No," I answer. "I like routine. I like the same thing."

"Maybe if you switched it up, you might be able to write another song."

"Switching up what I put in my smoothie will not help me hit the top ten on the Billboard list."

"You never know until you try," she replies right before she turns on the blender and smiles at me.

While my smoothie blends, my coffee finishes up, and I go to grab it, but she holds up her hand to me.

"I need to earn my money. You asked for a delivery, I'm going to give you a delivery." She picks up the mug and then holds it in front of her as if it's a diamond on a red velvet pillow and walks it toward me. "Your fuel, your mages—Oh mother of pearl," she screeches. "My toe, oh my God, my toe!"

"What?" I ask, trying to figure out what the hell just happened, but before I can hop off the counter to check on her toe, she stumbles and grumbles from the pain, and I watch in horror as the freshly brewed coffee tilts forward, brown liquid propelling out of the mug and onto my leg.

"Fuck!" I yell, leaping off the counter.

Crash.

The mug flies to the floor, shattering into pieces.

Burning-hot liquid sears right through my pants and onto the meat of my thigh.

"Motherfucker," I yell while shimmying out of my pants as quickly as I can.

"Oh God, are you burnt?" Hattie asks while bouncing on one foot.

The wet fabric clings to my leg, making it exponentially harder to get off. My leg is burning up. "Fuck," I scream.

"You *are* burnt. Oh God!" Hattie yells as she moves to the sink.

I finally free myself of my jeans, relieved from the razor-sharp pain piercing my skin. I let out a deep sigh of relief just as water blasts me in the side, drenching me from the waist down.

Standing there in nothing but a pair of black boxer briefs and an Aerosmith graphic T-shirt, I glance at Hattie as she sprays me with water, her eyes focused on my crotch as she doesn't let up on the faucet.

"What the hell are you doing?" I ask. "Do you think I'm on fucking fire?"

"I don't know," she says, continuing to spray me. "From the girly squeals you let out, I was afraid maybe you were . . ."

She looks up at me and smiles.

I frown at her.

She tries to smile more broadly.

I sneer.

And then our eyes both fall to the pool of water still gathering at my feet.

"Turn it off!" I yell.

"Oh right." She scrambles to turn the water off. She moves around the corner and toes the puddle of coffee and water. "Well," she breathes out. "What a way to start a morning, huh?"

Jesus fucking Christ.

———

ABEL: *Hey, I know I was kind of tough on you at dinner, so I want to make sure we're cool.*

Hayes: *You never have to send a text like that, you know we're always cool.*

Abel: *I don't want you thinking I'm taking Ryland's side. I'm looking out for you.*

Hayes: *I know you are.*

Abel: *And I know you probably don't want to hear this, but I don't know if keeping her around is a good idea. It won't end well. I'd cut ties now before word spreads, and Ryland finds out.*

I pinch the bridge of my nose as I stare down at his text because he's right. I really should fucking end it. Could I find someone to do the work she's doing? Yeah, I could. But two things make me hesitate. I actually trust Hattie. It's rare to know someone for a short time and trust her, but because of the history between us and because she's from my hometown, I trust her. A rare thing today. There's also the fact that I know she needs this, and as much as I want to say I don't care about Hattie, I don't think I could take away the one thing that is going okay—*decent*—in her life.

Hayes: *I understand where you're coming from, man, but she's going through a tough time.*

Abel: *It's not your responsibility to help her through that. Hell, you shouldn't even be talking to her.*

Hayes: *Just like how her family's currently not talking to her?*

Abel: *What do you mean they're not talking to her?*

Hayes: *I ran into her on the beach after she had pizza with Aubree. She's struggling, man. She thinks her family hates her. She keeps wanting to help them, to be a part of the new journey they're all on, and they're pushing her away.*

Abel: *I know Ryland and Aubree are being pushed to their breaking point right now.*

Hayes: *That's what she said, but they won't let her help. They keep telling her to focus on school, and dude, she failed out this semester. She can't go back to school right now.*

Abel: *Fuck, are you serious?*

Hayes: *Yes. She doesn't have a job, she barely has a place to stay. I'm pretty sure she's terrified of coming clean to her brother. If I cut her off, I don't know what she would do.*

Abel: *Jesus Christ.*

Hayes: *And to be honest, I saw the same look in her eyes that I see when I look in the mirror. Loneliness.*

Abel: *Hayes, are you trying to help her . . . or are you trying to help yourself by helping her?*

Hayes: *Maybe both.*

Abel: *This won't end well. You know that, right? Are you prepared for that?*

Hayes: *I have no fucking clue, man. But I'm struggling, and I feel like if I can help her at least one of us doesn't have to struggle.*

Abel: *You're crossing a line. Just . . . just be careful. And for the love of God, don't fuck her.*

Hayes: *I won't.*

I set my phone down and steeple my hands together as I stare at the ground.

Everything he said was correct. I am crossing a line.

Perhaps I'm trying to save myself by saving her. I shouldn't even be near her.

All fucking facts.

But . . . that's not stopping me from lifting off this couch and heading into the kitchen.

"How's your leg?" Hattie asks as I walk into the living room. Her surprising smile catches me off guard as I walk toward the kitchen. Coming from someone who wants to hate me, seeing a smile as a greeting is different.

"Sore," I answer.

I'll never fucking admit this to her . . . ever . . . but I think because I was able to tear my pants off quick enough, combined with her idiotic spraying of cold water, I didn't end up blistering. It's just a little sore, but she doesn't have to know that. She can sit in the fact that she nearly scalded my dick off with her mockery.

She shifts to face me in the midst of all of her letters. At this point, I've stopped worrying about her process, and I'm just going to let her do what she's doing even though it's taking over my entire living room.

"Do you need me to press a cold compress against it . . . maybe spray you with more water?"

"You've done enough," I say as I pick up a banana from the counter.

"Are you sure? Because I'm at your beck and call. Anything you need, let me be of service."

Let me be of service?

I can see that maybe she was feeling guilty about the whole coffee burning my leg thing, but . . . let me be of service? Nooo, that's not the Hattie I've come to know. So what gives?

I cock an eyebrow at her. "What do you want?"

"What?" she asks, her voice rising. "I don't want anything. I'm just here to help. Help my boss out. Yepper. Boss, boss, boss. Bossity boss. The bossest. Just giving him all the help."

"Bullshit," I reply, not buying a single second of this. "You want something. You're never this nice to me, even if you do try to sear the skin off my leg."

She holds a finger up to me. "That was an accident. I might not like you, but I'd never purposely try to harm you. And I'm just trying to make sure I'm fulfilling all of your needs. You are paying me, after all, and it would help to lighten the mood in this dark dungeon with a little niceness."

"You know, the more you lie to me, the less likely I'll give you whatever you want."

"What makes you think I want something? Honestly, can't a person be nice to another person without—"

"Hattie," I say sternly.

"Fine." She lets out a dramatic sigh. I fucking knew it. She makes her way to the kitchen island where I am and says, "My best friend Maggie is coming to visit me this weekend, and I was hoping I could use your kitchen to make cookies. I don't have a kitchen in the studio apartment I'm staying in and I promised her almond cherry cookies."

"That's all you want? My kitchen?"

She nods. "Yes."

"You don't have to ask to use it. Whatever is in this house, you can use it. Free range."

"Besides the studio," she says.

"Just because I can't be distracted, but if you wanted to go in there, you could."

"Well"—she heaves a sigh of relief—"I should have asked for something bigger if it was going to be so easy. Like letting Maggie stay in your house so we don't have to try to fit on the small bed in my studio. Next time I'll be sure to make the big asks."

"She can stay here," I say.

Hattie scoffs. "Okay, yeah, that's not going to happen."

"Why are you laughing?" I ask.

"Because that's ridiculous. I'm not going to bring my

friend to *your* house. We'll make it work in my studio. We tried making a reservation at the inn, but they're booked. We'll just cuddle in tight."

"Scared?" I ask her.

"Huh?"

"Too scared to stay here? Afraid your brother might find out?"

"No." She scrunches her nose up. "I'm not going to impose on you like that. Plus, I don't want to owe you anything."

"You wouldn't owe me," I say. "You're my employee. Matt would have been afforded the same courtesy."

"Would he?" she questions.

"Within reason," I answer with a cringe. "Probably not after I found out he was pickpocketing anything of mine he could get his hands on."

"That's what I thought. And no, the kitchen is good enough. Which if you don't mind, I'd like to make the cookies now so they have time to cool."

"If you're looking for ingredients, I have none."

"Don't worry, I brought everything required to make them. I mainly need your oven." She heads toward the front door, and I follow her. She opens the passenger side of my car and pulls out a cooler as well as a bag full of baking utensils and sheet pans.

"Let me help you," I say as I reach for her bags at the same time she grabs them.

Our eyes connect, and I watch her wet her lips as she's a short distance away from me. "I . . . I got them," she stutters.

"Let go, Hattie."

From the command in my voice, she lets go and then takes a step back, her eyes unblinking as she watches me.

After a few seconds, she says, "Stop doing nice things for me."

I ignore her as I bring her baking bags into the kitchen

and set them on the counter.

"Did you hear me?" she says as I unpack the bags, lining up her ingredients nicely for her. "I said stop doing nice things for me."

"I heard you," I say.

"Then why are you unpacking my bags?"

"It's called procrastination." I glance up at her. "Those in the creative field are experts at it. So, no, I'm not being nice to you. I'm just trying to find things to do to make sure I'm not doing the one thing I'm actually supposed to be doing."

"If that's the case, start looking through your letters."

"Ah, you see, if I were to do that, then I'd be pegging myself as an idiot."

I pull out her baking sheets and line those up on the stove top.

"How would that make you an idiot?"

"Because I'm paying you, right?"

"Yes," she draws out.

"So if I'm paying you, then why would I do a job I'm paying someone to do? Sounds pretty idiotic to me, but lining up this baking shit that truly is a pointless task. Now that's something I can do to keep me from writing. See how it works?"

She stares at me. "You're fucked in the head."

I chuckle. "Us creative types always are." Once I'm done, I set my hands on the counter and look her in the eyes. "Okay, what's next?"

"What do you mean, what's next?" she asks with a confused look on her face.

"We're making cookies, so what's next?"

"Uh, *I'm* making cookies, and you're headed back to your studio."

I pull on the back of my neck. "What did you not understand about the whole procrastination thing?"

"What do you not understand about me not wanting you

to be nice to me?"

"I can call you a dick while we bake. Will that make you feel better?" Clearing my throat, I ask, "What do we need to start with . . . dick?"

She relinquishes. "No one says dick as an insult anymore. Be more clever."

"What would you prefer me to call you?"

"I don't know, not dick."

"What is your go-to insult?"

She bumps my shoulder with hers, pushing me to the side as she picks up the butter and starts undoing the wrapper. "Make yourself useful," she says, tossing me a stick of butter. I smile to myself, knowing she's giving in to my procrastination technique. "And as for the insult, I go with the classic name-calling of anus."

"Anus?" I ask, laughing. "As in a butthole?"

"Yes. It's unexpected, rarely used, and gross if you actually think about it."

"So is that what you want me to call you?" I ask.

"Ew, come up with something yourself." She drops the butter in the large bowl she brought, so I do the same. She then unravels the cord to her hand mixer and hands me the cord to plug it in. Once it's set, she gives me the hand mixer and says, "Beat the butter."

"What do you mean beat it?" I ask.

She glances up at me in surprise. "Have you never made cookies before?"

"No, I haven't."

"Your grandma never taught you?"

"She was busier teaching me proper guitar chords than allowing me in the kitchen."

"Such a shame, think of all the baking songs you could have written if you had a touch of experience beating butter."

"Yes, greatest hits for sure."

"I know." She moves behind me, wraps her arms around

me and places her hand on top of mine that's holding the mixer.

"Are you trying to make a move on me?"

"No, you anus." I snort. "I'm trying to teach you, but you're far too big for this position. I'm going to have to mirror you."

She pushes me toward the end of the island, climbs on top of the counter, and then sitting cross-legged in front of me, she takes my hand again and looks me in the eye. "Are you ready?"

"I don't know. This contraption looks scary, and you seem to be irritated."

"Just know, if you piss me off, I can use these beaters on your crotch and turn your dick into straight up applesauce."

"What . . . the fuck?"

She doesn't reply. Instead, she turns on the mixer, and it flies against the side of the bowl.

"Christ, Hayes. You have muscles, use them. Steady the mixer."

Butter flies all over the bowl and the counter as I try to rein in the machine. "Well, warn a guy before you just turn it on."

"Wasn't aware you were so weak."

"I'm not fucking weak," I shoot back as we steady the mixer and together beat the butter.

"Technically, this is called creaming the butter," she says after a few moments of silence. "But I figured you would be massively inappropriate if I said cream the butter."

"You don't give me enough credit," I say. "I'm not that immature."

"Debatable." She turns off the hand mixer. Instead of getting off the counter, she stays seated and says, "Okay, sugar now. One cup of white, one cup of brown."

"That's a lot of sugar."

"Are you judging my cookies?"

"No," I say, shaking my head. "Just surprised."

"The reason they're good, Hayes, is because there's a lot of sugar in them, and of course, because of the almond extract."

"Question," I say as I measure the sugar. "Do I get any of these cookies?"

She rolls her eyes dramatically. "No, I'm just going to let you help me make them, use your kitchen, and then hoard them for myself. Honestly, Hayes . . . you really are an anus."

"Glad you're using that term loosely. And you're right . . . unexpected, funny, yet . . . gross."

She leans on one hand. "Stick around, I have so much more to teach you."

We spend the next few minutes adding eggs, the almond extract, and then putting together the dry mixture in another bowl. I had no idea making cookies was this intricate, but apparently, it's a treasured pastime for Hattie.

"Did Cassidy teach you this recipe?" I ask as she pulls out the maraschino cherries she dried last night.

"She did. She wanted a signature cookie she could sell at the shop, and when she was trying to figure out what would pair well with almonds, she knew cherries and white chocolate were going to be a great match. And before you ask, she didn't go with milk or dark chocolate because she was afraid the flavor profile was going to overpower the almond."

"Makes sense," I say. "The combination sounds good to me."

"It's delicious. The first time I brought Maggie back to Almond Bay, she had one and has been hooked ever since. I'd just grab some from Aubree, but she seemed inundated with work, so I figured making them would be just as fine."

"And you're teaching me, so basically a win-win for you."

"Is that what you'd call this?"

"Yup," I answer.

She winces. "I think you're pushing your luck, as I'd

hardly call baking with you a win. Now, gradually mix the flour into the batter. I'll hold the bowl for you. Turn on the hand mixer and go for it."

"Okay," I answer as I turn on the hand mixer and pick up the dry ingredients bowl with the other hand. I tilt it toward the wet ingredients, and when it doesn't move, I give the bowl a light tap and to my dismay, all of the powder falls into the wet bowl. Like a mushroom cloud, the dry ingredients puff right out of the bowl and straight up my nose and over my face.

"Oh my God." Hattie laughs hysterically as I turn off the mixer and set the bowl down. I wipe my fingers across my face, clearing off the flour, the chalky substance sticking to my skin. *This will warrant a shower.* "That's the best thing I think I've ever seen. Too bad we're not friends because I'd take a picture of you and send it to our friend circle."

"Such a shame," I say as I cough out some flour. "Wouldn't be the first time a white substance was up my nose."

Her eyes widen, and she leans slightly forward. Whispering, she cutely says, "Seriously?"

I chuckle. "Yeah, seriously."

"Hayes." She uses a reprimanding voice. "Are you saying you've done drugs?"

"What do you think?" I ask as I wet a paper towel and rub it over my face.

"Your grandma would be so disappointed."

I chuckle now. "I was young and stupid and hung out with the wrong people while on tour."

"Wait, so you don't do any drugs now?"

I shake my head. "No, learned my lesson after a night where I ended up in a hotel room in Kansas City, butt-ass naked, with no wallet or phone."

"Was Kansas City a party place for you or something?"

I shake my head. "I started the night in Atlanta, Georgia.

How I got to Kansas City, I'm still in the dark about that."

"Oh shit." She chuckles. "Yeah, so that's scary."

"Especially when I had to fashion a hotel sheet for pants. You learn pretty quickly after that."

"Was it hard to quit?"

"No." I shake my head. "I was never addicted, and I never did it that much, just occasionally. And it's been many years since the Kansas City incident, so I've been clean for a while."

"Thank goodness, I couldn't possibly work for a drug-hoarding anus. Could I work for a regular anus? Sure, I'll make accommodations, but not a drug-hoarding one." *This girl is a nut.*

"Glad to see you have standards."

———

I DRAG my hand over my face and lean back on my couch in my studio, my mouth watering from the smell of the cookies wafting through the house and the memory of Hattie laughing over the fact that I blasted the flour up in the air with the hand mixer. I'm pretty sure I still have some up my nose.

And I liked every second of it.

Not the flour, but the time spent with Hattie.

I liked the distraction.

I liked that she sat on the counter and helped me.

I liked that she didn't scoff at the fact that I've never made cookies but walked me through everything.

And when we were shaping the cookies, she held my hands and helped me mold them. *When was the last time I just . . . had fun like that? Pure, simple fun?*

Years?

Well, I fucking liked every second of it, and I shouldn't . . . for many reasons.

Reason number one, her brother hates me.

Reason number two, she's twelve years younger.

Reason number three, she's technically working for me.

But Jesus, none of that seems to matter as I keep wanting to go back into the living room to talk to her. To check out her progress. To just see if I can get her riled up.

Like right now, I want to go out there and just start a goddamn conversation for the hell of it.

I'm not going to, though.

Nope. Not going out there.

I take a deep breath and pick up my phone. I pull up my thread with Abel and shoot him a text.

Hayes: *I think I fucked up.*

If anyone can help me through these thoughts in my head, it's him. Thankfully, he must be between patients because he texts me back.

Abel: *If you tell me you fucked Hattie, I'm going to lose it.*

Hayes: *No. I didn't.*

Abel: *Thank Jesus. Then how did you fuck up?*

Hayes: *I know you told me to be careful, but I think the reason I can't seem to let her go is because I let her get under my skin.*

Abel: *What level under your skin are we talking about?*

Hayes: *I like being around her.*

Abel: *Jesus. Dude, I'm telling you, this is a bad idea. Really fucking bad. Okay, you do not want to get involved.*

Hayes: *I know, and there are other reasons I shouldn't get involved, many other reasons, but it's hard not to get pulled in by her charm.*

Abel: *Try harder. If you need to, go find someone to shake off these . . . feelings. Anything to get your mind off her.*

Hayes: *Yeah, you're right. I just think I'm spending too much time near her. She won't be here this weekend, her friend will be in town. That will help.*

Abel: *Perfect. This weekend, find someone to fuck.*

Hayes: *Okay, yeah. I can do that.*

Abel: *Good, and if you start to feel like this again, text me. I'll help you out. Even if that means you need to send me a dick pic to get that out of your system.*

Hayes: *Do you think that's something I do?*

Abel: *I don't know. I'm just here to serve.*

Hayes: *I'll spare you the dick pic.*

Abel: *Thank Jesus. Although, with the amount of old cocks I see in a week, I could use a fresher one.*

Hayes: *Are you calling my dick fresh?*

Abel: *Fresher than the eighty-year-old shriveled string cheese I saw today.*

Hayes: *Jesus fuck, man.*

Abel: *Was that a wet blanket for you? Because I have more where that came from.*

Hayes: *Keep it as ammunition for now. You might have to pull out your arsenal on me.*

Abel: *Locked and loaded.*

Knock. Knock.

I glance up at my door as if I can see through it, and I say, "Yeah?"

The door opens, and Hattie pokes her head in. "Uh, I want to eat a cookie. Now I know you made them, so I figured I'd give you the right to eat one with me before I started munching away. Consider this a courtesy."

"Are you inviting me to have a cookie with you?"

"Never," she says. "I'm telling you I'm eating a cookie whether you like it or not. Feel free to have one at the same time." And then she takes off, letting the door shut on its own.

I stare down at my phone and the texts from Abel telling me to stay away, but even though my eyes scan over his words, my body stands. With one toss of the phone to the empty couch, I forget everything he said and head out to the kitchen, where her music is playing on her phone again. This time, it's a cover of *Don't Stop Believin'*.

She snags a cookie from the cooling racks, and when she turns to find me approaching, I see a slight smirk pass over her lips before she hoists herself up onto the counter.

I grab a cookie as well and lean against the counter. Her

eyes land on mine, and then oddly, together, we take a bite. The moment the sugary goodness hits my tongue, flavors of cherry and almond popping off my taste buds, I know this has instantly become my new favorite cookie.

"Holy shit," I say. "These are good."

She checks out the cookie in her hand. "You know, I'd say you did a good job. I'm impressed."

"I'm impressed with myself." I take another bite. "How many of these did you say I could have?"

She eyes me. "Five, so pace yourself. Maggie is going to want at least two dozen. That's how crazy she is about them."

"Five won't be enough."

"Too bad, that was the deal." She shrugs.

"We never made a deal about the number. And technically, you made these in my kitchen. Therefore, they belong to me."

"Uh, wait a goddamn second," she says, straightening up. "We might have made them in your kitchen, but I was the one who bought the ingredients. Therefore, a percentage of them belong to me."

"Without my kitchen, there would be no cookies."

She levels with me. "Without my ingredients, there definitely wouldn't even be an inkling of cookies."

"Then we split them, half and half . . ." I pause as a set of familiar chords plays through her phone speaker. And then . . . a smirk lifts my lips as she looks at me confused. It takes her all of five seconds to realize why I'm smirking before she leaps off the counter and grabs her phone, turning off the music.

"It's not what you think," she says, phone in one hand, cookie in the other.

I move past the island and slowly walk up to her, feeling cocky as shit. "Not what I think it is? Because it sure as shit seems like your phone was just playing one of my songs. Why would it do that unless you actually listen to my music?"

"It was playing music from the seventies," she says.

"Funny, because my songs aren't from the seventies." I step right in front of her and shove the rest of my cookie in my mouth. I reach for her phone, but she pulls her arm away.

"What the hell are you doing?"

"I want to see your playlists."

"Why?"

"Because I want to see if you have one dedicated to me."

She rolls her eyes. "Conceited much? If you recall, I consider your music absolute swill. What you just heard was a complete coincidence. There is no way I'd dedicate a whole playlist to you."

"Then let me see them."

She shrugs. "Fine, have at it." She hands me her phone, and I open her playlists, scrolling through them.

There's Heart, Blondie, The Mamas & the Papas, Simon and Garfunkel, slow seventies, rock seventies, seventies covers, but nothing with my name.

Huh . . . shame.

"See, told you. I'd rather stick a fork in my ear than sit and listen to your music."

"Cute," I say as I hand her back her phone.

"Are you disappointed?"

"Slightly," I answer and move away from her. "I thought for a second that maybe you were harboring some secret fangirl status for me."

"Ha, in your dreams, Farrow."

"Apparently," I say and step over one of her piles of letters. I glance around. "I'm assuming you're leaving these piles like this through the weekend."

"Obviously. You need to know, if anything, I'm thorough."

"To a fault," I say as I walk away. "Half those cookies are mine."

"Once again, in your dreams, Farrow."

Chapter Nine

HATTIE

"You're here," I say as I fling myself at Maggie, her warm hug soothing my very soul in seconds.

"That drive was atrocious," she says. "Rained the whole way until I got here. What the hell?"

I chuckle. "Old granny couldn't handle the rain?"

"No, you know how I drive in the rain. White-knuckling it the whole time, even if it's just sprinkling."

"Well, you're here now. Let's get you upstairs. I have your cookies all ready for you."

"See, I knew there would be light at the end of the rain-soaked tunnel."

I take her bag and we go through the back of The Almond Store. Aubree has a lot of customers at the moment from the influx of tourists today, so I don't want to bother her, and we head up the stairs to my door.

"I had no idea The Almond Store had an apartment above it."

"Yeah, it's cozy in here, so prepare yourself," I say as I open the door and reveal my tiny studio.

Maggie pauses on the stairs, looking inside but not stepping in. "Um, what's this?" she asks.

"My apartment," I answer.

She shakes her head, still peeking in but never fully inserting herself. "No, this is not an apartment. This is a closet, Hattie, and a small one at that." Her eyes dart around the tiny space. "It doesn't have a kitchen."

"No, but it has a mini fridge, and that's a nice touch." I walk over to the dresser, where I have half of the cookies I made with Hayes. Yup . . . half. "And look, I made you cookies. Yum. Yum."

She sets her bag down on the top of the stairs and folds her arms across her chest. "Now, Hattie, you know I'm not a diva and I've slept on your dorm floor before, but I am a lady now. Do you truly expect me, as a lady, to sleep in this closet with you?" She glances over at the bed and points. "Are we supposed to share that? I don't think I could even squeeze in on the end because the slanted ceiling eats up half of the bed."

Huh . . . I didn't think about that.

"Yeah, it is sort of tight, isn't it?" I ask.

"It is," she answers.

Dammit.

"We can make it work," she says with an unsteady look. I know she's being kind, and Maggie isn't the kind of person who would care about something like where she sleeps, but if I look at it, with the ceiling, it would be as if we're sharing a twin bed.

"Um, I might have something different. Give me a second," I say as I pull out my phone.

"This is fine, really," Maggie says, standing at the top of the stairs.

"Says the girl who won't even enter the room."

She chuckles and says, "I'm getting acclimated."

Shaking my head, I turn around and text Hayes.

Hattie: *So . . . remember when you were nice to me and said I could bring Maggie to your house? Is that offer still available, or did it expire?*

Thankfully, he texts back right away.

Hayes: *Still available.*

Hattie: *Cool . . . so could I bring her over now?*

Hayes: *If you bring lunch.*

Hattie: *Deal. What do you want?*

Hayes: *And the other half of the cookies.*

Hattie: *Hayes! Those are for Maggie.*

Hayes: *Cookies or no bed.*

Hattie: *Fine! Now what do you want for lunch?*

Hayes: *Blue cheeseburger from Provisions with a side salad.*

Hattie: *A side salad? When they have the best fries ever?*

Hayes: *It's either fries or cookies, and I choose cookies.*

Hattie: *You're massively annoying.*

Hayes: *You realize you're saying that to the person offering their house to your friend.*

Hattie: *Why do I feel like you're going to hold this over my head?*

Hayes: *Because I wouldn't be the "anus" you think I am if I didn't.*

Hattie: *Facts.*

"Who are you texting?" Maggie asks. "Because you're smiling."

I look up at her and drop the corners of my mouth. "No, I'm not."

"Yes, you are," she replies. "You were smiling. So tell me who the hell you were texting, and if you say Matt, I'm going to scream."

"It wasn't Matt," I say, feeling slightly embarrassed that she caught me smiling when I didn't even know I was smiling. "It was Hayes."

"Hayes Farrow," Maggie silently whispers as she moves—I

mean floats, she's actually floating from the sound of his name —into my studio. "Why were you texting him?"

"He offered to let us stay at his place while you were here because he knows how small my apartment is."

"Well, what the hell are we waiting for?" she asks as she tugs on my arm toward the door. "Let's get the hell out of here."

Laughing, I say, "Wait, I need to pack my stuff first."

"Hurry up. We can't be wasting any time. Hayes needs us."

Good . . . God . . .

I can already tell this is going to be a bad idea.

"IT'S BEAUTIFUL," Maggie says, hands clutched together, looking up at Hayes's house, her face practically pressed against the window of his vehicle, which she gushed over as well.

"Maggie, what did we talk about on the way over here?"

"Being cool, I don't need a reminder. Trust me, I'm as cool as a cucum—oh my God, he's opening the door."

"Maggie . . . please," I beg of her.

"It's fine. I'm fine," she says as Hayes appears at the front door wearing black jeans and a worn Eagles T-shirt with some holes around the collar. And, of course, he's wearing a backward hat in typical Hayes fashion. "Ahhh," she screams as she pops out of the car and runs right up to him, hugging him.

Jesus.

Christ.

I watch as my best friend barrels into him and the surprised look on Hayes's face as he wraps his arms around her, her face burying itself into his chest.

Mortified, I get out of the car as well, just in time to hear Maggie say, "Oh my God, I love you so much. Everything about you. Your look, your attitude, your music. You breathe life into my soul on a daily basis. Without you, I'd be dead, absolutely dead. So freaking dead. But I'm not, because you exist and your magical guitar-playing hands exist." She lifts his hand and twiddles his fingers. "Ooo, look at those well-earned calluses. Calluses that have graced this world with your beautiful, bone-chilling music."

This was a huge mistake.

"And look at your eyes." She grips his cheeks and pulls him in closer to get a better look at him. "Holy shit, Hattie, have you seen his eyes? They're so much grayer in person like I'm almost staring into a mirror. Look at those things. I've never seen anything like it. And these pecs." She slaps the palm of her hands to his chest and gives him a solid fondling.

"Maggie, don't touch him." *This is so humiliating.*

"They're so beefy. You should really wear tighter shirts to show them off, or do more shirtless cologne ads. I mean, sure, I've bookmarked every single one I've seen for research purposes, but I think the world needs more. I'm a wedding planner, and sometimes the grooms tell me they want to get in shape for the wedding, so I send them some Hayes Farrow inspiration . . . that's a lie." She shakes her head. "The inspiration is for me, and me alone . . . if you know what I mean." She elbows him knowingly in the stomach.

"Maggie," I hiss.

"And honestly, I never would have known about you unless it was for Hattie. I remember the first time I heard your music."

Oh fuck!

No, Maggie, nooooo . . .

"Maggie, let's not—"

Hayes holds up his hand, a devilish grin on his face. "No, I want to hear this."

Dread envelops me as I feel all the color rush from my face.

Completely oblivious, Maggie continues, "It was in our dorm right before classes started. We just met each other and she was playing music when I returned from the bookstore. She asked if I wanted her to turn it off, and I told her it was fine. It was the first time I heard your rustic, earthy voice and I was addicted. I asked her who was singing, and she said Hayes Farrow and then proceeded to show me her secret playlist of your music. I remember the first night we tried pot, we stared up at the stars and listened to *The Reason* on replay." She leans forward and whispers, "I lost my virginity to that song."

And I want to be sucked into the earth as Hayes stuffs his hands into his pockets and looks past Maggie and straight at me as he talks. "I'm glad I could be of service . . . with losing your virginity and all."

Maggie goes into detail about the awkward night, but the whole time, Hayes stands there, staring at me, a satisfied look strung across his handsome face. It's official, I'll be looking for a new best friend starting tomorrow.

———

"WHAT THE FUCK, MAGGIE," I whisper to her once we're alone in her room, the room Hayes assigned her after she stopped gushing.

"Wow, this place is so nice," she says, smoothing her hand over the pristine white bedding. "I feel like we're in a five-star resort."

"Uh, hello, I'm talking to you."

"Huh?" She finally looks at me, and I notice the stars in her eyes. Jesus.

I pinch the bridge of my nose and say, "Do you even realize what you said back there?"

"No." She winces. "I swear I blacked out. I didn't embarrass myself, did I?" She nibbles the corner of her mouth, and I nearly fly out of my spandex to tackle her.

"Uh, you jabbered on for a solid five minutes while throwing me under the bus about liking his music."

"Why is that a bad thing?" she asks. "He's your boss, after all."

"Because he thinks I hate him."

"Why, though? Like, why does it matter?"

"Because . . ." I go to answer and then realize I don't have an answer other than because of Ryland . . . and pride.

"That's what I thought." Maggie shrugs. "As far as I'm concerned, I probably did you a favor. I saw the way he was looking at you. Can I just say, I'm jealous. If that man was looking at me the way he was looking at you, I'd have torn off my shirt and plopped my boob right in his hand, without question."

"There is something seriously wrong with you," I say as I flop back on the bed, the most comfortable bed I've ever lain on. Damn him.

She joins me on the bed, lies back, and clasps her hand with mine. "Let's forget about that and tell me why you need me because as far as I'm concerned, it seems like you have a friend in Hayes." *She's wrong.* If there's one thing that has been so abundantly clear since I landed back in Almond Bay, it's that I have no one in my corner. *Except Maggie* . . . before all her gushing. I've just felt so . . . lonely.

"He's not my friend and he hates my brother and my brother hates him and my brother hates me and my sister hates me and the only person in this town that seems to care a hint about me is Hayes and I don't like that. I feel like my sister and my brother should care about me, but all they care about is me going to school and I failed out this semester so what the hell am I supposed to tell them? The only thing they care about when it comes to me is something I failed. They barely talk to me now, they won't want to talk to me after this . . . oh my God, and if they ever found out about Hayes, they'd hate me even more."

Maggie takes a deep breath and says, "That's a lot to process. You've only been here for a few days. How the hell did you do that much in less than a week?"

"I work fast, apparently."

"You do," she answers. "Why don't we grab a drink, our burgers, and talk?"

I nod. "Okay."

———

"HERE YOU GO," Hayes says, carrying our drinks out to his patio overlooking the ocean.

"Thank you," Maggie says. "You're so sweet. And thank you again for allowing us to stay here. You should see the studio Hattie's been living in. There is no way we would have fit in there together."

"I told her she could stay here, but she refused."

Maggie whacks my arm. "Why would you refuse? It's so nice here."

"It's because she doesn't want me being nice to her," Hayes says, hands in his pockets again. "I'm known as the devil in her family, you know?"

"Oh, I've heard. You wronged Ryland in some way, right? At least, that's what I've been told."

"I'm sure you have," he says. "But she'd rather stay in a tiny studio than in a lavish house like this. Goes to show just how goddamn stubborn she is."

"You realize if I stayed here, my brother would legit lose his mind," I cut in.

"Seems like a fun game we should try, don't you think, Maggie?" Hayes rocks on his heels, enjoying this far too much.

"I mean, as her best friend looking out for her, I'd say no. But as a longtime fan of Hayes Farrow, I'd say let's try the drama."

"Your loyalty remains with me, remember that," I say.

145

"Alas," she sighs. "I must say, let's not piss off the brother, which means, stop being nice to my friend."

"Fine," Hayes says. "Guess I'll start kicking her in the crotch as a greeting every time I see her."

"That's all I'm asking," I joke, making him smirk in my direction. *It's a cute smirk.*

"Well, I'll leave you two to it. I'll be in the house, *not* seeing if you need anything else." He turns on his heel, heads back into the house, and shuts the door behind him.

Maggie shakes her head but doesn't say anything as she takes a bite of her burger. She doesn't have to say anything for me to know what she's thinking, it's written all over her face.

"Just say it," I finally say.

She glances over my shoulder, then leans in and whispers, "He would be great for you."

Yup, I knew she was going to say that.

"Maggie, he wouldn't. There is so much frustration and anger between him and my brother, and with the town involved, them picking sides, it would be such a Romeo-and-Juliet-type situation with an ugly ending."

"But . . . you like him, don't you?"

"No." I shake my head, even though in the back of my mind, it sort of feels like a little bit of a lie. "He has his good moments, but I don't think we would be good together, and honestly, I'm not sure he's my type."

"Extremely hot, great voice, and kind is not your type? Jesus, Matt really did a number on you, didn't he?"

"It's not that, Maggie, and you know it." I pick up my burger. "It's complicated, and I don't think getting involved or even thinking about getting involved with anyone at this point is a good idea. I can barely foster the relationships with my brother and sister, let alone someone else."

"I understand," she says, growing serious. "Tell me what's going on with Ryland and Aubree. Are they preoccupied?"

I nod. "Which I totally get, their lives have been turned

upside down with not only losing Cassidy but also taking on new responsibilities they were not expecting. And the pressure to keep Cassidy's spirit alive. I know they're struggling, but they just won't let me help them. I went to grab pizza with Aubree and it was almost as if she was horrified that I even asked her to share a meal with her, alone. But we barely started eating when she ditched me. Legit, got up and left. It was saddening and humiliating. And she just won't talk to me."

"Is the problem more with Aubree?" Maggie asks.

"Yes, she's the one pushing me away more. I think with Ryland, I feel so guilty with what I'm doing that I don't have it within me to face him, which is putting a gap in our relationship. I know this because he hasn't reached out since I had dinner there the other night."

"He's also busy trying to take care of a four-year-old," Maggie points out and gently places her hand on mine. "I truly believe their lives have changed, their perspectives, and their day-to-day operations. Maybe in the past, it would have been natural for them to reach out to you while you were in town, have meals, hang out, but I don't think any of it has anything to do with you, and a lot of it has to deal with what they're going through."

"Yeah, you're probably right."

"Doesn't mean you can't have feelings about it. I'm sure you're feeling left out, like you don't belong . . . fit in, especially since Cassidy was your person." Maggie takes my hand in hers. "That's such a valid feeling, Hattie, and you're allowed to experience the loss of all that. I truly believe you're going through some growing pains with your family, but I have no doubt it will all come together."

"You think so?" I ask.

She nods. "I know so. If I know anything about the Rowleys, is that no matter what, you're there for each other."

I nod. "Yeah, we are." Well, we used to be, anyway. It doesn't really feel like that anymore. *Not since we lost Cassidy.*

"And until they're able to peek their head up for some air, I'm here for you every step of the way."

"It's why I love you."

Chapter Ten

HAYES

I stare at the flames of my gas firepit in front of me, watching the dark blue embers fade into orange. The faint twinkling of stars just visible in the clear night sky, despite the fire in front of me. With my guitar in hand, I randomly stroke some chords, not really making music, just creating a soothing sound as I think about the day.

Maggie is fucking hilarious.

When she first approached me, I could tell she was about to fangirl, but I had no clue she was going to reveal Hattie's dirty little secret—she likes my music.

Nothing has given me as much joy as the moment I saw her face turn a dangerous shade of red while Maggie rambled on. It will go down in the books as one of the best moments of my life because Hattie will go out of her way to make sure I think she hates me. Completely out of her way, yet, all along she's been a secret fangirl.

A fangirl.

Has a playlist of my music.

Listens to the "swill" I write.

Hell . . . I hate to admit it, but it makes me feel damn good.

Really good.

"What are you doing out here?" her soft voice says, startling me as I look over my shoulder.

Wearing a pair of silk shorts and a University of San Francisco T-shirt, she has her hair up in a messy bun and her arms crossed over her chest.

"Couldn't sleep," I say, knowing it's way past midnight. "What about you?"

"Same," she says. "I went to the kitchen for a drink when I saw the fire. I was nervous you left it on, but then saw you sitting over here in the dark like a creep."

I chuckle. "Like a creep, huh?"

"Yup."

I nod for her to come sit next to me, and surprisingly, she joins me on the two-person bench I have in front of the firepit.

"Are you cold?" I ask her as she takes a seat and shivers.

"A little. I didn't think it would be cold out here, even with a fire."

"That's the ocean breeze for you." I set my guitar down and slip my favorite black sweatshirt over my head and hand it to her. "Here, put this on."

She glances at me and then down at the sweatshirt. "You're being nice again."

"I'll be sure to trip you tomorrow so you land face first into a wall."

"Deal," she says as she takes the sweatshirt and slips it over her head, the fabric nearly swallowing her whole. She groans in frustration. "It's annoying that this smells so good." She takes a deep sniff of my sweatshirt and lets out a sigh. "Ugh, you smell amazing. Why can't you smell like dirty fish guts or rotten compost?"

"Sorry, I'll work on that. I'll see if Coleman's has any dirty fish guts I can stick under my armpits."

"It's all I'm asking." She lightly chuckles and pulls her knees into her chest, her arms wrapping around her shins. "Thank you again for letting me and Maggie stay here. I'm pretty sure this is the highlight of her year."

"It was the highlight of mine too," I say as I lean back. "Found out the girl who spends every waking hour trying to convince me she hates me, actually enjoys my music. Wait, not enjoys it . . . obsesses over it."

Hattie buries her head in her hand and groans. "I think I need to resign from my job."

"You can't resign. All you've done is make a giant mess in my house with no rhyme or reason. You're not allowed to leave until that's sorted out."

"Like I said . . . I have a system."

"Can't wait to see how the system actually works," I reply.

"You'll be marveled."

"I'm sure of it." After a second of silence, I ask, "Is *The Reason* still your favorite song? Or is there a song for every year you've loved me that is your favorite? Maybe a song for every mood?"

"I hate you," she says, staring out at the fire.

"So you've told me." I nudge her with my hand. "Come on, tell me."

"No. I refuse to make your head any bigger than it already is. Let's just go back to pretending I don't like your music."

"That's not going to happen," I say. "Maggie has opened my eyes, and they'll never be closed after this."

"That's creepy."

"Perhaps," I reply. "But it's the truth." I nudge her again. "Come on, the least you can do after I let you stay here with Maggie is tell me about my songs. Maybe it'll help me write something."

"Oh, don't start with that, as if I have some magical power that will help you write."

"Maybe you do. Let's find out and see."

From her profile, I catch her rolling her eyes, but despite being annoyed, she says, "*The Reason* will always be my favorite song of yours for many reasons—no pun intended. I have a lot of memories connected to that song. But when I'm in a good mood, I'll play *Heartstopper* because it can keep the joy in my soul. It's upbeat, and fun, and despite Cassidy being team Ryland, she admitted to loving that song. And when I'm sad and just want to be sad, I listen to *The Day I Lost You* because it helps me sit in my feelings. After I lost Cassidy, I listened to that on repeat and cried for hours." I reach out and press my hand to her back, slowly rubbing my thumb in a soothing motion.

"And when I want to get work done and need the motivation, I listen to your *Black* album. It has the same vibes as Taylor Swift's *Reputation*, and it makes me want to fuck things up and get things done. I think I love all the songs on that album equally. But the first song I heard of yours that I loved and would secretly listen to was *Sinner Versus Saint*. I remember feeling so guilty listening to it, but I immediately fell in love with your voice because it was dark, dreamy, and edgy at the same time." She shrugs. "There you have it."

I drag my hand slowly over my mouth. "Wow, I was not expecting that."

She looks over her shoulder. "Consider it as a thank-you for letting Maggie stay here. It might have pained me to admit all of that, but I think I owed it to you."

I'm silent for a second because I'm genuinely floored by her honesty. It's such a rare gift these days, so much so that I've almost forgotten what it costs. True honesty. But this girl, apart from her fabrication about liking my music, has been honest. *Real.* "You realize you owe me nothing, right?"

She turns toward me and says, "Really, Hayes? Without

you at the moment, I don't know where I'd be. Probably speaking the truth to my siblings and sleeping in a studio above my dead sister's Almond Shop. At least with you, I have something to look forward to."

"Because I blackmailed you."

"If I truly didn't want to be here, I think we both know . . . you would have let me go."

I stare into her eyes and admit the truth, not stopping myself. "I'd let you do anything, Hattie."

She tilts her head to the side. "Why?"

I shrug but can feel the reason deep in my soul. *I'm fucking lonely.*

"Why, Hayes?" she asks, pressing me.

I drape my arm over the back of the bench. "I don't know, Hattie, maybe because it's fucking lonely out on the road. That I don't have as many people close to me as I thought I did. You push me away, but still stay close. You don't take when other people will . . . and that makes me realize you're not here to use me, especially since you know you could leave any moment you want, and I won't hold it against you."

She fiddles with her hands in her lap. "You're making it really hard not to like you."

"Maybe I'm not the kind of guy you should be hating," I say.

"With every day that passes, I'm beginning to think that." She turns away, and when I think she's about to get up and leave, she scoots back against the bench and leans against my arm. But then she scoots in closer and positions her body to lean against my chest and my arm.

Fucking hell.

It's not cuddling, but fuck, it's pretty damn close.

I press my lips tightly together as I stare up at the stars, the feel of her pressing into me creating a surprising inner turmoil. I like her. I'll admit it, I like Hattie Rowley when I know damn well I shouldn't. I shouldn't have invited her over this weekend. I shouldn't have offered her my sweatshirt just now, and I shouldn't allow her to lean into me like this. But hell if I'm going to stop her because if I'm honest, I was hoping something like this would happen.

I was hoping I could grow closer to her. I was hoping I could experience something more with her. Like when we made cookies, I felt something new . . . something exciting.

She sparked some light into my life.

But like Abel said . . . she's off limits.

So fucking off limits that what we're doing right now should be stopped, but when her head drops against my shoulder, for the life of me, I can't ask her to move.

I want her to move in closer.

I want her to stay here, staring into the fire with me until the early morning starts to rise.

"The stars are beautiful out here with the mountains as a dark backdrop underneath them," she says quietly. "Living in a city for so long, you forget to appreciate the little things like the stars."

"But the stars are the one thing that keeps us locked into home," I say.

"What do you mean?" she asks.

"No matter where you are in the world, you can always depend on the stars to keep you grounded, to remind you that you might be away from home, but you're still connected under the umbrella of the sky."

She sinks deeper into me as she says, "Did you look up at the stars while on tour?"

"Not at first," I answer softly. "I was too concerned with leaving. But even though I have a love-hate relationship with this town, there were times I felt . . . lost while on tour. The stars grounded me, gave me peace. I'd ask to be driven out to the country, and I'd hoist myself onto the roof of the car and stare up at the sky. Some of my most peaceful moments were spent there."

"Cassidy and I used to count the stars together. We'd spend many nights during the summer out on a blanket in the middle of the potatoes before she had Mac, counting and naming them. I haven't looked up at them since she passed."

"Naming?"

She nods against me. "We'd group them together and name them after things like . . . old rock bands, or vegetables, or TV stars. There was one time we both named the same star Jim Parsons and ended up laughing for five minutes straight with tears streaming down our cheeks."

I don't know what to say or how to respond that wouldn't make it seem hollow compared to what she just shared. I always strive for less is more, so I move my arm that's braced over the back of the bench to across her shoulders and tug her in closer.

She gently approves with a sigh.

After what seems like ten minutes, she quickly asks, "What did you do to Ryland?"

"I think that's something you should talk to your brother about," I answer. "Because there's his truth, and then there's mine."

"Well, let me hear your truth," she says.

"I don't want it to skew your brother's truth. You deserve to hear it from him and be on his side of the story, not mine."

"Why don't you let me be the judge of that?"

I sigh. "Hattie, if I tell you my side first, you're more likely to favor my story over your brother's, and even though things are strained between him and me, I'm not about to take the loyalty of his sister. So if you want to know, ask Ryland."

She shakes her head. "Just your response to that makes me want to believe you more."

"Don't," I say. "It won't be good for you."

She turns her head ever so slightly, her eyes matching up with mine, the light of the fire bouncing off her cheek. Quietly, she says, "Maybe it will be."

Jesus.

Those fucking eyes of hers. Soulful, but also so fucking naive at the same time.

Long, endless lashes frame the pale stones that are her irises.

And they're starving.

Starving for attention.

"You paint yourself in a light that's unflattering," she says, lifting her hand to feel the scruff on my jaw. Her thumb slowly works over it, and fuck, my heart beats faster than I've felt in a very long time. "Maybe you shouldn't anymore, because I'm not seeing the man you try to be. I see someone different."

Her thumb drags close to my lip, the temptation to suck it into my mouth is so fucking strong.

"You're seeing a lie." My breath feels heavy in my chest as she leans in an inch closer.

Fuck, don't kiss me, Hattie.

Please don't fucking kiss me.

I won't be able to stop you.

I won't be able to stop myself.

She moves in another inch, her eyes matching mine so we're at the same level.

"I think you're telling me a lie, and I'm seeing the truth."

Her tongue peeks out, wetting her lips.

My body stills.

My muscles tense.

My need skyrockets as she moves one inch closer.

Motherfucker, I want this.

I want those lips.

I want this girl.

I want every goddamn thing about her.

With nothing but a whisper of a breath between us, her thumb drags across my jaw. "Maybe you'll stop lying to me . . . to yourself."

And then she pulls back, taking the air straight from my lungs with her.

Standing, she takes off my sweatshirt, but I stop her while my pulse rockets through my body. My voice sounds garbled as I say, "Keep it."

"Keep your sweatshirt?"

"Yeah." I swallow hard as I stand as well.

She gathers the fabric at the collar and gently brings it to her nose before sniffing. When her eyes open, they dreamily look up at me. "I was hoping you'd say that."

Fuck . . .

"Yeah, you smell so good, Hayes."

I wet my lips as well, staring down at her, unsure of what to fucking say. This is bad. This is really fucking bad.

"You know, you could tell me that I smell good as well." She tugs on the hem of my shirt. "That would be the kind thing to do, though I know you hate being kind to me."

Not even the slightest.

I want to be nice to you.

You're the first fucking person, besides my grandma and Abel, I want to be nice to.

She peers up at me, waiting for a response, and because I'm the biggest dumbass in the world, I reply, "You smell really fucking good, Hattie."

With a satisfied smile, she loops her finger through one of my belt loops and tugs me an inch closer. "What do I smell like?"

I can feel the heat of her body up against mine and can practically taste her heartbeat.

"Are you trying to get us in trouble?"

"Maybe," she says, not looking shy at all, more ravenous than anything.

I'm tempted to lift my hand to her cheek, to deepen this moment into something more, but Abel's words pump through me, his warning to stay away. So I keep my hands to myself as I say, "You smell like electric sunshine."

"Electric sunshine?" she asks. "What exactly does that smell like?"

I shift, my body precariously growing closer. "Radiance with a zing, like soft summer meadows zapped by lightning. Like a sweet combination of fire and rain. Soft and edgy. Bright and dark all in one."

She stares up at me, a studying look in her eyes.

When she doesn't say anything, I ask, "What?"

"How many women have you said that to?"

"You want to know?" I ask.

"Yes." She nods. "I do."

I bring my finger under her chin, tilt it up and say, "None. That was for you and you alone."

Fucking leave . . . now.

If you don't, you will kiss her.

Don't fucking kiss her.

Jaw clenched, I step away, and she lets go of my belt loop as I move toward the back entrance of the house. I open the heavy sliding glass door for her, and she takes the hint—the night is over for us.

When I shut the door, she turns toward me, drowning in my sweatshirt, looking so goddamn beautiful it actually hurts. "Walk me to my room?"

"Do you think that's a good idea?"

"Why wouldn't it be?" she asks innocently, but there is nothing innocent in her eyes.

"You know exactly why," I answer as I step back and then nod toward the hallway leading to her room. "Go on, Hattie, go to your room."

She doesn't respond, not right away. She's almost to the hallway when she turns around and says, "You're not the dick I thought you were, Hayes. And that should be terrifying for us both."

Then she leaves, vanishing into the darkness of the hall-way. Her words beat rapidly through me.

Because she's right.

If Hattie doesn't think I'm the man she thought I was, yeah, that's terrifying for us both.

⸻

"ARE you going to get a haircut soon?" Grandma asks as I walk into her apartment.

"Good to see you too, Gran," I say. I set down a plate of the cherry almond cookies I can't stop consuming and offer Gran a kiss on the cheek. Hattie and Maggie helped me make more cookies this morning before they went off to have a pool day in my backyard. I knew the minute they headed to their rooms to change into their bathing suits, I needed to leave. No fucking way was I about to sit around and catch Hattie prancing around in a bikini.

No, that would destroy the crumbling resolve I've tried to desperately hold on to where Hattie is concerned.

A visit to my grandma's is exactly what I need.

They're always sobering.

"Well, are you?" she asks.

"Gran, I got one a few weeks ago."

"That can't be the truth. You look like you have a mop on your head."

I toss around my thick hair on the top that I keep longer than the sides. "This is how I wear it."

"Stop joking with me. It looks like there's a dead raccoon on your head."

See . . . sobering.

"What have you been up to, Gran? Besides counting the millimeters of hair growth on my head?" It's healthy to change the subject with her. It keeps the conversation fresh, or she'll drag down the same topic until it's dead and buried.

"Being smart with me, I see," she says as she adjusts herself in her chair to pull back her window curtain with her cane. She uses the end and points down to the house in front of hers. "See those children down there playing? The Macabees? They keep throwing rocks at the fire hydrant. I hope one of them knocks off the screw, and they get popped in the face with a blast of water."

Did I mention she's an old crotch?

Because she is.

The biggest of them all.

"I mentioned their disrespect to the Peach Society, and they said they'd have a conversation with the parents. But I don't think it's happened yet because I still see them throwing rocks. Is that what the world has come to? Throwing rocks at innocent fire hydrants?"

"It's almost as if they're forced to play outside rather than be on their electronics," I say.

"Exactly! We have screens for a reason. Stick them in front of one."

I chuckle and shake my head. "Some people might say that more kids need to be outside."

"Nonsense. Screens keep them out of trouble."

"Whatever you say, Gran."

"When are you going to give me great-grandchildren?"

Oh Jesus, here we go again. I swear great-grandchildren and her impending death are her favorite things to discuss. I don't think she sees the irony of the two things. *If she dies, there will still be no great-grandchildren.*

"Not for a while unless you want me having children out of wedlock."

"I don't care how you have them. Impregnate a giraffe for all I care. I just want great-grandchildren. I'm not getting any younger, you know. I broke my hip. Do you know what that means? I'm dying in six months."

Wow, she combined them today. I'm impressed.

I pinch the bridge of my nose. "If you're dying in six months, how could I possibly give you great-grandchildren if it takes at least nine months to make one?"

"I don't know. You have your ding-a-ling that's been around the block. Any accidents happen?"

Jesus Christ, did they give her an upper today?

"No accidents, Gran. I always wrap up."

She huffs her disappointment. "Well, that's upsetting. I'm going to die without great-grandchildren."

"Who says you're dying in six months?" I ask. "Abel didn't say anything about that. He said you've made a remarkable turnaround since I was called to come back home, making me wonder if you made it seem worse than it is."

Her mouth falls open, and she clutches her chest in surprise. "Do you think I'd do such a thing?"

"Yes," I say. "Yes, I do. I wouldn't put it past you."

"Well, you're wrong. I'm dying in six months, and when that happens, I'll watch you eat your words."

"How will you be able to watch if you're dead?" I ask her.

Her eyes narrow, and she points her cane at me. "Don't get smart with me, boy. I will haunt you so hard, you'll fear closing your eyes at night."

I truly believe her. This woman can pretty much will anything into fruition with an evil sneer and a call out to the universe, even her death in six months.

I hold my hands up and say, "Okay, so you're dying in six months. What should we do to make sure you have the best six months of your life?"

"For one . . . get you married." She brings both hands to the top of her cane and says, "Any prospects?"

Immediately, Hattie comes to mind, which fuck, that's annoying. She's never even been on my radar. Now she's the first fucking person I think of? Jesus . . . no, think of someone else.

Anyone.

Maybe that big-boob girl who never sucked your dick. What was her name again?

Hattie . . .

No.

Not Hattie.

Carla?

Annise?

No . . .

Hattie.

My inner turmoil gets the best of me because before I can think of some random girl's name, Gran stares me down, the maturity in her eyes like a pointed finger, demanding me to tell the truth.

"You're about to lie to me. Do not lie to me. You know I have my way of finding things out, so you might as well tell the truth."

I lean back in my chair and sigh. "Gran, there aren't any women in my life."

"Hayes Richard Farrow, I know that look in your eyes. There is someone. Now tell me."

Dammit. I tug on my hair that apparently needs to be cut. "Gran, I can't tell you because it's really not anything, and if it becomes something, it'll be bad."

"Is she married?"

"What?" I ask. "No. I'd never do that."

"Good." Gran nods her head. "At least I taught you something."

"You taught me a whole lot more than just that," I reply.

Her expression eases, and she shifts in her seat, puffing her chest. "Look at you flattering me, even on my deathbed."

"You're not on your deathbed, Gran."

"I broke my hip. That means I'm about to die. It happens to all the old people, so if you would please tell me who this person is so I can die in peace, I'd appreciate it."

Christ.

I scratch the side of my jaw. "It's complicated. I don't know how I feel about her, okay? So don't get all weird on me, and I swear, Gran, if you say anything, I might not come visit you on your deathbed."

She pokes me with her cane right in the quad, and fuck, it hurts.

"Ouch," I say, rubbing the spot.

"Don't you dare threaten me about my deathbed."

"You know what I mean. I need this to stay between us."

"Why?"

"Because it's highly sensitive, and you know this town. The minute someone says anything, it spreads like wildfire, especially with the Peach Society."

"I think you're overthinking it, but sure, this will stay between us. I can keep a secret like the best of them. Remember when you puked right before you went out on stage for the first time to perform at Five Six Seven Eight? I didn't tell anyone, did I?"

"You didn't. You just kicked the puke under the curtain and told no one, only for Ethel to find it later and scream bloody murder."

"Served her right. She deliberately wore pink that day because she knew I was wearing pink and then flirted with Rodney right in front of me. Too bad for her, he didn't find her flamboyancy the least bit attractive. No one constantly wants boa feathers flying in their face. Not to mention, he knew she was only interested in women and was using him as a tool."

"I think we might have gotten slightly off topic," I say.

"I don't like that woman." Gran crosses her arms over her chest and stares out the window. "She has perfectly working hips, and I bet she's going to throw that in my face. That's what happens when you're loose in the hips, always spreading your legs—"

"Okay, Gran," I say uncomfortably.

"You have loose hips when you're older." Okay, I guess we're not done here. "But I was a celibate angel for many years. So many years that I sneezed once, and a dustball flew into my underwear." Fucking Christ. "And do you know how humbling that is, Hayes? To find a dustball in your underwear?"

Lips pulled tight, I slowly nod and squeak, "Quite humbling."

"Exactly. And what do I get for being a born-again Virgin Mary? A broken hip that's going to kill me in six months. And there's Ethel, kick-ball-changing down the boardwalk with her loose, whore hips." She waves her fist toward the window out of pure agony. "Life is not fair."

And I think we might be done with the conversation about me, thankfully. I'll take her dustball talk over discussing Hattie any day. Because I still don't know what's going on with that, how I feel, and what the hell I'm doing, so telling Gran would honestly not make any sense.

"And do you know what else bothers me about that woman besides her whore hips?" Gran continues.

This will be one hell of a rant, so I might as well get comfortable. I snag a cookie from the plate, lean back in my chair, and say, "What else do you not like, Gran?"

━━━

CHRIST, I'm worn out.

Between Gran hating on Ethel to her complaining about the boardwalk planks and how they're not walker friendly— something I agreed to—and the agony of hearing what songs she wants me to sing at her funeral when she dies in six months—*Dream A Little Dream Of Me*—I'm exhausted.

I took my car because I knew Hattie wasn't going anywhere, so I parked it in front of the driveway and headed into the house through the front door. I toss my wallet on the entryway table, and just as I look up to head to the kitchen, I stop. Hattie's walking into the house through the sliding glass door, wearing a tiny yellow bikini.

She's fine as fuck.

Small triangles cover her small tits, and thin straps of her bottoms arch over her slim hips. The fabric's so thin that I'm not sure how it stays in place. Her toned body is basically on full display. The word *want* rushes through my mind.

When she glances up and sees me, a large smile spreads across her face as she says, "I'm drunk." And she throws her arms up as if we're supposed to celebrate this accomplishment. "I'm so, so drunk." She giggles and moves to the kitchen. "Want to get drunk with us?"

Yes.

And I want to tug that bikini off with my teeth.

"Uh . . . probably not a good idea," I say as she turns away from me, showing off the thong of her bathing suit.

I inwardly groan as my eyes fall to her pert little ass, cheeks smooth, the faintest stretch marks along the side. The girl is all-natural, just what I fucking like. And I'm not surprised she has them because compared to her body's structure, she has a juicy ass, something I can sink my fingers into and grip tightly while pounding into her.

"Are you staring at my butt?"

"Huh?" I ask, snapping my eyes up to see Hattie has turned around now with a pitcher of pink liquid.

"You were staring at my ass. Hayes Farrow, how dare you?"

I grip the back of my neck. "What did you expect me to do when you walked in here wearing that?" I ask.

"Be a mature adult."

"I'm mature and an adult, but that doesn't mean I'm not going to look at a sexy ass when I see one."

"Sexy, huh?" she asks as she spins around and jiggles her butt in my direction. "You like this?"

I smile and nod. "Yeah, I fucking do."

She turns back around and clutches the pitcher to her chest. With a smile on her face, she says, "Pervert." And then takes off toward the backyard. "You should join us. It might be fun to have a man to stare at. I like Maggie, but her boobs are just obnoxious. I'm getting jealous."

"Yeah, like I said, I'm going to pass," I say.

"Shame, you could have a good time with us."

"I'm sure, but I should work on some music," I lie. "Have fun." Without another look, I take off toward my studio, and when I step inside, I shut and lock the door behind me before flopping on my couch and dragging my hands over my face. Christ, the sight of her ass in that thong will stick with me for a very long fucking time.

Too long.

I reach for my guitar but then stop myself. Instead, I reach for my notebook as a thought pops into my mind. The color of her bathing suit matches the way she smells and the joy she seems to bring into the room. *Electric sunshine.*

I can't describe it any other way.

And that's what I write down in my notebook.

Electric sunshine, from there . . . I describe exactly what that is and how Hattie embodies everything about it.

⊏⊐

BOTTLE OF TEQUILA IN HAND, I lean back on my couch and let out a deep breath as I drunkenly stare up at the ceiling. The feeling of euphoria screams through me.

I did it.

I wrote a song.

A fucking good one.

It was as if something of greater power had taken over me, and the words flowed with the image of Hattie in my mind.

My pen flew across my notebook.

My mind was rabid with descriptions, with the need to taste her through my words.

The desperation.

The forbidden temptation.

The powerful yearning.

It drained out of me, leaving me spent and drunk.

And Jesus Christ, it's so good. Probably one of the best songs I've ever written.

The only problem is . . . since every last word is about Hattie, I can't share it with the world.

Why? Because she'd know. She'd know it was about her when she heard the lyrics. It's why I can't give it to the studio.

It's why I'm currently drinking.

And it's why I'm staring at Ruben's text, feeling agitated.

Ruben: *Just checking in.*

Yeah, that's all he's doing, checking in. And I know it's his job, but Jesus fucking Christ, I can't just perform when he says perform.

I tip my bottle back in my mouth, take a giant swig, then wipe my mouth with the back of my hand and text him back.

Hayes: *You're annoying the shit out of me. Fuck off, Ruben.*

There. That should do it. I set my phone to the side and clutch my bottle close to my chest just as my phone rings next to me.

Of course, the fucker calls. I shouldn't have expected anything less.

I lift the phone, answer it, then press it to my ear.

"What?" I say.

"Want to talk about it?" he says, knowing me all too fucking well.

"No," I answer.

"Hayes, come on . . . what's going on?"

Ruben is the type of guy who presses, who won't let you get away with not speaking your feelings—hence the phone call. Normally, I'd tell him everything is fine, but everything doesn't feel fine.

Everything feels out of control.

Uncomfortable.

Agonizing.

And I need to get it off my chest.

"What's going on?" I ask. "Well, besides the fact that I think I like a girl who I shouldn't like, and fuck is she beautiful, and sweet, and her freckles, fuck, Ruben, her freckles. She's . . . she's charming, and she listens, and she makes me feel less alone, and I don't like that because I shouldn't like her, I shouldn't want to talk to her, to be near her, but hell do I want to be near her, all the goddamn time. I want to go talk to her right now, and she smells . . . she smells so damn good, and the song I wrote, yeah, that's about her, but there is no way in fuck I can hand over the song to you despite it being really fucking good because if she found out I liked her then everything would be ruined, ruined for her and I can't ruin her, she's so much sunshine and promises, and I can't ruin that . . . so, yeah, despite that, everything is just fucking great."

"Okay," Ruben says calmly. "That's a lot to process. Let me see if I've got this right. You like a girl. You shouldn't like this girl. But you wrote a song about her. But you can't turn it in." Wow, he's good. "Why can't you hand over the song?"

"Because she'll know it's about her. Immediately. She'll know, and she can't know." I shake my head. "She can't know that I like her. No one can know."

"That's fair," Ruben says. "Can I ask, why can't anyone know?"

"It's Ryland's little sister," I say, dragging my hand over my face.

"Ryland, the guy who hates you?"

"Yeah."

"I thought his sister passed."

"He has three sisters. Hattie is the youngest. Fucking

twelve years younger than me, Ruben. Twelve years. Like . . . fuck, I'm a pervert for even looking at her."

"No, you're not." Ruben pauses. "Wait, is this the girl who's working for you?"

"Yup," I say, popping the P in yup. "The same girl. At first, it was easy just to ignore her, but she got under my skin. I think about her a lot. I catch myself staring, wanting to talk to her more. I thought maybe it was because I'm lonely. This job is so fucking lonely, Ruben. Everyone wants something from you besides friendship, you know? And she . . . she just stuck around. Talked to me. Joked around, despite us pretending to hate each other, and I saw her in a fucking bikini when I got home, one of those thong ones, you know what I'm talking about?"

"Yes, I do," Ruben says. "Hard to look away."

"Exactly!" I nearly shout. "And I couldn't look away. I just kept staring, and I lost it. I lost all will. I kept looking, and last night, fucking hell, last night."

"Dare I ask what happened last night?"

"She bombarded me outside by wearing my sweatshirt and cuddling into my side, and we watched the starry night sky, and that's when I realized how much she smelled like electric sunshine, and I just like her, Ruben, I fucking like her, but I can't. Abel will kill me. Ryland will kill me. I'd destroy her. She's so innocent and perfect. I'm not the guy for her, so I came into my studio and started writing. The more the words flowed, the more I drank, and now, I'm halfway done with a bottle and done with a song at the same time. And it's all about her, how she smells, how I'm desperate for one taste of her cherry lips, how I'd ask for one night to explore her and . . . and she would know it's about her."

"Which is bad."

"Yes, very bad," I say. "So bad."

"Okay, well . . . this is good."

My nose curls from his response. "What do you mean this is good?" I ask. "How is any of this good?"

"You've told me that you write your best when you're tortured, and it seems you're currently tortured."

"But I can't turn this song in."

"Then don't. But at least it got you writing. This is just the start. It might not feel good, but this is a good thing, Hayes."

I pause. "I want to punch you."

"I know." He chuckles. "Hang in there. This is where the good comes."

"Well, what the hell do I do about the girl?"

"That's up to you. I can't tell you what to do with your life, but if you're this tortured over it, you need to see which will be worse—not being with her or being with her and facing the consequences of that decision."

"Not . . . helpful," I say as I stand from the couch, bottle in one hand, phone in the other.

"I'm sorry, but this is a decision you'll have to make on your own."

"That's what I thought," I say. "I need to eat something."

"Okay, call me when you're sober."

"Doubtful," I say as I hang up and toss my phone onto the couch.

I open my studio door and bring my bottle as I make my way to the kitchen, the house sounding pretty quiet. Thank God they went to bed. I'm not sure I could take one more look at Hattie in a goddamn bikini.

I turn the corner to the kitchen and stop when I see her, leaning against the counter, a cookie in hand, wearing my goddamn sweatshirt.

Fuck.

When she sees me, she says, "I'm eating a cookie."

I lift my bottle to my lips and say, "I'm drunk."

A smirk passes over her lips. "Getting drunk all alone? Why didn't you join us?"

"Because I didn't want to," I say as I move into the kitchen and set my bottle on the counter. My eyes fall to her bare legs, then slowly climb to her eyes. "You're eating my cookies."

"We made them together, so our cookies."

"My house, my rules," I say as I take the cookie from her and shove the rest of it in my mouth, causing her eyes to widen.

"Hey, I was eating that."

"And now it's in my stomach. Your loss, my gain." I walk over to the fridge and open it up, looking for anything but pickles to eat, but of course I come up short, so I shut the fridge and lean against it as I watch Hattie pick up my bottle of tequila and bring it to her lips. She takes a swig and smirks at me. "That's mine."

"And now it's in my stomach. Your loss . . . my gain."

I close the distance between us and take the bottle from her, only to step away, my eyes remaining on hers the entire time. "You should go back to bed."

"Why's that?" she asks.

"It's not safe for you out here."

"Maybe I don't want safe."

"You do," I say as I take another swig of tequila, my brain feeling too fucking fuzzy to be close to her.

"Or maybe I want to do something dangerous for once."

I shake my head, but she moves toward me and dances her fingers up my chest. "I'm trouble," I say.

"Good," she replies as her hand trails down my stomach, but I stop her, my hand gripping her wrist. And then, in a flash, I twist her so she's pinned against the fridge, her arm extended above her head where I lock it in place.

Don't do it, man.

Don't play with fire.

Drop her hand and leave.

You're too drunk to even consider being near her.

But common sense never wins when tequila is involved.

"I told you I'm trouble," I say as I bring the bottle of tequila up to her mouth, and I slowly move the opening of the glass over her plump lips. She parts them, and I tip the bottle up so the liquid flows into her mouth. She swallows the small amount I give her and licks her lips, soaking up every last drop. "Don't you see that, Hattie? Don't you see that I'm trouble?"

"I do," she answers.

"So you shouldn't be out here with me, you should be in your room, sleeping."

"Maybe I came out here on purpose, knowing you were in your studio."

"Why didn't you just go to my studio?" I ask, lifting the bottle to my lips, wishing I could taste her lips on the glass, but I'm not that lucky.

She watches me swallow the tequila right before I set the bottle on the counter beside her. When she stares up at me, her hand still clasped by mine, she says, "I was too afraid."

"Good. You should be afraid," I say as I bring my free hand to her thigh and drag it up to her hipbone. Her breath hitches in her chest. Fuck, she's not wearing any underwear. "Are you wearing anything under my sweatshirt, Hattie?"

She shakes her head. "I'm not."

"Bad move." And then I slide my hand up her side, dragging up my sweatshirt until I reach her rib cage. "Tell me what you want," I say, my breath heavy, the feel of her soft skin under my calluses so goddamn extraordinary.

"I . . . I don't know."

"Wrong answer," I say as I spin her around so her chest and hands press against the fridge. I grab her elbows and push them up so her hands extend toward the ceiling, and then I force her to grip the top of the fridge. Speaking close to her ear, I say, "Don't fucking let go of that."

She nods as I take a step back and look her over. The

bottom of her ass is showing, giving me just enough of a view to make my mouth water, my body needing more.

In the back of my mind, I'm telling myself to walk away, to leave this girl alone, but my body has other thoughts as I smooth my hand under the sweatshirt and lift it to show off the rest of her ass.

"Spread your legs," I say, and when she does, I slide my hand down one globe to her hamstring and then to her inner thigh, causing her to tip her head forward and moan. "You planned this, didn't you? Putting on my sweatshirt, knowing it would make me feel possessive, not wearing anything under it because it would make me feel unhinged. This was all thought out so you could manipulate your way into my goddamn bed."

"I thought you didn't want me in your bed."

I push up against her, letting her feel my erection against her leg. "You know goddamn well that was a lie."

She sucks in a sharp breath. "Why are you so mad?"

"Because you're off limits," I say, dragging my hand down her ass again and then pulling up between her legs, getting so close to where I want to touch her that I feel the heat of her arousal on my fingers.

"I thought you make the rules."

"I do, and the rules are . . . you're off limits."

"Then why are you touching me?"

"Because you're tempting me," I growl and move up behind her, her ass pressing against my crotch as my hands fall to her hips.

"You're so hard." She wiggles her butt against me, turning me on even more.

"Don't do that," I say, keeping her hips still. *For the love of God, don't do that.*

"Afraid you might fuck me?"

"Afraid I might destroy you," I growl as I move my hands back to her ribs, feeling every bone, every divot.

Her lungs work feverishly under my touch, and as I slowly slide my fingers directly under her breasts, I can feel the pause in her lungs, the catch of her breath.

"God, Hayes," she groans, her ass pushing against me. "T-touch my breasts."

"No," I say, even though my need for her screams yes. I move my forehead to the back of her head and slide my index fingers up an inch, just so I can feel the slight plump of her breasts. "Fuck," I grumble as a war battles deep inside me.

Touch her.

Take what you want.

Don't . . . don't ruin her.

I bite on my bottom lip as my index finger slowly runs north until it hits the point of her nipples.

"Yessss," she moans, and I snap.

Momentarily.

I glide my index finger over the hot nub, flicking it back and forth a few times, making me so goddamn hard that my erection presses painfully against the zipper of my jeans.

"Tell me to stop," I whisper.

"No," she says. "No, I want this. Please don't stop."

The devil inside me wonders how much I could turn her on without touching her where she wants to be touched.

How much will she allow me to feel her, to experience her without giving her what she wants?

Only one way to find out.

Don't do it, a tiny voice in my head says, but I ignore it as I bring my hands back down her sides, past her ribs, to her hips. The sexy moan of betrayal that falls past her lips only spurs me on as I run my fingertips inward, right to her pubic bone, where she's completely bare.

Fuck.

Me.

"Touch me," she whispers. "Please, I'm so wet."

"Christ," I groan as I'm tempted to dip my fingers inside

her, so tempted that my pinky slips lower, passing over her slit just once. She sucks in a harsh breath, her hips seeking relief, but I give her none.

"Hayes, please."

"No," I say softly into her ear. "I refuse to touch you like that."

"Don't leave me like this. I'm so turned on. Stop teasing me," she complains.

"This is all you'll ever get," I say as I bring both my hands to her inner thighs and then drag them so dangerously close to her pussy, that the backs of my thumbs barely touch her labia. It's the lightest touch, but enough for her to groan in frustration.

"Please, Hayes."

"No," I say, my brain finally kicking in, taking over as my dick cries out in protest.

"Feel how wet I am."

"No," I reply as I drag the tips of my fingers to her breasts, allowing my index fingers to pass over her nipples one last time.

One flick.

One more.

Fuck . . . one more.

"God," she cries out in frustration as she turns around and faces me.

Her eyes are wild in the moonlight.

Her chest heavy with desire.

And when she stares up at me, I feel this demanding need to crash my mouth against hers.

To claim her.

Mark her.

I slap my hand against the fridge and prop myself up as I grip her hip, steadying myself.

"Fuck me," she says.

I drop my head and shake it. "No, Hattie. I won't."

Her response . . . she cups my length, taking me into the small palm of her hand.

"Mother . . . fucker," I cry out, a hiss passing my lips at the same time. When I open my eyes, I find hers wide, surprised.

"You're . . . huge."

"Another reason you can't have me. You won't be able to handle it."

I remove her hand and then say, "Spread your legs."

"Hayes, I'm not—"

"Spread them. Now. I will not say it again."

She spreads them. I cover the back of her hand with mine and bring it between her legs.

I won't touch her, but that doesn't mean I can't use her hand to touch herself and give her what I want.

"Have you ever touched yourself before?" I ask.

"Only . . . only when I'm alone."

"How do you like it?" I ask. The thought of her masturbating spurs my need for her.

"Two fingers," she answers.

I wet my lips and press her two fingers against her clit. She exhales sharply as her body leans against the fridge again.

"Tell me what your pussy feels like. Describe it to me." I move her two fingers in tight circles, rubbing against her clit. Her hand falls behind her, steadying against the fridge as she trembles from the touch.

"Warm," she answers. "So fucking wet, Hayes. Drenched."

"Hell," I mutter, leaning in closer.

"I've never been this turned on, ever."

"It's why I shouldn't be doing this," I whisper, picking up the speed, knowing she'll fall over quickly from the reaction I'm already getting from her. "This is dangerous. You'll want more, and I can't give that to you."

"Give me what you can," she says, her breathing more labored. I reach down and take her loose hand in mine. I clasp her hand with mine and bring it above her head while we massage her clit to the point of no return.

"This is it," I whisper. "Nothing else and never again. Don't ask for it. Don't beg. This is all it will ever be."

"Fuck," she says, her body shaking. I release my hand from between her legs and prop it against the fridge, not wanting to feel her come close to my fingers. I won't be able to withstand it. "Hayes, I need you."

"Make yourself come," I say as I release her other hand and step back.

Her eyes widen in surprise as I move all the way to the island and place my hands on the counter, holding myself in place.

"Hayes."

"Do it, Hattie," I say in such a dark, sinful tone that her hand pauses momentarily. "Make yourself . . . come. Now."

She gulps, and to my fucking demise, she slips her other hand under her sweatshirt, dragging it up until it reaches her breast. There, she cups her breast, kneading it and flicking her nipple. I stand there in fascination, watching the whole time as she brings herself closer and closer.

Her breath frantic.

Her legs shaking.

Her head falling back as her neck tenses . . .

"Fuck," she cries out as her fingers wildly fly over her clit, her body shattering before me as she comes. Once she catches her breath and her eyes meet mine, she says, "If I didn't do that, if I didn't make myself come, would you have left me like that?"

"Yes," I answer.

"Why?"

"Because I told you I was trouble, Hattie. You were warned." My brain snaps out of the haze I was just in, reality smacking me so hard in the face that it feels like I'm suffering from whiplash.

You stupid motherfucker.

What the hell did you do?

"You would leave me turned on? That's shitty," she says, her post-orgasm haze dissolving quickly.

"That's what I am, Hattie. A shitty person, I never tried to be any different."

"That's such bullshit, Hayes," she replies, stepping forward, but I move past her and grab my bottle of tequila. "You're not that man."

I lean in right next to her face and say, "And I've told you over and over again, I am that man. You're off limits, and that's all you'll ever be. Go to bed. Forget this ever happened."

And with that, I head toward my bedroom with one thing on my mind, getting my cock in my hand and the rest of this bottle into my stomach.

I fucked up.

And now I need to erase it from my memory. *Pathetic, Farrow, just pathetic.*

———

TEQUILA DID me fucking dirty last night.

Usually, we get along. Usually, we have a good time. Usually, we can easily forget the next day.

Not this time.

Tequila didn't let me forget one goddamn thing.

Not the sound of Hattie's gasps in my ear.

Not the feel of her tight nipple under my finger.

Not the way she shuddered under her own hand as she came.

Not one goddamn thing.

Instead, tequila imprinted every fucking moment of squaring her off against the fridge in my mind to the point that I woke up with such a huge erection that I had to take immediate care of it in the shower, despite making myself come last night the moment I got back to my room.

And I still feel uneasy.

I still feel like I could explode at any minute.

Like the key to the release of this pain, this pent-up desire rests *inside* Hattie only. *Fuck, to be inside her hot pussy.*

It's a brutal reality that forced me out of my house so I didn't have to see her this morning. Not sure I could withstand seeing her morning hair and the semi-unsatisfied look in her eyes.

It's why I'm in town right now, headed to The Sweet Lab for some coffee. Anything to get this crushing feeling out of me.

I set my helmet on my bike, pocket my keys, and then head toward the front of the store. Hands in my pockets, I round the corner just as another person collides with me, spilling coffee between us.

"Fuck," he says. "I'm sorr—"

But his voice dies off as we look up and make eye contact.

Ryland Rowley.

It was bound to happen. The town is small enough for us to bump into each other, but this . . . this feels so much heavier than when we ran into each other in the past. Because this time, I have the sounds of a turned-on Hattie lingering in my brain.

Ryland's brows drop, and he backs away. Luckily, neither one of us got coffee on our clothes, just over his hand and on the ground between us.

Unsure what to do, I tug on my neck and point at his coffee. "Want me to replace that?"

The man I once called my best friend scowls at me. "I don't need your fucking charity."

"Wasn't offering charity."

He transfers his to-go cup and shakes his wet hand to get the coffee off.

"Fuck," he mutters.

"I can grab napkins . . ."

His eyes snap up to mine. "Does it look like I want your help? Jesus, read the room."

That just makes me stuff my hands in my pockets as I let him figure it out on his own. And I don't know what comes over me, maybe it's the bitterness in me, or the internal burning from not being able to take what I want, or the fact that he treats me like such shit when I don't deserve it, but I say, "I see Hattie's in town."

That makes him lock eyes with me again. "Why the hell would you say that?"

"Just making conversation."

He takes a step forward, the smell of his coffee wafting between us. "Stay away from her."

"What makes you think I'd go near her?" I ask, standing my ground.

"To fuck with me," he replies.

"Yes, because my mission in life is to fuck with you, Ryland."

He gets in my face now, nose to nose. This man does not resemble the Ryland Rowley I used to know. I can honestly say he does not look good. Stressed. Beyond exhausted. *He was once so easygoing. He was once someone I knew better than anyone else.* But this guy is beyond angry. At me. *At life?* "Listen carefully, Farrow. Leave my sisters and my family the fuck alone. Got it?"

"Boys, boys, boys," Ethel O'Donnell-Kerr says as she walks up to us. "Now, now, I hope we're not getting into anything spirited here while we have visitors in our town only a whisper away."

Ryland stares into my eyes. "No, I was just leaving."

"Good," Ethel replies.

"See you around," I say with a smirk because if anything, I thrive for trouble when I feel out of sorts. He starts to move past me, and I lean into him, bumping his shoulder with mine. He shifts backward just slightly, but his eyes remain on mine.

"Stay. Away," he repeats and then takes off.

"Well, what a tense reunion," Ethel says.

Tense is a nice way of putting it.

Honestly, if I had it my way, I would have loved to feel Ryland's fist this morning. Craved it actually.

There's nothing better than physical pain taking away the mental pain. The physical pain I can draw on—I can live off it—but the mental anguish I'm going through right now . . . it almost makes it too hard to breathe.

But if there's one thing I learned from this interaction is that nothing has changed between me and Ryland. Backing the hell away from Hattie . . . it was a smart move.

Because he wouldn't forgive her. *And I don't want that on my fucking conscience too.*

Chapter Eleven

HATTIE

"How do you feel?" Maggie asks as I drive us back to my studio apartment, sad because I have to leave my best friend after our fun weekend. A weekend when I didn't have to worry about school, my family, or the loss of Cassidy. A weekend when we forgot, where we pushed the real world away, and now that we've popped our bubble of joy, all the problems in my life are resting on my shoulders again.

The weight of my lies.

The weight of my grief.

The weight of last night . . .

Frustration weighs so heavily on me that I actually feel sick to my stomach. I don't know what I was thinking, but the copious amounts of alcohol went to my head, and I nearly threw myself at Hayes—only for him to basically pat me on the ass and send me back to my room. It was humiliating and frustrating at the same time. All I could think about was how it felt to have him touch me. It was so maddening that I had to finish myself off.

And this morning, when he was playing his guitar out on his deck, I skulked out of his house, trying to put on a happy face for Maggie despite this war of embarrassment spinning through me.

How could he rev me up like that, get me so hot, and then just . . . walk away as if I have zero impact on him and don't matter? I'm not enticing enough for him to even finish the job?

It makes me feel undesirable, cheap, and like the age difference between us is a deciding factor . . . like I'm naive and far too inexperienced for him to grant me the time of day.

Humiliation is what I feel. But that's not what I say to Maggie to answer how I feel.

"Okay," I say.

"You're quiet," Maggie points out. "Which means you're thinking. You shouldn't be thinking."

"Hard not to," I answer as I turn down Almond Ave and head straight toward The Almond Store. "It was fun while it lasted, Maggie, but now I have to return to the regular world."

"I can understand that," she says. "But remember what we talked about? Ryland and Aubree are going through a lot of changes. Give them a moment."

And she thinks I'm talking about my brother and sister when, in reality, the perplexing confusion I feel now is all because of Hayes.

How he treated me with care last night but yet, set impossible boundaries . . . an impenetrable barrier.

The rift between him and Ryland. *It bothers him.*

Despite him not reciprocating last night, his restraint has made me like him that much more. *He cares.*

Fuck, I really do feel sick.

Not to mention the importance of this week . . .

Too sick to even talk about Hayes, I say, "Cassidy's birthday is this week. It'll be her first birthday since her death. I think Ryland and Aubree are doing something, but I haven't heard from them."

"Are you going to ask them?"

"Do you think I should?" I ask, keeping the subject on them and not on Hayes. That's why Maggie came here in the first place.

"Yes," she says. "They're still your brother and sister. Just because things are awkward doesn't mean you should pull away. If anything, you need to keep pushing to be close to them. Maybe offer to make dinner one night this week. Or to watch Mac. I'm sure Ryland could use a break. I know Aubree doesn't want help with the shop, but there has to be something you can do to support her. Maybe clean her house or do her laundry. You have spare time when you're not at Hayes's place, so why not find out what little things you can help with?"

"Yeah, I guess I can do that. Watching Mac would be a good one for Ryland. And Aubree, I think I might have to work on her, but there has to be something." It might also help me get my mind off everything with Hayes. Distraction. I need distractions.

"Exactly. Just keep trying. Maybe they'll stop pushing you away when they see how you can help."

"Smart," I say. "Okay, I'll text them and see what I can do."

"Perfect." We pull into the back parking lot of The Almond Store. When I put the car in park, Maggie turns toward me and hugs me. "And now about Hayes . . ."

Crap, and here I thought I was going to avoid that.

I wondered this morning if she heard us, if she heard me moan for him, but she never said anything. She just went about her morning as if nothing happened.

"What about him?" I ask, trying to play it cool.

"Don't get involved unless you can handle the ramifications."

"What do you mean? You were encouraging me to get involved with him this weekend."

"And that was advice built up on dreamy lust. You should know that about me. Now that we're out of his house and we don't have that haze over us—get it . . . haze." She wiggles her brows.

"Yes." I roll my eyes.

"I can thoroughly say if you want him, don't deny yourself, but you have to know he might hurt you if you go for it." He already has. "I want to give him the benefit of the doubt, but his reputation doesn't speak well for him. You're already struggling. Don't let him come into your life and break you. And not to mention, if Aubree and Ryland found out, it could quite possibly break any thread you might still have attached to them. If you're willing to risk that, then take what you want."

I glance out the window because I tried taking what I wanted and did a shit job at it. He played around with me, but in the end, he backed away. Probably because I was nervous, probably because I seemed inexperienced, probably because even though I've caught him glancing at me, he doesn't actually find me that desirable. He thinks I'm too young, and that could not have been more obvious last night.

"Why are you avoiding eye contact with me?"

A tear falls down my cheek as last night's embarrassment hits me harder than expected, and I'm unable to keep it to myself. I quietly say, "Because I tried taking what I wanted from him last night and failed miserably, and now I'm really freaking embarrassed."

"What do you mean?" she asks.

I turn toward her, more tears falling down my cheeks. "I mean, I saw him in the kitchen last night and came onto him. He touched me a little but never where I wanted, pinned me against the fridge, yet he wouldn't cross that line when I asked for more. He kept saying I was off limits. So I really don't think there's anything there."

"He touched you? In what way?" Maggie asks.

"I wasn't wearing anything under his sweatshirt, so he, you know . . . came close but never really went there. I was turned on to the point I was practically begging, and he still wouldn't do anything."

Her lips twist to the side as she thinks. "You know, if he almost went there, that means he wants it. He just needs to get past a mental block first." She wipes away my tears for me. "I don't think it's a matter of *if* he wants you, Hattie. I think it's a matter of *when* you'll break him. The question you need to ask yourself is . . . are you willing to break him, but in return, possibly lose your family?"

"You think I'll lose them?" I ask even though I'm pretty sure I know the answer to that.

She gives me a *get real* look. "The moment they find out you're working for him, they're going to lose their shit. If they find out you're actually with him, with him, I don't think they'll talk to you."

I bite down on the corner of my lip. "I know you're right. This all just . . . sucks. Everything about it. It's unfair because I was with Matt for many years and never felt like I do around Hayes. I swear, one look from him feels like an electric shock."

"I can only imagine. But I worry about you and your family. You were so close before. I think that's why you should build up your relationship with Ryland and Aubree first, then maybe, if you think it *won't* destroy what you've gained, ease them into the idea of giving Hayes a second chance. I think it's the only way to win both sides of this."

"Yeah . . . I think you're right. I'm sure there's a way I can get Ryland to open up, and when he does, I can show him how generous and kind Hayes has been."

Maggie nods. "I think that's a great idea." She grips the

handle of the door. "And you know, you can call me anytime. I'll try to come up here again soon. I have a few weddings but think I have some weekdays off."

"Sounds perfect," I say. "And thank you, Maggie."

"Anything for my girl." She hugs me over the center console and then gets out. I pop the trunk for her to grab her bag. She waves at me and gets into her car when she's done.

Instead of returning to Hayes's house right away, I decide to clear my head and head up the boardwalk.

Phone in one hand and wallet in the other, because I know I'll end up buying something at Pieces and Pages, I walk past The Almond Store, where I see Aubree helping a customer pick out some almond extract. I avoid the inn—in case Ethel waits at the window to jump out and talk to me—and cross the street, where I run directly into Abel on his way to work.

"Hattie, hey," he says with a smile. "How are you?"

"Good," I answer.

He nods. "Great to hear."

And then an awkward silence falls between us because there's a giant elephant in the room, an elephant so large that I honestly don't know how Abel can walk around with a monumental secret on his chest about both of his best friends.

"Have a good weekend?" he finally asks.

"Yeah, my friend Maggie came to hang out."

"Cool."

"What about you?"

"Oh, uh, went up to the redwoods with Ryland, Mac, and Aubree. Surprised you didn't head up with us. You were missed."

I feel my brow crease. "You went up to the redwoods?" *With my siblings . . . without me?*

"Yeah, but it makes sense why you weren't there with your friend in town."

"I wasn't invited," I say, feeling embarrassed.

187

He adjusts his messenger bag on his shoulder and looks visibly uncomfortable. "Uh, are you sure?"

"Positive."

"Maybe they didn't want you to have to choose between them and your friend."

"They didn't know she was visiting."

He sighs and glances down at the ground. "I really don't want to be in the middle of this."

"In the middle of what?" I ask. "Is there something you know that I don't know?"

"No," he says.

And then I stand on my toes and push my finger to his chest. "Did you tell them about who I work for?"

"No," he says quickly. "I wouldn't do that. You should know by now I'm not that kind of person."

He's right, he's not.

"I'm sorry." I tug on my ponytail. "I just . . . I feel like they're pulling away, and it seems I'm not crazy in thinking that from how they didn't invite me to the forest this weekend." I glance back at The Almond Store and say, "Maybe I should find out."

"Hattie," Abel says, grabbing my hand. "Please don't do something stupid."

"Like what?" I ask.

"Like . . . get me involved."

I roll my eyes and walk away. *Coward. Why is he only worried about himself here?* "Don't worry, Abel, you're safe."

I cross the street again and head right back into The Almond Store. The customer Aubree was helping moments ago walks out with a bag. I hold the door open for her and then shut it.

When Aubree sees me, she says, "Shouldn't you be at your internship?"

"Late start," I say as I approach the counter. "What did you do this weekend, sis?"

No reason not to get straight to the point.

She averts her eyes to her iPad, but I slap my hand on the screen, covering it up. "I'm looking for a second of your attention. I don't believe that's too much to ask for."

Her face contorts, irritation clear in her eyes. "What's going on?"

"I'm asking you the same thing. What's going on? Why didn't you invite me to go to the redwoods with you this weekend? And before you ask how I know, I ran into Abel. He casually mentioned what he did this weekend when I asked him."

"We didn't see your car, but we saw Maggie's in the parking lot. Thought you two were out and about, so we didn't want to bother you."

Oh . . .

Huh.

I guess that makes sense.

Jesus, Hattie, you're losing it.

"Oh, sorry," I say. I release her iPad.

"Care to tell me why the hell you're freaking out on me?"

Yup, that's exactly what's happening. I'm freaking out.

I'm feeling humiliated. Hurt. *Shut out of everyone's lives and interests as if I'm a fucking bother to them all.* Everything is so jumbled up, and the only person I can lean on just started driving back to San Francisco. Leaving me feeling so fucking alone. I have no idea how much honesty Aubree will tolerate, but I have to set these feelings free.

"Because . . . it feels like you don't want me to be a part of your life. When I heard you went to the redwoods without me, I assumed it was because of that. I've been here for two weeks, and . . . well, honestly, it feels like you and Ryland have been pushing me away."

Aubree sighs heavily and shuts her iPad. She rubs her temples and mutters, "This is why I wanted to tell you."

"Tell me what?" I ask.

189

"This can't be done with just me. It has to be done with Ryland too. Think you can come up to the farm for dinner?"

"Yes," I say. "I don't have anything planned."

A customer walks in, and she whispers, "Then see you tonight. Okay?"

"Yeah, okay," I say as I move to the back of the shop, the tension in my chest easing.

Maybe I'll finally get some answers tonight.

———

I PULL up to the dirt driveway of Cassidy's house—I don't think I'll ever think of it any other way—and gradually drive my car across the bumps in the road until I reach the front.

Today went by so freaking slowly that I almost lost it. I spent the entire day sorting envelopes. Finally shredded some piles that I didn't think warranted Hayes's attention, and all the while, I avoided Hayes at all costs by keeping my headphones on and my eyes down.

He slipped into the living room a few times, saw him moving around in the kitchen, but I think he had the idea I was avoiding him. Therefore, he should avoid me.

It worked.

My phone beeps with a text, and when I glance down, I roll my eyes.

Hayes: *Great avoidance today. Expert level.*

God, he truly is the most infuriating man.

Hattie: *Just getting work done.*

Hayes: *Liar.*

Hattie: *What do you want? You turned me down. Want me to get on my knees and beg?*

Hayes: *No, but I thought you could be mature about it. Guess that's what twelve years of difference does.*

My mouth drops open in shock as I stare at the blatant insult. What an ass!

Hattie: *Wow, Hayes. Resorting to being a dick. See, old age does that to you.*

Hayes: *Is this how it's going to be?*

Hattie: *You tell me, you came in guns blazing.*

Hayes: *If we're going to work together, I'd expect you to acknowledge me at the very least . . . and arrive on time.*

Hattie: *Yes, your majesty.*

Hayes: *And for the record, I denied you because I'm looking out for you.*

Hattie: *Whatever you need to say to convince yourself.*

The bubbles on his side of the text thread pop up and disappear. I'm about to tuck my phone away when it starts ringing in my hand.

Ughhh . . .

"What?" I answer.

"Surprised you answered," he says.

"What do you want?"

"Tomorrow, I have to drive down to San Francisco for work, and I need you to come with me."

"Uh . . . why?"

"Ruben won't be there, and I'll need an assistant on set."

"Set?" I ask.

"Shooting another fragrance commercial. It's last minute, hence why Ruben can't get there."

"What am I supposed to do?"

"Assistant things. Whatever production asks, whatever I ask, just be helpful . . . and not scowling with your headphones on."

"I wasn't scowling today."

"Did you look in a mirror?"

Growing irritated, I say, "You know, just when I thought you were a good guy, you change my perspective so quickly."

"Good, that's the way it should be," he says. "Since you don't want to be seen with me, meet me at the barn no later than five in the morning."

"Five? Have you lost your freaking mind? That means I'm getting up at . . . I don't even know what time."

"It's either that or we leave tonight and spend the night at my condo."

"Well, Jesus, I choose to leave tonight. What is wrong with you that you'd want to leave so early in the morning?"

"How about the fact that you wouldn't even look in my direction today? How the hell was I supposed to talk to you about it?" he asks, proving a point.

"You could have tapped me on the shoulder rather than sending passive-aggressive texts afterward."

"And risk getting my arm chomped off by the snarly beast? Yeah, I'm good."

"Aren't you just freaking humorous?"

"Speaking facts," he replies with his annoyingly quick wit.

"I have dinner with my brother and sister, but after that, I can meet up. I'll just have to grab some overnight stuff."

"Fine, but don't be too late, it's a two-and-a-half-hour drive."

"I know how long it is," I shoot back. "Just to be clear, do I need anything special to wear tomorrow?"

"Comfortable clothes. I'm sure you'll be running around."

"Perfect. Can't wait to spend a lot of time with you," I say sarcastically.

"Bitter much?"

"Goodbye." I hang up the phone and then get out of the car.

God, he's such an ass.

If he's trying to piss me off on purpose, he's doing a good job.

My humiliation about last night turns straight into anger, and I revel in it. It's such a better feeling.

I head up the stairs of the porch to Cassidy's farmhouse. Not needing to knock, I open the creaky screen door and walk right in, where I catch Mac playing on the floor with Chewy

Charles and some Duplos while Ryland is in the kitchen, pulling out a frozen lasagna from the oven.

"Aunt Hattie," Mac says when she spots me. She runs up to me and plasters her little body to my leg.

"Hey, kiddo," I say, squeezing her back. "What's Chewy Charles up to today?"

"Making friends with spiders," Mac answers. "But these spiders are special spiders."

"What makes them special?" I ask as I take a seat next to her Duplos.

"They like sucking blood."

"Oh my," I say. "Whose blood?"

"Duplo blood," she says in a menacing tone and then she runs her fingers—the spiders—over the Duplos, making sucking noises and then throwing her head back in a maniacal laugh. "Ha ha ha, sucking the blood."

I glance over at Ryland, clearly concerned about this new development, and he just shrugs as he sets the lasagna on the table.

Okay, so I guess we're not concerned about the blood-sucking finger spiders. Noted.

"Look at them. They're so full of blood," Mac says, moving her fingers in front of my face.

"Yes, plump and juicy with the red stuff," I say. I've never been super great with kids, kind of awkward actually, so I don't know how to handle or process blood-sucking finger spiders.

"Oh no, the spiders are falling," Mac says as she tumbles her fingers down in the air. "Chewy Charles, save the spiders." She picks up her horse and says, "Chewy Charles to the rescue. Catch those spiders. Place them on the ground. Lick them."

Ahh, the classic narration of MacKenzie. She started it around three, narrating her every move while playing make-believe.

We thought it was odd but also funny, and now, we're just used to it. I'm just so glad it continued after Cassidy died. One of the many things I'd feared for this little girl was that she'd lose her vivid imagination in her grief. *Are you watching your precious girl, Cassidy?*

"Good job, Chewy Charles," I say as I stand. "I need to talk to the captain of the house now—"

"This isn't a boat, Aunt Hattie. You can just say Uncle Ry Ry."

"My apologies," I say, working my way into the kitchen. "I need to speak to Uncle Ry Ry."

"Much better," she says, slowly nodding at me and smiling.

Ohh-kay.

I turn toward Ryland and say, "She's something else."

"Tell me about it." He keeps his eyes on the garlic bread that's in the oven, keeping the oven door partially open. "She screamed at me this morning because I sat on one of her imaginary spider babies. It took me fifteen minutes to calm her down. She was late to preschool, and I was late to school."

"Did you know the spiders were there?"

He glances over his shoulder at me. "Do you think I would have sat on them if I did?"

"True," I say and adjust my ponytail. "Uh, so I was just talking to my boss, and he said I have to go to San Francisco tomorrow. We leave tonight. Any chance we could talk and eat at the same time?"

"I don't want to talk in front of Mac," he says.

"Any chance she could watch a show and eat?"

"I guess so," he says. "It'll be her best night, that's for sure."

"Thanks, I appreciate it."

"Sure," he says as he slips on an oven mitt, eyes laser focused on the bread. "Are you liking the new internship?"

"Yeah, it's pretty good," I say, feeling awkward.

"Learning anything?"

"Uh . . . a little," I answer. "It's mainly condensing information. Elements of business." Facts. I've learned that women have no problem printing and sending naked photos to strangers, and I've also been very busy sifting through letters. "I'm gaining experience with the bonus of an income."

The front door opens, and Aubree walks in with a pastry box, most likely almond cherry cookies.

"Hi, Aunt Aubree," Mac says as she tosses Chewy Charles up in the air. "Flies into the air. Lands on his butt. Breaks his butt."

"Hey, Mac. I brought home some cookies."

"Yay!" Mac cheers and reaches for the box, but Aubree holds it high.

"Dinner first."

"And you get to eat dinner and watch a show," Ryland says as he removes the perfectly toasted garlic bread.

"*SuperKitties*! Can I watch *SuperKitties*? Please!"

"Sure," Ryland says. "First, potty and wash hands."

Mac takes off toward the bathroom, and we spend the next few minutes setting up our plates, then getting Mac situated with *SuperKitties* and her dinner. Once everyone is seated, I say, "I told Ryland I have to leave for San Francisco tonight. So I was hoping we could talk during dinner."

"Why are you going to San Francisco?" Aubree asks.

"For my internship."

She nods. "Oh, cool. Well, I'll let Ryland talk." She picks up a piece of garlic bread and takes a giant bite.

I turn toward Ryland, and he's cutting his lasagna as he says, "I don't even know where to fucking start."

"What do you mean?" Aubree says. "Start with the conversation Cassidy had with us in the hospital. That's all there is to talk about."

"What conversation?" I ask, looking back and forth between the two of them.

195

Ryland sets down his fork and knife. "It was a few days before she passed when you couldn't make it into town. She wanted to talk to us before you arrived because she knew her passing would take the biggest toll on you and Mac. She was worried about the both of you and how you would handle her death." Ryland takes a deep breath. "Her biggest wish for you was to finish school. She knew how hard you were working and how important it is for you to earn your degree, so she said she didn't want you getting distracted by losing her and trying to help out around the farm, the store, and with Mac. *She* wanted you to finish school. That was the top priority. She didn't care if the farm or store failed, but she wanted Mac to be loved and taken care of and for you to finish school. She made us promise."

"She . . . she did?" I ask, guilt swarming me, swallowing me whole. Oh great. *I'm letting Cassidy down as well? Fuck. Why the hell could I not have just passed the stupid courses?*

"Yes," Aubree says. "And so if we're distant, if it seems like we're pushing you away, it's because we're trying to get you to a point where you can finish, where you can accomplish that goal. You're not to worry about us here back at home."

"But that doesn't make any sense. We're family. Why wouldn't I help you?"

"Because Cassidy wanted you to focus on school," Aubree repeats.

"But why? It's not like I truly know what I'm doing after all of this," I say. "Why does it matter if I finish this semester or next?"

Ryland and Aubree exchange glances, and I know they're not telling me the whole truth.

"What's that look for?"

Ryland cuts into his lasagna again. "You just need to finish, okay? So this internship will give you the credit you need to graduate, right?"

"Uh . . . no," I say, causing both of them to snap their heads up.

"What do you mean, no?" Ryland asks.

"I mean . . . I'll have to attend another semester to finish up my master's."

"Why would you do that?" Aubree asks. "I was under the assumption that instead of classes, this was going to give you the credit you need."

Crap. The look of anger in her eyes sends a wave of nerves straight through me.

"No," I say in a shaky voice. "Like I said, my professors and I thought it would be best to focus on this rather than classes for now because of my grief. I just couldn't focus."

"Wait," Ryland says, holding his hand up. "So . . . you started your classes this semester and then just . . . stopped? Isn't that wasting money? Why wouldn't you just finish?"

Sweat trickles down my back as I realize I didn't fully think this through. I wouldn't even know how to begin to tell them the truth . . . the whole truth.

About failing.

About working for Hayes.

About my interest in Hayes . . .

"Hattie?" he asks, his expression waiting for an answer.

I swallow hard and realize that if I lie at this moment and they find out the truth, I might never be able to recover our relationship, so I decide to be partially honest, even though it's not going to be pretty.

Composed yet nervous, I say, "Well, I actually, uh . . . I didn't do that well on my midterms."

"What do you mean?" Ryland asks.

Oh God, here we go.

"I failed them . . . all of them."

"What?" they ask at the same time, their voices rising.

"I c-couldn't focus," I say. "Cassidy's death hit me hard, and before I knew it, midterms were here, and I wasn't prepared. I failed, and with my classes, if you fail the midterms, you have to retake the class."

"Wait . . . so you failed out?" Ryland says, looking angrier than I expected.

"Not because I was fucking around or anything," I say. "I was mourning my sister, Ryland."

He leans back in his chair and stares me down. "Why the hell did you lie to us?"

"Because I was too scared to tell you the truth. I thought that maybe if I took this internship near you guys, we could, I don't know . . . help each other out, and I could recharge for next semester."

"So we're talking like six to seven more months before you graduate?" Aubree asks, looking pissed.

"Yes," I answer.

"Jesus," she says, pushing back from the table. "You realize we're all mourning here, right? That you're not the only one?"

"Aubree," Ryland says under his breath.

"Come on, Ryland, all she had to do was graduate. That's it. And she couldn't even do that. You're taking care of a goddamn child, sleeping on a couch every night, barely making it day to day while putting on a happy smile. I'm drowning in responsibilities I never fucking asked for while helping you any chance I can, and all she had to do was graduate."

Caught off guard by her anger, I say, "I could help you, Aubree, but you won't let me."

"Because you can't!" Aubree says. "It's in her goddamn will."

What? I glance between my siblings. Ryland is pinching his brow, and Aubree looks like she's about to have a mental breakdown. What was in her will?

What is she talking about? And why don't I know about her will? And that's when it hits me. They shuttled me back to school before the will was read. *They pushed me away from them even then.*

"Aubree, enough," Ryland says.

"No, she needs to know." Aubree turns toward me and places her hands on the table, looking deep into my soul. "As much as we would all LOVE your help, we can't accept a goddamn hand from you until you graduate. Cassidy required it. She knew that instead of finishing school, you'd want to cling to her memory when she passed. And she was so fucking right." She tosses her hand in the air. "Ryland said to give you a chance to finish. It's why we didn't say anything at first, but like I told you from the beginning, Ryland, we should have said something because at least maybe she would have applied herself."

"You're not being fair," I say.

"None of this is fair, Hattie," Aubree says, tears forming in her eyes, something I've only seen a handful of times. "Losing Cassidy, taking on these responsibilities, working until we pass out every fucking day, none of it is fair. Trust me, if I could have you help, I would. I'd return to the things I love rather than running a store that was always a mere job to me before we lost Cassidy." She stands from the table, and as she walks away, Ryland stands as well.

"Wait," I say before he can leave too. "Ryland, I had no clue, I . . . I'm sorry."

"I know you didn't," he says as he goes after Aubree, leaving me to sit at the table, alone, stewing in my own thoughts.

In my own guilt.

Why did you do this, Cassidy?

Why wouldn't you let me help them?

You thought you were helping me, but in reality, you've just driven a wedge between me and my siblings.

A wedge that seems to get bigger and bigger with every day that passes.

BAG IN HAND, I get out of my car and lock it up before heading over to Hayes's waiting vehicle.

It wasn't long after Aubree left the table that I left. I waited for Ryland to return so Mac had eyes on her, but I took off. I thanked him for dinner and apologized one more time. He didn't say anything. I'm not sure he has much to say to me other than he's disappointed in me.

I don't blame him.

I'm disappointed in myself as well.

And I hate to admit it, but Aubree had very valid points. I'm not the only one mourning. I had one simple task—to focus on school. Aubree juggles two businesses that she isn't one hundred percent familiar with, and Ryland takes care of a four-year-old with spider fingers. In the grand scheme of it all, I was the one who got off easy.

Yet I'm jealous of them.

They have a piece of Cassidy, and I have . . . I have nothing.

I'd rather have the stresses they feel daily than the feeling of loss and disconnect.

I should have been part of the team to keep her memory alive.

Why didn't she allow that?

Why . . . why was she pushing me away as well?

I open the door to Hayes's back seat and set my bag down, only to move forward to the front seat, where I buckle up.

"No hello?" he asks.

"Not in the mood," I say as I stare out my window, my phone clutched in my hand.

"Care to talk about it?"

"No," I say.

"Okay," he says as he takes off down the road.

Tears well in my eyes as we drive south toward San Francisco, the conversation running through my head—Aubree's tears, her words of truth, the look of disappointment on both of their faces as they realized I failed out . . .

My lip quivers.

Not only did I fail them but I failed Cassidy as well. All I had to do was graduate, and I couldn't even fucking do that.

Before I can stop them, a tear cascades down my cheek. I wipe it away, but another follows.

And then another.

And then another.

I try to keep up, but it's useless.

"Come on, Ryland, all she had to do was graduate. That's it. And she couldn't even do that. You're taking care of a goddamn child, sleeping on a couch every night, barely making it day to day while putting on a happy smile. I'm drowning in responsibilities I never fucking asked for while helping you any chance I can, and all she had to do was graduate."

My heart feels like it's shattering all over again. I thought I'd only lost one sister . . . but I've lost them all. Tears stream down my face. *My brother's life is fucked up, my sister is drowning, and all I had to do was graduate.*

"Are you crying?"

"No," I say even though that one word sounds full of tears.

"Yes, you are," he says just as we leave town. He pulls off to the side, near one of the lookouts of Almond Bay, and puts the SUV in park before turning toward me. "Why are you crying, Hattie?"

I wipe at my tears. "I don't want to talk about it."

"Did I make you cry?" he asks in such a tender, caring voice that it actually makes me cry more.

"No," I say. "This has nothing to do with you."

"Okay . . ." He pauses. "Do you want me to take you back to your place? I can manage without you if I need to."

I shake my head. "I can't be there right now. Just drive, okay?"

"Okay," he answers as he puts the car in drive again and pulls out onto the road.

With one hand on the steering wheel, he remains silent, allowing me to just sit in my feelings, and surprisingly, I appreciate it. The last thing I want to do is talk about my brother and sister.

Thankfully, he turns on some music, and it fills the silence. Tracy Chapman filters through the speakers, her cool, raspy voice pulling me away from my thoughts as I focus on the lyrics and the instrumentals. I turn away from the window and face forward, more comfortable now, and just as I settle into my seat for the long ride, Hayes reaches over the console and takes my hand in his. When I glance at him with questions on the tip of my tongue, he doesn't lock eyes with me. Instead, he just squeezes my hand and remains like that . . . offering the support I never thought I'd find in him.

Chapter Twelve

HAYES

I don't like that she cried.

I don't like seeing it, and I don't like hearing it.

I thought it was me . . . the one she was upset with, and I wouldn't blame her if it was.

After I drove her desire to the point of breaking, then pushed her away . . . Yeah, I'd be pissed too. *Did she have to finish the job?*

But if this morning proved anything, it's best I didn't take it any further.

So when she showed up, quiet and subdued, I assumed it was because of me. But what's strange is that knowing I'm not the one who brought on the tears, I now want to know who did this to her.

Who made her hurt?

I want to take care of her, take that pain away. Knowing her situation with her family, that's my one guess.

Which means . . . fuck, did Ryland say something to her about me? Shit, maybe this really is my fault.

Did he warn her? Did he question her? Does he know?

Did they have a falling out?

Nerves creep up my neck, making my mind uneasy as I navigate the situation.

I started this entire interaction with her based on my need to control the people around me. I had no clue she'd take over my mind. That every second of the day, I'd be thinking about her.

And with every second I spend with her, I regret blackmailing her to work for me because, yeah, I might have been lonely, I might have needed the help—*she* sure as hell needed the help—but now, now I could have truly fucked her over.

Jesus, what's wrong with me?

And then practically forcing her to come with me to San Francisco? Technically, I don't need her there. The production company would have enough people on set to help me out . . . but I wanted her there. Ask me to explain that, and I can't.

I don't want to like her.

I don't want to touch her.

I don't want to get involved.

Yet I like seeing her . . . I need to see her.

I want her involved.

I want to hold her hand because she's sad, and I want to make her feel better.

I don't . . . fuck, I don't want to be lonely. Her silence today has been painful. I know she was mad from last night, but I still thought that maybe . . . she'd at least shake it off as a drunk thing and move on.

She moved on, all right, but she left me in the dust.

And it stung.

I didn't like one second of it.

So seeing her upset now has created a protective instinct

within me. And I felt like I could do nothing but reach over the center console and hold her hand.

And that's how it's been for the past half hour—holding her hand and listening to music.

"Are you okay with the music?" I ask her.

"Yeah, I love it," she says softly. Thankfully the tears are gone now. "I didn't know you listened to Aerosmith. When *Dream On* started playing, I was surprised."

"Love Aerosmith," I say. "I know my music is different from theirs, but if I ever did the rock thing, I'd want to be in a band like Aerosmith."

"Interesting," she says, her voice becoming lighter, not so distressed anymore, which puts me slightly at ease. "Is there a song you wish you wrote?"

"Yeah," I say as I keep my hand clasped around hers, glad she's talking. Talking and not fighting with me . . . because I feel like that's what we do, nonstop. "*More than a Feeling* by Boston. It's probably my favorite song ever. The premise of how a song can connect you to someone, past and present, is truly what music is all about. I often do a cover of it during my concerts. I have a rotation of a few, and that's one of them."

"I've seen it," she says softly.

"You have?" I ask.

She nods. "Yeah, for some reason, Instagram thinks I like to see videos of you. I was scrolling and stumbled across it. I watched because, well, I was hoping you fell off the stage or something—"

"Liar," I say, causing her to chuckle.

"Anyway, I thought it was good."

"Just good?"

She sighs heavily. "Fine, more than good. But the acoustic version is my favorite, if you need to know."

"I do need to know. I need to know everything you think about my music."

"I think Maggie told you enough."

"Not nearly enough," I say, loving that she's being playful now. "Did you have me under a secret playlist because you didn't want your family to know you like my music?"

"Exactly, but I'm pretty sure Cassidy knew. She never said anything, but she'd mention one of your songs every once in a while and give me a knowing look."

"Did you have a secret poster of me as well?"

"No," she scoffs. "I liked a few songs, that's it."

"Sounded like more than a few songs."

"We can move on from this. We've already talked about it, so there's no need to rehash it."

"I'm pretty sure I'll never let it go since you were so adamant about hating my music. Calling it swill."

"Well, now you know the truth, so drop it."

I chuckle. "Fair enough. But did you have any posters of any crushes on your wall?"

"No," she answers. "I was never really like that. You know, we were raised in a single-parent household. Dad never let us fantasize, especially Ryland and Cassidy. When he was at work, working extra shifts, they were taking care of me and Aubree. There wasn't much room for dreaming."

"You didn't dream at all?" I ask.

"Not about crushes. I dreamed about what I wanted to do when I got older."

"What was that?"

"When I was younger, I wanted to own a coffee house, which is so silly because I didn't even drink coffee, but I just thought it was this romanticized notion, a place where all the fun happens. I blame it on all the *Friends* reruns I was addicted to watching on TBS. I wanted my very own Central Perk. As I grew older, I held on to that idea, so I went to school for business. But the coffee dream faded as I spent more time at The Almond Store with Cassidy and helped her create every vision she had for it." She grows quiet and then looks out the window again.

"Everything okay?"

She shakes her head. "No. It's not, but nothing I want to talk about."

"Are you sure?" I ask.

"Yes," she says, shutting down quickly, which clarifies one thing. Whatever she was crying about earlier has to do with Cassidy. I don't want to push her, though. She normally doesn't shut down like this, despite our on-and-off friendship —if that's what you want to call it. She hasn't been shy about talking or holding back. Whatever is bothering her, she truly doesn't want to share.

I'll respect that.

For now.

━━━

"ADAM SANDLER," I say, breaking the half hour of silence. I couldn't take it any longer.

She glances over at me. "Huh?"

"Alphabet game, haven't you ever played it on road trips before?"

"Oh . . . yeah, but say that. Don't just say the actor's name."

"Go ahead. Your turn. And don't worry about repeating the previous answers. I just like hearing answers."

"Okay," she says, slightly skeptical. "Do we have to play?"

"Yes," I answer. "I'm bored out of my mind. And stewing in silence isn't going to help anything."

"Says the guy who let me stew in silence all day."

"That was your choice. You blocked me out with headphones."

"Because you were a jerk to me the night before."

I sigh. "Hattie, I wasn't a jerk. I was protecting you."

"I don't need you to protect me, Hayes. I'm a big girl. I know what I'm doing."

I grip the steering wheel tighter. "You have no idea what you'd be getting yourself into if I didn't hold back last night or the night before. When I said I'm trouble, I meant it."

"Yet you have no problem being confusing by holding my hand and trying to play a game to get my mind off things. I mean, what is it, Hayes? You're constantly giving off different signals."

"I'm just trying to be nice. Would you prefer it if I laughed in your face while you cried?"

"Don't be an asshole. You know what I mean."

"And you know what I mean when I say I'm trouble. You're better off moving on to something else. Someone else."

"Done," she says, her chin held high. I don't like the sound of that. "When we get back, I'll ask Abel out."

"Abel?" I ask. "My best friend Abel?"

"Yup. He's hot. He's a doctor. He's best friends with Ryland. Bet he would approve of our love affair."

"Don't say shit, Hattie, just to piss me off."

"But when you say things to piss me off . . . it's okay?"

"Jesus," I mutter. "What happened to playing the alphabet game?"

"What happened is that I'm calling you out on your bull-shit. You're a dick to me, then you're nice. Pick a lane, Hayes, and stay in it."

"Is that what you really want?"

"Yes," she nearly shouts. "That's what I want. I want something, anything, to just be normal in my life. If you don't want me, then be a dick to me, make me hate every second I'm with you. Don't let me cling to hope that maybe there's a chance."

"Don't ask for something you can't handle."

"I can handle it," she says. "Trust me, at this point, I can handle pretty much anything."

"Fine," I say.

If she wants me to be a dick . . . I can be a dick.

"WHAT DO you mean we have to share a bed?" she asks, staring at the king-sized bed in my condo.

For the rest of the drive, we sat in silence, my playlist thankfully filling the air. The entire time, I tried to wrap my head around the confusion of the last few days and brought it back to one thing . . . I fucked up.

I let her get too close.

I let her see how she affects me.

And I let her feel my desperate touch.

My will slipped and I haven't been able to handle the realization of that, hence confusing the shit out of her. Hell, I'm confused as well. Could I allow myself to indulge in her for one night? Of course. I'd love nothing more.

Fuck . . . I'd love to have her crawl between my legs and play with me right before I pushed her on her back and played with her . . . all night long.

But it can't happen.

It just can't.

I set my bag down on the dresser and say, "You could take the couch, but it hasn't seen an ass . . . ever so it might be stiff. And if you're expecting me to be chivalrous and take the couch, I must remind you, you told me to be a dick. So either sleep next to me or spend your night tossing and turning." Eyes on her, I reach over my head and grab my shirt, pulling it off.

Her gaze roams my chest for a moment before she turns away and walks into the living room.

The couch it is.

Less temptation for me.

I grab a pillow off my bed and walk into the living room where I toss it on the couch.

"There's a throw blanket in the drawer of the coffee table."

"Wait, you don't have sheets or anything?"

"On my bed, not for you."

"Not even an extra comforter?"

"Do I look like a five-star resort? Be happy I have soap to wash your hands with." I turn away and grab my toiletry bag before heading into the bathroom.

It's fucking late and my mind is exhausted from the constant rethinking of every interaction I've had with Hattie, so I need sleep. I rinse my face, brush my teeth, and I'm about to take a piss when Hattie charges into the bathroom with her clothes and toiletry bag as well.

"Uh, do you mind?" I ask.

"Nope," she says as she turns on the sink faucet and rinses her face.

Okay . . .

I turn my back toward her and whip my dick out to pee. I wait for her to say something to me, but when she doesn't, I finish up, give my dick a shake, and then stick it back in my briefs before flushing.

She's drying her face off as I wash my hands.

"Turn the light off when you finish," I say.

"Just because you said that, I'm not going to now."

"Is that how it's going to be?" I ask her.

"Yup," she says before shutting the door in my face.

Jesus.

I move over to the bed and plug my phone in to charge. I take a seat, not getting comfortable yet because I wouldn't put it past her to keep to her word. And instead, I set my alarm and then check the email Ruben sent me one more time with all the information I need about where I'm going tomorrow and the premise of the shoot.

Basically, shirtless bedroom scenes.

Nothing new here.

When I first signed this fragrance contract, I was excited to take on anything that offered me money. Who wouldn't be? But fuck, they've sexualized me on a whole new level, and there's nothing I can say about it. They make me great money, that's not the problem, but at some point, I want to move on from these ads and not have to take my shirt off for all the attention. I want to be taken seriously for my music. My craft. *Not just something superficial like my looks.*

The bathroom door opens, and I glance up just in time to catch Hattie walk out—leaving the light on—in a pair of bikini-style underwear that sits high on her hips and a thin crop top that is loose enough for her breasts to peak the fabric.

Fucking Christ.

As she retreats to the living room, she glances over her shoulder, my eyes on her pert ass, and she says, "Sweet nightmares."

I drag my hand over my mouth and stare down at the floor. Fuck, she's so painfully hot.

Good thing she's sleeping on the couch.

I push off the bed, turn off the bathroom light, and then crawl under the covers, letting them sit at my waist. I run hot, so submerging my body completely under the covers makes me sweat.

I prop one hand behind my head and stare up at the ceiling.

Jesus, I was just saying how exhausted I was, but after seeing Hattie in her version of pajamas, I feel wide awake. And from the creaks of the couch, it sounds like she's having a hard time getting comfortable. The couch was a shit purchase. I let an interior designer pick everything for this space because I truly didn't care. I just needed a place to sleep when I was in town, recording. I remember the first time I sat on the couch,

I immediately stood back up and vowed to never sit on the damn thing again.

"Ugh," Hattie grumbles in the living room, then she appears at the doorway of my bedroom. "You did this on purpose."

I sit up on my elbows to get a good look at her. Those curvy hips, propping up the strings of her underwear, her tapered waist and small belly button. Proportionate breasts that are just big enough to push at the fabric of her shirt. Yeah, she's so my fucking type.

Nothing fake about her.

"Did what on purpose?" I ask.

"Brought me here to create a one-bed scenario."

"What?" I ask, confused as she moves over to the other side of the bed and flips down the covers to get in.

"It's the oldest trick in the book, Hayes. You want me in bed, so instead of getting us two hotel rooms, you bring me back to your condo that only has one bed? What a coincidence."

"What are you implying?" I ask as she fluffs her pillow.

"That your horny ass wanted to get me into bed with you, and instead of just telling me you want me, you've created a scenario where we have to share a bed, giving you full access to tease me. Well, guess what?" She turns toward me and lies down. "It's not going to work."

I stare at her for a few seconds. "First of all, I brought you here because I'm not going to waste money on a hotel room when I have a perfectly decent condo to use. Second, I assumed you would be mature enough to share a bed without issue, but obviously, that was a misjudgment on my end."

"I can share a bed. That's not the problem. It's that I don't want to share a bed with you."

"Because you're too tempted, I get it," I say, being the dick she so desperately wants me to be.

"Oh fuck off, Hayes. You're not that appealing."

"Says the girl who's made two advances on me."

"Wow," she says. "You really do play the ass so well."

"You asked for it. I'm just delivering."

"The only thing you could probably deliver," she says. "And for the record, I could easily turn you on without barely trying."

"You think so?" I ask. "Because I specifically remember how quickly I made you beg with just a few touches."

Her eyes narrow. "If I allowed myself to touch you, you'd beg too."

"I don't beg . . . ever," I say.

"Prove it," she says.

"Prove it?" I ask. "How?"

She thinks about it for a moment and says, "Sixty seconds. We see who moans first in sixty seconds, point proven."

"You want to try to turn each other on in sixty seconds to prove a goddamn point?"

"Yeah," she says, a smile on her lips. "Scared?"

"No, worried about you, though. You won't be able to handle it."

"Way to deflect. You're worried you'll spend the night with blue balls once the sixty seconds is up."

"Trust me, that won't be a problem."

"Then let's see if you're so confident."

This can *only* end badly, but I get it. She's trying to feel something. Trying to prove something.

When I'm spiraling, I use the same techniques. I become unhinged and stab away at anything that will make me feel anything other than the agony I'm mentally going through.

And from the look on her face, I don't think I can back down. She needs this challenge. She's trying to fight some inner turmoil, and this seems to be one of the ways to do it.

And as we know, despite trying to stay away from her, I will also do anything to remove that frown from her face.

So stupidly, I say, "What are the terms?"

"No touching between the legs. No kissing. And when the sixty seconds is up or the first person to moan or touch themselves after . . . loses."

"Fine," I say and then turn over to grab my phone. I pull up the timer and set it for sixty seconds. "You ready?" I ask.

"Yup," she says with an insane amount of confidence.

Well, fuck . . . here we go.

I press start on the timer and then toss the phone to the side. Hattie scoots closer, and her hand finds the edge of my boxers, and immediately, I know I'm going to get hard in seconds.

This was a bad fucking idea.

Her finger runs along the thick elastic band of my boxer briefs, toying with the idea of what it would feel like if she slipped her hand inside. And I realize at that moment, I could make this easy on me. I *could* let her do the hard work and strike when the moment's right. So I lie flat on my back and place one hand behind my head as she moves in closer. My arm moves around her as her warm body becomes plastered against mine. I clutch the strap of her underwear in my fist, possessively holding her close to me.

She glances up at me, slightly surprised, but then focuses back on her task and drags her fingers up my stomach, paying attention to every divot and curve of my abs, swirling around, rubbing and then moving up to my pecs. I watch her pull on her bottom lip with her teeth as her finger runs over one of my nipples.

Yup, I'm hard. One swipe of my nipple and I'm fucking gone.

But she said the first to moan or touch themselves. I haven't lost, I'm just on an uphill climb now.

I grip her a little tighter, tugging on her underwear so she can feel my possession. She swallows tightly and then rubs her pointed nipples against my chest as she flicks my nipple.

Fuck, it feels amazing.

Everything about this feels amazing.

Her tight body up against mine.

The way she's touching me.

The possibility that I could just flip her on her back, claim the loss, and fuck her into the headboard until she's crying out my name.

She has me turned on. Easy.

But I won't let her know that. Ever.

She wants a challenge, so she's going to get one.

I remain stoic, unmoving, as she brings her hand back to my abs and down to my boxer briefs, where she slips one finger past the elastic.

Fuuuuuck.

I maintain even breathing, reject the need to tighten from her touch, and remain as calm as can be even though my cock presses against my boxer briefs, looking to play.

And I can tell she's getting frustrated as she glances at the timer.

Her mouth works to the side, clearly trying to think of something nuclear that will tip this game in her favor. *Unless you plan on grabbing my dick.* I'm not sure she'll think of anything else, so I need to make a move.

I tug on her underwear, pulling her back, but before I can move on top of her, she brings her chest close to my face. And then to my surprise, she lifts her crop top to reveal her gorgeous tit.

Fuck.

Me.

Jesus, it's perfect.

Small, but it still makes my goddamn mouth water. And with her tightened nipple, pointed and looking for someone to suck on it, I feel my chest grow heavy as my hand itches to take her into my palm.

In my mouth.

Lap at her with my tongue.

But despite what my body wants, I don't move. I tighten my grip on her underwear, my fingers digging into her hip now as she brings her pointed nipple right to my mouth.

Yes. Fucking. Please.

And I realize what she's doing. She's pulling the nuclear card.

I'm such a tit man, I want it in my mouth.

My lips part slightly as she rubs the nub along them.

I nearly flip her onto her back in desperation but remember to hold it together as I choose subtlety for the biggest impact.

As her nipple tantalizes my mouth, I barely part my lips and gently wrap my lips around her nipple.

Her eyes connect with mine in shock, and that's when I bring it home. I suck on the nipple, just enough of a pull to ignite a flame within her, and then I let the nub go, pulling my mouth away.

Subtle, barely a touch, but the damage has been done.

To my fucking satisfaction, her head falls back, her teeth clamp over the corner of her mouth, and the lightest moan falls off her tongue just as the timer goes off.

Winner.

Her head snaps forward, and when she looks down at me with surprise in her eyes, I smirk in response.

I reach for my phone and plug it back in before painfully turning to my side, facing her, and tucking my pillow under my head. I might have won this game of hers, but it doesn't negate the fact that she turned me on as well. I just did a better job of masking it.

"Nice try, Hattie," I say, taking steadying breaths to regain some semblance of control over my body.

She just stares at me, breathing heavily for a few moments before she huffs something under her breath and turns away, curling into her pillow.

Do I feel bad?

No.

She brought this on herself.

Do I wish I could rip that shirt off her and pay more attention to those delicious tits?

Yes.

But instead, I'm going to drive home the storyline she wants me to play out between us, the one where I'm the dick who tortures her.

I reach across the bed, curl my hand around her waist, and then with one pull, I bring her straight to my chest on a gasp.

"What are you doing?" she asks as her ass lines up with my hard-on.

Speaking closely to her ear, I say, "Do you feel that?" I press her in even closer. "Do you feel what you did to me?"

"Y-yes," she says, her voice shaky as I slide my hand up her stomach. The rise and fall of her chest spurs me on as I brush my thumb lightly across the underside of her breast. "God," she says as I do it again, enjoying her reaction and the softness of her skin. I could easily get lost in her. She's so responsive, needy, the perfect combination for what I want when it comes to a woman.

I move my palm up to her breast and cup her, rolling my thumb over her nipple, just a brief pass, but it elicits a moan from her as she presses her ass against my painful erection. I move my hips against hers, seeking friction, just enough to make me starve for more.

With my forefinger and thumb, I gently pinch her nipple, the tiny nub pebbled, begging for more. I want to give her more. I want to tear this top off and bury my head between her small breasts. I want to lick them, suck them, play with them until she can't breathe anymore and all she can focus on is her release.

"Fuck, Hayes. More," she begs, the sound of her throaty voice such a turn-on, but . . . fuck, what am I doing?

The point of playing with her was to show her I have control and she doesn't, yet with every grip of her breast, every roll of her nipple, my control is slipping.

And it can't.

I can't fucking lose. Not with so much on the line. Not with the thought of Ryland in the back of my head.

So I pause, and even though I can hear the beat of my own heart in my ears, as well as the need to fuck this woman deep in the marrow of my bones, I say, "This is the difference between you and me . . . I know how to control myself, whereas you don't." I push away, putting distance between us and scooting to my side of the bed.

"Are you fucking kidding me?" she asks as she turns toward me in bed, a furious look on her face highlighted by the moonlit room. "What the hell, Hayes?"

"Do you have a problem?"

"Yes," she says, her eyes now furious. "You're messing with me."

"No, I'm being exactly what you wanted. You asked for this. You started it."

"I did not ask for you to lie next to me and tease me." She shakes her head. "Do you truly think you can fuck around with me?"

"I told you, I'm not interested in you in that way."

"Then why even bother with all of this?" she asks, waving her hand about.

"You're here for a job. You're the one who brought on the intimacy."

"And you keep feeding into it," she practically yells. "And not to mention, you're the one who held my hand almost the whole drive down here. So tell me what that was about."

"It's called comforting someone. I thought you needed it."

"That's not comforting. That's sending mixed signals."

"Believe what you want, Hattie."

She shakes her head and says, "This is so fucked up,

Hayes. And I don't want to deal with it anymore. After this trip is over, I'm done with you, done with this job."

She turns away from me, as far away as she can go, and curls into her pillow, silent for the rest of the night.

She's done with this job?

Done with me?

Not sure I like that.

Actually, I know I don't like it.

I like knowing she comes to my house every day and is there if I want to talk. I like that she's organizing my life even though it's made my house more chaotic, and I hate to admit it, but I like that she's been able to help me break through my writer's block.

She's peace, but she's anarchy.

She's a challenge, but she's effortless.

She's simple . . . yet complicated.

And I like all of it.

I've become accustomed to her presence.

Tempted to pull her back into my chest, I turn away so I don't make another mistake. Apparently, I've made so many already, but as I try to get some sleep, I know one thing for sure—she's not going to be leaving this job.

Not going to happen.

———

HATTIE WALKS BESIDE ME, falling in line with my stride as we work our way through the sound stage where we'll be working today. On the drive over, where she remained silent just like the rest of the morning, I told her what we'd be doing today and what was expected of her. Basically, to help out with anything that needs to be done.

She didn't acknowledge me, so we'll see how today goes.

I didn't get much sleep last night, constantly in turmoil over Hattie.

I like her. There's no questioning that. The problem is, she seems to be already having issues with her family, and if they find out that she's been working for me, if I . . . if I made a move or worse, gave in to her temptation, they'd never forgive her. I've known Ryland long enough to know he's not one to forgive. And for Hattie to lose her family, that's not something I can stomach.

But fuck, I've found myself making stupid decisions. Like last night, like holding her hand, like pinning her against the fridge and exploring her body. Like *tasting* her. Fuck.

I've pushed it too far, I've pushed her too far, and now, even though I don't want her to move on to another job, it *might* be best.

Fuck . . . I'm so confused.

"Do you have any questions?" I ask her as we near the director.

"Nope," she says as Kevin approaches us.

"Hayes, thank you for coming in on such short notice. We truly appreciate it." He shakes my hand.

"Not a problem at all," I say with a smile. "This is my assistant, Hattie. She'll be able to help with whatever we need."

"Wonderful," Kevin says as he greets her. "Hattie, it's very nice to meet you."

"Nice to meet you as well," Hattie says, life coming back into her face for the first time this morning. "If you need anything, just let me know."

"We will. We're short-staffed because this wasn't planned, so we'll use you all day." Kevin turns his attention to me. "Hayes, I'd like you to meet who you'll work with today." Kevin turns to the group and says, "Odette, can you come over here and meet Hayes, please?"

From the group of people, a woman in a black silk robe turns around, her wavy brown hair floating around her shoulders as her gaze locks with mine. Deep-brown eyes peer up at me as a beautiful smile crosses her pouty lips.

Hell . . . she's . . . she's gorgeous.

"Odette, this is Hayes Farrow. Hayes, this is Odette Jenkins, the wonderful woman you'll be working with today."

"It's so nice to meet you," Odette says as she holds her hand out to me. I take it and give it a soft shake.

"It's nice to meet you as well," I say. "And I'm going to apologize in advance for anything Kevin makes us do."

She chuckles. "It's okay. I've done quite a few of these types of shoots. I'm well seasoned at this point."

"Maybe you can walk me through it then," I say, sticking my hands in my pockets. "And this is Hattie, my assistant."

Odette looks over at Hattie and offers her a genuine smile. "Hattie, what a beautiful name. It's nice to meet you."

"You too," Hattie says as she moves an inch closer to me.

"Well, why don't we get you into hair and makeup, Hayes? Wardrobe, as you know, is pretty much nothing." Kevin glances up and says, "Ah, there's the bed, they're rolling it in now. Let me go check on it. Freddie, can you show Hayes and Hattie to makeup? Odette is all set."

"Sure thing, boss," Freddie says, coming up to us. "Right this way." He directs us down a hallway and to the first door on the right.

The door is already open, so the makeup artist stands to attention when I step in. "Hayes, how are you?" Jacklyn says. I've worked with Jacklyn a few times on different projects.

"Great. How are you, Jacklyn? How are the kids?"

"Annoying as usual," she says with a laugh. She gives me a quick once-over. "Been working out a lot lately? You look bigger."

"Can't hear that enough," I say as I sit down in the makeup chair. "This is Hattie by the way, she's my assistant."

"Hattie, great to meet you," Jacklyn says. "What happened to the annoying guy who used to follow you around?"

That makes Hattie snort right before I say, "He was stealing from me. So I fired him. Luckily, I was able to hire Hattie on short notice."

"Lucky girl," Jacklyn says as she starts wiping down my face. "Hayes is one of a kind, one of the sweetest in the industry. You couldn't have found a better boss."

Hattie presses her lips tightly together as she glances at me in the mirror. "She's right. I'm pretty awesome," I say, hoping it gains a response from Hattie, even if it's just a smile. But nothing.

Instead, she asks, "Would you like me to get you some coffee?"

Jacklyn shakes her head. "No coffee for this guy. Just water and some mints. Given the intimate close-ups with Odette, you'll want nothing on that breath of yours."

From the corner of my eye, I catch the look of surprise on Hattie's face. I didn't explain the shoot to her, just that she needed to be here. But these fragrance shoots usually have limited clothing, lots of oil, and smoke. Close-up shots of my abs, of my arms, of me tugging on my hair . . .

But this shoot is for a fragrance that both men and women could wear. Ruben sent me the premise yesterday, and when I read through it, I realized how different it would be.

It's going to be intimate.

"Then would you like some water?" Hattie asks me.

My eyes connect with hers, and I say, "That would be great. Thanks."

Chapter Thirteen

HATTIE

"How long have you been working for Hayes?" Odette asks as she comes up next to me at the drink station.

I glance in her direction, taking in her soft features, plump lips, and dark lashes. God, she's so pretty. Talk about feeling inferior.

"Uh over a week?" I answer, unsure of the timeline. I think it's been almost a week, but honestly, I can't be sure. It's all meshing together.

"Wow, congrats on the job. I've heard nothing but great things about Hayes. I've met my fair share of assholes when it comes to this business, so when my agent told me I'd be working with Hayes and affirmed his kind reputation, I was excited."

I nod and smile, unsure what to say as I grab a bottle of water.

"To be honest, I'm a touch nervous. I've done intimate scenes before, but I've sort of crushed on Hayes for a bit, and

I want to make sure I remain professional, you know, not let my fangirl get the best of me."

"Understandable," I say awkwardly because my mind is still trying to wrap itself around the whole intimate thing. Like . . . how intimate are we talking? And why is this bothering me? It shouldn't. Especially after last night, I shouldn't care less what Hayes does or who he touches, but my brain doesn't seem to get that memo. Not as a sickening feeling forms in the pit of my stomach. As much as I want to hate him and ignore the man and act like he doesn't affect me, that would be a massive lie.

With just one glance, he can make me weak in the knees.

"I'm just glad it's a closed set," she says. "Being naked in front of a lot of people is uncomfortable."

N-naked?

Like . . . no clothes?

"You have to be naked?" I ask.

She nods. "For the most part. I'm wearing a nude G-string right now and some nipple pasties that are uncomfortable. But other than that, I'm naked."

"Wow." I swallow hard and quickly glance down at her, noticing her larger chest pressing against her robe. "I, uh, I don't know how you do it."

"Normally, it's not that big of a deal, but I don't know, it just feels different with Hayes, you know? He's so popular, and everyone seems to have a crush on him. It's like I'm fulfilling every girl's fantasy today."

Tell me about it.

"Well, I'm sure you'll do great. And if you need anything, just let me know."

"That's so sweet of you. I appreciate it. Normally, other women on set haven't treated me this nice, so I'm happy you're here."

I smile at her and then move away from the drinks. "Break

a leg . . ." I wince. "Is that what I'm supposed to say in situations like this?"

"I can't be sure, but I'll take it." She smiles back, and dammit, she's just so freaking pretty.

Dimples and everything.

I wonder what Hayes must think of her. She's older than me and clearly has her life together if she has a great job like this. She's breathtaking with her dark features and sultry-sweet voice. Not to mention, from what I saw with her robe covering her, she makes my curves look like a stick figure.

If we stood side by side and Hayes had to pick, there's no doubt he would pick her based on that alone, which makes me feel so inferior . . . and so young.

When I return to the makeup room, Hayes has his shirt off, and his hair is styled in a sexy, messy way while Jacklyn bronzes his face. He glances in my direction and says, "Everything okay?"

"Yes," I say as I hand him the water. "Is there anything I can do to help?"

"Yes," Jacklyn says as she finishes up. "I could use your help with oiling his skin."

"Oi-oiling?" I ask as I watch Hayes sip his water, the column of his neck contracting as he swallows, making him look even sexier than before.

"Yes. It isn't baby oil or anything like that. It's a special lotion we use, but I like to go in with some highlighter once it's applied, so it would be great if you could rub him down, and then I can follow you."

Hayes smirks at me. "You asked if you could help."

Yeah, but I didn't think oiling him was going to be the answer.

"Where's the lotion?" I ask.

"Right over there on the counter," Jacklyn says as she finishes up his face. "The blue bottle."

I find the lotion, and just as I turn around, Hayes stands from his chair, and I get a good look at him.

His chestnut hair is pieced out, styled slightly to the side but messy. A sexy, purposeful style that would stop anyone in his path. Jacklyn didn't do much to his face, but what she did only highlights his light eyes, making them seem more dangerous and mysterious. And then there's his bare chest, not a fleck of hair on it, smooth, thick, contoured . . . just impossibly attractive. God . . . I hate him.

I hate him so much for being that attractive.

I hate him for bringing me into his life because I was doing fine without him.

I hate he won't even look at me the way I wish he would.

And I hate that even though he's broken me a few times, I still very much want him.

Especially at this moment.

I want to walk up to him, wrap my hand around his neck, and bring his lips down to mine. And I want to not just kiss him, but I desperately want him to kiss me back . . . and that's why I hate him the most.

He's made me desperate for him.

It's why I need to stay away.

After today of course.

"Everything okay?" he asks, a quirk to his brow.

"Yup," I say as I squirt some of the lotion on my hand, the consistency not what I expected. It's thinner and has that oily texture, but it's not pure baby oil, which I'm sure will make it easier for him to get off.

I set the bottle down, rub the lotion in my hands, then step up to him. Jacklyn is busy cleaning one of her brushes, so it's almost as if we have a small moment of privacy. I lift my hands to his pecs and then press my palms to his heated skin. I focus on anything but his face as I gently rub the lotion over his thick, strong chest. A chest I've never felt on a man before.

Matt's body had nowhere near this kind of physique, and anyone I dated before Matt was just a child.

Hayes is on a different level.

A much different level.

"Don't do that," he says quietly, catching my attention.

I look up at him and say, "Do what?"

"Bite the corner of your mouth like that."

I didn't even realize I was doing it.

"I wasn't doing it on purpose."

"Well, don't."

"Why not?" I ask as I move my hand down his abs. He sucks in as my hands skim over the individual stack of muscles.

Through clenched teeth, he says, "Because it's hot."

My eyes shoot up to his in surprise just as Jacklyn joins us. "Okay, sorry about that," she says. "I had to clean my brush, but I'm ready. Looks like you've done his chest so far, perfect. I'll follow in closely."

And then, for the next few minutes, I rub lotion over Hayes, rubbing it in as Jacklyn teaches me, and she follows along with her highlighter. The entire time, I feel Hayes's eyes on me, following my every stroke to the point that my heart's nearly beating out of my chest when I finish.

When I step away, I can still feel every contour and flex of his muscles against my palm. I can hear his soft intakes of breath when I pay attention to a new part of his body. And I can feel the blaze of his eyes on me when Jacklyn goes to wash her brush again.

Unable to stand here under his stare, I give myself a few moments to collect myself as I wash my hands. *Pull it together, Hattie. Be professional.* No one else is on the verge of panting while in his presence.

"We're ready for you," Kevin says, popping his head in.

"Coming," Hayes says but doesn't move toward the door.

Instead, he steps toward me and places his hand on my lower back before whispering, "You ready?"

His fresh mountain scent, mixed with the lotion, swirls around me, pulling me out of my safe space and right back into his world, where I find myself drowning and searching for any air to breathe.

"Are you?" he asks again, reminding me that I'm on a job.

"Yes," I answer, attempting to hold it together.

"Then follow me." He heads out of the room, and I follow close, watching each muscle in his back flex and contort with his every step.

When we step into the main space, there is now a four-poster bed in front of an ombre screen of pink to purple. Sheer curtains are draped around the bed, hanging off the posts, and a large fan is placed just behind the bed as well as a smoke machine.

As we approach, Odette stands nervously next to Kevin, still wrapped up in her robe. Her eyes land on Hayes, starting at his chest and moving up to his face. I catch her gently licking her lips as she practically eats him alive with her temptress eyes.

Hayes places his hand on my lower back and leans in close as he says, "Mind holding my water for me?"

"Nope," I answer, and when he places the water in my hand, his fingers brush against mine right before he steps up to Odette, wearing nothing but a pair of jeans. Not even shoes.

There's no doubt every woman in this room is thinking the same thing as me . . . *I wish I was Odette.*

"Wonderful," Kevin says. "Can you undo your jeans?" he asks Hayes. "I think it would look less formal that way."

"Sure," Hayes answers, and I watch his large hands undo the button of his jeans and unzip them halfway. "That good?"

"Perfect." Kevin brings them closer to the bed, and I take a step forward as well, wanting to hear everything he has to say. "Now, this will be simple. We're doing all of the shots right here. We'll start in the bed because that's where most of it will happen, and then a few individual shots of you walking in the smoke toward the camera. It shouldn't be very long. But we'll need you to hold your positions as we get close-ups as well as distants."

Hayes places his hands in the front pockets of his jeans, which tugs them down just enough to show off his boxer briefs. "Not a problem."

"Okay, let's get into position. We'll have Hayes sitting on the bed at first. Odette, you straddle his lap. This shot will be from behind, and I'll just need to see your hands sliding up her back. Odette, I'll need you to arch and play with your hair."

"Sure thing," she says. She then turns to me and asks, "Hattie, would you mind taking my robe?"

Yes!

I'd prefer you keep it on actually.

"Um, sure," I answer while she undoes it, giving me a full frontal view of her naked body other than a thin strap of fabric between her legs and two pasties right on her nipples. Jesus, her tits are perky and huge, and everything I could ever dream of. Her stomach is flat, toned, and her legs are long and lithe like a ballerina. Quietly, she asks, "Do I look okay?"

I swallow, my jealousy rearing its ugly head as I realize I'm going to have to watch Hayes fondle this woman, this gorgeous, everything-I-wish-I-was woman. I smile kindly at her and say, "You look amazing."

She places her hand on my forearm and whispers, "Thank you."

She then turns and faces Hayes. I watch his eyes as he slowly takes her in and then clears his throat as she gets up on the bed and straddles his lap. His hands immediately fall to her hips and his eyes fixate on her face.

I fist the robe tightly as Kevin positions the camera behind them, and he calls around for production to turn on the smoke machine and for the music to start, which is Taylor Swift's *Don't Blame Me*, and he instructs Odette to lift her hair as he calls action.

Odette reaches up and grips her hair as she tilts her head back. Hayes's hands slowly slide up her back, and Kevin calls out, "Move in close to her, Hayes, and press kisses to her neck."

Pardon me?

He's going to kiss her?

And as if he doesn't even have to think about it, he leans closer and gently moves his mouth along her neck, kissing and sliding his hands up farther.

"Just like that," Kevin says. "Keep kissing her and . . . ugh, Hattie, can you jump in and lower her G-string? I'd love to see a little of her ass."

"I can," Hayes says as he slides his hands down Odette's body and moves his hand under her G-string, lowering so you get a full picture of her butt.

"Great. Now go back to kissing her neck. Slide your hands up her back, then down to her ass. Yes, perfect, Hayes. Dig your fingers into her backside. Let's get a zoomed-in shot of that. Great." Kevin continues to direct them until he calls cut. Hayes leans back against the headboard, and Odette whispers something to him.

I see him nod and then say something back to her, but I can't tell what it is. *He's probably apologizing for being hard.* Because how could he not be hard? Odette is breathtaking, and he's kissing her, feeling her up while she straddles his lap. He has to be hard.

And that makes me sick to my stomach.

As much as I'd love to say watching him fondle another woman doesn't bother me at all, I'd be lying. This bothers me.

Tremendously.

Because Odette is getting everything I wish I could have with Hayes without even trying.

"Jacklyn, makeup check before we get to the next position. Hattie, bring Odette her robe," Kevin calls out.

"I'm good," she says as she moves to the side of the bed where Jacklyn touches her up. My eyes fall to Hayes, with his head propped up against the headboard, staring up at the ceiling as he takes a few deep breaths.

Why did he think I needed to be here? I'm a certified coatrack and cup holder. Was it really necessary for me to come with him? Is this another way of him showing me just how much I don't fit into his world? If so, it's cruel.

"Hattie," he calls out. "Can you come here?"

Stiffly, I walk up to him as Jacklyn tends to Odette. "Yes?" I ask him.

"Can I have some water?"

Trying not to flare my nostrils over the menial task I was brought here for, I hand him his water, and he thanks me, his eyes connecting with mine. After a gulp, he hands me the bottle and then leans back on the headboard again.

"Anything else?" I ask him.

"No, that's it."

I step away, so irritated with him that I clutch the robe tighter as Odette gets back into position. I watch his hands slowly move over her skin as if he's committing the feel of her to memory.

"Now, I'd love to see you flip her onto her back," Kevin says, "and hover above her."

"Sure," Hayes says over the music.

Smoke billows around them, and Kevin calls out to me, "Hattie, grab one of those hand fans and wave the smoke around them."

I set the robe and water down and snag one of the large flat fans and start waving it lightly over the smoke, swirling it around Odette and Hayes as Kevin calls out action. Hayes grips Odette tightly and then flips her onto her back. I watch her breasts jiggle from the sharp movement and hear her gasp over the music from her surprise. Why is she gasping? She knew exactly what he was going to do.

"Again," Kevin says, and they perform it a few more times. Every time, her body becomes more and more sexualized with the arch of her back, the press of her boobs in the air, and the way her fingers slide up his thick biceps. "Great, next position." Kevin moves the camera to the side now, where they get a better shot of Hayes on top of Odette. "Okay, from here, I want you to wrap your legs around Hayes's waist, and Hayes, I want you to run your hand up her side and then over her breast where you lightly grip it." Excuse me? Kevin turns toward Odette and says, "Are you still okay with the instructions from the intimacy coordinator?"

Odette nods, of course, because who wouldn't want to be in her position right now?

"Hattie, keep wafting the smoke." Oh shit, right. *Your job isn't to scowl.* It's to blow smoke around them. I lift the large fan and start waving it up and down as Kevin calls action, and I watch there, in horror, as Hayes's hand slides up Odette's body to her breast, where he grips it, causing Odette to arch her back and dig her hand into his hair. "Perfect," Kevin calls out. "Again."

My stomach roils with nausea.

My eyes are glued to every single thing he's doing.

My heart rips out of my chest with every kiss he places on her cheek, her jaw, her neck.

My breath escapes me every time his palm connects with her breast, gripping tightly.

My hope shatters as she gasps every time his jean-clad pelvis pulses into her.

It's all too fucking much, and I feel tears starting to tickle the backs of my eyes.

This . . . this right here is torture.

I've become hopelessly attached to this man, something I truly didn't expect. Odette is wrong about him. He's arrogant, conceited, and drives me mad most of the time. But, at this moment, I realize how much I've craved his touch. His affection. *His friendship.* Him. But this has shown how far out of his league I am. Physically. Emotionally. I feel so . . . unsophisticated. *I couldn't even graduate from college.*

And I can't help think of one of the first things he said to me when I first started working for him: he has no interest in me physically.

I'm not his type.

That much is clear.

Stunning Odette, with her beauty and maturity, is.

I take deep breaths, willing back the tears and telling myself to look at anything else other than the two of them.

After what feels like hours, Kevin finally calls the shoot a wrap, and in a catatonic state, I robotically walk over Odette's robe to her while Hayes offers Kevin a handshake. "I'm going to take a quick shower," he says to me and then takes off, leaving me with Kevin.

Odette walks off as well, and I don't know what to do until Kevin asks me to help collect the linens on the bed and stuff them in carts to be laundered.

Sighing, I assist the other production assistant, and we clean up while the smoke slowly dissipates from the set. The entire time, I feel broken, cut, and so raw . . . *I just want to go home.* So once I know there is nothing left for me to do, I walk back to Hayes's dressing room. I'm about to knock on the door when it opens, and Odette stands in the doorway.

"Oh," I say. "Sorry, I thought this was Hayes's room."

"It is." She smiles. And when I glance over her shoulder, I catch Hayes slipping his shirt over his head.

Right . . .

Fuck . . . I feel the tears wanting to form again, but I take a few deep breaths. Not here, not now. Hold it together, Hattie.

I try to smile, but I know it doesn't come off that way. Luckily, Odette is oblivious as she says, "Thank you again for your help and encouragement today. It meant a lot. And congrats on the job again. You couldn't have found a better guy to work with." She looks behind her and says, "Catch you later, Hayes."

Hayes nods at her but doesn't say anything as he sits on the couch to put his shoes on.

When Odette takes off, I stand there in the doorway, feeling like . . . like a child, waiting for the adult to be done with his . . . adult things.

He stands from the couch and says, "You ready?"

"Yes," I answer as I step aside, letting him out of his room, but instead of walking in front of me, he once again places his hand on my lower back and guides me toward the exit. He says goodbye to a few more people, and then we make our way to his SUV. I expect him to go to his side, but instead, he follows me to my side and opens the door for me.

I move past him to get in, but he doesn't put much distance between us. Rather, he steps up to the door and places both hands on the top edge as he leans in.

When I don't look at him, he grabs my chin and forces me to look him in the eyes.

That's all it takes, one look from him, and the tears fill my eyes.

Dammit.

I don't want to cry in front of him.

I don't want him to know how today affected me.

But it's next to impossible to hold back the feelings raging through me.

I'm embarrassed. Humiliated. And my heart . . . it feels broken.

"It was a job," he says softly as a tear rolls down my cheek.

He wipes it away from my cheek and repeats, "That's all it was, Hattie. It was a job."

"I know," I say.

"Then why are you crying?"

I shake my head, hating myself at this moment for letting him see my weakness. "It's stupid. Nothing you need to worry about."

"I'm worried," he says. "So tell me." When my eyes connect with his, he whispers, "Please, Hattie."

Damn him. A tear falls down my cheek, and I wipe it away as I say, "You don't care about me, Hayes. So please don't pretend that you do."

"That's where you're wrong. I care about you more than I should."

"Stop." Another tear falls down my cheek. "Don't bullshit me, Hayes. I saw Odette walk out of your dressing room. If you remotely cared about me or my feelings, you wouldn't have had her in your room. And please, don't act like nothing happened in there."

"Nothing happened," he says, his eyes never wavering from mine. "She tried to make a move, but I stopped it . . . because of you." He lifts my chin again when I try to look away. "Because I can't stop thinking about you, Hattie." He blows out a heavy breath and says, "I can't do this. I can't be the asshole you want me to be. Not when . . . not when I care so much about you."

I shake my head. "Just . . . stop. I can't do this, Hayes. I can't hear you say things like that, but turn me down and grope another woman right in front of me. It doesn't add up."

"It was for a job," he repeats.

"I understand that." I wipe my tears. "But this job comes right after last night after you groped me and then made it a fucking point to tell me you have no problem controlling yourself around me. Do you know how undesirable that makes me feel?" I wipe another tear. "And you can't tell me you didn't feel anything when kissing her, cupping her beautiful breasts, basically dry-humping her in front of the camera."

"What do you want me to say, Hattie? That I got an erection while on camera? Yes, I did. I got fucking hard, but only because the entire time, I was picturing you under me, not her."

"Oh bullshit, Hayes. Don't feed me lies. After last night, there's one thing I know for sure. I'm just someone to play around with but never someone to desire."

"Because I wouldn't go through with what you wanted?"

"Exactly why, Hayes. You say you can't stop thinking about me, yet you turn me down every chance you get."

"Because you shouldn't be mixed up with me," he yells at me, his body taking up the entire opening of the door. "Because you'd lose that relationship with your brother, with your sister, and I'm going to tell you right now, Hattie, I'm not fucking worth it." He grips my chin, forcing me to look at his steel-gray eyes. "I'm not worth it."

I'm not worth it.

He's said this to me numerous times already, but given that Ryland and I haven't touched the subject of Hayes since I've been in Almond Bay, I still have no clue what happened between them. And it's been years. And despite how much Ryland and Hayes loathe each other, Abel's still friends with both of them. *It can't have been that bad.*

It seems that Rowleys are the masters at holding grudges, though. I've heard nothing from Aubree all day, so any sisterly love I sought with her seems to be irrevocably destroyed. Because of the damn clause in Cassidy's will, and my own failure, I can't see any chance of restoring a relationship with my siblings. So right now, while I'm feeling so raw and wrecked and so alone, why not lose everything? Why not tell this man that I've seen below the surface and what I see, I like. I want more of. *He* says he's attracted to me, so what can I say to show him that I want him? That he is "worth it."

I wet my lips, his gaze nearly tearing me apart as I say, "What if . . . what if I think you're worth it?"

He shakes his head. I thought I saw a moment of relief on his face, but it's as if he's been conditioned to think only the worst of himself. Which he confirms when he says, "You don't know me well enough to make that kind of decision. Trust me, I'm doing you a favor." *Right. A favor. There it is, folks.* His shields are up. Again.

"I don't need your favors, Hayes." I press my hand against his chest and attempt to push him away, but he doesn't move. "Please, just get in the car and drive me back to Almond Bay."

Of course he doesn't listen. He brings his hand to my thigh and smooths it up my leg. Quietly, he says, "If I gave myself the opportunity to give you what you wanted, *what I want*, I'd dismantle every thought you ever had of being with a man. I'd break you. Then I'd slowly worship every inch of your heavenly body until you realized that no other man will ever give you the unequivocal pleasure I'll give you. There'd be no going back for you." He wets his lips as he stares down at my mouth. "And despite desperately wanting to bury my dick so far between your legs, I won't. I won't fucking break you. Because, Hattie, it would fucking break me too."

He pushes off the car and shuts my door, leaving me breathing heavily in my seat, my mind whirling with his proclamation.

He would break me . . . I believe that. *But how would I break him?*

I've already experienced short bursts of pain from him casting me aside. But knowing it would break him?

I know I shouldn't want that. But I've had small tastes of Hayes-given pleasure . . . and sadly, my body still yearns for him.

Time to give up, though, Hattie—something you seem very capable of doing.

237

———

HAYES DROPPED me off hours ago.

The car ride back to Almond Bay was quiet. We just listened to music but didn't say anything to each other. When I got out of his car, he asked me to come by tomorrow to finish what I started in the living room. If I wanted to leave after that, that was fine.

I agreed that I'd clean up the rest of the living room and finish that bag of letters, but when I was done, I wasn't returning. For my own sanity, I can't go back.

Now in my small studio apartment, I stare up at the ceiling while lying in my bed, thinking over the past twenty-four hours, hell, the past week. How did I go from dating one man to being infatuated with the wrong person? Is that the kind of effect he has on people? Must be, especially if Odette tried to make a move on him. I'm not surprised by that, but I am surprised Hayes denied her.

She was everything I'm not. I assumed he wanted to be with her, to finish what they started in that bed—*especially because she's everything I'm not*—but I was wrong.

I was so wrong.

My phone beeps next to me, and I glance down at it, seeing that it's a text from Ryland.

Perfect.

Ryland: *We're going to Cassidy's grave tomorrow for her birthday. Want to meet up and drive together?*

Holy shit . . . it's her birthday tomorrow. How did that slip my mind? I knew it was happening this week, but Jesus, I completely forgot about it. What kind of shitty sister does that make me? Guilt swarms me as I text Ryland back.

Hattie: *Yes, let me know when and where, and I'll be there.*

Ryland: *I took tomorrow off to be with Mac. Aubree is leaving Glenda to run the store as well. Mac wants to make Cassidy's cookies and sing her happy birthday.*

I suck in a sharp breath as I think about what that's going to be like, seeing a little four-year-old girl sing happy birthday to her dead mother . . . fuck, not something I want to witness. But I don't really have a choice in the matter.

Hattie: *Okay. Want me to drive out to the house?*

Ryland: *Probably be best. Grab a strawberry rhubarb pie from The Sweet Lab and a new puzzle. Mac mentioned those were Cassidy's favorite things to do with her.*

Hattie: *Sure, I can do that. Anything else?*

Ryland: *That's it. I'll see you tomorrow.*

I look at the time and realize if I don't get out of bed now, the stores will close, and I won't be able to get the puzzle and pie. So I slip on a sundress and shoes, feeling far too emotionally exhausted for any of this.

I head up Almond Ave toward Pieces and Pages. To the left, Five Six Seven Eight is bustling with music as an outdoor salsa class takes place on the lawn. With a pink feather boa wrapped around her, Ethel waves to me and motions for me to join, but I politely smile and shake my head.

No way will I be doing any sort of salsa dancing right now.

I pass Sozzled, the saloon, aka bar, in town and consider popping in for a quick drink. Maybe I will tonight. Nothing like getting drunk alone to block the feelings of having to deal with your dead sister's birthday.

Rodney's Railroad Museum is next, a small red shop plastered between two buildings. It's one of Almond Bay's treasures because Rodney has spent countless hours building a replica of the town in model train scale. It's really cute. There's even a person with a pink boa near Five Six Seven Eight. Ethel was "tickled" by the addition.

I skip past The Sweet Lab because I don't want to carry a pie around while looking for a puzzle and head straight for Pieces and Pages, my favorite store in town. And that's where I get lost for the rest of the afternoon.

HATTIE: *Pie and puzzle has been secured.*

Ryland: *Thank you. What are you up to?*

Hattie: *Going to get drunk.*

Ryland: *Think that's a good idea?*

Hattie: *No. But after attempting to find a puzzle Cassidy would like and picking up her favorite pie, I need some shots in my system.*

Ryland: *Be careful.*

Hattie: *It's Almond Bay, Ryland. What can happen?*

"Haven't seen you in a while, Hattie," Joe, the owner of Sozzled, says.

I take a seat on a barstool and sigh. "School will do that to you."

"What can I get you?"

"Something that will get me drunk," I answer. "And before you question me, tomorrow is Cassidy's birthday. I need something strong."

Lucky for me, this is a moment when everyone in the small town knows each other, and that simple request is understood without any more questions.

Joe gets to work, mixing a drink, and I pull up my text thread with Maggie.

Hattie: *I'm about to get drunk.*

What I wouldn't give to have her here with me. She's my rock. Unfortunately, she has her life together, something I'm struggling with.

Joe hands me a concoction and winks at me before heading to the other side of the bar to serve someone else. As I take a sip, Maggie texts me back.

Ooof, that's strong, just the way I need it.

Maggie: *Alone?*

Hattie: *Yup. Just me and my phone.*

Maggie: *Cassidy's birthday?*

Hattie: *Yeah. I had to pick out a puzzle she might like and her* *favorite pie. I dropped them off at my apartment and then came straight to the bar.*

Maggie: *Understandable. Is there any other reason you're drinking . . .*

Hattie: *If you're referring to Hayes, the answer is no.*

Maggie: *Good. He doesn't deserve your drunkenness.*

Hattie: *He doesn't! He deserves nothing. Even though he said this one thing to me today that made me want to simultaneously punch him in the esophagus and pull down his pants to suck his dick.*

Maggie: *That's quite a spectrum. What was it?*

Hattie: *Just how much he wants me but won't have me because of Ryland. Anyway, I don't want to talk about him. I just want to drink.*

I tip back my drink and quickly gulp it down. Yup, it's going to be one of those nights. I flag down Joe with a wave and point at my empty glass. His eyes read shock, but he nods, letting me know he'll fill me right up.

Maggie: *What are you drinking?*

Hattie: *Can't be sure, but it's strong.*

Maggie: *Please don't drink too much that you end up sifting through a dumpster looking for food.*

Hattie: *That happened one time, Maggie. And I thought the dumpster was a fridge, so you can't blame me.*

Maggie: *Yes . . . yes, I can. I've never seen anything so vile in my life. You smelled like rotten cheese curd when you finally resurrected.*

Hattie: *Some people like that smell.*

Maggie: *No one likes that smell.*

Joe brings me another drink, and I thank him before taking another large sip. He then returns and places a bowl of pretzels before me. Smart man. I pick one up and take a bite as I text Maggie back.

Hattie: *Did you know there are jobs where you can be practically naked and dry-hump famous people?*

Maggie: *Are you talking about strip clubs? Because I know what those are.*

Hattie: *No. That girl, Odette, rode Hayes hard today. I got to watch him palm her huge boob.*

Maggie: *Nooooooo, you did?*

Hattie: *Yup! A big old breast, right in his hand. But it's okay. She was wearing nipple pasties.*

Maggie: *That was the fragrance commercial? Did they happen to say when that's coming out? I'd be interested in viewing it.*

Hattie: *Maggie!*

Maggie: *Sorry, you're right . . . how dare he! How big was the boob?*

Hattie: *Like three of mine put together.*

Maggie: *Oof, that's a blow. I know how much you wish your boobs were bigger.*

Hattie: *Would it have hurt them to grow a touch more? I mean . . . when I was a teenager, I'd push hard, focusing all my efforts on my chest to make them sprout more.*

Maggie: *That . . . is something I could have done without hearing.*

Hattie: *Aubree told me once to put Miracle-Gro on them . . . and I did.*

Maggie: *I can imagine how that played out.*

Hattie: *Not well. I was so worried I would blossom weeds right out of my nipples.*

Maggie: *LMAO. Did you?*

Hattie: *I think you know nothing has ever blossomed on my chest by now.*

Maggie: *Your boobs aren't that small.*

Hattie: *Compared to Odette's, they're seedlings.*

Maggie: *Were they natural?*

Hattie: *Very. I honestly wanted to squeeze them myself.*

Maggie: *I'd probably have been the same.*

Hattie: *And get this, he admitted to being hard. Granted, I think I was even hard watching it all go down, although I was too ripe with jealousy, anger, and nausea to notice just how hard I was.*

Maggie: *Can you stop saying you were hard? I don't like that.*

Hattie: *It's facts.*

Maggie: So he said he was hard. That was generous of him to share that with you.

Hattie: Sort of pried it out of him. It's a long story. Either way, he said it was because he was thinking of me the whole time. I'm going to tell you right now, if he was thinking of me while squeezing that volup-tuous tit, he's going to be disappointed . . . well, I mean, not that he will ever squeeze my boob. Huh, actually he did . . .

Maggie: Uh, what now?

Hattie: **SIGHS** It was last night. We ended up sharing a bed, another long story, and he squeezed my boob in another one of those teasing situations. I'll be honest, I was ready to sit right on his face.

I down the rest of my drink, and Joe, the good man he is, brings me another.

Maggie: I haven't ever sat on a man's face, but the bridal party I was working with the other day talked about sitting on faces.

Hattie: Did you get any good detail on how to execute the face sitting?

Maggie: They just texted their guys. They did it while at knitting club.

Hattie: Does knitting give you confidence?

Maggie: No idea, but it makes me want to try it.

Hattie: What about crochet? What kind of confidence does that give you?

Maggie: I feel like knitting gives you more confidence because you're using two sticks instead of one.

Hattie: Hmm . . . how about needlepoint? What does that do to you?

Maggie: Make you lose your eyesight.

Hattie: Maybe that's the way to go then. If I lose my eyesight, I won't ever have to look at Hayes again.

Maggie: Frankly, it's a solid plan. What about his songs, though?

Hattie: I can escape those easily.

I lift my glass just as a chord strikes through the speakers. What the . . .

I glance over at the stage, and sure enough, Hayes sits on a stool, a spotlight highlighting him in that stupid backward hat of his, holding a guitar.

"What the fuck?" I mutter to myself as people in the bar start cheering and growing closer to the stage. What happened to this town not liking him?

Not quite seeing that.

Hattie: *Dear God, Mags . . . he's here.*

Maggie: *Who? Hayes?*

Hattie: *YES! And he's on stage, about to sing a freaking song.*

Maggie: *What are the odds? Just when you claim you can escape his music. It's almost as if an author is fucking around with your life, pulling all the strings.*

Hattie: *What do I do?*

Maggie: *Well, depends. You can show him how much you hate him by taking your shoe off and throwing it at him.*

Hattie: *Tempting.*

Maggie: *You can boo him off the stage, but that might get you kicked out of the bar, and from what I've been able to gather, our goal tonight is to stay as close to alcohol as possible.*

Hattie: *Correct.*

Maggie: *So then, the shoe seems promising, or you can just listen to him . . .*

Hattie: *And think about the fact that he's turned me down like three times at this point? That seems like fun.*

Maggie: *Three times? Okay, I think we need to have a different goal when it comes to this man. He's clearly not helping.*

Hattie: *No, he's not, and why is he even playing music at the bar? He always says no one likes him, so what's he doing?*

Maggie: *Maybe trying to spark some creative juices. Isn't he struggling with writing?*

Hattie: *Can you not defend him? I know you have a hard-on for him, but come on, Mags.*

Maggie: *Stop saying women have hard-ons! And I wasn't defending him, just trying to state the facts.*

"Thanks for having me tonight," Hayes says into the

microphone as he strums his guitar. "This song is dedicated to a girl I can't seem to get out of my head."

My stomach drops, and I watch as he glances in my direction before dipping his head and focusing all his attention to his guitar.

No fucking way.

Hattie: *OMG OMG OMG!!! He just looked at me and dedicated the song he's singing to me.*

Maggie: *He said your name?*

Hattie: *No, but he said it's dedicated to a girl he can't get out of his head, and even though he spent his morning groping perfect boobs, I know he's talking about me.*

Maggie: *Dear . . . God . . .*

His fingers play along the guitar strings and then a familiar melody starts forming. The back of my neck tingles as I realize exactly what he's playing. I set my drink down and turn toward the stage, my eyes fixated on him as he begins singing the acoustic version of *More Than a Feeling*. The acoustic version I told him I was absolutely in love with.

Hattie: *He's . . . he's playing More Than a Feeling.*

Maggie: *Uh-oh.*

Hattie: *Uh-oh, is right.*

I place my phone in my lap and focus all my attention on him, watching as his throat contracts while he sings, his eyes close when he hits the higher notes, and how his fingers so effortlessly slide along the guitar strings.

I feel myself fall into this transfixed state where there is no one else in the room, just me and him, and he's singing to me, his voice feeling like a warm blanket wrapping me up into a gentle hug.

My phone buzzes in my lap, but I ignore it. Nothing could tear me away from this moment, from listening to him.

Not my brain telling me to pay him no attention.

Not the audience around me, probably noticing just how enamored I am.

Not even the texts from Maggie.

Because he's singing to me.

"Here's another one, Hattie," Joe says next to me, and I take it without looking, bringing the drink to my lips. The alcohol's starting to cloud my brain. *Just like I wanted.*

While he plays the instrumental section, my eyes zero in on his fingers, how they expertly press against the strings of the guitar, on the concentration on his face, the way his teeth pull on the corner of his lip, the muscles flexing in his forearms. He's everything I want, and it hurts my very longing and desperate soul that I can't have him.

That he's off limits.

That he won't give in to temptation like I so easily have.

He finishes the song, and the crowd around him claps and cheers as he sets down the guitar and thanks the room. His eyes on me, he says, "I appreciate it. But I know you're really here to listen to Jacob Latter. So put your hands together for him." The crowd cheers as Jacob . . . Dee Dee Coleman's son —the owner of the general store—walks out onto the stage and shakes Hayes's hand.

"Thank you, Hayes," he says into the microphone. "Couldn't have asked for a better opening act." The crowd chuckles and then Jacob goes into what he'll be playing, but I block him out as I watch Hayes work his way through the crowd and straight to the end of the bar.

He glances over in my direction and that's when I take a moment to give him a long once-over.

Worn jeans that aren't too tight but not too loose, accompanied by a pair of stylish dark brown Timberlands. He's wearing a heather-gray T-shirt tight around his chest but loose around his waist and a faded backward hat. His heavy, dark five o'clock shadow makes his steely eyes seem much more dangerous. And in the back pocket of his jeans is a piece of paper, barely hanging out the back. I wouldn't have noticed if it wasn't for the contrast against his jeans. When my eyes draw back up to his face, I also catch him looking in my direction.

When I got home after he dropped me off, I took a shower and changed into a simple navy-blue sundress sans bra because when you have little boobs like me, you can get away with it. I also let my hair dry naturally, which has led to soft waves framing my face.

His eyes remain on mine from across the bar as he licks his lips.

"You doing okay?" Joe asks.

"Yes," I practically shout. Good God, Joe startled me from my need to walk up to Hayes. But the problem with a small town is everyone is watching everything you're doing, so I turn toward the bar and glance down at my phone to read Maggie's text.

Maggie: *Is it weird that I'm playing the acoustic version on my phone while you hear it in person? Have to admit, I'm hard for you.*

I chuckle and text her back.

Hattie: *I thought we weren't saying women can be hard.*

Maggie: *You know, I think we need to think of this as an equal opportunity thing. Everyone can be hard! Also, from the delay in texts, I'm going to guess you either started drooling while listening or fell off your chair from being so captivated.*

Hattie: *Neither. But he keeps looking in my direction. He's at the bar now.*

Maggie: *I can feel the tension from here! Are you going to do anything?*

Hattie: *No. What can I do? There are too many eyes in this place for anything to happen. And I don't think it's a good idea. I can't keep throwing myself at him.*

Maggie: *So what are you going to do?*

Hattie: *Get completely wasted.*

Maggie: *It's not a great plan, but it's a plan. Bottoms up, bestie.*

247

"JOE," I say, leaning over the bar now, half my body on the counter, the other parts dangling in the air. "I'm thirsty. Why won't you give me more drink drink?"

"Because you're calling it drink drink," he says.

"Just squirt it in my mouth," I say, picking up his bar gun. "Right here, in the gullet." I press one of the buttons and shoot a stream of water right into his bucket of ice. "Oopsie doopsie." I giggle.

"Hattie, I suggest you get off my bar or I'll have you removed."

I perk up and whisper, "By the cops?"

"I've got her," a male voice says before two hands grip my waist and pull me back into a seat. When I glance up to see who dares interrupt my fun, I come face to face with Hayes Farrow.

"Gah!" I scoff. "The enemy touched me, Joe." I slap the counter. "Are you going to let the enemy touch me like that?"

"As long as you're not hanging off my bar, I'm going to let him do whatever he wants to you."

"That's not safe," I mumble and cross my arms at my chest. "What if he wants to tie me up in his sex dungeon? Would you let that happen?"

Joe wipes down his bar, where I must have over-sprayed some liquid. "I trust Hayes. If he took you to his sex dungeon, he'd be gentle."

"My God," I say as I tip back and start falling off my stool.

Hayes is immediately at my side and propping me back up.

"See," Joe says. "Gentle."

"Maybe you should go back home," Hayes says quietly.

"Maybe you should mind your own business," I reply, shaking him off me.

"Hattie."

"What?" I ask, turning toward him.

He glances around the bar and says, "People are looking."

"Oh . . . heaven forbid you're seen with me, right?" I look around as well and catch a few people staring. I wave to them, a smile plastered to my face. "Nothing to see over here. Just the enemy touching me."

"Hattie . . ." he says in a warning tone.

"He never wants to touch me," I shout. "Never ever, ever—"

Before I can finish, he scoops me up, tosses me over his shoulder, and he turns to Joe. "Put her on my tab."

"Sure thing," he says as Hayes walks away.

"Put me down, you anus!" I yell. "People are going to see up my skirt. Hey, what are you looking at?" I say to an old lady I've never seen before, most likely a tourist. "Keep your eyes to yourself."

"Hattie, please," Hayes says, working us through the bar.

"And you didn't want to draw attention. You carrying me like a sack of vodka potatoes isn't going to lessen the staring. Look, there's Ethel. Ethel, yoo-hoo," I say, waving my hand. "Yup, this is happening. This right here is happening. Sound the sirens. Alert the press. Hayes Farrow is touching Hattie Rowley. Weeee-oooo, weee-ooooo."

"Shut the fuck up, Hattie," Hayes says just as he pushes through the door of the saloon and walks me down the street.

"Unhand me, you monster," I say, scratching at his back.

He doesn't say anything but walks me across the street and behind the back of The Almond Store. It's nearly pitch-black besides the streetlights lining the boardwalks. The town is silent, the only establishment open being the bar.

"This is ridiculous," I say. "You're treating me like a child."

"Because you're acting like one," he says as he reaches the back of The Almond Store. "What's the pin code to get in?"

"As if I'd tell you that. Turn me around, and I'll plug it

in." He spins so I face the pin code, and I plug in the number, unlocking the door.

He pushes through and then with ease, climbs up the steps that lead to my apartment. When he jiggles the doorknob and it opens, he grumbles under his breath. "You don't lock this?"

"We lock the store. What's the point?"

He steps into the apartment and finally sets me down. I stumble backward for a second, but he catches me and rights me on my feet before I take a spill. Once steady, I slap his hands away and push down my dress, holding my chin high.

"How dare you manhandle me like that?"

"A thank-you would suffice."

"I would never," I reply as I catch him looking around my space. "Stop observing my room."

"It's small in here."

"I know," I say. "But I don't need much. Not all of us need mansions like you, Hayes."

I walk over to my dresser and pull out an oversized shirt, only to stumble against the dresser and crush my finger in the drawer. "Motherfucker!" I yell as I hold my finger with my other hand. "Oh fuck, that hurt." I stumble to the ground, unable to keep my wits about me, and Hayes is quickly at my side, taking my finger into his hand.

"You okay?" he asks, examining it.

"No," I say as I slouch on the floor. "I hurt my finger."

"I can see that," he says softly. "Do you want some ice?"

"No. I want to change and get ready for bed."

"Do you need help?"

I shake my head, my anger dissipating as he holds my finger, the throbbing starting to settle. It takes me a few seconds, but I finally say, "That's better."

"Good." He stands from the floor and pulls me up with him. He hands me my shirt, and I hold it close to my chest. "Sooo, are you going to change?"

"Yes," I answer but don't move.

"Do you want me to do it for you?"

I shake my head but still don't move.

He bends at the knees to look me in the eyes. "You're not moving, Hattie."

"I know." I sigh.

"Is there a reason?"

I shake my head, the alcohol doing funny things to my brain. "You . . . you made my finger feel better."

Yup, I'm drunk.

His eyes soften.

"Matt never made my finger feel better." My eyes meet his. "But you made my finger feel better."

"Hattie," he practically whispers.

"I know." I nod. "You're trouble, but how can someone be trouble when they make your finger better? I don't under- stand." I twist my lips to the side. "I just don't get it." And then I head into the bathroom. I shut the door behind me and strip out of my dress, crashing into the cabinet with my knee, unable to keep my balance.

"You okay?" he asks. Of course he wants to know I'm okay because . . . because past the trouble, past the denial, past the fact that he's my brother's enemy, he's . . . he's amazing and sweet and kind, and cares about me. That's what he said—he cares about me.

Maybe the only person besides Maggie who cares for me.

"I'm okay," I say as I right myself.

I spend the next few minutes going to the bathroom and brushing my teeth. Once I change into my shirt, I head out of the bathroom to find Hayes standing in the middle of the room, waiting for me, his hands in his pockets. He looks so handsome, so sexy, his triceps popping.

"Well"—I pull on the hem of my shirt—"I guess I should get to bed."

"Yes, you probably should," he says.

Our gazes lock, and this heavy, electric energy passes

between us both, this gravitational pull dragging us together, but where he's doing everything in his power to pull away, I could easily give in.

"I'm tired."

"I'm sure you are," he responds.

"You know, lots of drinks and all."

"Yeah, I could tell."

I bob my head, unsure of what else to do.

"Here," he says, reaching out his hand. I take it because I have no self-control, and he moves me to my bed where he pulls back the covers for me. He's already plugged my phone into its charger, which is extremely thoughtful.

As I settle on my pillow, he takes a seat on the edge, having to duck just because of the angle of the ceiling. He rubs his thumb across my cheek.

I feel myself lean in to his touch as he says, "Why did you drink so much tonight?"

"Do I need a reason?" I ask.

"No, but it doesn't seem like something you'd normally do. Was it because of what happened today?"

I shake my head. "No, not everything is about you, Hayes." Although, a little bit of what happened today motivated me, maybe half and half. Definitely after he sang his song, I went full on *let's get plastered* mode.

"Then what?" he asks.

"Do you really care?"

He nods. "I fucking do, Hattie." His voice grows soft. "I care far too much about you than I should."

"Is that why you dedicated your song to me tonight?"

"Yes," he answers without looking away.

"Ugh," I groan. "You're so frustrating. You realize that? I don't want to like you, Hayes, but you make it hard."

"I'm sorry." He strokes my cheek again.

"Are you really?" I ask.

He nods. "I am. Trust me, if circumstances were different, you wouldn't be frustrated with me."

"What would I be?" I ask.

His voice grows dark as he says, "You'd be full of me."

I squeeze my eyes shut, hating how one sentence made my muscles tighten and go from loose drunk to full on aroused.

I bite down on my lip. "How full?"

His thumb drags over my jaw. "Fuller than you've ever been, that's for damn sure."

"Show me," I practically beg him.

"You know I can't, Hattie. I can't cross that line."

"But you want to . . ."

He breaks eye contact for the first time and drops his hand from my face. "Not a question I should answer." To my surprise, he leans down and places a soft kiss on my head, the kind of kiss that screams friend zone. There's nothing passionate about it. And all it does is anger me. "Get some sleep." He pulls away, but I grip the nape of his neck, holding him in place. When his eyes meet mine, they plead with me. "Don't, Hattie."

I tug him an inch closer.

"Hattie . . ."

I sit up some more, making it so our faces are at eye level.

"Tell me you don't want this," I say to him, taking one more risk.

"I . . . I . . . think you need to sleep."

"That's not saying you don't want this."

The space between us zaps with the electric need bouncing between us, and as I close the space, making sure there's only a whisper between our mouths, I feel the stuttering in his breath and the heat of his body.

"Please . . . don't." His voice drips with desperation, but he doesn't pull away. He remains still, and the moment he wets his lips, I know I'm not going back.

This is it.

I'm taking what I want.

And I do.

My mouth covers his for the first time, my kiss shattering the fine line that's been drawn. He stiffens under my touch, but it's only for a millisecond as I work my mouth over his. With every kiss, he relaxes, and then to my absolute pleasure, he presses his thumb under my jaw to angle my mouth how he wants it.

And he kisses me back.

The fullness of his lips.

The demand of his mouth.

The energy he gives me.

The passion.

I melt under the feel of him taking control, finally giving in to my need for him . . . and it's the best feeling I've ever experienced.

His lips part, and I reciprocate, then he's kissing me with such intense passion that I'm panting. The sharp scruff of his five o'clock shadow rubs against my sensitive skin as he opens his mouth, looking for more, his tongue seeking out mine. I let out a long moan, swiping against his tongue as well, trying to soak up every moment.

But that one swipe is all it takes to wake him up, and before I can kiss him one more time, he's standing from the bed, shoulders tense, a look of disbelief in his eyes.

"Fuck," he says, dragging his hand over his mouth. "Shit, Hattie, I shouldn't have done that. You're . . . you're drunk."

"Not that drunk," I say, desperation clawing at me, telling me to pull him back down.

He shakes his head. "Your eyes are glassy, and you're having a rough night. I shouldn't have . . . fuck, I shouldn't have done that."

Of course.

This is how it always goes, right? I take one step forward, and he sprints two miles away.

I know he enjoyed that kiss. I felt it with how tightly he gripped me and with the way his mouth worked over mine. If he wasn't into it, he never would have kissed me back, and never with tongue.

But this is how it is with us—he won't let this attraction between us be something.

I stare up at the angled ceiling, frustrated, and say, "Just leave, Hayes." The short euphoria I just experienced evaporates with every look of guilt I see flash through his eyes.

I don't want his guilt.

I want him.

All of him.

His hands.

His kisses.

His heart.

Feeling his gaze on me, I turn away and bring the blankets up to my chin, tucking myself away from the world.

"You know why, right, Hattie?" he says. Credit to him for at least sounding tortured.

"Yes, you don't have to repeat yourself, but you do have to leave. Don't bother locking up."

I hear him step away from me, his shoes sounding against the hardwood. I squeeze my eyes tight, holding back the tears until I hear the door shut behind him, but when the light turns off, and I hear the distinct plop of his shoes coming off instead of hearing him walk down the stairs, I grow confused.

What is he doing?

I turn around just in time to see him grab a pillow from a chair in the corner, and he plops it on the floor next to the bed. With a throw blanket in hand, he lies on the floor.

"What are you doing?" I ask him.

"Going to sleep."

"Why aren't you leaving?"

"Because I don't want to leave. Not when you're drunk.

Not when you're clearly going through something. I want to be here for you."

"But that's the thing, Hayes," I say, unable to hold back my emotions clawing at my tight throat. "I don't want you to be here for me. I don't want you near me, not when . . . not when I can't have you."

"Trust me, Hattie, you have me in every fucking way. Whether you want to believe it or not."

"If I had you, then you wouldn't be sleeping on the floor."

"You're right." He stands from the floor and lifts the covers to my bed. When I look up at him, he nods toward the slanted ceiling. "Scoot over."

"Hayes."

"You want to see how you own me? This is it. Now scoot over."

I bite on my bottom lip and contemplate the implications of this. If I scoot over and he lies down next to me, I don't think I'll ever be able to get over the feel of him tucked in behind me, but if I don't scoot over, I give up the chance of being able to feel him wrapped around me all night.

My muddled brain can't quite seem to figure out just how bad this might be, so instead of properly weighing the pros and cons, I scoot over, and he slips in behind me, wrapping his bulky arm around my waist and pulling me in close to his chest.

"This is what you want, isn't it?" he asks, his mouth right next to my ear.

"I want more," I say.

"I can't give you more, especially when you're drunk. But I'm willing to give you this." His hand slips under my shirt, and his palm presses against my stomach. The warm feel of his grip soothes my aching soul immediately.

"If this is all I can get, then I'll take it," I say right before turning toward him and taking one more chance. I kiss his lips, and thankfully, he doesn't turn away. He lets me explore for a few seconds before I pull back.

He sighs heavily, his teeth tugging on his lower lip, and when I start to turn around, he stops me, bringing his hand to the back of my head and covering my mouth again with his.

I melt into his hold, knowing this is temporary because he doesn't part my mouth with his tongue. He doesn't deepen the kiss, just skims the surface of what could be so much more before he ends the kiss.

His eyes bore into mine, the expression in them so sad that I can't take it and turn back around.

His grip on me tightens as he buries his head into my hair.

"Fuck . . . I like you, Hattie."

My heart nearly shatters. His rough, tortured voice pierces me to my very core.

"I like you too, Hayes."

And that's the last thing we say to each other before we fall asleep.

Chapter Fourteen

HATTIE

The slam of a door wakes me from a cold, dead sleep. I pop my head up just as I hear feet storm up the steps to my apartment, followed by a banging on my door.

Hayes stirs awake behind me and pops up his head as well.

"Hattie, open this goddamn door."

Fuck . . . it's Ryland.

Hayes and I exchange looks at the same time as fear creeps up the back of my neck.

There is no other way out of here than that door—the one Ryland is pounding on.

And if I open that door, and Ryland sees Hayes in here, there is no way Hayes will be leaving.

"I will break this fucking door down. Now open up." He bangs again, and I scramble to get out of bed. Hayes helps me by lifting me over him and placing me on the floor.

"He's going to murder you," I whisper.

"I'll be fine," Hayes says.

"I don't think you understand just how bad this is."

Hayes stands from the bed, towering over me with bedhead and sleep still in his eyes. "I'll be fine, I promise. Open the door before he knocks it down."

"But . . . how does he know?" I ask, the night fuzzy in my head.

"You pretty much announced to the bar that I was taking you away. Probably took two seconds for someone to text him."

"Hattie!" he yells, pounding.

"Fuck," I mutter before I brush my shirt down and walk up to the door, fear clutching my chest. I don't want to open the door. I don't want to subject Hayes to whatever Ryland might do to him, but I also know I can't let him break down the door. So with a deep breath, I unlock the door and open it an inch. "Ryland," I say as he stares at me with murderous eyes.

He places his palm against the door and pushes it open, just enough to see Hayes standing in the middle of the apartment, hands in his pockets.

"You motherfucker," Ryland growls right before he charges toward him.

"No," I say to Ryland as I reach for his arm, but he shrugs out of the way, cocks back his arm, and lunges toward Hayes.

The sound of Hayes's jaw crunching under Ryland's fist makes me physically ill.

"What the hell are you doing?" I yell as Hayes stumbles backward. I grab Ryland's hand, but he shakes me off as he goes in for another punch.

"You think you can just fuck my sister and get away with it?" Ryland screams, the veins in his neck popping, looking so terrifying that I don't even recognize him. His fist plows into Hayes's stomach, and he buckles over, letting Ryland get another punch into his side.

Oh my God!

Why isn't Hayes fighting back?

"Stop," I scream at Ryland before he can truly do some damage if he hasn't done so already.

I hop on his back, trying to limit his ability to attack Hayes, but Ryland pulls me off and pushes me to the side, causing me to crash into my dresser, my back slamming against the hard wood. "Fuck," I cry as my eyes connect with Hayes. Fury takes over him, and just as Ryland goes to strike him again, Hayes blocks Ryland's fist and returns the punch straight into Ryland's stomach.

Ryland steps backward, crippling over just as Hayes uppercuts him into the jaw, the crunching sound deafening. "Don't you dare fucking hurt her," Hayes says as he closes the distance between him and Ryland, gripping Ryland's shirt. He cocks back his arm, and I scream at him.

"Don't, Hayes. Please. Don't."

Hayes glances in my direction, which is enough time for Ryland to punch Hayes in the side of the head. As he loses his balance, Ryland hops on Hayes's back, tackling him to the ground, where they start wrestling each other.

Two large, grown men, rolling around on the floor, tossing punches, grunting, swearing at each other, and all I can do is watch in horror, crying, begging them to stop.

Shirts are ripped.

Punches are thrown.

Blood splatters across the room.

I jump onto the bed because as they roll around, they take out the dresser and the chair, ruin the rug, and destroy the entire apartment. *Cassidy's apartment.*

"Please stop," I cry out, tears streaming down my face as I watch two important men in my life try to kill each other. "Ryland, stop. Hayes," I sob and, just when I think there will be no end to this, Abel appears at the door, his chest heaving as he takes in the scene in front of him.

"Get Hayes," he says to me as he sacrifices himself and

pulls Ryland by the shoulders. I take a moment when Ryland and Hayes aren't on top of each other and throw my body onto Hayes, knowing damn well he won't hurt me. I clutch him, my arms and legs wrapped around him as he breathes heavily against me.

"Let me the fuck go," Ryland says, and when I glance over at him, my stomach twists with nausea as blood drips down his eye, across his face, and under his lip.

"You're going to kill each other, and you have a little girl to take care of," Abel says, the voice of reason. That's all it takes for Ryland to let go of the tension and to fall backward on the ground, where he clutches his forehead.

Hayes relaxes as well while his arm snakes around my back soothingly, my heart still pounding erratically. Quietly, he whispers in my ear, "Are you okay?"

I shake my head because I'm not okay.

Nothing about what just happened is okay.

I feel so hopeless. *That was so . . . brutal.*

I have no idea what I would have done if Abel hadn't shown up and pulled Ryland off Hayes.

I put a few inches between me and Hayes and look him in the face for the first time. His eye's already swollen, and blood drips from his nose and a spot above his eye.

Tears stream down my cheeks as I run my thumb over his cheek.

"I'm fine," he says, understanding my concern. "Promise."

I turn toward Ryland now, his hands still clutching his head as he breathes heavily.

"Ryland . . . I—"

"Don't," he says as he sits up, the murder in his eyes gone, and in its place . . . emptiness. "I don't want to hear your apologies because they'll fall on deaf ears. Nothing you say will make this right. You're dead to me, Hattie." He runs the back of his hand over his nose as he bends forward, still catching his breath.

D-dead to him?

Without even letting me explain?

My lip trembles, a sob on the tip of my tongue just as Hayes says, "I did nothing to her. Nothing happened between us. I . . . I wouldn't let anything happen."

"I don't fucking believe you," Ryland snaps back, the anger pouring off him.

"Of course you wouldn't," Hayes says defensively. "You've never believed anything I've told you because you've decided to assume the worst about me instead of hearing me out."

"Why would I hear you out when you got my girlfriend pregnant?" Ryland shouts.

Uh . . . what?

I turn to Hayes. "You got his girlfriend pregnant? You have a kid? Is that why you guys don't talk? That's the reason? Wait . . ." The dots start connecting as I think about when their friendship dissolved. It was a few summers after their high school graduation. Ryland was dating his longtime girlfriend and crush, Samantha Horbach, while trying to make it in the big leagues. Hayes was playing music in small bars, trying to get noticed. Both of them trying to make something of themselves. "You got Samantha pregnant?"

"He did," Ryland says. "And then left her to fend for herself. She ended up having a miscarriage and then left town. Losing her was the downfall of my goddamn career and all because he betrayed me."

I crawl away from Hayes just as he says, "I didn't do it." His eyes stay on mine the entire time, never wavering. "I didn't fuck her. I wouldn't do that to a friend."

"Don't call me your friend." Ryland stands, and so does Hayes.

"Ryland," Hayes says, his voice full of sincerity. "I didn't touch her. At the summer party, she tried to make a move on me while you were in Pittsburgh for a game. I turned her down, and she was pissed about it. She ended up fucking Nick that night in the back of his Jeep. I swear on my goddamn life, it wasn't me."

Ryland pauses, and I can see him thinking it over, questioning himself and his assumption.

Abel steps up and places his hand on Ryland's shoulder. "I swore I'd stay out of this, but what Hayes is saying is the truth. I spoke to Nick a few years ago, and he admitted it. I've wanted to tell you, Ryland. I've wanted to get the truth out between you for years, but then Cassidy got sick . . . Hayes, this should have been settled years ago. I shouldn't have listened to you and kept quiet. I'm sorry I've held on to it, for both of your sakes."

Feeling like I've been through a car crash with terrible whiplash, I sit down on my bed and glance between the desperate look on Hayes's face and the confused look on Ryland's face. I can tell by Hayes's expression that he wants to be trusted. And Ryland? He's believed a massive lie . . . for over a decade.

"But . . . she said you got her pregnant."

"She lied," Hayes says softly.

More confusion wraps around Ryland as he takes a few steps back, his hand on his head. "I . . . I can't fucking deal with this right now," he says as he wipes the back of his hand over his mouth, smearing blood across his cheek. "It's Cassidy's birthday, and I have a little girl wanting to celebrate."

Hand still on his shoulder, Abel says, "Come to the office, I'll clean you up."

"Ryland . . . wait."

He glances over his shoulder, not a single ounce of brotherly love directed at me. "Be at Cassidy's grave at nine. Don't be late."

And then Ryland and Abel walk out of the apartment and down the stairs.

Silence fills the room as regret, guilt, and sorrow consume

me in a chokehold, making it impossible to fully fill my lungs with air.

"Are you okay?" Hayes finally says.

"Does it look like I'm okay?" I ask as I swipe at my tears.

"I don't want to hear your apologies because they'll fall on deaf ears. Nothing you say will make this right. You're dead to me, Hattie." He's done with me. His own sister. What the hell was all this for? I look at Hayes, and once again, I see his contrite expression. *I am so fucking over this. My heart has just been torn apart.* "You took a brutal beating from him . . . all for what?" I toss my hands up in the air. "You said it all along, to stay away from you, not to get involved, yet there was no point. There was no reason for it all, for all of this." Snot drips from my nose. "This . . . this feud was pointless. The agony I've been going through, it was pointless. The trashing of this room was all pointless." I gesture to the floor, taking in the blood splatter, the mangled rug, the . . .

My eyes narrow in on an envelope on the floor. A familiar envelope.

"What is that?" I ask as I stand from the bed and pick up the envelope, the handwriting shocking me to my very core. I hold it up to Hayes. "Where the hell did this come from?"

He swallows. "That's what I came to give you last night, but you were drunk."

Hand shaking, I run my fingers over the return address: Cassidy Rowley.

The envelope is addressed to Hayes Farrow.

"How long have you had this?" When he doesn't answer, I yell, "How long, Hayes?"

"A few months." His hands fall in his pockets.

"You've had a letter from my sister for a few months, and you're just now mentioning it?"

"I forgot about it. Matt gave it to me on tour. I stuffed it away somewhere, and I found it yesterday when I was shuffling through some of my shit."

"Why didn't you mention it? I would have helped you look for it."

"I didn't want to make any promises in case I couldn't find it."

I flip it over and see that it isn't open. "You didn't read it."

He shakes his head. "Anything Cassidy wanted to say to me, I didn't think I needed to hear."

I check the postmark date and notice it's from a week before she passed. My throat closes in on me. "This . . . this was important. You should have opened it. You should have told me."

"Hattie, I'm sorry. The moment I found it, I brought it over to you."

"No, you didn't." I shake my head. "You watched me get drunk at the bar." He takes a step toward me, but I back away. "You shouldn't even have sung a song. You should have texted me the moment you found it and told me it was important." I clutch the envelope to my chest. "But you didn't. Instead, you tried to what . . . get on my good side? I'd say seduce me, but we both know how last night went. I just . . . I don't get it, Hayes. If you cared about me—"

"I do care about you."

"No, you don't," I shout at him. "If you cared about me, you wouldn't have ever fucked around with my feelings. You wouldn't have strung me along. You would have found a way to make things right with Ryland rather than let him believe you were a horrible man, which affected me."

"I didn't think I was going to . . . going to—"

"Going to what? Fall for me?" I ask. "God, you can't even say it."

He pulls on the back of his neck, staring down at me. "Hattie, I'm . . . I'm sorry."

"Just leave, Hayes." I shake my head.

"Hattie, please," he says, his crushing tone drawing my attention. His shirt is ripped across the chest, giving me a glimpse of his bare skin. There are blood smears across his face, and his eyes are full of sorrow. "Please, don't shut me out."

"Don't shut you out? Coming from the man who has done nothing but that to me this entire time." I press my hand to my chest. *I'm so fucking sick of crying over this man.* I am so, so done. "I don't want to even look at you right now."

His lips seal together as he slowly nods. Quietly, he picks up his hat from my nightstand and heads toward the door, his shoulders slumped, and when he makes one more attempt to get my attention, I feel my body turn to stone, unwilling to give him a second look.

"I'm sorry," he says one last time before he exits my apartment, leaving me in the wake of the destruction.

But I don't care.

I don't care about the blood splattered across the floor and the rug that used to lay flat across the floor. I don't care about the broken dresser or the upturned chair, or the pictures that somehow fell to the ground while they were wrestling.

The only thing I care about is the letter in my hand. *Why did Cassidy write to Hayes? Did she have something going on with him?*

With shaky fingers, I slide the envelope open from the back and slowly pull out a folded piece of paper. On a deep breath, I unfold it, and the moment I see her handwriting scrolled across the paper, more tears fill my eyes, clouding my vision.

I tip my head back, not wanting to get any of my tears on the paper and ruin her letter. It takes me a moment, but I hold the paper up and read once I've gathered myself.

Dear Hayes,

I know I'm probably the last person you expected to hear from, but as you might know—or might not know—I'm really sick, and I'm getting my affairs in order. Morbid, I know, but as I lie here in my bed, knowing my time is coming to an end, I realize I don't want to leave this earth without at least trying to make my mark.

I know about Samantha, I know about the miscarriage, but what I don't know is why. You were a part of the family growing up. Aubree and Hattie were too young to truly know you, but I knew you. I knew you well. Some of my best moments in high school are from bonfires on the beach with you, Ryland, and Abel. The Samantha thing never made sense to me, and I know I'll leave this earth without knowing why, but you know why.

And this is where my request comes in.

I'm asking the world from Ryland, to take on the responsibility of raising my child. And I know he's too much of a proud man to ask for help, but he's going to need it. So from my bed where I'll take my last breaths, I ask you, please, please reach out to him. Please break this feud.

Give me the peace of mind knowing I can trust that you two can move past your differences and be the friends you once were. If anything, do it for Mac because the more strong, passionate, loving people in her life, the better.

Thank you, Hayes.

Cassidy

P.S. I know you don't know Hattie very well, but she could do with a friend like you too. Our whole family has grieved your loss. Please be someone in her life too.

P.P.S. She's also a huge fan. She pretends she isn't, but she is. I hear her playing The Reason all the time.

I cry and snort at the same time.

Why, Cassidy?

Why didn't you leave me any part of you? Your baby girl . . . your store . . . a letter. Anything.

Ryland and Aubree have such big parts of Cassidy and knew what she wanted. But I was sent away with nothing but the largest hole in my heart that nothing will ever take away. I've felt so alone in my devastation. With nothing but silence.

And even fucking Hayes Farrow got a letter.

But why couldn't you have written to me too, Cass? All I've wanted was your words.

And why, of all the days for Hayes to find this, to give me this letter, does it have to be today?

———

"UNCLE RY RY," Mac says, tugging on his hand. "I think I had too much pie." Ryland turns toward her where he's sitting at the dining room table and places his hand on her belly.

"Are you full?" She nods.

"I feel sick."

"I told you a third piece would have been too much."

"But I needed to eat my piece and a piece for Chewy Charles and a piece for Mommy."

"I understand," Ryland says. "How about we rest you on the couch, and then we can make the cookies when you're feeling better?"

"Can I watch a show?"

"Yes." He glances at Aubree. "Can you help her out?"

Aubree stands, patting her stomach. "I could use the rest too." Together, they walk off to the living room, leaving me alone with Ryland.

We didn't mention anything about the early morning wake-up call when I arrived at the grave earlier. He explained to Mac that he ran into a door, and that's why his face was bruised and he had a stitch above his eye. She asked him why on earth he would run into a door, and he told her it was because he wasn't paying attention.

Meanwhile, I felt Aubree staring me down, not necessarily angry but confused. I think we're all confused at this point. We were able to honor Cassidy. I silently sobbed as I watched Mac hug Cassidy's gravestone for what seemed like forever, telling her how much she misses her. I thought my heart was shattering all over again. *It's not fair.* This little girl needs her mommy. At the glass beach, Mac picked out a few stones for the collection she started with Cassidy. We then made grilled cheese sandwiches and had pie at the farm. *It's exactly what Cassidy would have wanted.*

All the while, the awkwardness from this morning floats over us, and now that Mac is off in the living room with Aubree, I know it's my time to talk to Ryland.

"Can we talk?" I ask him.

"Yeah," he says, surprising me. I thought I'd have to work a little harder to get his attention. But I'm sure he's emotionally exhausted and has no fight left in him. *He looks so exhausted.*

He stands from the table and brings the empty plates to the sink before nodding toward the back porch. Following him, I open the squeaky screen door and step out onto the small back porch with a view of the potato fields.

He sits in one of the white wicker chairs, and I take a seat in the other.

He doesn't give me a chance to speak as he starts the conversation. "Are you seeing him?"

I shake my head. "No. But I'll be honest, Ryland, it's not from my lack of trying. He wouldn't make a move. He's told me no several times."

He glances up at me. I can see anger in his expression, but there's also heart-wrenching pain. *This has been a weird day for him.* "You were trying . . . given everything between me and Hayes?"

Yeah, this won't be easy because technically, I betrayed my brother, but I figure I should at least try to explain to him.

"I want to tell you the truth, Ryland, but I need you to stay and listen to the whole thing, okay? Promise me, you won't walk away."

His jaw clenches, but he leans back in his chair and nods. "Promise."

"Thank you." I smooth my hand over my leggings and mentally tell myself I can do this. "So as you know, I failed out of this semester. I didn't know what to do, so I came back to be with Matt, and I was going to figure out my path from there. Matt broke up with me immediately and told me he only stayed with me because Cassidy was sick. He told me to gather my stuff, and that's when I found the Grammy he stole from Hayes. Technically, I was there when he stole it, but I thought I'd be the bigger person and return it while trying to get Matt fired because I'm spiteful, apparently."

That causes Ryland to smirk, but only for a moment. "It's why no one wants to cross your path."

Seeing that he's a little more at ease than this morning, I feel better with my story as I move forward. "Hayes caught me dropping the Grammy off and told me that he knew I was a part of it. He had already fired Matt, and well, he told me he needed help with some stuff around his house. He was going to pay well, and I needed money. So I took the job." Ryland rubs the side of his jaw but doesn't say anything, so I keep going. "I was organizing his life, and he was trying to write some new songs. Pretty sure he still is. To keep it a secret, I lied about where I was going every day because I didn't want you to think I wasn't on your side with whatever had happened between you and Hayes. But the more I got to know him, the more I saw a different side of him, a side that I'm sure you saw in him before you two lost your way. I'd never known that side of him, so it was fascinating, and I started to like him."

Ryland glances at me, and I shrug.

"I'm sorry, but I did. And the more I showed him that, the more he pushed me away. The more he told me he wouldn't go there. The more he told me that you, Ryland, you are the one who matters, not him. He wouldn't let me grow close out of fear that it would ruin my relationship with you."

Ryland slowly nods as he goes back to staring out at the potato fields.

"Yesterday, I was upset about a lot of things. I won't get into it, but I decided to get drunk. I made an ass of myself, and before I could hurt anyone or myself, Hayes brought me back to my apartment. He stayed the night because he knew I was drunk and wanted to keep an eye on me. Trust me when I say he wouldn't make a move. He made it clear he'd never cross that line with me. What you saw today, what you heard about last night was just him taking care of me."

"I got a text from Ethel that she saw you and Hayes walking back to your place last night. I saw the text this morning and saw red."

"I completely understand. I wasn't honest with you, and it must have been a shock. I'm sorry, Ryland. I should have told you the truth from the very beginning, but I was embarrassed."

"So this entire time, you've been working for him? It hasn't been an internship?"

I shake my head. "No, no internship. I've been sorting through fan mail."

"Jesus, Hattie."

"I know, I'm sorry. I didn't know what to do after I failed my midterms. I was scared, nervous to tell you. You and Aubree were already dealing with so much. When Hayes offered the job, I knew it would at least give me an excuse for being back in town. Trust me, I know it's not right, and I felt guilty when I lied to you."

He rubs his temples with his fingers. "So you've been sorting mail."

"Mainly." I swallow hard. "And trying to figure out what I want to do with my life." He leans back in his chair again and sighs. "I'm sorry, Ryland."

"I know you are," he says softly. "None of this has been easy on us, and navigating through what I can only describe as a masterclass of how to fuck over a family has been a goddamn nightmare."

"Mostly for you and Aubree."

"For all of us," he says, now looking me in the eyes. And there he is, my older brother. The anger is gone. The betrayal has disappeared, and to my surprise, he reaches over and takes my hand in his, offering me a gentle smile. It's enough to cause tears to well in my eyes. "Don't cry," he says.

"Hard not to," I say. "I thought . . . I thought you were going to hate me forever."

He shakes his head. "No, I could never, and I'm sorry I said some shitty things to you. I never should have said any of it."

"I get it," I say. "I probably would have reacted the same way if the roles were reversed."

"Nonetheless, it was uncalled for, and you must know, no matter what, I'll always love you, Hattie. That will never change."

"Thank you," I say softly.

He pulls his hand away. "How did, uh, things end with you and Hayes when I left?"

I shake my head. "Not well. I found this on the floor. I think it was in his back pocket and fell out when you two were wrestling." I hold out an envelope and watch his eyes fall on it.

"What's that?"

"It's a letter from Cassidy. She sent it to Hayes. He knew about it and never told me. We got in a fight over it, and I told him to leave."

Ryland scratches the side of his jaw. "What did she say? That she wants me to be friends with Hayes again?"

Stunned, I ask, "How did you know?"

"She said the same thing to me in my letter," he replies.

"Wait, you got a letter too?"

"I did. Aubree and Abel as well."

"What?" I sit taller. "Did she leave me one?"

Ryland shakes his head. "Not that I know of. There was nothing given to us to give to you."

"Really?" I ask, feeling the wind knocked straight from my lungs. "Why wouldn't she leave one with me?"

"Can't be sure." Ryland pushes his hand through his thick

hair. *She really didn't write me anything. Why? Why was school the only thing she thought I needed?* They all got letters. Everyone but me. "She told Aubree she believed she could make the farm bigger and better than it is, since Aubree cares so much about the earth and plants. She told me that I'd make a great father, and it's why she chose me to take care of Mac, and then she told me to clear things up with Hayes because I needed the help." *But what could Hayes offer that I couldn't? He's off touring the world . . .*

"What did she say to Abel?" My throat is tight, so I can only whisper the words out.

"That she would always love him," Ryland says, his voice tightening. "They were close, closer than I think you ever knew. I truly think they were in love at some point, but he never made a move because she was my sister." He pulls on the back of his neck, looking sick about it. "Abel and I never talk about it because I know how much it hurts him that she's gone." He pauses. "Those flowers you saw at Cassidy's grave were from him. He visits often. It's why he's so involved in Mac's life because he wants to hold Cassidy close to him."

"Jesus," I say, my throat tight from the emotions running through me.

"But she also told Abel to help bring me and Hayes back together."

"She did?"

He nods. "She did. She's told everyone."

"So why didn't you listen?"

"Taking care of Mac, working at the school, and coaching the baseball team is hard enough as it is. Reaching out to someone touring around the country would only add to the mess of my life. It was easier to ignore it. Easier to stay angry."

"Are you angry still?" I ask.

"I don't know what I am," he answers. "This entire time, I was convinced it was Hayes. The transgression had him written all over it. At that point in our lives, he was drinking a lot, doing some drugs. He wasn't in the right frame of mind, so when Samantha said he was the one who got her pregnant, it was easy to believe. Especially since he started to get noticed by some labels, and I . . . well . . . I was struggling to make something of myself. Sam's confession—her infidelity—did me in. I was done. I settled back into Almond Bay and clung to my grudge, not willing to let it go."

"Are you willing now?" I ask.

"I don't know." He drags his hand over his face, avoiding the laceration over his eye. "I think I might need some time."

"I understand."

"I need some time with everything," he continues. "I know why you lied, but I'm still trying to comprehend it all." His eyes meet mine. "But in the meantime, you can stay here, at the house, in Cassidy's room."

"What?" I say, confused.

"Do you really think you can live in that apartment after we trashed it?"

"I guess I haven't thought about it."

"Well, you're welcome here unless you want to go somewhere else."

"I mean . . . I don't have anywhere else to go."

"Not Hayes's house?" he asks me with a quirk to his brow.

"Yeah, I don't think that's going anywhere." I twist my lips to the side, thinking about the dejected look on his face as he walked out of my apartment. "Plus, I don't think I'm his type."

Ryland shakes his head. "Not from what I could tell. The moment I pushed you off me, he went feral." Ryland touches his sore jaw. "Not sure I've ever taken a punch that hard." He turns to me. "Sorry about pushing you away. I was out of my mind. Are you okay?"

I nod. "I'm fine." And then, for some reason, looking in my older brother's eyes does something to me. I get emotional, and tears well up in my eyes. I wave my hand in front of my face and say, "Jesus, I don't think I've ever cried this much."

He reaches out and takes my hand in his again. "You're allowed to cry, Hattie. To feel emotion."

"I know, but I don't know what I'm crying over." I let out a deep sigh as Ryland squeezes my hand. "I just feel so lost. I failed at the one thing Cassidy wanted me to succeed at. I fell for a guy I shouldn't have fallen for. I betrayed your trust and made a complete fool of myself." I shake my head. "I'm just . . . I'm not in a place I should be mentally, and I don't know how to get out of it."

"Maybe you need to slow down," Ryland says. "Take some time to find yourself again." He wets his lips and adds, "And if you like Hayes, maybe you pursue that."

"Ryland—"

"I'm serious." He looks me dead in the eyes. "Life is too short, Hattie, not to go for the things that matter. Cassidy didn't go after what she wanted out of fear that it might hurt me. And I don't want the same thing to happen to you. If you like Hayes, go for it."

"But what about your relationship with him? Cassidy wanted you two to figure things out, to reconnect. If I get in the way of that—"

"You won't," he says, squeezing my hand again.

"Does that mean you're going to try to make things right with him?"

"I mean, for Cassidy, I probably should, but it won't happen overnight. I see the toll it's taken on Abel, and I'll be damned if I get in the way of the happiness of another one of my sisters. Because you, Aubree, and Mac are all I've got. You're my core. I might have been absent, strict, and bossy over the past few months, but this morning, with the fight, with watching Mac's heart pour into her mother's grave, it's been a swift kick to the balls. You're what I care about. You three are what makes me happy. And I can't lose that."

275

"I don't want to lose you either," I say, tears streaming down my face. "I thought . . . I thought you and Aubree were moving on without me. Getting Aubree to slow down and take a breath felt impossible. You were both guarded when I came back, and I know we talked about it, but I don't know, our lives are headed in different directions. I feel like I'm clinging on . . . holding on to a part of yours."

"I'm sorry we made you feel that way," Ryland says. "But in all honesty, I think Aubree and I have both been trying to just stay afloat. It's not an excuse, it's just a way of life right now."

"Then let me help."

Ryland shakes his head. "You need to focus on you right now. Because you're only as good to us as you are healthy. You were so close to Cassidy. You need to mourn. You need to find who you want to be after the death of your sister. We'll be here, but we need you to find you first. If failing your midterms has taught us anything, it's that."

"How is that fair?" I ask. "You're sacrificing so much."

Ryland shakes his head. "No, we're finding a new normal, and I think I'm starting to come around to it." He dreamily looks toward the porch screen door. "The other night, Mac came up to me and cuddled on my lap, resting her head on my chest. She told me she loved me and that I'm her best friend." That, of course, brings more tears to my eyes. Ryland's eyes well up too. "I love that little girl, and I think we're finally starting to find a new normal, even if it's hard. I'm not saying we're fully there yet, but there's promise. Aubree is the same way. You don't need to worry about us. Worry about you."

I bite the corner of my lip as I realize he's right. How can I possibly help if I'm struggling with who I should be. I've lost so much in the last couple of months—my sister, my school, my tool of a boyfriend . . . *my purpose.* I might need to take a second to breathe.

I might need to take a second away from everything, even Hayes, so I can truly find some inner peace.

"Thank you, Ryland."

"No need to thank me. That's what big brothers are for." He stands from his chair. "Now, let's go check out that room."

"Why don't you take it?" I say. "I can take the couch."

He shakes his head. "I can't stomach it. But I know it's something that might help you, being close to Cassidy again. Who knows, maybe you might find what you need in there."

He tugs me to my feet, and together, we walk into the house.

Chapter Fifteen

HAYES

I strum my guitar as I lie against the couch in my living room, surrounded by the piles Hattie made and a bottle of tequila next to my propped-up foot on the coffee table.

It's been one of those days.

Yesterday was . . . well, it was something else.

Ryland has one hell of a fucking right hook, and today, I'm feeling the effects of it. Abel did a house call last night, checking in to make sure I didn't need any stitches or anything like that. He just told me to ice my whole face and then went on his way.

We didn't talk about what happened exactly.

We didn't even talk that much at all, and I know it's because he's trying to stay out of it. I don't blame him. If I was in his shoes, I'd be the same way.

I lost control yesterday. The minute I saw Hattie get pushed into the dresser, I saw red, and I unleashed. Ryland was my punching bag and we both took full advantage of the opportunity, all of that pent-up anger between us, all of the miscommunication, the years of not talking, it all was brought out at that moment. I'm not sure what would have happened if Abel hadn't stepped in, but when I felt Hattie drape herself across me to get me to stop, I immediately regretted it all.

And the look on her face, the scared look, it's been on replay in my head ever since.

I thought about texting her, about apologizing again, but I figured there was a reason she hadn't reached out to communicate with me, and it was probably because she didn't want to see me after seeing the monster I became. After the information I withheld from her.

Which has led me to drinking alone in my goddamn house while mindlessly strumming my guitar and writing down everything I like about her in my notepad.

Her freckles.

Her mesmerizing eyes.

Her strong will.

Her temper.

Her patience.

Her ability to see right through me, to my very soul.

Her fucking lips . . .

Jesus Christ, those lips.

I knew the moment she kissed me, I was supposed to pull away, but nothing would stop me from at least tasting her. She was tentative and nervous, but the moment I reciprocated the kiss, she gained confidence and rocked my goddamn world.

It was soft, tender, and irresistible. I didn't want to part from her, but I didn't want to take advantage. She was drunk, and I knew the kiss had to end because she wasn't of sound mind.

And yesterday morning, when I woke up with her still in my arms, I had a moment of euphoria before it was all flipped upside down.

"You fucking idiot," I mutter as I lean forward and grab

my bottle of tequila. I take a large swig just as a car pulls up in the driveway. I try to get a read on who it is, but I can't tell. A car door slams, and I pray it's Hattie.

I want to see her.

I need to see her.

I need to make sure she's okay.

That she doesn't hate me even though I hate myself.

When there's a knock on my door, my heart skips a beat and I set the tequila down. I straighten my shirt and adjust my hat to make sure it's not askew or hanging off my head. Thinking I look somewhat presentable, I open the door to a resigned Ryland.

Fuck.

His eyes lift to mine, and he says, "Can we talk?"

"Do I need a bodyguard?"

He shakes his head so I let him in.

Hands in his pockets, he steps inside and looks around, taking in the piles of fan mail that Hattie has made.

"Fan mail," I say as I move toward the couch and take a seat. I nod toward the chair that is clear of paper, and Ryland sits down as well. His eyes fall to the bottle, and I can feel his judgment, so I say, "Rough two days."

He touches his jaw. "Same."

Awkwardly, I sit there, wanting to reach for the bottle but unsure if I should. After another few seconds of silence, I ask, "Want some?"

"Was waiting for you to ask."

I head to the kitchen, where I grab two tumblers and bring them to the living room. As I pour us a generous portion, I think about how much Ryland has changed since the last time we hung out. He's taller, oddly, with at least thirty more pounds of muscle packed on, and he has a full beard, making him seem more mature and older. It's as if we've time-hopped, and there's no evidence of what happened in between.

I hand him his drink, and we both take a swig before settling into our seats.

Unable to take the silence, I say, "How's Hattie?"

Yup, I'm desperate for any information, even if it's from her brother who hates me.

"Okay," he says. "She moved into the house."

"Oh . . . cool," I say even though I know the main reason she did was because the apartment is covered in our blood and abuse. "So you two talked? She's not—"

"Dead to me? No, of course not, Farrow. I love my sister. What I said was wrong, and I've apologized."

"Good." At least there's that. Hattie's not completely alone.

Ryland rests his arms on his legs and looks up at me. "I came here because . . . well because of this." He hands me the letter from Cassidy, the one I gave to Hattie. The flap to the back has been unsealed, and there's a splatter of blood across the corner. "Read it," he says.

My pulse races as I unfold the piece of paper.

My stomach drops from the first paragraph.

I know I'm probably the last person you expected to hear from, but as you might know—or might not know—I'm really sick, and I'm getting my affairs in order. Morbid, I know, but as I lie here in my bed, knowing my time is coming to an end, I realize I don't want to leave this earth without at least trying to make my mark.

Fuck.

I couldn't imagine being in that position, knowing I'm leaving so much behind and preparing for it. And what does she ask for? *To make things right. To fix things.* To look past myself, and find a way to help Ryland—help him with *her* baby girl— and be there *for* him. Guilt swarms me because she's right. I should have offered to help the moment I found out about Cassidy. I should have tried to bury the hatchet then with Abel's assistance, but my pride got in the way.

And then . . . the little nugget at the end of Cassidy

throwing Hattie under the bus. I inwardly smile. Hattie, the secret fan, I fucking love it.

When I look up at him, he says, "I don't know how to move on from here, how to patch things up between us, and I'm sure as hell not making any promises, but there's one thing I know for damn sure. I'll do anything for my sisters, just like they'll do anything for me."

"So . . . do you want to be friends or something?" I ask awkwardly.

He lifts his drink to his lips. "Not sure if we could ever get there again, but I can work on not wanting to punch your face in whenever I see you."

"Fair," I say and then take a sip of my drink as well. "For what it's worth, I was telling the truth. I never made a move on Samantha . . . ever. I know I was going through a rough time when it all happened, but there's one thing I can stand by, and that's not fucking over my friends."

He stares at his drink and says, "I think I can believe that. Abel said the same thing, but you know how it is. You believe something for so long, it's going to take a second to process."

"Yeah, I get it."

He meets my eyes. "But I'm going to work on it."

"I appreciate that."

He stands from the chair and sets his drink on the coffee table. "Okay, I need to get out of here and pick up Mac before practice."

I follow him to the door. "What you're doing, taking care of MacKenzie, it's really admirable, Ry."

"I wouldn't have it any other way." He pulls my front door open, but before leaving, he turns back to me and says, "Not sure what's going on with Hattie, but I'll tell you this, you fuck her over, you hurt her, and I won't have one single problem having a repeat of yesterday. Understood?"

I nod.

And with that, he takes off.

What do I make of that? Is he suggesting he'd be okay with me pursuing Hattie?

After the crap we've been through—after I've pushed her away several times—would *she* even want that? Me? I have my doubts. I've missed her, but I'm fairly certain I brought that on myself.

▭

I PACE MY BEDROOM, staring at my phone.

It's been a week since I've spoken or seen Hattie, and now I'm starting to lose my mind.

I wanted to give her space, some time to come to terms with how I acted, but now that it's been a week, I'm in panic mode. At the very least, I want to have a chance to speak with her and explain myself. To convince her I'm not the barbarian she saw. That I didn't hold out on telling her about the letter to keep her from connecting with her sister.

That's why I'm staring at my phone, trying to figure out how to text her.

I quit my pacing and read over my text one more time.

Hayes: *Hey, Hattie. I know it's been a week since we last spoke, but I just wanted to reiterate how sorry I am. I'd love to see you or at least talk to you.*

It reads a little desperate, but then again, that's exactly how I feel, so why mask it?

Not fucking caring at this moment, I send the text, and then I wait.

I take a seat on my bed, watching, waiting, and when the text says it's been read, I feel my chest expand with hope, but with every second that goes by, I find that hope slipping away.

And after what feels like an hour with still no response, I realize, maybe . . . maybe she just doesn't want to talk to me, and that, fuck, that hurts.

"ARE you sure you don't want to go out for a walk?" I ask my grandma, who's sitting in her chair, staring out the window.

The moment I walked into her room, I realized how stuffy it was and opened the window for her. She was happy to see me, but also distracted. She can't stop looking outside, and for the life of me, I can't figure out why. I came here for a distraction, but she's barely talking to me.

"I can't walk, remember? I'm dying."

This again . . . Jesus.

I spoke to Abel about it, and he said she might be dying because she's losing her mind. But other than that, she's recovered from her fall remarkably well, thanks to her nurse aide. So . . . my rush to come back to Almond Bay wasn't really necessary. In hindsight, I'm glad I did even though the main reason I want to stay isn't talking to me at the moment.

"You're not dying," I say, dragging my hand over my face. "Abel said you were fine."

"What does he know?" she huffs.

"He's a doctor. He knows a lot."

"A small-town doctor, they aren't as educated."

"Abel graduated from Stanford."

"Is that supposed to impress me?" she asks as she watches a couple walk along the street. Jesus Christ, she looks like a dog ready to pounce on anything that crosses her turf.

"Some people might find graduating from Stanford impressive," I reply.

"I don't. Anyone can get into Stanford these days."

Also not true, but there's no use in fighting her. She's in a spiteful mood today, so arguing will get me nowhere.

"So is that a no to walking outside? I can push you around in a wheelchair."

Slowly, she faces me and folds her hands on her lap. "Is

there a reason you're being incessant about going outside when I'm perfectly content looking out the window?"

"Uh, I just thought that you might want to experience outside firsthand rather than from a window. Fresh air might help prevent you from dying so soon."

"I enjoy being outside like this. That way, I don't have to bump into that tart of a woman, Ethel, who inserts herself in everyone's business."

"I can understand that," I say, just recently being a victim of Ethel's meddling.

"But if you aren't content with just staring out the window with me, I suppose you can tell me what's going on in your life."

That's one way to put it.

"Perhaps you can tell me why your face has scratches on it? Are you getting into trouble again? There was a ruckus that you were fighting. Is that what happened? You got in a fight?"

"I did," I answer honestly. "With Ryland Rowley."

"The Rowley boy?" she asks, sitting a touch forward now, her eyes now on me rather than the streets. I see how it is.

"Yes. The Rowley boy."

"Why on earth would you get in a fight with him? Isn't he taking care of a little girl now? You can't be punching his face in."

I chuckle. "I didn't punch his face in, but we did get a few jabs on each other. And it's a long story, but he thought I slept with his sister."

Grandma's eyes widen. "Hayes, you didn't."

"I didn't," I say. "But I was hanging out with her, and well, he didn't like it. We got in a fight, and then we worked things out. It's all good now."

"I guess that's how men solve their problems, with fists rather than words."

"We used words . . . after the fists, but we used words."

She gives me a *not buying it* look. "So what about the girl?

Are you with her?"

"No," I say on a sigh as I glance down at my hands. "I think I scared her. She's not talking to me. Probably for the best, you know?"

"Why?" Gran asks, true concern in her voice.

"Well, she's twelve years younger than me, and she's been struggling with a few things, not to mention I've turned her down several times, so I think she's given up. I just don't think it was meant to be."

"So why are you sad?"

"I'm not sad," I say.

"Do not lie to me, boy," she says, holding out her shaky finger. "I know when my grandson is sad, and you are sad."

I tug on my hair, trying to put this into words. "I don't know, Gran. I just . . . I liked her. She was different. There's a lot more about her to know, but what I do know, I like."

"So go for it then."

"She's not talking to me."

Gran waves her hand in dismissal. "That means nothing. Sometimes I wouldn't talk to your grandfather because he was an idiot, but that didn't stop me from loving him. You just have to find a way to mend the bridge between you two. Unless . . . does the brother not approve?"

"No, I think he does. I mean, he told me not to hurt her."

Gran nods her head. "Ah, then yes, he's given you permission. Therefore, take it."

"I don't know."

She lifts her cane from the side of her chair and pokes me with it.

"Ow," I say, rubbing my leg, but she does it again. "Gran, what the hell."

"I said go get her. Now don't you dare disappoint me. Understood? Remember, I need great-grandbabies before I die."

Right, it always comes down to that.

"Now leave, I don't want to see you again until you've fixed things with her."

"But—"

She points her cane toward the door. "I said . . . leave."

Okay . . .

"HAYES, YOO-HOO," Ethel says from the balcony of Five Six Seven Eight. "Are you coming to the talent show this Friday?"

After the conversation with Gran, I didn't quite find the courage to approach Hattie, so instead, like the self-destructive person I am, I ignored life, drank, and described Hattie's eyes in great detail in my notebook . . . over and over again. After the fourth round of talking about her freckles, I decided I was losing it and needed some fresh air. I met up with Abel at the Hot Pickle for a sandwich, and he told me about his day of removing a boil, a few warts, and giving Rodney a testicle exam. I told him to fuck off with his disgusting stories, which only made him laugh.

"I don't think so, Ethel," I call out as I glance toward The Almond Store, hoping Hattie's in there. Yup, that's what I've resorted to. Casually strolling the streets of Almond Bay, looking for her.

"Shy?" she asks with a cheeky grin.

"Yeah, that's it." I smile back.

"Well, we'd love to see you, and of course, if you happen to regale me with some gossip of what's happening between you and the Rowleys, I wouldn't mind that either."

"I'm sure you wouldn't," I say as I step up to The Almond Store and pull on the door, the bell above ringing as I enter. Aubree is at the counter, hovering over an iPad as she looks up.

When she sees me, her expression remains neutral. "Can I help you?" she asks.

I stand there like an idiot, unsure of what to say because I came in here hoping to see Hattie, but now that I know she's not in here, I feel stupid. "I don't know why I'm in here."

She folds her hands together. "Really? Because it seems like maybe you're looking for my sister."

Jesus, nothing gets past these siblings.

And I'm not going to stand here, bullshitting her when clearly that's the reason I came into the store.

"Is she here?"

Aubree shakes her head. "Nope."

Dammit.

"Okay . . . well, I don't want to bother you."

"The least you could do is buy something now that you're in here." She smirks, and I have a feeling she's about to milk this moment.

But she's right. I'm in here, so I might as well buy something. "What do you want me to buy?"

"From the looks of the dark circles under your eyes, I'd assume you've gone through a decent amount of alcohol over the past week or so. Maybe replenish with some almond vodka. And that shirt, it's nice and all, but an Almond Store shirt might look better on you, especially the light blue one. Oh, and you can't come into the store without purchasing a few bottles of almond extract, some cookies, and on an unrelated note, maybe hire someone to clean the apartment upstairs since you destroyed the little sanctuary that Cassidy and Mac used to sleep in."

Shit. How could I have forgotten about the apartment upstairs? That's the reason Hattie's now living with Ryland, right? Because the place she used to stay in is destroyed.

I pull on the back of my neck and step forward. "You're right. I'm sorry about the mess—"

"Oh, don't worry, I know you're not entirely at fault, but Ryland doesn't have the time to clean it up given the fact that he's raising a child, coaching the best baseball team in the state, and teaching, but you know, since you're strolling the streets of Almond Bay at three in the afternoon, it seems like you might have a little more time on your hands."

I haven't spent that much time with Aubree, especially since she's grown up, but Jesus, is she straightforward. Just like Hattie.

"Yeah, I can do that."

"And purchase those other items, right? Because I do have a business to run, after all, and it's all about the bottom line."

"Put whatever you want into a bag, and I'll buy it."

"Risky, I might ring you up for five hundred dollars' worth of items."

"I really don't care, Aubree."

She tilts her head to the side, studying me. After a few seconds, she says, "You like her, don't you?"

No use in hiding it. I nod. "Yeah, I do."

"Interesting." She moves away from the counter and walks around the store, grabbing vodka, almond extract, and a bag of almonds. After picking out a shirt, she pauses and says, "Are you a large?"

"Yeah."

Then she goes back to shopping, even grabbing me a cookbook, something I know I probably won't ever use. "This should do it." She brings everything back to the counter and starts packing it up in a brown paper bag. "You know, if you like her, you should probably ask her out. I heard Ryland wouldn't necessarily chop off your dick if you did."

"She won't answer me."

Aubree glances up, a hint of surprise in her eyes. "Hmm, that's interesting as well." She taps away on her iPad and then turns the screen toward me. Two hundred fifty dollars.

Yup, Aubree is a sly one.

I pull out my wallet and stick my credit card into the card reader.

"She's been a little lost lately," Aubree says. "Stuck in

Cassidy's room. Not saying much. I think she needs to have some fun."

The chip reader beeps at me, and I remove my card. "Receipt?" Aubree asks.

"No, I'm good."

She hands me the bag. "I'd say clean up the apartment and see what happens from there. If she does approach you, show her some fun. She needs to find herself again, and even though it pains me to say this, you might be the person to help her."

"Okay." I turn to walk away, but she calls out to me.

"Where do you think you're going?" she asks. "The apartment is that way." She thumbs toward the back of the shop.

Right . . .

I head to the back and up the stairs to the apartment, where I open the door and take in the mess in front of me. The area rug is twisted up into a ball with dried blood splattered around the floor. One of the drawers on the dresser is crooked and broken, the chair in the corner is upturned, and pictures that once hung on the wall are broken on the floor.

Jesus. *It's a mess.*

Kind of like me.

I'm a successful solo artist with a shitload of money to my name, but being back here has confirmed something I've partied and fucked to keep at bay. *I'm a mess.* Apart from Gran and Abel, I have no one else who gives a shit about me. And I'm not exactly surprised by that, either.

Maybe cleaning up this room reflects what's needed in my life too.

Looks like I have my work cut out for me.

I've never shied away from hard work, though, and if Gran is right, repairing this room—*repairing me*—might be the bridge needed to also set things right with Hattie. Because I want that.

I want that with every piece of my heart.

Chapter Sixteen

HATTIE

I stare up at the ceiling of Cassidy's room, unmoving.

Not sure I've moved from this position in over a week, other than some food and bathroom breaks.

The moment I walked into Cassidy's room, I was broken.

Just destroyed.

I spent hours crying on her bed, her scent surrounding everything I touched or looked at.

Her little trinkets around her room like the jewelry box I used to play with when I was a little girl, the same jewelry box Mac will play with. Her picture frames lined up along her dresser. Pictures of me and her at my high school graduation, where she told me how proud of me she was. Pictures of her and Mac when Mac was first born. A picture of all of us in front of The Almond Store with a now open sign in our hands.

Then there's the quilt we made together with all our old T-shirts. The scrapbook I made for her of Mac's first year of life. The table runners we found in an antique store on our trip to the redwoods. Her favorite perfume she only used for special occasions. And so many more things that I've just laid here and stared at, remembering, reminding myself of what a beautiful human she was and crying over the fact that it isn't fair she was taken so soon.

But despite falling into a deep hole of depression, I've made dinner for Ryland and Mac every night until Ryland told me I didn't have to anymore. When I asked him why . . . he said because he couldn't eat one more burnt thing, and he meant that in the nicest way.

I couldn't even argue. I struggled to eat my own food.

So now, as I lie here, staring up at the ceiling again, not helping with dinner, I try to think about what I should do with my life. And just like every other time I think about it, I'm blank. Because I'd have spoken to Cassidy about this. "I know you wanted me to finish school, Cass, but what then? You were meant to be here with me, lending your immeasurable wisdom into my life. *What should I do next when breathing without you feels too utterly painful?*"

My phone beeps to notify me of a text, pulling me out of my thoughts. I lift the screen up to see a text from Maggie. She's been a freaking saint through all of this. She's checked up on me every day, multiple times during the day, and has made me laugh. She's listened and even used some tough love on me when Mac was complaining that I smelled at the dining room table.

The overnight delivery of hygiene products from Maggie pushed me right into the shower.

I open up her text.

Maggie: *My bride for this weekend just told me she slept with the best man, and she was wondering if I could help break the news to her fiancé.*

I flip to my stomach, relieved for the break in my thoughts.

Hattie: *Stop. Are you serious?*

Maggie: Dead serious. She showed me the text messages from the best man who's begging her not to say anything, but she feels guilty.

Hattie: Are you going to help her?

Maggie: I mean . . . I know I said I was full service, but I think this is slightly outside the parameters of my job. I pride myself on happily ever afters, not breaking people up.

Hattie: When did the bride sleep with the best man?

Maggie: Years ago. She and the now-fiancé were broken up for a day. Like a whole Ross and Rachel type thing. She got drunk with the best man, and they did it. Well, just oral. She went into detail about the whole experience, and I learned a trick or two. According to her, the best man has a crooked wee wee, which now, when I see him, I keep looking at his crotch to see if said wee wee is trying to fit in his pocket.

Hattie: LOL. Is it?

Maggie: Haven't been able to confirm yet, but I shall keep you abreast.

Hattie: Obviously that would be appreciated. And to circle back, if it happened years ago, I'd tell her not to say anything. The best man is already struggling with the crooked wee wee, so he's suffered enough.

Maggie: Great advice. Also, it will only ruin what they have, so I don't think it's smart to say anything. I mean, the moment to say something would have been when they got back together, but she missed the mark on that.

Hattie: If I were in her shoes, I'd have probably been so happy I was back together with the non-crooked wee wee that I wouldn't mention the mishap. So I get where she's coming from. But the best man . . . I mean, that's rough. Does he have feelings for her?

Maggie: Not that I'm aware of. He's been super helpful and willing to do anything when it comes to setup, carrying things, directing. He's been the VIP.

Hattie: Guilt will do that to you.

Maggie: Exactly. Well, this was helpful. How are you? Burn anything lately?

Hattie: Ryland took that responsibility away from me.

Maggie: *Smart. I'd have done the same. Are you still catatonic in Cassidy's bed?*

Hattie: *If I tell you yes, are you going to yell at me?*

Maggie: *Hattie! You know I love you, but lying around in your dead sister's room isn't going to do anything for you other than continue to put you in a deeper state of sadness.*

Hattie: *And it has. I honestly don't want to do anything.*

Maggie: *Not healthy.*

Hattie: *I know, but I don't have anything to do, anywhere to go. Ryland and Aubree won't let me help with anything because they said I won't be here for long, and they don't want to rely on my help only to lose it, which I get.*

Maggie: *Well, why not go back to work, you know . . . with Hayes?*

Hattie: *I quit that, remember?*

Maggie: *Have you spoken to him at all?*

Hattie: *No. I know Ryland has, but I honestly don't know what to say to him. I don't know where we stand. It's all just . . . up in the air.*

Maggie: *Well, that won't change if you KEEP STAYING IN BED!*

Hattie: *Are you trying to tell me something?*

Maggie: *If I have to drive up there to drag you out of bed, I'm going to be VERY, VERY angry. Do you understand? It won't bode well for you.*

Hattie: *Are you talking about pulling back on your best friend card?*

Maggie: *Yes, and I'm not even afraid to say it. Now, get your ass out of bed and do something!*

———

I WALK through the screen door of the house, and both Ryland and Aubree look up from where they're eating breakfast at the dining room table. They exchange glances and look back at me.

Aubree swallows her eggs and says, "Were you . . . were you outside?"

I grip my shoe and stretch out my quad as I say, "Yes, I went for a run."

"Like . . . exercise? Outside?" Ryland asks before taking a bite of bacon.

Mac comes running into the room, her hands still wet from going to the bathroom, and she stops as she takes me in. "You know how to walk?"

Dear God, if a four-year-old is insulting me, then it was definitely time I got out of bed.

"Yes," I say, as I reach for her, but she jumps away and goes over to Ryland, who wraps his arm around her and pulls her into a hug.

"She's sweaty," Mac says.

"Better than smelly," I say.

"I can guarantee you smell right now," Aubree says.

"Aren't you a welcoming family?"

"We do the best we can." Aubree takes her plate to the sink and then walks up to me. "Glad to see you out of the room. Think you could stop by the store today?"

"Really?" I ask, excited.

"Yeah, I'd appreciate it," she says before waving to everyone and taking off.

I head into the kitchen for some water. "What was that about?"

Ryland shrugs his shoulders. "I don't know. She's a wild card."

"She is." I take his plate from him and rinse it off in the sink, then place it in the dishwasher. "Do you need anything today? I can run by the store or run some errands."

Ryland shakes his head. "We're headed over to By the Slice tonight, right, Mac?"

She nods as she ducks under the dining room table with

Chewy Charles. "Yup, and we're going to The Talkies to watch *Frozen*."

I glance over at Ryland, who dramatically rolls his eyes. I think the poor guy has seen that movie at least three times a week since taking Mac under his care. Sometimes, I swear it looks like he enters a room like Elsa, chest forward, arms spread, but of course I'd never say that to him. I keep that tucked away, at least for now.

"That sounds like fun."

"We'd invite you, but it's just for me and Uncle Ry Ry," Mac says as she rolls on her back, kicking her feet up in the air.

"Well, I wouldn't want to impose on your date."

"And Uncle Ry Ry said I can have Sour Patch Kids."

"If you eat all of your veggies first," Ryland says. "Don't forget that part."

"Piece of cake," Mac says.

"So you don't need me to do anything?" I ask Ryland.

"Take a shower. That's what I need you to do."

"Stop." I push at his shoulder. "You're going to give me a complex."

"Good, you need one to get you out of that bedroom." He leans against the counter and takes a sip of his coffee.

"Hey, I went for a run. That should be something."

"It is something," he says, growing serious. "And I think you taking the time to mourn is good. I'm not sure you did that when you were at school, but hiding out all by yourself in a room when you're going through something like that is also dangerous. So I'm seriously glad to see you doing something for you."

"What about you and Aubree?" I say. "You haven't had time to mourn."

"We have in our own way," Ryland says. "Hey, Mac? Go get your shoes on."

"Okey dokey," she says, taking off.

Ryland turns toward me. "I've had the chance to mourn with Mac. Sure, I had to take care of her while mourning, but I've still had that connection to Cassidy. Aubree has mourned while running the farm and shop. It's kept her busy, and I think both you and I know she does things her own way at this point. She's not one to really *be* in her emotions. But you, you're different, and even though I'm sad you didn't get to graduate this semester, I think it's important to get your head on straight."

"Thanks. And for what it's worth, I'm sorry about not graduating."

"I know you will," he says. "That's something Aubree and I have come to terms with."

"Do you think I'm letting her down?"

"Aubree?" he asks.

I shake my head. "Cassidy."

Ryland sets his empty cup in the sink. "No. I think she'd appreciate you taking small steps. Losing someone is one of the hardest things a human ever has to endure. Cassidy was always about being your authentic self, and that's what you're doing. If that means pretending to take an internship with my mortal enemy behind my back, then that's being you." He offers me a teasing smirk that makes me laugh.

"And you know what? I'd do it all over again."

"I wouldn't doubt it." He pulls me into a hug but then regrets it immediately. "Fuck, you're gross."

"Shut up." I push at his chest, making him laugh.

OKAY, so I don't want to admit it, but those soaps Maggie sent me smell amazing. I'll obviously never tell her that, but I keep sniffing my skin. And it's not like I haven't been showering, but stepping out of Cassidy's room, all stuffy and sucking in the air I keep recycling through my body, invigorates you. I swear my eyelashes have some natural lift now from experiencing fresh air.

After a nice, long shower where I scrubbed and shaved every orifice of my body, I lotioned up, added a touch of mascara, and let my hair air-dry into waves, only adding a touch of oil to the ends for some texture. I threw on a pair of jean shorts and one of my favorite Boston shirts. When I looked in the mirror, I was impressed with myself. I looked like a human.

And now that I'm headed into The Almond Store, I think Aubree might keel over from the sight of me.

I push through the door and notice a few tourists milling about, but when Aubree catches sight of me from behind the counter, her eyebrows shoot up.

Smiling, I walk up to her and say, "What do you think?"

"Am I supposed to compliment you?"

"Yes."

"I'm glad you smell better."

I roll my eyes and then join her behind the counter. "So what do you need help with?"

"I don't need help with anything. But I do think you should see something." She nods toward the back. "Go check out the apartment."

"You mean the trashed apartment? If you wanted me to clean it up, I wouldn't have worn my nice shirt."

She glances at my shirt and then back up to my eyes. "That's your nice shirt?"

"Glad you have no problem being a dick to me."

She chuckles. "Just go look at it."

Confused but also intrigued, I head up the stairs to the apartment. I open the door and—*oh my God.* It's spotless. Freshly painted. *Pristine.*

There is a new dresser to the right, next to a pink, retro mini fridge and matching microwave. A new beige and fluffy area rug covers the hardwood floors, while a soft olive green is fresh on the walls. A new bed positioned under the angled ceiling is now made up in soft white bedding, with one of Cassidy's quilts folded on the end. Pictures of the family in black and white hang around the space, and the chair in the corner has been reupholstered.

It's . . . gorgeous.

I can't believe she did this.

I walk back down to the store. Once Aubree's checked out the customers in front of her and sends them on their way, I pull my sister into a hug. "I can't believe you did that. When did you find the time?"

"I didn't," she says.

"What do you mean you didn't?"

She smirks. "Hayes has been working on it the last few days."

I feel my stomach dip from just the sound of his name. "H-Hayes did that?"

Aubree nods and leans against the counter. "Yup. I think he likes you . . . a lot. He asked me constantly if what he was picking out would be something you'd like. He even asked for pictures of the family. Did you notice the one picture with the lyrics of *The Reason* on it?"

"What? No."

"I suggested that. He was hesitant at first, but he ended up doing it. Super cute."

"So . . . he did that? For what? For me?"

She nods. "Yup. Now, I'm not saying to run over there and have his baby, but I do think there's an opportunity there, and if you're ready, you should at least explore it."

"I don't know, Aubree. I'm such a mess."

"You are," she says, not sugarcoating a damn thing. "But sometimes when we're a mess, we need someone to help us clean it up. Hayes might be that person."

I bite down on my lip, thinking about it. In all honesty, I've missed seeing him. I've missed going to his house, hearing him lightly strum his guitar in the background. I've missed his teasing and his interest in the little things like how to make cookies.

"I can see you're thinking about it," Aubree says, cutting through my thoughts. "How about this? When he was done, he begged me not to tell you he did it."

"He did?"

She nods. "Yup, he didn't want to take credit for it, but I don't know, I'm feeling generous. I think he deserves the credit."

"What am I supposed to do?" I ask.

"I think you go over there and at least talk to him. There's no doubt in my mind that he'd be relieved to see you." When I don't move right away, Aubree walks up to me, takes my hand in hers, and drags me toward the door.

"What are you doing?"

"Giving you the push you need. Now get out of here."

"Aubree, wait." She pauses, and I turn toward her. "What is this?"

"What is what?"

"This." I motion between us. "You're being . . . nice."

She looks at me confused. "Am I supposed to be mean to you?"

"When I first arrived in Almond Bay, it was almost like you couldn't even be in the same room as me, but now you're . . . well, you're talking to me. *Engaging.* What's with the change of heart?"

Understanding falls over her face as she says, "You know, sometimes when you're trying to stay afloat, you put blinders on to keep you from getting distracted. Ryland just helped me lift those blinders." She offers a soft smile. "Sorry if I made you feel like you didn't belong."

"You don't need to apologize. I can't imagine the kind of stress you and Ryland have been *and* are going through. I just wish you would let me help more."

"You will," she says. "In good time, but for now, you fix you. That's what Cassidy would want the most." I know she's right. "Now get out of here. I have a call with a lawyer, and I don't need you distracting me."

"A lawyer?" I ask. "Everything okay?"

She rolls her eyes. "Yeah, just some semantics to work out. Nothing you need to worry about."

"Okay," I say. "But you would tell me if something was wrong."

"Always. And nothing is wrong, okay? Don't come back here unless you have a story to tell about Hayes." *I can only hope it's a good story and not another one where I feel like I've failed you and Ryland.*

I GLANCE over at the Adirondack chair on Hayes's porch out of habit. Once you're scared twice, you don't forget it. During the whole drive over here, I was a ball of nerves.

Do I want to see Hayes? Of course. My heart has wings whenever he's around, and I feel it takes off with just one glance from him. But he's also turned me down so many times at this point that it's easy to fall under the impression he would do the same thing all over again.

With a very unsteady breath, I raise my hand to his door and knock loudly in case he's in his studio. From the living room, I hear him say, "Come in."

Was he expecting me?

That would be weird if he was unless Aubree told him.

Either way, I open his door and walk in only to find him sitting on his couch, guitar on his lap, his head turned down toward the strings, and the stacks of paper I made look untouched.

"Hey," I say softly, causing him to whip his head to the side in surprise.

"Hattie," he says, straightening up.

Okay, so he wasn't expecting me.

"Can I come in?"

"Yes, of course." He sets his guitar to the side and goes to stand, but I wave him off.

I move around the piles and approach him, taking in the soft waves of his hair on top of his head, the sharpness of his beard, and the surprise and awe in his eyes. *Hell, I've missed this man.* I'm not sure how it happened, but I grew attached to him over the small amount of time we spent together. And now that I'm near him again, I feel my pulse pick up and my mind begin to hope all over again.

Maybe this time will be different . . .

"How are you?" he asks as I stand in front of him, nervous.

I push my hair behind my ear. "Did you redo the apartment?"

He shifts uncomfortably but lightly nods. "I did."

"Why?" I ask.

"Because I ruined it, and I didn't want you to feel like you couldn't return. I wanted it to be a place for you to feel comfortable to stay."

"You didn't do it for any other reason?" I ask, still standing in front of him.

He pushes his hand through his hair. "What reason would that be?" he asks.

Taking one last chance, I push him back on the couch and straddle his lap so I'm facing him. I rest my hand on his chest, and his hands immediately fall to my legs.

"Did you do it because maybe you were trying to impress me?"

"Impress you? No." He lets out a heavy breath, and from where my palm rests, I can feel the rapid beat of his heart. "Did I want to show you how much I care about you? Did I want to show you I'm not the monster you last saw? The one who attacked your brother? Then, yes."

"And why wouldn't you want me to see you as a monster, Hayes?"

He wets his lips right before saying, "Because I really like you. Because I want to have the chance at dating you, taking you out, doing this the right way."

A much-needed smile passes over my lips. "Really?"

He cups my cheek and nods. "Really. It's never been a question if I want you, Hattie. That's been apparent since the moment I saw you dropping off that box at my front door."

"But you said—"

"I lied," he says. "Every chance I had, I lied because I knew if I gave in to the temptation that is you, I wouldn't be able to let go."

"So why now?" I ask, my fingers moving up to his face where I drag them across his coarse beard.

"Because of Cassidy," he answers.

And that's the exact answer I needed. I take his face in both my hands and crash our mouths together. His hands slide up my back, bringing me in tight and holding me in place as he reclaims my lips, but nothing is between us this time. It's just me and him. No restrictions. No fears.

And he commands every second of it.

His tongue traces the plumpness of my lips, edging me to open, and when I do, he doesn't dive his tongue in right away. Instead, he gently runs his tongue against mine until the embers between us ignite into a burning inferno.

Hungry, he delivers open-mouthed kisses, his grip moving all the way up to the back of my head, his tongue dancing across mine, owning every inch of my mouth.

This kiss is unlike anything I've ever experienced.

The passion.

The demand.

The pent-up need. It crashes together. It's in the way he

holds me and the way his mouth possesses mine. It's addicting, making me want so much more.

"Fuck," he says, releasing my mouth and pulling away, his eyes falling on mine. "I don't want to push you too far."

My body begs him to take anything he wants—to strip me down and make me his—but my mind, my fragile, barely healed brain is pumping the brakes . . . because he's right. If I went any further, it would be pushing me further than I want to go. Further than I'm ready.

I lean back and take a deep breath. "I want to take it slow."

"That's totally fine," he says.

"Are you sure?" I ask.

"Yes, Hattie." He cups my cheek. "Do I want to fuck you until you don't have a voice anymore? Of course." I gulp. "But I want to do it when you're ready."

Not sure I'd ever be fully prepared for that.

"I'm just barely getting my mind straight," I say honestly. "I've spent the last week or so letting myself live in my feelings, remembering Cassidy and letting myself mourn. Today's one of the first days I've gotten out of bed, put some makeup on, and gone into town. Aubree showed me the apartment, and I just . . . I had to come over here and thank you."

"No need to thank me, Hattie."

"What you did was really sweet. I appreciate it. I'm not sure I'm ready to stay there yet. I'm still kind of attached to Cassidy's room right now."

"That's fair."

"But I know I can't stay there forever, especially since Ryland has been sleeping on the couch for months now. I was actually thinking of clearing it out for him and giving him a bedroom. He needs one badly."

"Do you want me to help you?" he asks.

"Oh, you don't have to do that."

"I'd like to," he says, sincerity ringing through his tone.

"That's not something you should do alone, and if you haven't noticed, I have some experience fixing rooms."

I chuckle. "Is that going to be something on your résumé now?"

"Might as well add it." He smiles and then brings his hands to my thighs. He rubs his palms along my skin. "So would I be able to take you out on a date sometime?"

"I think we can arrange that."

"Yeah?"

I nod. "Yeah. As Ryland said, I need some fun in my life."

"I can provide the fun. I can provide whatever you want."

I tug on the collar of his shirt playfully. "So all those times you turned me down, it really was because of Ryland?"

"Yes, Hattie. Trust me, I was fucking burning for you."

My smile grows wider. "Oh my God, wait until I tell Maggie that. She's going to be so jealous."

He laughs and then brings me down on the couch so my back is on the leather, and I'm staring up at him. He pushes a strand of hair out of my face as he lightly presses another kiss to my lips. "I will say this. We're not working on that bedroom until you clean up my fucking living room. The papers are making my skin itch."

"Why didn't you clean them yourself?"

"You made the mess," he says, his nose sliding up the column of my neck, the feel of him so close, making my nipples hard. "You clean it up yourself."

"Where's the chivalry in that?"

"No chivalry when I was paying you to do a job. A job you didn't finish."

"Because my boss was a maniac, demanding coffee at seven in the morning."

He kisses my jaw, my cheek, my nose. "A task you never completed correctly."

"Should have fired me then," I say as I bring my hand up to his face, in disbelief that this is happening right now. That

I'm allowed to touch him, kiss him, feel him without guilt swarming me.

"And miss out on being able to see your fuckable ass in those bike shorts every day?"

My eyes widen. "Fuckable ass?"

He smirks and then pushes off me. "I have a lot to teach you, Hattie."

Oh dear God.

———

"TELL ME HOW THIS IS FAIR?" Hayes asks as he digs into the sack of fan mail and places them in front of us. "This is your job."

"But isn't it more fun when we do it together?"

"No," he deadpans, causing me to laugh. "I prefer to watch you do it."

"These are your fans, Hayes." I pull out a letter and another naked picture falls out, this one from one of his serial fans. The tenth naked picture from this particular lady. I flash him the picture. "You need to appreciate them."

He swats the picture down. "You're doing this just to torture me."

"No, I think we should spend more time together, and if you happen to help me with this task while spending time with me, then it's a win-win."

"For you."

I shrug. "Best you realize now that I'll win more in this relationship."

He undoes a letter and says, "Is that what this is? A relationship?"

"What else would you call it? Romantic involvement?"

"Yes, that's much more eloquent." He chuckles, and I nudge my shoulder against his.

"You act like this is new to you. You found Cassidy's letter, which means you were looking through things."

"Not through these bags of mail. I was looking through my tour shit," he says. "I was pissed the night I found it and ended up kicking a box. Her letter fell out."

"Pissed about how things went down in San Francisco?"

"Yeah, that trip was . . . fuck, it was miserable. So many things went wrong. I couldn't comfort you the way I wanted. And then you told me to treat you awfully, and because I'm a stupid, prideful man, I decided to do just that, only hurting you more." He takes my hand in his and brings my knuckles to his lips. "And then . . . Odette. The . . . job. Jesus Christ, I'm surprised you're letting me hold your hand right now after all of that."

"It was a breaking point, that's for sure," I say.

"For me too. I was so mad at myself because I pushed you away too much. When you said you were quitting, the realization that I wouldn't see you every day, that hit me really fucking hard." His battered eyes plead with me. "Would you have not come back?"

"Probably not," I say. "It was too hard being around you and not being able to give in to my feelings."

"Same, but I was taking every second, every moment I had with you. I was not giving that up."

"Good thing we don't have to worry about that now." He kisses my knuckles again. "So when you found the letter from Cassidy, what did you do?"

"Had a minor meltdown because I was so fucking grateful." He chuckles. "Then I went to The Almond Store, but when you weren't there, I decided to go to Sozzled because Joe told me to come sing a song whenever I wanted. I thought it might help with my writing, getting out there again, but then I saw you, and well . . . I decided to sing you a song instead."

I feel my cheeks blush. "You did such a beautiful job. I was transfixed. I think it's the main reason I had enough courage to kiss you that night."

"I'm glad you did. It's been more than a feeling for a while with you, Hattie."

I look to the side at him. "You're going to make it hard for me to ever think of another man, aren't you?"

"It's my number one priority right now."

⸻

"YOU CAN SIT on one of the barstools, you know," Hayes says as I cross my legs on top of his island counter.

"I like it better here." I lift my piece of pizza and take a bite. "Thank you for dinner, by the way. Would you consider this to be our first date?"

He shakes his head as he stands next to me, not taking a seat either. "Nah, I'd need to pick you up, bring you flowers, the works. Make it official."

"You don't have to bring me flowers, but I bet Mac would like some."

"Yeah, get on her good side?" He smirks. "But to answer your question, this is just a hangout."

I love that smirk so much. It's odd seeing him use it so freely. It makes me realize how guarded he was before. It was so rare to see his smile. But this Hayes, he's relaxed, like a weight has been lifted off his shoulders, and I'm sure it has. "Okay, so when is our first date?"

He picks at the cheese on his pizza. "Whenever you're free."

"Do you think I have a complicated calendar? I just got done crying in my sister's room for a week. I'm pretty free."

His lips soften. "How about tomorrow night?"

"Wow, don't you think that's a little soon?" He gives me an exhausted look, and I chuckle. "Just kidding, that would be perfect. What do you have planned? Do I need to dress up?"

"Nothing fancy," he says. "But you know . . . if you want to wear a dress like you wore when you were at Sozzled, I won't be mad about it."

"Ooo, you liked that, did you?"

He nods, the sultriness in his eyes making me feel all warm inside. "I did. You looked really pretty."

Really pretty.

Can't tell you the last time someone said that to me. Matt never doled out any compliments.

Head tilted down, I quietly say, "Thank you."

His finger lifts my chin as he says, "You know, you blush a lot. It makes me think you're shy around me."

"I wouldn't say shy." He releases me as I wipe my fingers on my napkin and pick up my Diet Coke to take a sip. "But you know . . . I've never been spoken to how you speak to me. You're honest—well, when you're not trying to push me away—"

"Not because I wanted to," he adds.

"I know. But you're honest. You say what's on your mind, and before, with Matt or any other guy I've dated, they weren't particularly vocal about my looks. They rarely complimented me. Not that I needed them to survive, but it's always nice to hear every once in a while. So yeah, I might blush because I'm not used to someone telling me I'm pretty or that they liked my dress." I shrug, feeling awkward.

His brow pulls together. "Those *boys* you were with before clearly didn't know how to treat you the way you deserve. Their loss, my gain."

And that's the kind of answer I'd expect from Hayes. He's passionate and possessive, everything Matt was not. I know this will be different. I have a feeling that being with Hayes will be unprecedented, and I'm excited to see where it goes.

"What about you?" I ask as he picks a pepperoni off his pizza and plops it in his mouth. "What kind of women have you dated?"

"Not many," he answers and leaves it at that.

"Is that all you're going to say, or will you be honest with me?"

"Do you want me to tell you the truth?"

"I do. The more I know, the better." I've seen the tabloids, and I'm actually hoping he tells me it hasn't been as . . . lurid as that.

He leans his hip on the counter and wipes his mouth with his napkin before tossing it next to his plate. "Had a girlfriend back in high school. You were probably too young to even know who it was, but she was my first for pretty much everything besides a kiss."

"Who was it?"

"Flavia Gotchen. Did you know her?"

"Nope."

He chuckles. "Didn't think so. But yeah, we were each other's first everything. We fumbled a lot, but we also learned. She broke up with me when we were seniors because I cheated on her."

"What?" I ask, surprised by this information.

"Listen, I'm not proud of it. It was the one and only time I've ever cheated. I learned my lesson quickly after her brother nearly beat me to death. I apologized to her multiple times, but the damage was done. I still remember the look on her face when I told her I cheated. If it wasn't for her brother's fists, her expression of utter defeat would have prevented me from ever doing that again."

"And you haven't?"

He shakes his head. "No, I haven't. I've also never been in a serious relationship. You might have seen love connections in the media throughout the years, but that was all press. Nothing serious. I got into drugs, alcohol, and fucked a lot of roadies."

My nose curls up from his confession. I know I asked for the truth, but I wasn't ready to hear that. His sordid past is out there for everyone to know. He's done his fair share of drugs —he even admitted to it when we were baking—and it doesn't take a genius to realize he probably has a lot of sex on the road. But it still doesn't make his confession any less impactful in my head.

"Want me to stop?" he asks.

I shake my head. "No. I asked for the truth. I'd rather hear it from you than someone else."

He nods and folds his arms across his chest. "There was a brief relationship, and I mean brief, with a girl who used to open for me on tour, but it was short-lived because I quickly found out . . . she had a boyfriend back home. I ended it immediately. Like I said, I cheated once. I was never going to be involved in it again."

"Oh God, really? Who was it?"

"Karla Moore."

"Oh, she's beautiful," I say, thinking of her killer legs. "I tried her leg workout once that was posted on one of those lifestyle blogs. I got halfway through and gave up."

He chuckles. "She used to do that workout every single day. It was impressive. But after her, it was just random fans that I'd fuck. Nothing serious at all. The only woman in my life was my grandma."

"That's sweet," I say.

"She keeps me grounded."

I turn toward him, my pizza now a second thought. "So why change now? Why ask me out? Why give us a chance?" I ask. "I mean, I'm assuming this isn't a fling for you. Because it's not a fling for me."

"It's not a fling." He takes my hand in his and brings my knuckles to his lips. His mouth lightly rubs against them before he says, "I changed because I realized quickly that I'm fucking lonely." He pauses for a moment, pressing a kiss to my knuckles. "I was struggling with finding my voice again, my writing voice, and I realized it was because I had nothing to write

MEGHAN QUINN

about. No one to write about. My life was . . . empty. It's been empty for a while. And then, well, you popped into it and things started to change."

"Wait . . . are you saying I've helped you write a song?"

He holds up two fingers. "Two, actually. I haven't sent any to Ruben, my agent, yet because they were about you, and I didn't want you to think I wrote songs about you."

"Why not?"

"Because you weren't talking to me. It would have looked desperate. I didn't want to make you uncomfortable."

"It wouldn't have made me uncomfortable," I say. "It would have been really sweet." I pause and then add, "Actually no, not sweet. It probably would have melted me into a puddle of nothing. I don't want to admit it, but . . . there were many nights, listening to your music through my headphones that I thought about you singing them to me."

"Seriously?" he asks in disbelief.

"When Maggie said I had an obsession, she wasn't kidding. I played your songs on a loop during some of my darkest times."

He moves in closer. "Did you play my songs this past week?"

I shake my head. "I couldn't. I wouldn't have been able to stomach hearing your voice, not when I was trying not to think about you."

He tugs me to the edge of the counter, where I drop my legs, and he steps up between them. "While you weren't thinking about me, I was thinking about you every goddamn second." He pushes a strand of hair behind my ear. "Thinking about holding your hand, looking into your arresting eyes, running my finger over the pulse in your wrist . . . counting your freckles. Fuck, Hattie, I thought about you so much."

"Is that . . . is that what you wrote in your songs?"

"I did." He cups my cheek.

312

Staring up into his shadowless eyes, I ask, "Think you'll play them for me one day?"

"I want to," he answers as his thumb strokes my jaw. "But they need some finessing. They're pretty raw right now."

"Can I be the first one to hear them when you're ready?"

"Of course," he answers.

"Thank you." I lift my chin, searching for his lips. He places his hands on my hips and offers me a soft, gentle kiss.

When he pulls away, he asks, "So I didn't scare you away with my past?"

Is his past different from anything I've experienced? Of course. Is that something I'll hold against him?

Never.

I shake my head. "No. I think we all have the opportunity to change, and from the sounds of it, you've changed."

"I have." He picks up his pizza again. "The only vice I have now is alcohol, but that's not every day, just apparently when I'm trying to forget you."

"Well, I hope you don't pick up a bottle then. I'd be devastated if you tried to forget me now."

"Not going to happen," he says with a wink.

━━━

WHAT A FREAKING DAY.

Woke up to run and spent the day with Hayes, but not like every other day. I got to hold his hand, lean into his embrace, kiss him whenever I wanted . . . guilt free. It's been one of the best days I've had in a long time. In fact, if I think about it, it's probably the most at peace I've felt since before Cassidy was diagnosed. Every day since has just been . . . hard. Today was like taking a deep, full breath.

Hand in hand, we walk to my car. The night settles above us, a dark blanket of sky and stars. He gently presses me up against the car door with his hands on my hips while I smooth my hands up his chest, staring into those beautiful eyes of his.

It was a really fun evening.

When I came over here earlier, I didn't expect to stay so long. I didn't even expect to leave with his lips imprinted on mine, but that quickly changed the moment I saw him. We spent the evening talking, joking, learning more about each other, and the more he told me, the more I liked him.

Hearing that he cheated on his girlfriend stung a bit, but I liked that he was honest about it, putting it all out there so nothing was hidden between us. I think it takes a big man to recognize when they've fucked up and the changes they've made to avoid making that mistake again. I appreciate that about him. It has given me more faith that he wouldn't cheat on me.

I learned about his love for his grandma. His love for model trains because of his grandma's close relationship with Rodney. His first love song was written about this girl he had a crush on back in middle school. *How cute.* He told me how he once stole one of Ethel's boas—Abel dared him—and they buried it in Abel's parents' backyard, so scared that Ethel would find out and then kick-ball-change them all the way down to the police department.

And I loved every second of his stories, watching how animated he became, the expressions on his face, such a vast difference from the serious—guarded—man I spent time with.

"I wasn't expecting this at all today," he says, stealing the thoughts right from my head. "I planned on getting drunk tonight, writing some more lyrics that pertained to your eyes, your freckles, your idiotic piles of papers." I chuckle. "But then you gave me the best fucking surprise ever by coming over and kissing me."

The best surprise was him kissing me back rather than telling me no and he can't do this. I'm so glad I didn't have to beg and plead for him to give me a chance. *Us. Give us a chance.*

I play with the hem of his shirt, tugging on the thin fabric. "After I saw the way you redid the apartment above The Almond Store, I had to see you. Thank you, Hayes. I really love what you did there."

"You're welcome, Hattie," he says, moving in closer. "It was cathartic, actually, and gave me some space to think on things too." I wrap my arms around his neck, and he connects his forehead to mine. "Tomorrow. I'll pick you up around six, okay?"

"Okay," I say as I lift on my toes and press a kiss to his lips.

He sighs against my mouth before parting his lips and pressing into me.

It's a delicious kiss, full of promises of what's to come.

"Why are you smirking?" he asks when he pulls away.

"Nothing."

He tilts my chin up. "Tell me."

"I was just thinking how I want to take things slow, but now I'm unsure how slow I can really go when you kiss me like that."

His eyes turn dark, hungry. "It will be torture, but I'll go as slow as you want. Snail's pace. Even though right now, if it were up to me, I'd have you bent over the hood of your car, pulling down your shorts, and sucking on your clit in seconds."

Dear God.

I wet my lips as my chest grows heavy. I can practically *feel* him doing that. He'd own me, every inch of me. His hands would hold me down while his mouth did all the work, and it would be the best orgasm of my life. Just from the way he kisses me, I know it would be the best.

"Hattie," he says in warning.

"What?" I ask, my gaze snapping up to him, falling out of my thoughts.

"Don't look at me like that."

"Like what?"

"Like you *would* let me drape you over the hood of your car."

I run my fingers through his hair. "I wouldn't be opposed."

He groans and steps away, making me sad. "No, you said we're taking this slow. That's anything but slow. Shoving my tongue into your pussy until you're screaming is not taking it slow."

God, why does he have to talk like that? It makes me all itchy and needy inside.

"I know . . ." I close the distance between us. "But that doesn't mean we can't . . . I don't know, dry-hump or something."

His brow raises in question, and it's so cute, it makes me laugh. "No one dry-humps past high school."

"Then they're missing out." I lift on my toes and press a chaste kiss to his lips. "See you tomorrow."

I reach for my car door handle, but he beats me to it and opens my door for me, hanging on it. "See you tomorrow."

He shuts my door, and I turn on my car as he walks back to his house. I wave and then pull out of his driveway. The minute I hit the road, I call Maggie.

"I have about ten minutes," she says into the phone. "Please tell me you showered today."

"God, why is everyone so concerned about my hygiene? I wasn't *that* bad."

"That's cute, keep telling yourself that," she says. "So did you?"

"Yes. I showered, shaved, did my hair, put on mascara and real clothes, and then I went to Hayes's house and sat on his lap and kissed him, and he kissed me back and asked me out on a date."

There's silence on the other end of the phone.

"Maggie, you there?"

"Ummm . . ." she draws out. "Is this Hattie? I feel like this is a prank call because the last time I spoke with Hattie, she was still contemplating why fuzzy socks are so popular, and I had to say because they're fuzzy repeatedly."

I laugh. "It's me, Maggie."

"Okay, because something funny just happened. I thought you just told me you kissed Hayes, and he asked you out."

"I did."

"Hmm, I don't know how to take that."

"Maggie," I groan, making her laugh. "Can you tell me you're proud of me?"

"Of course I'm proud of you, but excuse me for being slightly shocked. You went from not doing anything to seizing your life. I'm just trying to connect the dots."

"Well, nothing is truly seized, but I feel good. I feel like I'm on the right path."

"Uh, if your tongue is down Hayes Farrow's throat, then yes, I can guarantee you're going down the right path. Care to explain how this happened?"

"Simple. He renovated the apartment."

"Oh God," Maggie says, a hitch in her breath. "I think . . . I think I just had a mini orgasm."

"What is wrong with you?" I laugh.

"I don't know. Weddings make me emotional and a little nuts. But God, how sweet. So what, are you a couple now?"

"I mean, I think we're taking it one step at a time, but I do know that after today I feel happy."

"Good. I'm glad to hear it."

"But I told him I wanted to take it slow." Saying it out loud makes me cringe because God, there's nothing more that I want than to hump that man . . . let him pleasure me until I'm a puddle of a woman in his bed.

"What?" she yells into the phone. "Have you lost your mind? When I stayed at his place with you, I had sex with him in my head at least a dozen times, and I know he wasn't ready for that, but it happened anyway."

"Why are we friends?"

"You have me questioning that very statement right now." She huffs. "Why aren't you having sex with him?"

"Nervous, unsure of myself. I think I've been through a whirlwind of events the past few months, and I just need to slow down, you know? Find myself, figure out what the hell I'm doing with my life."

"What the hell you're doing is graciously taking your clothes off for Hayes Farrow. You can find yourself while holding his dick in your mouth. You're multitalented. You. Can. Multitask. Have I not taught you anything?"

"You haven't," I say on a laugh. "You've literally taught me nothing."

"Clearly," she replies in exasperation. "Okay, so you're not having sex with him. Well, good luck with that. Tell me how it goes and how long it lasts because, according to my calculations, it won't last long."

"And what calculations are those?"

"Easy, I take your neediness to experience a well-executed orgasm by a real man, combine it with his mad sex appeal, and blamo, two days tops."

"Is that real math?"

"The most real."

I chuckle. "Well, we'll see. It might be fun to just . . . tease around a bit."

"Ha!" She laughs so loud that I can feel my phone shake. "Teasing, uh-huh, you were ready to pounce him in San Francisco. There is no way you'll be able to 'tease around a bit,' whatever the hell that means. But I think it's honorable that you're putting up a front. Shows character."

"I'm going to go now."

"Best that you do. I need to go direct a flower girl on how to toss flower petals down the aisle, not eat them. Love you."

"Love you."

Chapter Seventeen

HAYES

Shit, I'm nervous.

I haven't been able to focus all day. I attempted fine-tuning a melody in my head but gave up after an hour and resorted to mindlessly watching reruns of *The Office* while doing a set of push-ups and then sit-ups every ten minutes.

Now I'm sore as fuck, slightly exhausted, and still nervous.

Before I left my house, I changed my outfit seven times.

Yup, seven.

And guess what? The shirts I rotated through were all variations of black and gray. There wasn't much difference at all, but it didn't prevent me from getting all fussy in front of a goddamn mirror and checking the sleeve length of each shirt to make sure it showed off enough bicep to entice Hattie, but not too much that I look like Danny fucking Zuko strutting down the high school hallway.

And my hair, out of all days to try to style it and not wear a hat. I fidgeted with it for twenty minutes, threatened to flatten it with a hat multiple times, then finally rewet it and started all over.

And I'm still not happy, but I didn't want to be late picking up Hattie.

I'm also concerned that I put on too much cologne. It's all I could smell while driving to the farm. I even rolled down the windows to air some of it out, but I went by a cow farm that smelled like last week's garbage under the hot sun, which caused me to close the window, capturing the hot garbage smell in my car . . . so . . . it's hot garbage cologne in here.

In addition to the parade of monochromatic shirts, the endless tousling of hair, and the dip into a pool of cologne, I've taken down ten Altoids.

Ten!

I no longer have taste buds. I fried them right off.

Jesus Christ, what is wrong with me?

Oh, I know.

I care about Hattie. She's probably the first girl I've cared about in a long time, and I'm on the fence with her brother, whose approval I now need to win. And I thought it would be a good idea to win his approval by bringing him flowers like a goddamn nimrod.

Yup, fucking flowers.

It was funny at first, but now, now I'm concerned it might come on too strong.

I put my car into park as I stare up at the farmhouse. Small and quaint, it's seen better days under the sun with the chipping paint on the exterior and a cracked floorboard on the porch. I can't imagine the kind of pressure Cassidy was under while living here. The farm, the store, taking care of a child . . . while being sick at the same time. She truly was Superwoman.

I grab my flowers and step out of my SUV and walk up the front steps of the porch where I knock on the screen door.

It immediately opens, and a little girl with bouncy brown curls stares up at me.

MacKenzie Rowley.

Hell, she's adorable.

"You're here for Aunt Hattie, aren't you?"

I squat down in front of her, and I nod. "Yup." I hold my hand out to her. "I'm Hayes."

She stares me down, one eye deeply examining me while her hands prop up on her hips. "I know who you are. We aren't supposed to like you."

Looks like I've got my work cut out for me.

I hold one bundle of flowers in front of her and say, "What if I gave you these? Would that help?"

She looks down at the flowers and then back up at me before snagging them. "Chewy Charles loves flowers." And then she takes off, leaving me in the entryway.

Who the hell is Chewy Charles?

I stand up and step farther into the house, the open floor plan offering a view of the tight living room with one couch and a TV. It's decorated modestly with mainly pictures of family and the farm. To the left is the dining room attached to the kitchen, where cabinets all line one wall and a wheelable butcher's block is in the middle. Decorated with blue gingham curtains and stone pottery, I can see how this could easily feel like home.

"Hey," Ryland says as he comes down the stairs.

"Hey." I wave awkwardly because seeing him not curl his nose whenever we're in the same room is still uncomfortable. "Uh, here." I extend the flowers toward him, and he pauses mid-stride and looks at them. When he gives me a confused expression, I clear my throat. "I got you, uh, flowers."

"Me?" He points at his chest.

"Yup. Thought it would be nice." God, kill me now.

He doesn't move, doesn't reach for them, doesn't take

another step forward, and I know it's because I look like an absolute moron.

Here you go, Ryland, I got you flowers—what a fucking idiot!

"They're daisies. I thought you liked daisies." *Stop talking, Hayes, you're not doing yourself any favors. You have no fucking clue if he likes daisies or not.*

"What makes you think I like daisies?" he asks as a tiny trickle of sweat forms on the back of my neck. *See, that's why you should have stopped talking.*

"Uh . . ." I swallow. "Your eyes."

"My eyes?" he asks.

Yeah, Hayes, how exactly do his eyes remind you of daisies? They're neither shaped like them or white or yellow for that matter.

"I mean, your complexion."

"My complexion?" He raises his brow.

And yup, that sweat trickles down my back.

"You know, did I say complexion? I meant your smile. Your smile reminds me of a daisy."

"When was the last time you saw me smile?"

Great point.

"I don't know, man," I say, giving up because the more I talk, the more I'll embarrass myself. "Just take them." I step toward him but fail to notice the pink fire truck right in front of me.

I trip over it, attempt to catch my balance, but step on a smaller car and fly forward, bouquet stretched out in front of me and plaster the flowers right into Ryland's chest, sending us both tumbling to the floor together.

"Ooof," Ryland exhales while I mutter, "Christ," under my breath, our arms and legs getting tangled together.

"Noo!" Mac screams at the top of her lungs and runs over to us. I have about one second to figure out what happened before a plush ball whacks me over the head with surprising force. "You get off him. Don't touch Uncle Ry Ry."

"Ouch, fuck," I say as a hard piece of plastic surrounded by fur hits the side of my head.

Ryland struggles beneath me. I struggle on top of him with the flowers sandwiched between.

"Get up," Ryland says, pushing at me.

"I can't with the whacking."

"Don't hurt him. Don't hurt him!" Mac screams, walloping me in the head over and over again.

"Jesus Christ," I say as I attempt to roll but can't navigate with the beating I'm taking to the head. I locate the floor with my hand and move my leg forward just as Ryland screams at the top of his lungs.

"Shit, that's my dick."

"What's your di——" *Klunk.* I'm smacked in the eye with what I'm assuming is a stuffed animal. "Motherfucker," I yell as I grip my eye. She caught it when it was open.

"Your knee," Ryland groans. "Your knee is on my dick."

"Get off his dick!" Mac screams.

"I don't want to be on his dick." I scramble but take another beating to the head, a one-two knock-knock.

"Don't say dick," Ryland groans.

"What the hell is going on down here?" Hattie says just as she pulls Mac away, ending the abuse and allowing me to roll to the side and lie flat on my back. As I stare up at the ceiling, my head pounds.

Ryland rolls the other way, giving us just enough room between us to no longer have any issues.

"That man was on Uncle Ry Ry's dick."

"Mac," Ryland groans, crunched over. "I said don't say dick."

"I don't even know what a dick is," Mac replies, tossing her hands in the air. "How am I supposed to know?"

"Because I said don't say dick."

"Can we drop the dick talk?" Hattie asks.

From the horse snout to the eye, my vision is a little blurry, but from what I can see, Hattie is dressed in a pale-yellow floral sundress with thin straps and brown buttons all the way up to the middle. It's tight around her torso but flares at her waist. *Really fucking pretty.* Her hair is down in soft waves with half of it pulled back on top into a messy bun, and her eyes look greener than ever with the way she accentuated them with her makeup.

Fuck, she's gorgeous.

And she's giving me the stink eye.

Shit.

"Were you two fighting again?"

"Yes," Mac says while Ryland and I both say no. "They're lying. I saw that bad man we're supposed to hate attack Uncle Ry Ry. He tackled him to the ground."

"Seriously, Hayes?" Hattie asks. "What is wrong with you?"

"No," I say. "I didn't attack him. I was handing him flowers."

"You were what?"

I catch my breath and lower my hand from my eye as I try to blink a few times, begging for it to work again. "I brought him flowers as a peace offering. See?" I hold up the flowers, but the bouquet sags to the side from the crush of two grown men's bodies. "I thought it would be nice, but then I got fucking nervous trying to explain why I brought them, decided to just shove them into his chest so I didn't say anything else stupid, wound up tripping over toys, and face-planted into Ryland's nipple."

"Right into the nipple," Mac says, her arm jutting up.

"Don't say nipple," Hattie says.

"The bad man said it," Mac argues.

"I'm not a bad man, I promise," I say.

"He kneed me in the dick while on the ground," Ryland says, the pain seeming to ease just enough for him to chime in.

"See?" Mac points at me. "I told you he was attacking Uncle Ry Ry's dick."

"Don't say dick!" Ryland and Hattie say at the same time.

Hattie then presses her fingers to her brow. "Mac, please go upstairs and play in your room for a moment, okay?"

"Fine." She grabs her horse stuffy, the half-mutilated bouquet, and heads toward the stairs. "I didn't want to be here with the dick stuff anyway."

"Jesus," Ryland mutters before lying flat on the ground and taking a few deep breaths.

"Are you okay?" I ask him.

"No." He drags his hands over his face. "You kneed me several times. I nearly threw up in front of Mac."

"That would have been the icing on the cake." Hattie moves over to the kitchen, pulls an ice pack from the freezer, and then tosses it at Ryland. "Here, ice your balls. I'll get Aubree to come over and watch Mac while you nurse your manhood."

"Nah, don't bother her," he replies while slowly trying to rise to his feet. When I notice him struggling, I get up, grip him under the arm, and aid him. He's crouched over but standing now, so I help guide him to the couch where he sits, spreads his legs, and puts the ice pack right on his crotch. Not sure that will help, but when a man's in that situation, we will pretty much do anything to make it better.

When I turn around, Hattie has her arms crossed, and she says, "So you're telling me you accidentally tripped and fell into Ryland while handing him flowers, and while you were trying to get up, you kneed him in the dick?"

"Apparently, and in my defense, I was getting pummeled in the head over and over by your niece, so my vision was blurred, and my wits weren't quite there."

Hattie turns to Ryland. "Is this true?"

Ryland glances at me and then nods.

"I mean, if he just took the flowers, none of this would have happened," I say in my defense.

"I wasn't expecting to receive flowers from someone I haven't talked to in over a decade, let alone a man who is supposed to be taking my sister out, not me."

"It was a kind gesture," I say, exasperated. "Can't we just accept that? I brought some for Mac too."

"Aw, really?" Hattie asks. "That's cute."

"So it's cute when I bring them for Mac, but not for Ryland? Why can't we be comfortable in our masculinity and accept flowers from another man?"

"It's not that they're from another man," Ryland says. "It's that they're from *you*."

"So if Abel brought you flowers, would you have been okay with that?" I ask.

Ryland shrugs. "I would have asked him what the occasion was, but I would have accepted them."

"So you're telling me we're not at flower-exchanging level yet?"

"Dude, I can barely look at you, so no, we're not at flower exchanging yet."

I nod and stuff my hands in my pockets. "Good to know."

Hattie clasps her hands together. "Well, this is not how I expected to start this date, but I guess we should get going before anything else happens like you slip and fall and I find your head in my brother's crotch."

Ryland shakes his head. "We're definitely not at face-to-crotch level."

"Not sure we should ever be at that level," I say.

"For the love of God, I hope not." Hattie moves toward the stairs. "Let me grab my things, and I'll be right down."

She jogs up the stairs, and I turn back toward Ryland. I nod at where he holds his ice pack and say, "Still shriveled up?"

"It's going to take a week for my dick to release itself from my scrotum."

"Fair," I say. "And hey, sorry about that. Your niece has quite the beating arm on her. She can hold her own."

"Good to know. Your eye looks a little swollen. Do you need some ice?"

"Nah, I think it's just a little shocked right now. And if I get a black eye from your niece, I'll wear it with pride."

"You better," he answers just as Hattie comes down with a small backpack draped over her shoulders and a smile on her face.

"Ready?" she asks.

"Yeah, ready," I answer. I nod at Ryland. "Nice seeing you, man."

"Remember what we talked about." He gives me that older-brother glare, reminding me that I might have brought him flowers, but he's nowhere near ready to trust me with his little sister.

Fair. I get it.

I'll have to earn that trust back, a task I have no problem putting the time into.

I open the front door to the house and let Hattie out first before taking her hand in mine and bringing her over to her side of the SUV. Before I open the door, I twirl her toward me and say, "You look really fucking good." I run my finger over the strap of her dress. "I like this. A lot."

Her cute cheeks blush as she says, "Thank you."

I lean in and press a soft kiss on her lips before pulling the car door open. I help her in, then grab the seat belt and buckle her up. I smile up at her and then shut her car door.

Once inside the car, I place my hand on her thigh and back out of the driveway with one hand on the wheel.

"How was your day?" I ask her, my nerves starting to ease. I mean, it can't get worse than getting whacked in the head by a horse and kneeing her brother in the balls several times. Can only be up from here, at least that's what I hope.

"It was good. I was full of nerves all day in anticipation of tonight, so I kept myself busy with cleaning up Cassidy's room. I started to go through her clothes, deciding what should be kept and what could possibly go."

"Wow, really?" I ask. "That's a big step."

"I know. I talked to Aubree about it briefly. She said she wanted to go through everything before I donated it, but she also thought it was time. There's an old cardigan with large flowers on it that Aubree wanted. Cassidy used to wear it whenever she got cold. It has some holes in it, and I thought I'd get it dry-cleaned for her and take it to Elizabeth Gomez."

"The veterinarian?" I ask. "One of four members of the Peach Society? Why would you do that?"

"She's an expert crocheter, and I'm pretty sure she could help patch it up. I want it to last forever. I know one of the reasons Cassidy stopped wearing it so much was because it started to unravel. Thought it would be a nice present for Aubree."

"Thoughtful, Hattie."

"Thank you."

"So tell me why you were nervous?"

"Why did I think you would let that little snippet go?"

"Not sure. It's not my style, though." I squeeze her bare thigh and slide my hand an inch higher. "Why are you nervous? You've been alone with me plenty."

"I know, but this is different. I feel like I have to impress you."

"Untrue," I say. "And hey, want to know a secret?"

"Yes," she answers.

"I was nervous too. I changed my shirt seven times."

She glances at me. "And you went with plain black after seven choices?"

"The others were also black and gray."

She leans her head back and laughs. "So what you're telling me is that you don't have any other clothes?"

"Pretty much," I answer.

"I'm glad you were nervous too. That makes me feel better."

"I was also nervous to give your brother flowers."

"Oh my God, I can't believe you did that."

"Me neither. I think he might hate me more now. Not sure that won me any brownie points."

"I don't think it did either," she replies.

"Looks like I'm going to have to give him candy next time."

"Just don't trip over toys and smash it in his face." She chuckles.

"Trust me, I've noted to look where I'm walking in that house from now on."

I HAD a few thoughts when I thought about where I wanted to take Hattie for our first date. I know she likes By the Slice, but we just had pizza. And I wanted to do something more intimate. So I stopped by Coleman's and picked up some cheeses, crackers, and her favorite pickles to make a charcuterie board. I also stopped by The Sweet Lab for some assorted cookies. I considered making some of the almond cherry cookies but didn't want to burn them, so I thought better of it.

There's this spot over in Almond Bay, the actual bay where it's dry, where there's a beautiful view of the ocean and the cliffs that flank the west side of Almond Bay. Not many people go down there, so I'm hoping it's uninhabited tonight.

"You okay?" I ask Hattie as we make our way through the sand. I have my backpack full of food and a blanket. I thought about bringing my guitar but decided not to at the last moment. I don't want this to be about me. I want it to be about us learning more about each other.

"Great," she says as she takes my hand and smiles up at me.

"We're almost there."

We round the corner that leads into Almond Bay, and thankfully, it's abandoned. Like I said, not many people would be here or even know about it, for that matter. There are more old people in Almond Bay at this point than young, and the older residents would never make the trek.

"I'm sorry if this was longer than you expected, but this is one of my favorite places."

"I don't mind at all. It's beautiful down here. I can see why it's your favorite."

I lead her to the very center of the bay and set my backpack down. Cliffs as tall as five-story buildings surround us, an almond-shaped opening leading out to the ocean, giving us the perfect view but also seclusion at the same time.

"I also brought a light in case we're still out here when it's dark." I pull out the blanket, and I lay it down on the sand.

"You thought of everything," she says while taking a seat.

I pull out the pickles. "I tried to."

Her eyes soften as an appreciative smile passes over her beautiful lips. "Oh God, you're going to make it really hard to keep my hands to myself, aren't you?"

"Just trying to show you that I care about you is all. I haven't really done this, at this capacity, so tell me if I do something wrong."

I take a seat next to her, and her hand slips behind my neck as she says, "You're doing pretty great so far." She presses a kiss to my lips, and I inwardly sigh as her soft mouth moves over mine. I could easily sink into this, lie down on my back, and drag her with me, but that's not the point of this date. So I pull away and take a deep breath as my head spins with desire for this woman.

Christ, ever since she walked into my life, I hadn't allowed myself to taste her and now that I've broken the seal, it's like I'm crazed and unable to get enough.

"Jesus," I mutter as I reach into my backpack.

"What?" she asks.

"Your mouth." I meet her eyes. "It's what sins are made of."

She smirks. "I could say the same about you."

"Something you'll find out about soon." I wink and then pull out the cheese I put in a small cooler, as well as the drinks and crackers with some grapes. I lay everything out and say, "I wish I had some fancy plating for you, but this will have to do."

"It's perfect," she says as waves lapping the shore set a relaxing soundtrack for the evening. I don't think I could have picked a more perfect spot for us.

"This looks delicious," she says as she picks up a piece of Colby jack cheese and pairs it with a cracker.

"I also brought a fork for your pickles so you don't have to dip your fingers in the juice, leaving you with a pickle hand."

"Is there something wrong with pickle hand?" she asks.

"Depending on what kind of pickle you're touching," I answer with a wiggle of my brows, causing her eyes to widen.

"Gross." She pushes at me, making me laugh. "That was such a typical male response."

"Oh . . . fuck, sorry, did I not mention I'm a man? That must have slipped by me."

"Is this how it's going to be? You're going to be a smart-ass?"

I push a loose strand of hair behind her ear. "Unfortunately, for you, yes. You want to know the real me? This is it."

"If that's the case." She stands, but I tug on her hand.

"Sit the fuck back down."

She laughs and then crosses her legs, draping her dress in just the right way so nothing shows. "Guess I'll stay then."

"Damn right, you'll stay."

———

"I KNOW NOTHING ABOUT YOUR PARENTS," Hattie says as she leans back on her hands. We just finished eating, and I packed up the empty bins. We joked around a lot, talked about Mac and how strong-willed but sweet-hearted she is, like Cassidy, the loss of her dad—I'd had no idea he died in a tour bus accident when Mac was one—and how she's doing since she's lost Cassidy.

"What do you want to know about them?" I ask as I pull her closer to me, our shoulders now bumping up against each other.

"I'm assuming they're not really in your life. You speak to your grandma, though."

"Because she raised me," I answer. "My dad wasn't a great guy. Didn't know much about him, only can truly remember seeing the taillights of his car as he drove away. Haven't heard from him since. He didn't have the balls to try to come back into my life when I started hitting it big. My mom, well, she just decided one day she didn't want to be a parent anymore. Told me that in a letter she gave me and left me with my grandma."

"Oh my God," Hattie says, turning toward me. "That's awful. How old were you?"

"Twelve," I answer. "She went to live in Arizona with Ray, her now husband. They own a pawn shop together. The first time she heard me on the radio, she called me to congratulate me and asked if I wanted to celebrate. I told her to fuck off. She's come back a few times since then, wanting to celebrate my accomplishments, but I haven't let her. The night Samantha cheated on Ryland, I actually got in a fight with her on the phone. I resorted to old habits, got so fucked up. It's why Samantha found it easy to say I fucked her, because she didn't think I'd remember either way. But trust me, I remember everything from that night. Every goddamn thing." I pause. It took me so long to see that my mom was in the wrong, but it certainly wasn't that night. I've never told a soul, as who have I had to tell? *But now I have Hattie.* "That was the night my mom told me she should have never had me in the first place because I was a selfish prick who wouldn't help her out with money. You don't forget things like that."

"I'm so sorry," Hattie says softly. "I . . . I didn't know. I shouldn't have asked."

"I'm glad you did," I say, taking her hand in mine. "I want to be honest with you about everything. The more you ask, the more I'll tell you the truth, and the more you'll know."

"Well, you deserve better," she says. "I'm glad you have your grandma. I assume you're close."

"We are. She has her moments when I know she resented me at points in my life. I mean, I was a twelve-year-old punk broken by abandonment. I lashed out every chance I got. It's probably why I haven't had any real relationships, and most certainly why I didn't fight for Ryland, because if he wanted to leave too and not listen to my side of the story, then I was good with him leaving. Wouldn't be the first person, wouldn't be the last."

"Do you still have that mindset?" she asks.

"I like to think that I don't since it's something I've worked on, but I can't make any promises. I struggle deeply with abandonment."

"I can see why." She gets on her hands and knees and crawls between my legs, leaning her back against my chest. I wrap my arms around her and as she turns her head up to look at me, she puckers her lips. I place a soft kiss on her mouth, and she turns back around.

I grip her tightly, soaking in the comfort from her warm, soft body, the sweet scent of her perfume, and the understandable hold she has on my heart. *I have no idea how I've existed without this level of closeness.* Hattie's showing me exactly what's been missing in my life. Genuine care and affection. Warmth. Acceptance. *And I never want to lose this.*

"I never knew about that side of your life because you were shunned from the family by the time I was old enough to be a part of these conversations. Did Ryland know?"

"Ryland and Abel know everything. The only thing Ryland doesn't know is what my life has been like since the fight."

"Has anything changed since then?"

"Nothing of significance," I answer. "Honestly, it's almost as if I've been walking around in a haze for the last decade or so. There aren't many things that stick out to me other than professional accomplishments. Those are great and all, but not when you don't have anyone to share them with."

"You had your grandma and Abel."

I nod. "And Ruben, he's my agent. But that's pretty much it."

"How do you feel now? Still feel like you're in that haze?"

"No," I answer. "The moment you stepped onto my porch with a box, it was like the haze lifted. I was intrigued that you were Ryland's sister. The dangerous side of me wanted to play around to fuck with him, but as I spent more time with you, I realized the damage I could do, and that's when I started to pull away, which proved to be too hard. I tried to return to that haze, but it was impossible with you walking around the house every day."

"Well, I'm glad you're not back there now."

I kiss the side of her neck gently and ask, "What about you? Do you ever miss your parents?"

"Sometimes," she says. I can't imagine what losing your mom to breast cancer and then your dad to a heart attack does to such a little girl. She was lucky to have Ryland and Cassidy, who stepped up and took care of their younger sisters. "I didn't know my mom all that well, but from what I heard, she wasn't entirely the most loving, caring mom. And Dad, well, secretly, I was kind of glad he died. He was . . . just awful."

I hold her tighter. I have strong memories of how Mr. and Mrs. Rowley treated their kids. *That's what I had to refer to them as too.* They weren't warm people. The day Mr. Rowley beat Ryland with his own glove after a game where he struck out three times has been imprinted on my mind. He berated him behind the dugout, telling Ryland he wasn't working his way to the grave to see his son strike out. Their parents might have put a roof over their heads and food on the table, but they were cold. Mean. I place a kiss on Hattie's forehead, hoping desperately she never received her father's wrath, something that got worse after Mrs. Rowley died.

"Dad . . . well, you probably know this, but he hit Ryland. He never raised a hand to me, but he was awful to Ryland. Would make sure Ryland had a hard time waking up the next morning. It's why I was so attached to Cassidy, because she was the main adult figure in my life who offered me the comfort and love every little kid desired. Even when she got married and had Mac, I was still very much a part of her life."

"I'm glad you had her and I'm sorry that she was taken away."

"Thank you," she says softly. "There are days where I still can't believe she's gone, like this is some sort of sick prank, but after spending a week in her room, I think it's starting to sink in."

"Do you think it helped?"

"Yes," she says. "I think I needed to have that connection with her, that moment. She passed when I was still at college. She wouldn't let me come home. She said she was fine and she was going to make it. Well, I think we know how that turned out. Coming back into town, not feeling her warm hug, or seeing her brilliant smile, or hearing how proud she is of me . . ." I hear the waver in her voice so I pull her in even closer.

"It's okay, Hattie."

She sniffs. "Sorry."

"Don't apologize. It's good to talk about it. It's good to cry."

"But on our first date? That doesn't seem right."

"There are no rules about first dates. We can make it how we want it." The wind picks up the edge of the blanket, flipping it over her feet, but she doesn't move. Instead, she cuddles in even closer.

"I just miss her, Hayes. I wish I could have spent one more day with her before she left."

"What would that day have been like?" I never really saw them together, but I do remember how maternal Cassidy was. She always seemed to just . . . *know* what people needed and when.

"It would start with our favorite breakfast of eggs, bacon, and donuts from The Sweet Lab. She loved the maple ones. Then we'd spend hours going antique shopping. She collected vintage tablecloths and runners, but only certain ones. They had to be stained and well loved."

"Why's that?" I ask.

"Because the pristine ones, someone would buy, but the stained ones with tears, those still needed a home. After that, probably pick up a puzzle at Pieces and Pages. She loved puzzles just as much as I did and we'd have spent the rest of the day eating pizza, pineapple and pepperoni of course, watching old-school movies from the early '90s, and putting together our puzzle. She would have talked about how Jake Ryan from *Sixteen Candles* was the best movie boyfriend of all time, and I'd have argued with her that it was Ronald Miller from *Can't Buy Me Love* because Patrick Dempsey is so hot."

I chuckle. "I don't know, Jake Ryan had the car. Ronald Miller had a lawn mower."

"It was endearing," she says, exasperated as if she's had this conversation a million times.

"Well, either way, it sounds like the perfect day to me."

"It would have been."

She shivers under my arms, and I ask, "Are you getting cold?"

"A little."

I kiss the side of her head and say, "Let's pack up."

"But I don't want the night to end."

"It won't," I answer as I stand and pull her up with me. "I still have other things planned."

———

"COMFORTABLE?" I ask.

"Very," she says as she snuggles into me.

After we packed up and made the trek back to my car, I warmed her up with my heated seats and pre-controlled climate so she didn't have to wait long to be warm. I then drove her north to a spot just past my house, where the field grass is high, there's zero light pollution, and the sound of the ocean still fills the air.

I laid out two cushioned mats on the ground, covered them with blankets, added two pillows, and then helped her down onto the makeshift bed so we could stare up at the stars.

"This is beautiful, Hayes."

"I've been here many times, especially when I need to clear my head but don't want to be directly on the beach. It's the best place to watch a meteor shower."

"Have you ever taken a girl here?"

I shake my head. "Never. You're the first."

"I'm honored," she says. "Your sacred spot. I can see why you've gatekept it for so long."

"Not afraid of sharing it with you, but you better not take anyone else here."

She chuckles. "Who would I take here?"

"I don't know . . . your brother?"

"Ew." She pokes my side. "What is wrong with you that you think I'd take my brother to a romantic spot like this?"

"Honestly, I don't know. I'm still recovering from the flowers incident."

"I think we'll all be recovering from that for a while, including Mac."

"I don't know. She seemed to shake it off pretty quickly. But good luck getting her to stop saying dick. I think that's ingrained as a core memory now."

"Something Ryland will have to deal with. He started it, so he'll have to try to take it back," she says, her hair brushing against my chin as she snuggles.

"I still can't believe he's technically a dad."

"I know. Despite being a teacher, he never showed interest in having kids, but he's always had a soft spot for Mac. I think Cassidy knew he'd be able to step into the role naturally. I'm not saying it's been easy for him, but he's finding his way."

"And are you finding your way?" I ask.

Her head tucked into my shoulder and chest as her hand rests on my pec, she says, "Umm, not really. I mean, I'm getting my master's in business management, but I don't know what to do with that. I always thought after I was done, I'd come home and help Cassidy at the store. But I don't know now. Maggie has told me I should help her with her wedding business, but in all honesty, I don't think I want to stay in San Francisco, and I'm also not into her hours. I swear she's always working and I'd always feel I should work the same hours."

"I can understand that. Not to mention, you should never go into business with friends."

"I've heard that as well. So that leaves me with no ideas regarding what direction I want to take."

"You have time to figure it out."

"Not really," she says. "I mean, it's not like I'm swimming

in cash over here. I'll have to get a job. And after a failed semester, my scholarship is on the line."

"You have a job with me," I say.

"I feel weird working for you now. When we hated each other, I had no problem taking money from you. It felt great, actually." I chuckle. "But now that we're, you know, seeing each other, it doesn't feel right."

"Listen," I say, tilting her chin up to look at me. "My house is a goddamn disaster because of you. You started a job, and you will finish it. After you're done with that job, you can do whatever the hell you want, until then, I own you."

She laughs. "Do you really think that kind of attitude will get you what you want?"

My hand that's wrapped around her back slides to her hip, and I tug on her dress, pulling up the hem so I can feel her skin under my palm. "Yes, I do."

"Why did you bring me out here?" she asks, her fingers making a slow circular motion on my chest.

"Remember when we were sitting by the firepit when Maggie visited?"

"Yes. That was one of the first times I felt butterflies in my stomach. I've always heard Cassidy talk about that feeling you get in your stomach when something truly excites you. Do you remember giving me your sweatshirt because it was chilly? The moment I put it on, it felt like my stomach was being lifted by thousands of butterflies."

"Fuck, if only I knew that," I say, sad that I couldn't capitalize on that moment.

"You wouldn't have done anything. You and I both know that."

"True, I wish I could have."

She tilts my face toward hers with her fingers. "Do something about this moment."

My teeth fall over my lip, and my hand draws up to cup her bare ass. The solid palmful immediately makes me hard.

But I control myself as I say, "That night, as we stared at the stars, I told you how they'd become the key to keeping me sane, to remembering where I'm from and who I am." She nods, her fingers toying with the collar of my shirt. "I wanted to bring you out here so I can add another grounding spot. So I can look up at the stars and remember this moment with you."

"Hayes," she says softly.

"We had a brutal beginning, Hattie. I hurt you several times. And I don't want you to recall those moments when you look back at us. I want you to remember this moment, where we lie under the stars, grounding us in time to this spot, and started something new." I cup her face. "I don't know where this will take us or what's going to happen in the future, but I do know I like you, a lot, and I want to try with you. In the future, there will be moments like commercials with Odette, or tours, or my attention being pulled in different directions, but this right here, us under the stars, it's what I'll always come back to in my mind. You, me, and a blanket of the peaceful night sky."

She wets her lips and shifts so her delicate mouth can find mine. The smell of dried grass and the damp night air surrounds us. I get lost in her heated touch, her passionate kiss, and her tentative tongue.

Our bodies press together, our mouths part wide, and my tongue dives against hers, tangling as her grip on me grows stronger.

Fuck . . . her mouth is so delicious. Naive but sexy.

And with every dip of her tongue, every move of her hand, my control starts to slip further and further until I knowingly pull away before I do something she's not ready for.

"Hattie, we need . . . we need to take a second."

Her dreamy eyes open, and as she stares down at me, her teeth roll over the corner of her mouth and her hand lowers down my stomach.

Fuck.

Me.

"Careful," I tell her. "You don't want to start something you can't finish."

"But I haven't finished in so long," she coos into my ear as her hand finds the waist of my jeans.

"Hattie." I breathe heavily, feeling my pants grow tight just from the thought of her hand slipping past the waistband. "Seriously, I won't be able to control myself."

"Good," she says as her fingers dip under my jeans and my boxer briefs.

"Fuck. Hattie, seriously." I smooth my palm over her thong-covered ass, gripping the string tightly.

"I'm being serious," she says as her hand slips farther and farther . . . and farther . . .

I focus on the courage in her eyes as her fingertips pass over my erection. Then the most delicious expression crosses her face.

Joy.

Nerves.

An appetite for me.

They're all there, and unfortunately, nothing can stop me as I growl and flip her to her back so I'm hovering over her. She spreads her legs, welcoming my body.

Surprised at first, it takes her a second to adjust, but when she feels my pelvis press against hers, she asks, "What can you do to me that will make me come but will keep our clothes on at the same time?"

"A lot," I say, my control completely gone, my dick leading the way now. "Name what you want. It's yours."

I hike her dress up around her waist so the fabric isn't in our way.

I lower my mouth to hers, not pressing all my weight into her but just enough so she can feel me. Languidly, I kiss her, taking the lead, not using tongue at first, but teasing her with my lips.

Her hand drives through my hair, tugging on the strands as her legs wrap around mine, pulling my pelvis closer to hers, but my jeans can't possibly feel good rubbing against her, so I lift and stare down at her.

"Undo my jeans and push them down."

"Wh-what?" she asks, looking cutely nervous.

"Keep my briefs on but push down my jeans. It'll feel better."

"Okay," she says. She reaches for my jeans and undoes them, then slowly pushes them down my thighs until they're out of the way, leaving me sitting up on my knees in my boxer briefs and my massively large bulge stretching for release.

"Oh my God," she says quietly as her hand runs along my length, her fingertips tantalizing me. I can feel my cock twitch under her touch. "You're so big, Hayes."

"Get used to it," I say. "When you're ready, I'm going to fill you up with my cock . . . in your mouth, pussy, and ass."

Her eyes flash up to mine, and before she can make a retort, I carefully lower her back down on the cushion and blankets and then settle myself between her legs. This time, I press into her with my length, causing her to gasp out and grip my shoulders tightly.

"Hayes," she says breathlessly. I thread my hand into her hair, grip the strands, and pull her head back so I can run my tongue along the column of her neck. I drag it down and then kiss my way up, nipping at the same time.

I move over her jaw and say, "There's one thing you need to know." I bring my mouth to just above hers, and I nip at her lower lip, giving it a light tug before saying, "This body, these lips, this pussy"—I thrust into her, and she gasps loudly —"they belong to me now. If we're doing this, we're doing it my way, meaning you"—I drop kisses down her neck—"are . . . mine." I run my tongue along her collarbone and then to the juncture of her shoulder, where I bite down on her skin while driving my cock over her pussy, dragging and pressing into her at the same time.

"Fuck," she whispers as her fingers dig into my T-shirt.

"That's it, Hattie. Don't hold back," I say as I drive into her again. This time, her legs widen more. "Hold your knees, and spread your legs wider. I don't want anything in my way."

"H-how?" she asks. I'm starting to realize she's not as experienced as I thought she was.

I lift and spread her legs wide, then push them up. I glance down at her barely-covered pussy and feel my mouth water at the sight of it. I want to bury my head between her legs, taste her, make her come on my tongue. I want to hear her moans, feel her shiver beneath me from just my mouth, but I also know she wants this. She wants the friction, the passion, the temptation without going too far.

"Grip your knees and keep them like this."

She nods and places her hands on her knees while she leans back on the pillow. Her eyes are wild as I bend down, my head falling between her legs. I might not lick her, but that doesn't mean I can't at least get close. I run my nose along the fabric of her thong and see the shake in her body as I slowly climb up until I reach her mouth. I glide my tongue over her lips, parting them, and then thrust my tongue against hers while I thrust my hips as well.

She groans against my mouth and then matches the strokes of my tongue with hers, so they dance, suck, and tempt. She's an expert with her mouth, how she kisses, and how she teases. *How good would she be at sucking my cock?*

My guess . . . really fucking good.

I tear my mouth away again and move it over her jaw, this time going down the other side of her neck, past her collarbone, just above the swell of her breast. I drag my tongue over the top of her dress and then suck her skin into my mouth as I thrust onto her.

"God, Hayes," she says, her voice breathy now. "Feels . . . so . . ." Her words are cut off with a moan as I bring my mouth over the fabric of her dress and suck on one of her hard nipples, the floral material inconvenient. It doesn't seem to bother her because her back arches, moving her breast deeper into my mouth. "Fuck," she says, her body starting to tense, so I move over to the other breast, where I do the same thing. I bring her nipple into my mouth and then she arches her back so I can suck it harder.

Unable to keep my hands to myself, I grip the breast I'm not sucking on, igniting the flame for both of us. I'm such a tit man, any size, and Hattie's are fucking perfect. Not too small, not too big, just right, and it takes everything in me not to pull down her dress and expose them. Instead, I pick up the pace of my hips, creating more heat, driving up the friction until she's panting, squirming beneath me.

"Fuck, Hayes . . . fuck, I—"

"Tell me, baby," I say. "Tell me you're going to come." I pause on her breasts, prop my hands on either side of her and focus only on my hips, driving them up and down, rubbing against her clit, putting her in a position of no return. Her head tilts back, her mouth falls open, and a long moan falls past her lips as she shatters beneath me.

I pump against her a few more times, letting her ride out her orgasm until she releases her arms and she relaxes. That's when I pull off to the side, my back toward her, and whip my cock out. I smooth my hand over the precum on the tip of my dick and use it as lubricant while I pump my length, the sound of her orgasm still fresh in my ears. It takes me a few seconds, but I'm coming in the grass, my back tensing, my groan loud enough to draw attention from anyone nearby. When I finish, I sit back on my knees and slip my cock back in my briefs, catching my breath.

I glance over my shoulder at Hattie, watching me from behind. I lift on my knees, pull my pants back on, and then I hover over her, dipping my head down and kissing her on the lips.

"Fuck me, you have the sweetest lips," I say, cupping her cheek and letting my mouth take over. *I need to taste her. Just one taste.* So I move down her body, between her legs, where I slide the thin piece of fabric to the side and drive my tongue up her slit, tasting her arousal with one swipe. *Fuck. She's so sweet.*

She gasps, and just as quickly as I tasted her, I cover her up and bring her dress down. Her eyes wide, she stares up at me, and I take the moment to wet my lips, dragging her arousal over my mouth.

"Fucking delicious."

And just like that, even under the moonlight, I can see that sexy blush of hers.

Fuck, I'm going to have so much fun with her. And this is only the beginning.

Chapter Eighteen

HATTIE

Maggie: *HE WHAT?!?!*

I curl up on my bed, knowing it's late, but I can't possibly sleep, not after the night I had. I texted Maggie the moment I got home, and thankfully, she was still awake.

Hattie: *You read that right, he dragged his tongue over my slit and then said I was fucking delicious.*

Maggie: *Call the fucking fire department because my nether regions are on fire.*

Hattie: *I think mine are still burning up. Every time I think about it, I get all . . . hot and tingly.*

Maggie: *I was hot and tingly the moment you told me he came in the grass. I don't know why, but I find that incredibly erotic. Couldn't come on you because you're far too precious, so he came on the grass. Hot!*

Hattie: *It was really hot, the most intense sexual experience of my life, and he didn't even penetrate me.*

Maggie: *Which can only mean one thing . . . you need to get over* this whole taking it slow thing. You're missing out, girl. Think of all the orgasms this man can deliver. They are world-class.

Hattie: I know. After tonight, I'm not sure I'll be able to hold back.

Maggie: See, told you. Men like Hayes don't come along very often. Take advantage of it.

Hattie: I really want to do this right, though. I don't want to end up being another one of his roadies.

Maggie: You know that's not the case. I doubt he's had intimate conversations with those women. You're different.

Hattie: I think I am too, but I want to be sure, you know?

Maggie: I get it. So how did the date end?

Hattie: We stared up at the stars a while longer. He told me about the meteor showers he used to watch, and then he took me back home. He walked me up to the front door, gently kissed me, and told me he'd see me tomorrow.

Maggie: What's tomorrow?

Hattie: Apparently, I'm still working for him.

Maggie: Oh, what a shame.

Hattie: You don't think it's weird?

Maggie: Uh, co-workers to lovers, yeah, I'm not complaining about that. Don't bend over in front of him too much, might entice him to plow you from behind.

Hattie: Seriously, what is wrong with you?

Maggie: Frankly, I don't know. I think this business is getting the best of me. Plus I was reading a book one of the bridesmaids recommended to me about a hockey player and a ten-year age gap. **Whispers** He fucks her in her dorm. I've never been more turned on.

Hattie: What have you done to my best friend?

Maggie: She's overworked, exhausted, and horny. This is what you get.

Hattie: Fair. Do you need help? I mean, I don't really want to work with you, I'm too scared it could hurt our friendship, but I can always assist in any way you need.

Maggie: I appreciate it, but I think you're right. We need to keep *things separate. I'll be okay. I have the next two days off, and I'm going to do nothing but read and binge Only Murders in the Building. Selena is queen.*

Hattie: *She is. Okay, I'll let you get to sleep.*

Maggie: *I'm so happy for you and your clit. Live in the moment and don't overthink it, okay?*

Hattie: *Thank you. Love you.*

Maggie: *Love you.*

I THOUGHT WORKING with Hayes was distracting before, but now that he's more comfortable with me in his house because we're dating, seeing him walk around with his shirt off in nothing but a pair of jeans, strumming his guitar, I'm getting nothing done.

And I mean nothing.

"Can you put a godforsaken shirt on?" I yell over his guitar playing.

He pauses and looks up at me from where he's sitting on the hearth in his lounge room.

Hair all mussed, no socks on, just jeans, and his perfectly toned chest on full display, he's so handsome that it actually hurts to look at him.

"What?"

I pinch the bridge of my nose. "I can't focus with you playing your guitar shirtless, so if you would please go in your studio or dress yourself, that would be appreciated."

The proudest of smiles crosses his face as he rests his arm on the top of his guitar and stares into my very soul with his alluring eyes. "Are you saying you're having a hard time concentrating because you can't stop staring at me?"

"That's exactly what I'm saying, and no, I don't need you to rub it in."

"Oh, I want to rub something, that's for damn sure," he says as he stands and sets his guitar down.

"Stop right there, mister," I say, holding my hand up. "There will be no touching or humping while I'm on the job. I will not be paid for sex."

"Fine, you're fired. I'll rehire you after." He steps over a pile of papers, and I stand, backing away.

"I'm serious, Hayes."

His eyes are hungry and dangerous. "So am I."

Oh dear God.

He lunges toward me, and I scoot out of the way, a scream falling off my tongue as I run behind the kitchen island.

He glances in my direction, hair falling over his forehead, determination clear. "Hattie," he says, straightening up. "We can either do this the easy way or the hard way." He walks toward the kitchen, his jeans loose on his narrow, ripped waist, his chest proud, and those boulder-like arms pulling my attention. He's so hot.

And I'm just distracted enough to forget I'm keeping him away. He moves to my side of the island, and I quickly round the corner to the other side.

Both hands on the counter, palms flat against the cold surface, he stares me down. "Hattie, you won't like what happens if you don't give in easily."

"Are you threatening me?" I ask, slowly backing up.

"I am," he answers as he turns and runs toward me.

I scream and sprint down the hallway, his footsteps close behind, so close that I juke to the left to try to throw him off but realize it's a huge mistake because I juked right into his bedroom. I pause for a millisecond to figure out what to do, but that's all it takes. He scoops me up from behind and then tosses me on the bed.

Shocked, I look up to see him kneel on the bed and practically crawl toward me, looking like a desperate wolf about to eat his prey. I scoot back on my butt and hands until I reach the headboard.

"Nowhere to go," he says as he grabs my ankles and yanks me between his legs where he presses his weight on top of me.

Breathless, I say, "I did not come to your house to be sexualized, mister. I came to work."

"Oh yeah, I forgot." He lowers his head and speaks directly into my ear. "You're fired." And then his lips press against my neck.

I sigh into his touch as his hands work up my shirt, tugging the fabric until he can't move it anymore. That's when I lift, and he pulls it over my head, leaving me in nothing but my bra.

His mouth floats up to my jaw and then to my lips where he controls my mouth like he has done every other kiss he's given me. Demanding. He's possessive with his movements, reiterating the narrative that I belong to him and only him.

From the touch of his warm palm to the slickness of his mouth and the press of his bulge into me, there's no way I could ever want anyone else, not when Hayes makes me light up like this in seconds.

He groans as he releases my mouth and then bites down on my neck, probably leaving another mark like he did the night before. I woke up this morning with several bite marks I had to cover up, marks I had no problem touching, marveling at.

He travels past my collarbone and then straight to the swell of my breasts. His hands fall to my A cups, and he squeezes them as he buries his face between them, licking, sucking, biting.

He's ravenous.

"Jesus," I whisper as I grip the back of his head, my hips now seeking some relief.

He pulls back, flips one of the cups of my bra down, exposing my breast. "Fucking hell," he mutters right before he laps at my nipple with the tip of his tongue. The sensation immediately causes me to buck up my hips.

"Yes," I say, wanting so much more.

"You like that?" he asks as he moves to the other breast.

"Yes," I answer, squirming beneath him.

"Are you wet?" He's flicking so rapidly that I don't even have to check. I know I am.

"Yes," I cry out when his teeth tug on my nipple.

"Good," he says as he sucks my nipple between his lips and then releases me, pushing all the way back and leaving me there, stunned.

He gets off the bed, the bulge in his pants unmistakable as he tugs on his hair.

"What are you doing?" I ask, sitting up on my elbows.

"I told you, you could come to me the easy way or the hard way. You chose the hard way, so now you'll have to live with the consequences."

He turns away from me and heads out of his bedroom.

I'm so quick out of the bed that he barely leaves the room before I tug on his hand, spinning him toward me. He presses his hand to my stomach and pins me against the wall.

"Do you have a problem?" he asks.

"Yes," I answer, the wind nearly knocked out of me. "You can't just leave me like this."

"You should have thought about that earlier," he says as he rubs his nose across my cheek, still turning me on.

Two can play this game.

As he moves his nose over my jaw, I reach down between us and cup him in my palm.

"Motherfucker," he whispers as he rests his forehead against my cheek.

"You need this just as much as I do," I say, bringing my other hand to his jeans and undoing them.

"Shit." He breathes heavily just as I push at his jeans, and they fall past his ass. He lifts, his eyes locking with mine, and before I can take another breath, he's slipping his fingers past the waistband of my spandex shorts and peeling them down my body until I step out of them. Once free, his hands grip my thong-covered ass, and he lifts me against the wall, only to settle me right over his cock. The only thing between us is the fabric of our underwear.

"Hayes, you're so huge," I say as he lifts my arms, and then pins them against the wall above my head.

He thrusts his hips into me, and I wrap my legs around his waist, holding him close, the friction between us already hot, already bringing me to the edge.

"I can't fucking wait to get inside this pussy," he says, thrusting harder. "I'm going to destroy it."

His mouth finds mine, and he parts my lips with his tongue before diving it against mine. He releases one of my hands, grips my cheek, and angles my mouth better.

"Ride me," he says.

I slip my arm around his neck for more support, and then I lift up and slam down.

"Fucking yes," he grunts as a wave of arousal beats with my pulse, running rampant through every last inch of my body.

Continuing the same movement, I find his lips and continue our kiss, rubbing against him, letting the outline of his length bring me higher and higher to the point of no return.

God, I want his cock. And I know I said I was going to take this slow, but hell, what would it feel like to have him inside me, to see what he can do with all our clothes off?

Amazing. I know it would be.

I also want to feel his cock in my hands and my mouth. I want to run my tongue over it, suck the tip, play with his balls, make him so crazy with need that he can't think of anyone else but me.

That he never wants anyone else . . . but me.

"Bite me," I say as his mouth releases mine.

His teeth clamp over my shoulder, and he bites down hard, the sensation pouring through me like liquid lava. I've never had it this hard, this passionate before. It's as if we're both rabid for each other, unable to get enough or satisfy our need until we both fall over.

I pump harder over him, his body helping me. The girth of his cock rubbing over my clit gives me everything I need, lighting up my body and shooting it into a numb state where the muscles in my core pull and tighten.

"I'm . . . close," I say, moving faster.

"Fuck, me too," he grunts out, his breath heavy on my ear as his free hand clutches my ass, and he holds me in place against the wall as he pulses harder now, driving into me.

"Fuck, Hayes," I say, my muscles tensing.

Thrust.

My stomach bottoms out.

Thrust.

My pussy clenches.

One more thrust.

And I shatter against him, my moan silenced by his mouth as he captures my lips again, driving his hips more and more and more until he tenses, groans against my lips, and then says, "Fucking hell . . ."

He stiffens and shudders against me while we both slow down and take deep, long breaths.

His forehead presses against mine, and he says, "I could get used to the dry-humping."

I let out a shaky laugh. "And you were making fun of it."

"Why dry-hump when you can have the real thing?"

"Because this drives the tension. Makes the need much higher."

"Trust me, babe, the need is at an all-time high. Can't get much needier over here." He presses a chaste kiss to my lips as he lowers me. "But I'll take what I can get. And what I can get is making me lose my mind." He steadies me with both hands on my hips. "I need to go change."

I smirk. "Make a mess, did you?"

"You did," he says, tilting my jaw up and kissing me again. "You made this mess."

"Uh, you're the one who chased me."

"And you were the one looking at me as if you could eat me right there on the floor," he counters.

"And you're the one walking around here without a shirt on, so . . . this is on you."

"I'm only walking around without a shirt on because you came to my house, acting professional, as if I didn't just make you come under the stars the night before. I needed to make sure you were still interested."

"Needy much?" I ask, arms crossing in front of me.

"I think we went over this. When it comes to you, yes, I'm the neediest motherfucker you'll ever meet." He gives me one more kiss and then pulls away. He heads toward his dresser but looks over his shoulder and says, "By the way, you're hired again. Now get to work."

Smiling, I say, "I don't think I can work under these conditions."

HAYES: *Why is your thong on my bed?*

Hattie: *In case you missed me tonight.*

Hayes: *Fuck, Hattie, you can't do shit like that.*

Hattie: *Oh . . . was it weird?*

Hayes: *No, it was hot, and now I wish you were here.*

Hattie: *I wish I was too. Currently, Chewy Charles is gnawing at my feet and starting to get aggressive.*

Hayes: *Who's Chewy Charles?*

Hattie: *Mac's horse stuffy. According to Mac, he likes eating mold, and my toes are full of mold. Still trying to decide how I feel about that.*

Hayes: Moldy toes, huh? Thank God I don't have a foot fetish.

Hattie: Lucky you. Do you have any fetishes?

Hayes: Not really. I am sort of a boob guy, though.

Hattie: Ooof, sorry I can't help you out in that department.

Hayes: What are you talking about? Your tits are perfect.

Hattie: They're an A cup.

Hayes: I don't care. They're sexy as shit. Tight, little nipples that are super responsive. Perfect for me to play with. Hell, I'm getting hard just thinking about them.

Hattie: Really? I've never been a fan of my boobs.

Hayes: Well, baby, I'm their number one fan.

Hattie: That's the third time you've called me baby.

Hayes: Better not have a problem with it.

Hattie: I don't. Matt was never into terms of endearment.

Hayes: Was he into anything?

Hattie: Big boobs, which I didn't have. He also really liked it when I'd pinch his scrotum.

Hayes: Wait? Really?

Hattie: No. LOL. But I wouldn't put it past him if he developed a love for that. He was always weird in bed.

Hayes: Sometimes weird isn't bad.

Hattie: This weird was bad. Like I said, he took forever to find my clit. He was adventurous but not in a good way.

Hayes: Explain.

Hattie: Like doing it in the bathtub. It would result in us sliding around everywhere, water sloshing onto the floor. He'd come, and I'd be left to clean up the mess.

Hayes: What a douche.

Hattie: Yeah, and I thought I was going to marry him.

Hayes: Fuck, that's depressing. Imagine what your life would be like with the guy who likes his scrotum pinched.

Hattie: I was joking about that.

Hayes: Doesn't matter. It's stuck in my head, and that's how I'll forever remember him now.

355

MEGHAN QUINN

Hattie: *Who? Scrotum Pincher? Hopefully you never see him again then.*

Hayes: *Doubt I will. He won't want to show up anywhere near me, especially with how much he stole.*

Hattie: *Why did you let him steal so much?*

Hayes: *I didn't let him. I think I was just too goddamn out of it to even care.*

Hattie: *I thought you stopped doing drugs a while ago.*

Hayes: *I did, but that doesn't mean I wasn't in a fog. I've been in one for a while. Going through the motions, never letting myself feel anything.*

Hattie: *Why?*

Hayes: *A year-long tour desensitized me. I just started shutting down after a while. The demand was high from the label. I lost the love for it all, and I just . . . shut down.*

Hattie: *That's so sad.*

Hayes: *It is what it is.*

Hattie: *I wish I was there so I could give you a hug.*

Hayes: *How about I come by tomorrow and help you with Cassidy's room? You can give me a hug then?*

Hattie: *I'd love that.*

Hayes: *Good. I'll see you tomorrow then.*

Hattie: *See you tomorrow. XOXO*

Chapter Nineteen

HAYES

Hands in my pockets, I wait in front of the farmhouse screen door for Hattie to answer.

I slept like shit again, but it's because I anticipated coming over. Since kissing this girl, I feel like I'm losing my goddamn mind. I want to be near her all the time. I think about her constantly, and I'm trying not to look pathetic by begging her to spend every waking moment with me.

She still has work to do at my house, but I think it would be good to switch it up and go to Cassidy's house. I know that if she came over to my house, I wouldn't be able to keep my hands off her. At least here, I'd feel weird fucking her where Ryland sleeps.

It's a good cock block.

The door opens, and Hattie's beautiful smile shines through the screen door. "You're here," she says as she opens the screen door and flings her arms around me.

Chuckling, I return the hug and tilt her chin up so I can get a taste of her perfect lips.

"Hey," I say softly.

She presses the side of her head to my chest and gives me a hug. *This. Her hugs.* How can *her* hugs feel like everything I need in life? I can breathe easier. *She cares about me.* The sky seems bluer when she's in my arms. *She listens with her whole heart.* I can actually hear the birds chirping. *She's filled my emptiness with her bright light.* And the beating of my heart in my chest reminds me just how fucking alive I am. *It's like the bland, monotonous headspace I've been trapped in has evaporated.*

All from a hug . . . from her.

Her arms release me, and she brings her hand to mine. Smiling up at me, she says, "Want to go see the room?"

"I do," I answer.

She brings me into the house, and I scan the floor for any toys that might trip me, but it's all cleaned up. She leads me up the creaky staircase to the second floor. The house is not very big at all, truly perfect for a small family. We move down the cream hallway, past what I'm assuming is Mac's room with the pink flower door, past a decently sized bathroom and to the end of the hallway.

The door is already open, so Hattie pulls me in, and I take in the soft, comforting room. This room *is* Cassidy. With its light colors of creams, blues, and greens, picture frames lining the tall oak dresser, the simplicity of a lone jewelry box and bottle of perfume. Cassidy, like Hattie actually, was light and sweetness. *Such a brutal loss to this family, to this world, to lose someone with so much goodness to give.* Makes me wonder if there was a way to epitomize her in a song somehow.

The closet door is open, and clothes are separated into piles. "Looks like you've done some work," I say.

"Yes, I have a pile of clothes Aubree has to go through, I set aside a few items for myself, and then that pile over there, the big one, is all donation. Aubree and I set aside a few key pieces for Mac when she gets older, but we're pretty much done with the clothes."

"How do you feel about it?" I ask her, understanding that this could be a really tough thing to do.

"Okay. I've had my moments here and there, but I think this needs to happen. Ryland's been sleeping on the couch downstairs in the living room ever since Cassidy passed. I can't imagine that being comfortable. He keeps his clothes in the downstairs closet. He's just occupying the space, but this is his home now. I think he deserves a space of his own and hope it will help him settle somehow, if that makes sense."

"It does," I say. "He had a house, right?"

Hattie nods. "It was closer to the high school, but he didn't feel right pulling Mac from the house she knows. He wanted to keep things as normal for her as possible. Although, it was bigger than the farmhouse and it didn't smell like potatoes."

I chuckle. "I kind of like the smell."

"I could do without it." She picks up a large potato sack and hands it to me. "Help me put the clothes in this."

"Did you wash this?" I ask as I look into it.

"Yes, of course. I'm not about to donate a bunch of potato-smelling clothes."

"Just checking." I hold it open for her and she starts gently placing Cassidy's clothes in it. She falls silent and just to make sure she's okay, I say, "Hey, you good?"

She glances up at me, tears in her eyes as she nods. "Yes. This is good."

"Are you sure you're ready for this?"

"Yes. It's just sad is all. But this needs to be done, and I know Aubree and Ryland aren't going to do it. I think this project was meant for me."

"I think so too," I say as she places the last of the one pile in the sack. "Want me to place this in the hallway?"

"That would be great."

I move the sack of clothes in the hallway, and when I'm

back in the bedroom, I find Hattie working on another stack, but I stop her and take a seat on the bed. I pull her on top of my lap and brush a loose strand of hair out of her face when she looks up at me.

"What are you doing?" she asks.

"Letting you know that you don't have to go through this alone, that I'm here for you. For anything you need. Even if it's just a hug."

A small smile tugs on the corner of her mouth. "God, what Cassidy would think if she saw this. You holding me, in her room . . . I don't think she'd believe it." She leans in and presses a kiss to my lips, more for comfort than anything. "And thank you. I'm glad you're here."

"Me too." I connect her hand with mine and say, "You know, before everything went down with Ryland, Cassidy and I were good friends. It was Ryland, Abel, Cassidy, and me. We all hung out together. She'd tag along, and we didn't mind at all. So honestly, I think she'd be happy about this, about you and me, at least, that would be my hope."

Hattie's eyes soften. "I think you're right. She would. She did suggest you be my friend in her letter to you." Hattie places her hand on my cheek, and she leans in, lightly kissing me. When she pulls away, she says, "Okay, let's get this place cleared out. I want to get everything ready so I can paint and set up to surprise Ryland tomorrow."

"Tell me what to do. I'm yours."

She hops off my lap. "First, take your shirt off. I prefer to look at my hired help with no clothes on."

I chuckle and shake my head. "Nice try. I'm not taking anything off. It will only distract you and to hell if I'm doing this alone."

"It was worth a try."

I scoop her around her waist and bring her back to my chest. Speaking close to her ear, I say, "Maybe later, though."

"Something to look forward to."

I kiss her neck and then release her, but not before she gives me the most sultry stare down of my goddamn life.

"Don't do that," I say, pointing my finger at her.

"Do what?" She smirks as she hands me another potato sack.

I open it wide and reply, "Look at me like you would have no problem dropping to your knees right now and sucking my dick."

"I wouldn't." She bats her lashes, and I shake my head.

"Jesus Christ." I stare up at the ceiling as she puts the clothes into the sack. "You know, I have no problem tossing you over my shoulder and dragging you out to my SUV. I might not fuck you in your sister's bedroom, but I have no problem fucking you in my car."

"Mmm, that sounds like fun."

"Stop it," I playfully yell at her, causing her to laugh.

"A little testy today, are we?"

"I'm trying to be good, Hattie. You're making it hard."

"Making your penis hard?" She smirks when she finishes with another pile.

My nostrils flare at her. "Keep bending over in those spandex shorts, and it's going to be really hard."

"Oh really?" She leans over to pick up a shoe off the ground but keeps her eye on me while her ass is directed right at me. "You mean, bending over like this?"

I set the potato sack down and move toward the bedroom door. "I'm out of here."

Her cute laughter bounces through the room as she grabs my hand and tugs me back. "You're not going anywhere. Now be a good boy, work hard, and if you're lucky, I'll reward you in the end."

"I'm holding you to that," I say as I smack her ass. The snap of the sound is exactly what I need to hold me over.

"STORAGE?" I ask Hattie as she sifts through a box from under Cassidy's bed.

She looks up at the photo albums in my hand. "Are those from our childhood?"

"Yes," I answer.

Hattie nods. "I'm sure Mac would want to look at them one day. Cassidy put them together. I remember her working hard on them one summer, and she showed our dad, and . . . well, he told her it was a huge waste of time. She didn't think so, though. And I'm glad she didn't. Now Mac will get to enjoy her hard work."

"And you too," I say as I put the albums in a plastic container.

After sifting through the closet and dividing the clothes up, I told Hattie we should pick up some plastic containers for anything she wants to store in the attic for Mac later on. That way they'll hold up well over the years. She agreed, and we made the short trip to a Walmart about twenty-five minutes away. We ate sandwiches, listened to some music, her choice—she went with the best of Heart—and then we came back to the house where we've been delicately sifting through Cassidy's memories. And with every new thing we find, Hattie seems to be growing stronger and stronger. I think I expected her to be sad this entire day, but it seems going through everything is therapeutic for her.

"Okay, these are all photos as well. I'm going to put this shoebox with the photo albums." Hattie hands me the box, and I put it with the albums. "One more shoebox." She wiggles under the bed and pulls out one last shoebox. She flips the top open once she sits up and then gasps out loud, shutting the shoebox quickly. A smile cracks over her face as she looks up at me.

"What?" I ask.

Still smiling, she turns the shoebox toward me, flips it open, and shows off a box full of sex toys.

"Holy shit," I say as she closes it. "Wait, was that a picture of Abel?"

"What?" she nearly screams and turns the box toward her. She flips it open and looks around. "I don't see a picture of him."

"I know, I was just kidding."

"Oh my God!" She shuts the box and kicks it across the floor. "You almost made me dig through my sister's sex toys."

"Just wanted to see your reaction. It was everything I needed. Thank you."

"You have issues."

I just shrug. "So what do you want to do with the box? Feels weird to donate."

"Feels even weirder to keep!"

I chuckle. "True."

She quirks her lips to the side. "Is it weird . . . that I have the same vibrator?"

My eyebrows shoot up. "You have a vibrator? I wouldn't peg you as that kind of girl."

"Uh, don't you remember? Matt couldn't find my clit. I had to get off somehow."

"True," I say. "Do you have that vibrator here with you?"

She slyly smiles as she stands and carries the sex toy box to the closet, where she puts it on the top shelf. "I do, and I've used it."

"Fuck," I say softly.

"It's my favorite thing ever. Gets me off in a minute or less."

I wet my lips. "I want to see that."

"Maybe you will."

I nod toward the closet. "Why did you put the box up there?"

"Oh you know, something fun for Ryland to stumble across later."

I laugh. "You're evil."

"Consider it payback . . . for you."

"Finding his sister's sex toys? That might be too much of a punishment."

"Mmm. Think about it, Hayes. If Ryland hadn't perpetuated that feud with you, and you'd made a move on me sooner, think about how many times your cock could have been in my mouth by now."

"Can you not fucking say stuff like that?" I beg as I shift uncomfortably, trying not to think about that perfect mouth on my dick.

"Are you getting hard again?"

"Yes," I say. "Jesus fuck, Hattie. Everything you do makes me hard."

"Might want to get that checked out." She moves to the dresser and starts picking up the picture frames.

"Maybe you should check it out."

She dismisses me with her hand. "Enough, horn dog. We still have to finish packing these things and then head up to Target and the paint store. Get to work."

I roll my eyes and grab one of the full bins and take it to the attic.

———

"UM, why is your shirt off and tucked in the back of your jeans?" Hattie asks as she sits cross-legged in front of a bin that she's filling with some of Cassidy's personal effects that she's saving for Mac.

"Because the attic is hot, and I don't want to be a sweaty mess since we'll be going to stores after this."

"But . . . that's distracting."

"Says the girl who's been purposely bending over right in front of my dick the entire day."

"That's different," she says.

"How?"

"Because whereas that sexually frustrated you, you without a shirt on sexually frustrates *me*."

I tilt my head back and laugh. "Oh, I see how it is. It's fine for you to torture me, but it's not allowed when the roles are reversed."

"Glad you see it that way. Now if you could please put your shirt back on, that would be appreciated."

"No fucking way," I say as I take a seat on Cassidy's bed that has now been stripped of all linens. Hattie plans on washing them at my house. They're currently in a potato sack in the back of my car.

We're almost done. I'm impressed with how much we've accomplished. There are just a few things here and there, but for the most part, we could paint tomorrow and surprise Ryland.

"What are you looking at?" Hattie asks as she finishes up with the bin she's working on.

"How much we were able to do. I'm impressed."

"I don't think I could have done it without you."

"Nah, you could have. It just would have taken you longer."

She pauses in putting a jewelry box in the bin when she says, "No, I think I would have gotten lost in the memories, lost in my emotions." Her soft gaze connects with mine. "You've been my rock, helping me through this. Thank you."

Aw, hell. How does she do that? Make me like her even more by saying something so simple. *Unlike my mom.*

"God, I wished I'd never had you, Hayes. You're so much like your dad. Useless. Why did God give me such a hopeless son?" Thanks for that, Mom.

I was made to feel less than what I am until Mom left. Not that her words after that were much better. Had I not had Gran, had she not intervened, I wouldn't have turned out half decent as a human. But someone to call me their rock? Never would have expected that.

Not after watching my father leave without a second look back and listening to my mom constantly berate me for not being a good son . . .

It changes a person's perspective.

"No need to thank me, Hattie. I like being here for you."

She walks up to me and presses her hands to my chest as she leans in for a kiss. "I'm glad you are." She releases me and then surveys the room while I survey her matching spandex shorts and tank top set. Hands on her hips, she says, "I think we just need to clear out the nightstands, and that's it."

"She would be proud of you," I say, which draws her attention back to me.

Hattie shakes her head. "No, I don't . . . I don't know about that. I mean, the one thing she wanted was for me to finish school, and I didn't."

"Yet. You haven't finished school yet. You lost your sister. It's not because you weren't applying yourself. You're allowed to mourn her."

"It's not just that," she says. "I . . . I was struggling in school as it was before she passed. It's why my adviser suggested I take a second, because . . ." She bites down on her lip. "I haven't told anyone this, not even Maggie."

"Hey, come here." I tug on her hand and move her onto my lap. My hand goes to her back, holding her in tight as I direct her chin in my direction, forcing her to look at me. "What haven't you told anyone?"

"I think . . . I think I want to quit school." I can feel her entire body wince from the confession, and I know I need to tread lightly. School is a hot-button issue for her.

"Okay. Why do you think that?" I ask.

"Because I'm not interested in it. I don't know what the point is. I'm getting a master's in business, and for what? It's not like it's teaching me anything I don't already know. I hate being away in San Francisco even though Maggie is there. I want to be here, in Almond Bay. I wanted to be closer to

Cassidy before we lost her. I felt like Mac was growing by the second, and I was missing every bit of it. I want to be a part of the store. I want to run it. That was the goal, for Cassidy and me to run it together. I see Aubree struggling . . . I just . . . I don't want to go back to a world where I wasn't comfortable. Where I wasn't learning anything of substance. I want to be here. Stay here. Live here."

"I can understand that," I say, soothingly running my hand over her back. "This is home."

She nods. "And the whole time I was lying in Cassidy's room, staring up at the ceiling, all I could think about was how much I wish I didn't have to go back to school at the end of the summer." She shakes her head. "I really don't want to go back, Hayes."

"Then don't," I say.

"I wish that were the case, but . . . something in the will says I can't help Aubree until I graduate. Like how can that even be enforced? And I get that school was important to her, especially since she never went, but . . . it's almost like I'm being punished." Tears start to cloud her eyes. "You know I helped Cassidy build the store, right? I spent a whole summer laying down flooring, painting, stocking, and baking hundreds and hundreds of cookies. The Almond Store was a product of us both."

"I know," I say softly.

"And . . . and she just left it to Aubree. I don't understand. She left everyone something. She sent you a letter, Abel, Aubree, Ryland . . . but nothing for me. Why?" Tears start falling down her cheeks. "I'll be honest, Hayes. One reason I've gone through everything so carefully in here was because I was looking for something, anything from her that might have been addressed to me but got lost in the mix." She shakes her head. "Nothing. She was . . . was practically my mother, the one who raised me, loved me, made sure that I understood what love was, yet she left me with nothing."

"I'm so sorry," I reply, not sure what else to say, because what is there really to say? Hattie's right. Cassidy left her nothing, and she's allowed to have those feelings of discontentment. I know she's not jealous about not getting anything financially, because Hattie isn't like that. But sentimentally, I agree with Hattie. Why didn't she get a letter when everyone else did?

"Ugh, I'm sorry. I was doing so great and then I just lost it on you at the end."

"Don't apologize," I say, forcing her to look me in the eyes. "I'm here to support you for moments like that. And your feelings are valid, Hattie. I wish I could tell you why she didn't leave you a letter or put restrictions in the will, but I can't. All I can say is that you doing this, you taking care of your brother and giving him a space to be while he takes care of Mac, this is something Cassidy would be proud of. This is something she'd be smiling about. So focus on that, because you don't want to cloud your thoughts with the negativity, with questions about something you can't change. It will drive you crazy. Trust me on this. I've been there."

"You're right." She nods. "I'm finally finding some peace with Cassidy's passing. I don't want to add anything negative to it." She sighs. "And she should be proud of this, proud of how I took deep care of her items, the thought that went into how to preserve everything for Mac. She would have loved this, especially since the end goal is to give something to Ryland that he'd never give to himself."

"He wouldn't." I've known Ryland long enough to understand that he'd sleep on that couch for the rest of his life if he had to. He's always put family first, friends first, everyone else first besides himself. It's time someone put him first. "And hey, the whole college thing, that's something we can cross when the time is right."

"We?" she asks, a raise to her brow.

"Yes . . . we," I reply. "I'm in this for the long run, Hattie. As long as you'll have me, I'm here."

She rests her head on my shoulder, and I bring her in even closer. "I knew you had a heart beyond all of the blackness you try to hide behind. Why do you not show it?"

"Afraid of getting hurt," I admit.

"Why trust me then?" she asks.

Because you have a heart of gold. Because you are such an unexpected wonder in my life.

I want to say many things to Hattie, but perhaps this is the most honest answer I have.

"You haven't given me a reason not to."

I kiss the top of her head, and we spend the next few minutes just like that, with her on my lap and me holding her close.

⊏⊐

"THANK YOU FOR YOUR HELP," Hattie says as I set down a reusable bag full of food and some toiletries Hattie needed to pick up.

Our last stop of the day was Target where we spent an exorbitant amount of time looking over bedding, curtains, sheets . . . pillows. We went back and forth over table lamps, nightstands, rugs, even an extension cord because there isn't an outlet close enough to the bed for Ryland to plug his phone in, but Hattie wasn't sure which one to get. And then of course, she decided he needed an alarm clock that would help him sleep better, not sure how that works, but Jesus Christ, I nearly lost my mind in there.

The only reason I survived was because halfway through, I went and got myself some popcorn and a drink and enjoyed Hattie second-guessing every choice she was making because she needed to make the room perfect.

And in the end, when she went to pay, I handed her my card and said it was on me.

She refused . . . dramatically.

But I won because no way in hell would I allow her to pay, not when I forced her to put a record player in the cart, as well as two of my records which, frankly, I thought was hilarious. Ryland and I haven't hung out in a while. He needs to catch up on what I've been doing.

"You're welcome," I say as I slip my shoes off.

She glances down at my feet. "What are you doing?"

"Oh, did you think I was going to head home?" I shake my head and reach into the bag only to pull out a toothbrush. "Forgot to pack myself this, but I'm good to go now."

"What do you mean you forgot to pack that?"

I walk over to the door that leads to the stairs and hold up a small bag. "My overnight shit."

"So were you planning on staying here the whole time?" she asks, arms folded.

"I wasn't planning on letting you out of my sight," I say. "Not when I've slept like shit the past few nights. I need some sleep, and I know you're the only way I'll get it."

"You're just inviting yourself over?"

"Yup," I reply. "Problem with that?"

"Maybe I do have a problem with that." She places her hands on her hips.

"Too damn bad." I move past her and straight into the bathroom, where I get ready for bed.

She texted Ryland to let him know she'd be staying at the apartment tonight so he doesn't worry about where she is. Everything we bought for Ryland's room is stored in my SUV, and we've already had dinner, so now . . . now it's time to relax.

I turn on her shower and wash my body quickly from today's hard work, and then find a towel under her sink. I dry off, brush my teeth, and then slip on a pair of fresh boxer briefs before exiting her bathroom, where I find her sitting on her bed. A look of disbelief in her eyes as they take me in, starting at my thighs and traveling up the way to my face.

"That was quick."

"I don't want to waste any time." I nod toward the bathroom. "Your turn."

She stands from the bed and moves past me to the dresser, where she pulls out a few things. "You smell good," she says. "Did you bring your own body wash?"

"Yeah, thought if I went to bed smelling like you, I'd have a hard dick the whole night, which would negate the fact that I want to sleep tonight."

She just smirks and slips into the bathroom. I hear the shower turn on as well, and as she's washing up, I lie across her bed and click on the red notification in my text messages.

Ruben: *Haven't heard from you in a while. Getting nervous.*

Love the guy, but also hate him so fucking much.

Hayes: *What would it take to get out of this contract with the label?*

The bubbles on the text thread appear so fast that it makes me chuckle. I can only imagine he's been sitting by his phone, waiting for my response.

Ruben: *If you're serious, I can look into it.*

Hayes: *Is it even an option?*

Ruben: *Anything is an option. Can I call you?*

Hayes: *Not at a good place where I can talk.*

Ruben: *Okay, can you tell me why you want out of the contract?*

Hayes: *Tired. Worn down. I want to do something for myself. I like staying here, at home.*

Ruben: *You've worked tirelessly for the last year. I'm sure you're enjoying the break.*

Hayes: *I am, and I met someone. Not saying I want to give things up for her, but I want to at least take a break from it all so I can just live my life. Enjoy my life. Enjoy the money I've made.*

Ruben: *I can completely understand that. If you want out of the* contract, I know there's a loophole I can work on. But you know they won't ever sign with you again if you cut out without delivering another album.

Hayes: I know, and I'm okay with that.

Ruben: How about I give you a week to think about it. And then if you tell me you're ready to cut out, I'll make it happen. Does that sound okay?

Hayes: I think that's fair.

Ruben: Good. What's this change of heart?

Hayes: The girl who was working for me, Hattie? Yeah, we're seeing each other, and for the first time in a really long time, I feel peaceful.

Ruben: I thought you weren't allowed to be with her . . .

Hayes: Things changed. Her brother and I have come to an agreement. It's a long story, but needless to say, we're dating, and fuck, man, it feels good. I like her so fucking much. When she's around, it actually feels like I'm able to see the world again.

Ruben: Then you have to work on that relationship. I know I bother you about songs and schedules and sponsorships, but in the end, you're my friend, and I want you happy. If she makes you happy, then I'll do whatever I have to so you can keep that happiness.

Hayes: I appreciate it, man. My career isn't over, but fuck, I'd love the break.

Ruben: Then we'll give you a break. I'll check back in, just in case you change your mind.

Hayes: Sounds good, and hey, if you make it out here, you have a place to stay. Might be nice to finally show you around Almond Bay.

Ruben: Only if you make me some of those almond cherry cookies.

Hayes: If you get me out of my contract, I'll make you enough cookies to fill a bathtub so you can bathe in them.

Ruben: Hard to turn that down.

I smile just as the bathroom door opens. I glance to the side only for my mouth to fall open. Standing in the doorway, one hand hanging on the doorframe, Hattie takes my fucking breath away.

Wearing what I can only assume is a thong, the strings

high on her hips, and a cropped tank top, she stares me down with one thing on her mind . . . me. I can see it in her rapturous gaze.

"Jesus fuck," I mumble as she turns off the bathroom light and struts toward me. "Hattie," I say just as she straddles my lap.

My hands fall to her backside, and I was right . . . she's wearing a thong.

"You look hot," I say as my thumbs slip under her crop top and brush against her breasts. "Please tell me this is what you always wear to bed."

"When I'm alone, yes."

"You're not alone right now," I say as she moves over my hardening dick.

"You don't count." She pushes me back on the bed. I have to dodge the slanted ceiling, but I lie on the soft mattress and look up at her as she straddles my lap. Her hands fall to my chest, and she slowly rocks over my cock.

"Fuck," I groan as I get a glimpse of the underside of her breasts as her body undulates over mine.

"Mmm, you're already so hard," she moans, moving slowly over my cock.

"With you, it takes a second," I say as I run my hands up her thighs.

She leans down and places a kiss on my jaw, my cheek . . . my lips. I open my mouth for more, but she moves to my neck and then my collarbone.

When her fingers pass over my nipples, I lock my mouth shut from groaning, but when her tongue flicks over them, I can't hold back. "Fuck, baby."

"You like that?" she asks, almost surprised.

"I like it all," I answer, giving her the go-ahead to do more, to take what she wants. To explore.

She continues to rock over me as she plays with my nipples, dragging her tongue over them, up my neck, back to my jaw, teasing me with her lips across mine until she moves back down my neck again, the trail of wetness igniting a deep sense of need inside me—a burning sensation that I know dry-humping will not take care of tonight. I'm going to need more.

More of her.

Whatever she'll give me, I want it all.

Her kisses land against my heated skin, between my pecs, across my nipples where she sucks on one, and I groan in response. She smirks and then drags her tongue to my stomach, where my breathing halts, and my body stiffens. She swirls her tongue over every one of my abs, and when she reaches the last one and moves down between my legs, I lift just enough to look at her. "Hattie . . ."

But she doesn't stop. She takes the waistband of my underwear and drags it down, revealing my full erection. Her eyes widen as she watches it stretch up my stomach.

I'm about to tell her she doesn't have to do anything, but she pulls my briefs all the way off and then pushes my legs open. Her tentative hands run up my thighs and then inward until they almost touch my cock, but don't. Instead, my dick jolts from the near touch, and I groan.

"Baby, don't tease me."

A maniacal smile passes over her lips. "Don't tease you? What about all the times you teased me?"

"You're stronger than I am. I won't be able to take it."

That makes her laugh right before she drags her fingers under my cock, the backs of her knuckles touching my length. She doesn't grip me.

Fuck.

"Seriously, Hattie."

She sits up so her mouth grows close, and my cock twitches in anticipation, precum already on the very tip. That's how she affects me. That's how much I want her.

"You have the sexiest cock I've ever seen," she says right

before dragging her tongue over the underside, all the way up to the tip.

"Ahhhhh, fuck," I hiss, my hands gripping the comforter beneath me.

Her hands smooth under my erection again, across my stomach as her tongue flicks across the large vein that extends up my length. "How many women have sucked your cock, Hayes?"

"Hattie," I say, not wanting to answer that.

"Too many to remember?" She presses light kisses all over my shaft, down to my balls where she gently licks the seam.

Fucking hell, what is she doing to me?

"Answer the question, Hayes. How many?"

"Fuck, I don't know," I say, my chest growing tight as she moves her lips back to my tip where she hovers, waiting for me. "Hattie, come on."

"How many?"

Jesus Christ, does she really want to know?

"Too fucking many," I say, causing her to smile.

"Good, and this is the only one you're going to remember." Then she opens her mouth wide and takes my cock all the way to the back of her throat.

"Holy fuck," I nearly yell as her teeth drag along the sensitive flesh, adding a whole new sense of pleasure. My stomach contracts, my abs firing off as her mouth works up and down over my length.

Wet.

Hot.

Addicting.

One of her hands grips the base while the other fondles my balls, and together, she works my cock with her delicious mouth to the point that I can barely breathe, the sensation of her tongue combined with her sucking has me fucking panting.

"Hattie, wait," I say as she pumps harder. My legs start to

go numb. Fuck, this is happening faster, faster than I care to admit. "Hattie. Stop." She sucks harder, causing my stomach to bottom out and all of my attention to fall to my cock and the imminent pleasure. "Hattie . . ." I squeeze my eyes shut.

Fuck, hold off, man.

Don't fucking come. Don't you dare fucking come.

Shit . . . just as my balls start to tighten almost to the point of no return, she releases my straining length from her mouth and scoots away from the bed where she stands. In absolute agony, I watch as she smirks and runs the back of her hand over her mouth.

My head flops back on the mattress, my cock dangerously jolting on my stomach as a painful, "Motherfucker," slips past my lips.

Christ, talk about edging. I've never been brought that close only for the woman to stop. But Hattie, she literally has me by the goddamn balls.

When I get enough strength to sit up on my elbows and watch my swollen cock seek relief, I catch Hattie in front of me, a heated smile on her lips as she lifts her shirt over her head and drops it to the floor. Then she runs her hands under the string of her thong and pushes it down until she's completely naked, revealing her sexy, bare body.

"Jesus," I say as she moves toward me again, but this time, she doesn't get control. She had her chance and nearly made me weep as a grown-ass man. It's my goddamn turn. The moment she's close enough, I pull her onto the bed, and I move on top of her, my wet, aching cock resting on her thigh. "Is that your payback for all the times I never gave you what you wanted?"

She nods.

"Call us even then," I say right before I bring my mouth to hers and dive my tongue against hers, possessively claiming her.

She'll be marked as mine tonight. I might remember the

way she sucked my cock until the very fucking day that I die, but tonight, nothing will ever compare to what she's about to experience.

I pin her wrists above her head with one hand. She gasps as I run my other hand down her side and palm her breast, squeezing it hard.

"God . . ." she moans, her teeth falling over her bottom lip.

My fingers come together, and I pinch her nipple, letting it roll between my forefinger and thumb, the sensitive nub causing her to jut her hips up and her head to thrash to the side. I love how responsive she is. It's such a turn-on. And it's not fake, either. There is nothing fake about her. Her reactions are genuine, and I know that because when I pull away to look down at her, I see that beautiful blush on her cheeks, staining them red.

"This pussy is fucking mine tonight," I say as I bring my mouth to her jaw, where I drag my tongue along the slender bone. "I want you bare. I want to see my cum dripping down your leg." She swallows hard. I bring my mouth to her ear and whisper, "Do you give me permission?"

She nods.

"No, baby, I need to hear it. Tell me what you want."

"I . . ." She gulps. "I want you to fill me with your cum."

"Mmm." I drag my nose over her cheek. "Good fucking girl."

Keeping her hands pinned above her head, I kick her legs farther apart with my knee, making room for my body. I grip my cock and bring it to her slit, where I slide it along her slick opening.

"Fuck, you're so wet, baby."

I run my tip along her clit, and she bucks up in response, so I do it again, the slickness of her pussy creating this euphoric effect to swallow me whole. I get lost in the feeling of gliding my cock over her to the point that I let go and just use my hips to pump along her arousal.

"Hayes, I don't . . . I don't want to come like this. I want you inside me."

"Are you close?" I ask, surprised.

She nods. "Very." So I lift, leaving my drenched cock to rest on her thigh again as I catch my breath. She groans in aggravation as I don't do anything. I just let her sit there, pleasure hanging on the edge. "Hayes," she complains. "Please."

"You want this cock?"

"Yes."

"Then let that greedy pussy take it," I say as I move to her entrance and slowly slide in.

"Oh my God!" she shouts, and I pause because I don't want to hurt her.

Because she's so fucking tight.

Because she's so tense. I can't move any farther in.

"Jesus," I mutter as I feel a bead of sweat break out on my lower back. "Hattie, relax."

"I . . . I can't. You're too big."

"Baby," I say, my teeth clenched as I try not to black out from how tight she's squeezing half of my cock. "Deep breaths." She doesn't even try, so I release her hands, and they immediately come to my chest, where she braces herself, and then I bring my mouth to hers. Instead of demanding her tongue and roughly taking what I want, I slow down and gently run my tongue along her lips, parting them and then offering her a more sensual kiss, a kiss that shows her I'm here at this moment with her and there's nothing she needs to be tense about.

After a few kisses, our mouths lightly gliding against each other, her hand floats up the back of my neck into my hair and her body relaxes, and the vise-like grip her pussy has on my cock eases, allowing me to breathe as I move an inch farther. This time, she doesn't tense.

I continue to make out with her, now twisting my tongue against hers, kneading her breast.

She moans into my mouth, and I take that moment to move another inch, and then another . . . and another. Her legs open wider for me, wrapping around and digging her heels into my back. Still not fully inserted, I dive my tongue into her mouth, and her legs spread a little wider, giving me the rest of the room I need.

With one more deep, sultry kiss, I press my cock to the hilt, bottoming out. Both of us moan together. "Fuck, feels so good, Hattie."

She brings my mouth to hers and continues to kiss me, her mouth going wild now, moving rapidly over mine. She gets lost in the kiss. She relaxes when she's in charge of something else. So I let her control our lips while driving the friction between us.

I pulse my hips in and out of her, slow at first, barely moving, but as she becomes more aggressive with her mouth, I drive harder inside her, to the point that our mouths separate, and we both gasp for air as my hips drive in and out.

In and out.

In and fucking out . . .

"Oh God," she says, her back arching, her breath growing heavy.

Hands on her hips, I sit back on my heels and bring our connection with me, guiding her up and down. I stare down at the way my cock slips into her wet pussy, the narrow space I have to work with so fucking amazing that my fingers and toes start to tingle with my impending orgasm.

"I want . . . your . . . mouth . . ." she pants. I pull her up so our chests meet, her hard nipples rubbing against my pecs as she bounces up and down over my cock, barely escaping the angled ceilings.

Her fingers tangle into my hair, and her mouth connects with mine as I move her over my cock, this new angle rocking my goddamn world as she sinks farther and farther every time she rises.

"Fuck, Hattie. I'm close," I say before biting on her lower lip and then soothing it with my tongue.

Her fingers claw into my skull, her hips moving faster as her mouth pulls away from mine. Her head falls to my shoulders, her breath erratic as we both work to the point of no return. She assists in moving up and down, I help her by gripping her hips and together, we fuck each other.

We fuck hard.

She bites into my shoulder.

I reach up and tug on her hair.

She claws into my back.

I pinch her nipple.

"Ahhh, Hayes!" she says as her head falls back, exposing her neck. I take advantage, and I bite down on the sensitive flesh. "Oh God," she says, her body tensing around mine. "Oh fuck, Hayes. Oh God, I'm . . . I'm . . ."

She screams out a feral sound as her entire body convulses over mine, her pussy squeezing my cock so tight with the orgasm that rips through her that I don't have a second to even think about it. My orgasm hits me hard, and I yell out her name as I come inside her violently, both of our bodies shuddering.

"Fuck . . . me," I cry out as my dick continues to twitch inside her because her pussy won't stop squeezing me. "Baby," I say gently as I lay her down on the bed and hover over her, still connected. "Jesus, are you okay?"

Sleepily, she nods. "I'm more than okay." When her dreamy eyes open and she looks up at me, I feel this twinge of protection cover me in an instant.

This is my girl.

I just claimed her.

Marked her.

Let everyone know around us that she is not to be fucked with.

I slowly ease out of her and then place a kiss on her forehead before helping her up. I hop off the bed and then scoop her up in my arms.

"What are you doing?" She chuckles.

"Carrying you to the bathroom so you can take care of things."

"I can walk."

"Not with the amount of cum I just shot in you." *It has been a while since I've come inside a woman. A while for me, anyway.* At least I know I'm clean. I never would have taken her bare had I not been recently tested.

Her cheeks flush, and it's the cutest fucking thing. I kiss the tip of her nose and set her down in the bathroom, where I grab a washcloth for myself and then give her some privacy.

After I clean myself up, I go back to the bed where I scoot in close to the ceiling, this bed not big enough for two people, but big enough if I plan on having Hattie plastered to my body the whole night, and I do.

Resting on my back, I push my hand through my hair. *What just happened?*

Hattie fucking Rowley just rocked my goddamn world.

And now I don't think I'll ever recover. This is it for me. I've reached the pinnacle. Nothing and no one will ever be better than her. That's a shocking revelation because I'm still getting to know this girl, but fuck, I don't ever want her to leave my life. Not when she made me . . . hell, she made me feel again.

She's made me realize what a heartbeat feels like again.

A pulse.

She's made me breathe.

Lifted my chin.

Opened my eyes to the world around me when I'd done

nothing but kept my head down since the moment my mom abandoned me.

The bathroom door opens, and I turn my head to catch Hattie walking toward me, her perky tits on full display, her body marked by my mouth, my scruff, my hands, and the first thing that pops into my head is the word: *mine*.

She's all fucking mine.

I lift the covers for her, and she slips into the bed. I wrap my arm around her waist and pull her into my chest where I place a kiss on her shoulder.

"Everything good?" I ask.

"Everything's perfect," she answers.

"I wasn't too rough?" I press a kiss to her neck.

"No, I loved it. Everything. I loved everything."

"Good," I say as I nibble up her neck *because you're not getting any sleep tonight.*

Chapter Twenty

HATTIE

Hayes shifts behind me, his morning erection plastered against my backside, his heavy arm draped over my middle, and his head buried in my hair, lightly sleeping as the morning sun streams through the window. It's the most amazing feeling.

I feel amazing.

When he said I wouldn't be getting any sleep, he wasn't lying. The moment I started to drift off to sleep, his hand would caress my breast or move down between my legs. His lips would find my neck, and within seconds, I was at his beck and call, waiting to see what he would do next.

And he did everything.

Something I found that he loves to do . . . oral.

God, does he love it. And he loves when I do it to him too, which was such a huge turn-on for me. I came on his tongue twice, and he came in my mouth once. I can still feel the way he tugged on my hair as his entire body strained during his orgasm, the feral moan that flew out of his mouth was so sexy.

There were moments when he took his time, and other moments when he was ravenous, twisting and turning me in all different positions, especially when we wound up on the floor, giving us more room. I very quickly found out that he loves fucking me from behind. And I worked out that I didn't mind him lightly spanking me. It caught me off guard at first, but then I got into it, just like everything else he introduced to me.

And for the record, he had no problem finding my clit. He spent a great deal of time playing with it, playing with me, trying to get me to come every chance he could get.

Now this morning, it's clear how much time he spent between my legs because I'm sore. But sore in the best way.

I reluctantly slip out of his grasp and tiptoe across the floor to the bathroom, where I shut the door behind me. I catch myself in the mirror, and the first thing I see is my hair, which has somehow accumulated at least three inches of volume throughout the night . . . most likely thanks to Hayes and his wandering hands.

The next thing I notice are the dark bite marks on my neck, my shoulders, and along my chest.

"Holy shit," I whisper as I lean closer, my fingers running over the marks he left on me. God, they're everywhere, even on my boobs. My teeth drag over the corner of my mouth as my lips curl up into a slight smile. Call me crazy, but I like them. I like having "battle wounds" from the night before; it shows me just how much his words ring true.

You drive me crazy, Hattie.

It's what he whispered to me when we were on the floor. He was behind me, hands on my hips, driving into me viciously until we both came simultaneously. I felt it at that moment when he was ravenous and out of control. But seeing the evidence from it this morning makes me smile more.

Stepping away from the mirror, I take care of business, flush, and then wash my hands, my eyes traveling over my body, taking in the marks all over again. I drag my fingertips over them, and with every new spot I find, I grow increasingly desperate to wake him up and ask him to add to my collection.

I give myself one last look before I open the bathroom door, where I come face to face with Hayes standing on the other side. A small squeal pops out of my mouth from the surprise of him standing there, but then my eyes roam his lickable body. The cutest sleepy smile crosses his face as he tugs on his messy hair. His chest has a few marks from me, there's a scratch mark near his right nipple, and then . . .

Oh.

My.

God.

His fully erect cock strains between us.

When my eyes meet his, I say, "How?"

He chuckles. "You, that's how." And then he tugs on my hand and brings me toward the bed where he takes a seat on the floor, his back up against the side of the bed. He spins me around so my ass is right in front of his face. His hands start at my ankles and move up until they round over my butt. "Bend over, baby."

Unsure what he wants this time, I bend over, exposing my entire backside to him. He grips my ass, and before I know what's happening, he drives his tongue against my pussy.

"Spread your legs more."

Already starting to feel breathless, I spread my legs and then he goes back to flicking his tongue over my clit while I reach down and touch my toes, giving myself some semblance of balance.

"Fuck, you taste so good in the morning," he says before using his thumbs to spread my pussy and give him better access. He flicks his tongue in short, brief strokes, building up the base of my orgasm. He does it in layers. *He loves it.* He gets me to the point that I'm dripping wet, begging, then he pulls back and builds layers of pleasure until I'm thrashing, pleading with him to let me come.

His mouth pulls away, and he slides his fingers along my slit, making them wet, only to slip them inside me, curling them as he reaches the hilt, hitting me in just the right spot that my arms immediately go numb.

"Hayes, oh God."

"Mmm, there's that sound I like to hear," he lazily says before scooping his fingers inside me again. His other hand rubs over my ass cheek right before he slaps it, just hard enough to catch me by surprise with the sting, but then he smooths his palm over my skin, soothing it. "I didn't like waking up alone in bed." He spanks me again, causing me to groan.

"I had to go to the bathroom," I pant.

"Doesn't mean I didn't like it. I wanted this warm body next to me." He scoops and spanks at the same time, and I start to lose my balance, but he steadies me. "I wanted to feel your tits, play with your nipples, turn you onto your back and suck them into my mouth until you were ready to come." He scoops and spanks. "But you weren't here." He spanks me harder, and I cry out in pleasure, for the first time actually feeling my pussy convulse around his fingers. God, what is he doing to me? "Don't do it again." He spanks me and then releases his fingers, only to drive his tongue against my clit with harder, faster strokes this time.

"Oh God, Hayes." My legs shake beneath me, this position so hard to hold for an extended period, but I can't . . . I can't stop him because it feels too damn good. His amazing tongue vibrates across my clit, giving me exactly what I want. What I need.

And when he spanks me again, my eyes widen, noticing his erection, precum dripping down the length.

"I want your cock," I say before I can stop myself. "I want it bad."

His mouth lifts away. "Can't fucking hear that enough." He soothes his hand over my ass and says, "Grab your vibrator."

"W-what?"

"You heard me. Grab it." He leans his head against the bed as his large hand moves up and down his length. Watching him sitting there, watching me, stroking himself, his cock glistening from his arousal, has to be one of the sexiest sights I've ever seen.

I'm in a whole other world with this man. There's no denying it.

I move to my nightstand on shaky legs, my entire bottom half sore, and grab my vibrating wand. I hand it to him, and he says, "Turn back around and squat over my dick."

Confused about what he has planned, I turn away from him and lower myself, thankfully with him guiding me.

"That's it, baby," he says as he positions his cock at my entrance. "Now sit down."

My back against his chest, I rest on his lap, his cock fully entering me, filling me up in the most delicious way. I take a few deep breaths, letting myself settle in because when I say he's big . . . he's big.

Long.

Thick.

And he knows how to use it.

"That's my girl," he says as his lips run up the back of my neck, making my nipples hard. "Hike your legs in close on either side of my legs. I want you wide and exposed."

I bring my feet in close and place them outside of his legs, exposing my pussy.

"Such a good listener," he says. He turns on my wand vibrator and brings it to my nipples, where he lets it vibrate the little nubs. *God, that feels incredible.*

As he focuses the vibrator on my breasts, he runs one finger up my slit and then sucks his fingers.

"I could eat you every morning, that's how fucking good you taste." And then he goes in for seconds.

Thirds.

On the fourth one, I'm breathing so heavily that my chest is heaving.

"I . . . I need to move," I say, his cock twitching inside me with every taste he has of me. How can he do that? Just be submerged inside me and not lose his mind? Because that's how I feel right now, like if I don't start creating friction, I might pass out.

"No, don't fucking move," he says as he moves the vibrator lower, and when I think he's going to bring it to my clit, he lowers it farther until he's pressing it against his balls. "Ahh, fuck yes," he says, his body relaxing beneath me. "Oh fuck, Hattie." His hips shift as the vibration against his balls travels up to me, up his length, vibrating inside me. He pinches my nipple with his other hand, causing my pussy to clench around him. "Fuck yes," he groans. "Jesus, I'm going to come so hard."

His hips start moving as he continues to vibrate his balls. Those light pulses are driving me insane. *I need to come.*

"I need more," I say, my hand falling between my legs to press into my clit.

"Don't you dare fucking touch yourself," he says. "Loop your hands behind my neck."

"Hayes."

He pinches my nipple hard in warning, so I entwine my hands behind his neck, giving him free range to my body. And I fully trust him because as I sit on his lap, full of his cock, he focuses his attention back on me despite how much he loved using the vibrator on himself. He glides the wand up my inner thigh, across my clit briefly, and then to the other inner thigh.

"I won't last, Hayes," I say. "Please."

He nibbles on my neck and whispers, "I won't either."

Then he brings the wand to my clit, and I scream so loud

that I nearly fly off him because, Jesus fucking Christ, it's the most intense sensation I've ever experienced. Full of him, pressed against his chest with my back, clawing at his neck as the vibration sears through me.

My orgasm climbs at a rapid rate, my pulse skyrockets, my legs start to give out, and a sense of euphoria takes over me as I feel him twitch inside me.

"Yes, Hayes. Yes," I yell. "Oh my God."

"That's it, baby," he groans into my ear. "Squeeze my cock."

He holds the vibrator steady, right where I need it, right where I can't escape it, and it starts at the tips of my toes. It screams up my legs and tightens every muscle in my body, pulling together, tying in a deep knot in the pit of my stomach and my hips buck up as it crests over me, a splash of pleasure like a tidal wave, hitting me so hard that I cry out his name as I come.

"Hayes, fuck . . . oh my God."

"Ahh, Jesus, baby," he groans as he moves the vibrator lower. "Pump my cock."

I rock up and down on him, my legs doing most of the work, the vibration still creating this afterglow of pleasure through my body as he tenses, the vibrator falling to his balls again. His chest tightens beneath me, his cock swells, and then he's coming, his groan turning into a bite mark on my shoulder as he rides out his orgasm.

It takes a few seconds to come back to earth, but when we do, he switches off the vibrator and tosses it to the side before I drop my legs down, and he wraps his arms around my waist, just under my breasts.

"Fucking hell, Hattie," he says while squeezing me tight. "I'll never get enough of your pussy. Never."

I rest my head against his shoulder, and I'm about to tell him I'll never get enough of his cock when there's a knock on my door.

Oh shit.

What time is it?

"Hattie," Aubree's voice comes through the door. "I know you're in there . . . everyone knows you're in there."

"Oh my God," I whisper, forgetting a freaking business is below us.

My sister just heard us.

Customers probably heard us.

The town will soon know what I sound like when I come.

Feral.

Loud.

And out of control.

The freaking humiliation.

"Hattie," Aubree calls again.

Cheeks heated from embarrassment, I lift from Hayes and rip the comforter off my bed as I walk to the door, feeling his cum start to drip down my leg, just the way he likes it. I wrap the blanket around me and part the door open a smidge.

Smiling nervously, I say, "Uh . . . hey, sis."

Her expression is flat as she says, "I don't care what you do in your private time, but during business hours, for the love of God, I don't need the entertainment of your bedroom extracurricular activities. Got it?"

"Yup. Sorry about that. Lost, uh, track of time."

"Well, you're going to apologize to Ethel because she left the store with bright red cheeks and a horrified look on her face."

Great. Out of all people to hear us, it had to be Ethel. Now the town will think we're some sex sycophants.

Although, after the past twenty-four hours, maybe we are.

"Sorry," I say again.

Aubree shakes her head and moves down the stairs without another word. When I shut the door, Hayes wraps his arms around me from behind, not the least bit apologetic.

"They heard us, Hayes."

"So?" he asks, kissing my neck.

"So . . . people are going to think we're sex fiends when they talk to Ethel. I mean, I screamed when I came. Actually screamed. My voice is a little hoarse from it."

"You did. It was really fucking hot."

"Hayes," I complain as I turn in his embrace. He pushes down the blanket and pins me against the door.

"What?" he asks as he bends at the knees and takes one of my breasts into his mouth, momentarily distracting me.

"You . . . you can't . . . we can't . . ." He tugs on my nipple, and a small moan falls past my lips again.

"If you don't want them thinking we're sex fiends, you have to be quieter than that." He scoops me up and lays me down on the bed, with my legs dangling off the bed. He spreads them and swipes at his cum, only to smooth it across my stomach.

When our gazes match up, his markings now all over me, I know I'll have to cover my mouth with a pillow because he's not going to take it easy on me.

Poor Aubree. *Well, she did tell me to go after what I want . . .*

⸻

HAND ON MY THIGH, Hayes drives his SUV toward the farmhouse with the other, the back of the SUV piled up with everything we need to redo the room today.

After he made me come again on his tongue, I convinced him to shower, which he'd only do if I joined him, which of course meant I went down on him.

Maybe we are sex fiends . . .

Either way, we finally made it out of the apartment, clothed, and avoided Aubree altogether. I'm pretty sure I was quiet when he had me on the bed, but honestly, I can't be sure. He tends to make me forget everything when he's between my legs.

And now that we're driving, breakfast sandwiches ready to be consumed when we arrive, I can't help but notice just how right it feels to sit next to him, his hand on me, claiming me every chance he can get. It almost feels like this was meant to be. Me and him.

"Why did you cover up my bite marks?" he asks as he glances over at me.

"Are you serious?" I ask.

He nods. "Yeah, you should be proud of those."

"I am," I say. "But I'll also be seeing my niece and brother later, and I don't want it to be obvious that you spent the past twenty-four hours licking, kissing, and biting every inch of my body. Do you really think Ryland will be cool about it?"

He pauses for a moment and then chuckles. "Jesus, I completely forgot about his reaction. He's going to murder me."

"No, because I covered everything up. You're welcome."

He sighs heavily. "I completely forgot about the world around us." He glances over briefly. "I didn't hurt you, did I?"

I shake my head. "No, not at all." I feel a blush creep up my cheeks as I say, "I liked everything . . . and I mean everything." I had absolutely no idea sex could be so . . . animalistic. *Wonderful. Euphoric.* That squatting position . . . using my vibrator . . . I need to stop thinking about it. I doubt I've ever been that turned on in my life. I've never felt so connected to someone during sex either.

A smirk pulls at the corner of his mouth. "Good answer. But if I'm ever too rough, you have to let me know. I feel like I lost my mind around you last night. I couldn't get enough."

"I could tell."

"Are you sore?"

"Yes," I answer, and he squeezes my thigh. "But in a good way."

"I'm sorry," he says softly.

"Don't apologize."

"No, I'm sorry, because the moment I can get my hands on you, I'm not going to take it easy."

That makes me laugh. "God, Hayes. You're so old. Where do you get the energy?"

"Excuse me?" he asks in disgust. I laugh even louder. "I'm not fucking old. Watch your mouth or I'll shove my dick in it the minute we stop this car."

"As if that's a punishment."

"Watch it," he says in a threatening tone. "Your brother might kill you if I fuck you in his house, but it will be well worth it."

I place my hand on top of his and slip my fingers under his palm so we're holding hands. "Is this how it's going to be? You just fucking me every chance you get?"

"Do you have a problem with that?"

"Nope, not as long as you still wine and dine me. Just don't want to be treated like a fling."

"Trust me, babe, you're anything but a fling." He pulls down the dirt road to the farmhouse and parks in front of it. Everyone is gone at this point, so we have the house to ourselves.

I go to exit the SUV when he keeps me in place. When I turn toward him, he cups my cheek and sincerely says, "You heard me, right? You're anything but a fling."

"I heard you," I say.

"And I mean it." He moves in an inch. "I might be fucking greedy with your pussy right now, but that doesn't negate the fact that I like you, a lot. I like your mind, your heart, your quick wit, the way you care for me, and the way you make me feel when you walk into the room. There's so much more to us than just sex, and I don't want you to think I lost focus of that."

"I didn't," I say. "But it's good to know."

"Good." He closes the space between us and brushes a

very light kiss on my lips. When he releases me, he says, "Stay there."

He exits the car and rounds the hood, where he opens my car door. Before pulling me out, he leans in and rests his forehead against mine.

I loop my hand behind his head and whisper, "You okay?"

"Perfect actually," he answers when he looks up at me. "So fucking perfect, Hattie, that it doesn't feel real. This doesn't feel real."

"I know what you mean," I say. "I woke up this morning feeling so happy that I almost didn't trust it."

"Same," he says. He lowers my hands from his neck, and he grips them as he looks me in the eye. "I'm scared I'm going to fuck this up, Hattie."

"Why?" I ask as I actually see the fear in his eyes.

"Because the only other relationship I was in, I fucked up. I don't have good examples of love in my life, and I don't have a good fucking track record."

"That doesn't mean anything," I say. "That's all in the past."

"I know, but I still have this looming fear." His scared eyes meet mine. "This is too good to be true. Like . . . I don't fucking deserve you."

"Yes, you do." I never would have thought that such a confident, charming . . . *virile* man could have any self-doubts. "Why would you say that?"

"Because when it comes to relationships in my life, I tend to lose them. You're loyal to your core."

"So are you," I say. "Look at your relationship with Abel. That's stood the test of time through some really rough patches. You cheated on your girlfriend back in high school. That was a long time ago. And you said you learned from your mistakes."

"I did." He sighs. "Fuck, I'm sorry. I shouldn't be

worrying you with this. Let's . . . let's get the stuff in the house and get painting."

"Hold on," I say, keeping his hands in mine and not letting him leave. "Hayes, look at me." When his eyes match up with mine, I say, "I trust you with my heart. You haven't done anything to prove me differently. In fact, every chance you've had, you've protected me. You've put me *and my needs* first. The pickles, the job, letting Maggie stay at your house, my relationship with my brother, the apartment . . . you've always put me first, no matter what. This isn't too good to be true. This is real because we've worked at it. You've worked at it. Okay?"

He reaches around me and pulls me into a soft hug before tilting my chin up and pressing a light kiss to my lips. "Fuck, I like you, Hattie."

"I like you, too," I say. "A lot."

He kisses me again. "Good, because I'm so fucking attached to you that I'm not sure I could let you go at this point."

"You better not," I say, and he smiles that beautiful smile of his.

As he helps me out of the car and we start unloading everything into the house, I think about how different Hayes is compared to the image I had of him in my head. Growing up, I didn't know much about him, just that he was my older brother's friend, and when everything went down between him and Ryland, he became the Antichrist in our house. That summer, it was Ryland's downfall. He stopped playing baseball and came back to Almond Bay. Dad treated him like absolute shit every chance he could get, and we all thought it was because of what Hayes did. In reality, it wasn't Hayes at all. So I developed this image of him in my head that he was a bad person. A terrible person. *I felt so guilty for liking his music.*

And now that image has been completely obliterated. Hayes is not that person at all. He's very loving and caring with a heart of gold if he lets you in to experience it. He's protective, loyal, fierce. And he's sensitive and slightly inse-cure, which makes him human . . . and makes me like him that much more. If he wasn't a little insecure, he'd almost come off as pompous. Like he's better than everyone, and given his popularity and profession, that would be under-standable.

But he's not like that.

He's anything but that.

And it's one of the reasons I'm falling fast and hard for this guy.

⎯

HATTIE: *It happened.*

Maggie: *What happened?*

Hattie: *The sex.*

Maggie: *Whhhhat?!? Like . . . penis met vagina last night? And shook hands?*

Hattie: *How could they possibly shake hands?*

Maggie: *I don't know . . . tip and clit?*

Hattie: *God, Maggie!*

Maggie: *You asked!*

Hattie: *I honestly think there's something seriously wrong with you.*

Maggie: *Stop diverting me from the real meat of this conversation. You had Hayes Farrow's penis inside you.*

Hattie: *You don't need to put it like that, but yes . . . multiple times.*

Maggie: *Dear God, where's my fan when I need it? Tell me every-thing. I want to know length, girth, rotation.*

Hattie: *What the hell is rotation?*

Maggie: *How did that boat float? Was the motion of the ocean good?*

Hattie: *If you keep talking like that, we're not having this conver-sation anymore.*

Maggie: Help a girl out! It's been so long for me. I need this. Tell me, please.

Hattie: Fine, but don't be creepy. He was very long, I mean, stretched passed his belly button.

Maggie: *whispers* Jesus.

Hattie: Girth was really tight. Like, he had to pause for me to relax so he could fit.

Maggie: *wipes drool* Mother of God.

Hattie: And "rotation," not sure how to describe whatever this is for you, but he was bottoming out every single time.

Maggie: And I am now weeping in my purse. Thank you for that.

Hattie: And that's just his penis. That's not the rest of him. His hands, his mouth . . . his demanding, unyielding voice. He kept asking for more and more.

Maggie: I'm legit sobbing into an old peanut butter cracker wrapper because that's all I have at the moment. I am JEALOUS!! I'm assuming he had no problem finding your clit.

Hattie: None. Maggie, it was so freaking good, like I didn't think sex could be like that. And the things he whispered in my ear when he was deep inside me. I can't stop thinking about it. Ugh, and then this morning, I completely forgot where we were, and he had himself fully inside me while using a vibrator against my clit, and I screamed so loud . . .

Maggie: Where were you?

Hattie: Above The Almond Store. Aubree came and knocked on the door. Ethel heard everything.

Maggie: Oh my God! The old crotch probably had her spirit reawakened.

Hattie: Probably. But seriously, he makes me forget everything around me, and it's just us. I think I'm falling hard for him.

Maggie: Aw, that makes me so happy.

Hattie: But don't you think it's soon? I mean, I'm still a few weeks out from Matt breaking up with me. This isn't a rebound thing, is it?

Maggie: No. Not from the way I've heard you talk about him. This is so much more, and let's be honest, it's not like you and Matt were fully immersed into each other's lives. You were drifting apart.

Hattie: We were.

Maggie: And with Hayes, it seems you guys are on a different journey. You have a deeper connection. With Matt, it was more of that high school type of love, which sometimes grows stronger with years or, in your case, faded as you grew up. With Hayes, you're in a more mature relationship.

Hattie: True, and he told me this morning how much he likes me. He made it known he had no intention of ending what we have.

Maggie: Eeep, really?

Hattie: Yes, and he wants me to meet his grandma. There's a town gathering at Five Six Seven Eight that Aubree texted me about. Mac wants us all to go, and Hayes said we could take his grandma as well because she needs to get out of her apartment.

Maggie: Oh, Ryland and Aubree must be THRILLED about a town gathering. Aubree especially.

Hattie: I think she'd rather listen to me and Hayes go at it in the apartment above. But you know Aubree, she'll do pretty much anything for Mac. All of us will.

Maggie: So this is good. You're all going to hang out together. Even Ryland and Hayes?

Hattie: I think so. I mean, things aren't comfortable between them, but I think they'll get to a point where it's not awkward.

Maggie: It should get better once you reveal the bedroom, don't you think?

Hattie: I think so. I also think it's a peace offering from Hayes.

Maggie: How's it coming along?

Hattie: Good. Hayes is touching up some paint—with his shirt off—and I'm resting on the bed, texting you because I just got done ironing curtains.

Maggie: Send me a picture. I want to see him with his shirt off.

Hattie: That's my boyfriend! You can't drool all over him now. And saying things like he impregnated you in your mind.

Maggie: My thoughts are my own thoughts. You can't take those away from me. And are you actually official? Is he calling you his girlfriend?

Hattie: I don't know, I mean . . . we haven't had the chance to do introductions, but I'd assume he'd call me that after the conversation we had this morning.

Maggie: And the multiple orgasms.

Hattie: So many orgasms.

"What are you doing over there?" Hayes asks, startling me so badly that I nearly toss my phone in the air.

Hand to chest, I say, "Jesus, you scared me."

He sets his paintbrush down and walks up to me. "Whoever you're texting, I don't like it."

"Why?" I ask as he lays me down on the bed and hovers above me, his pecs flexing.

"Because you have this smirk on your lips that's only meant for me."

"That smirk was because of you," I say. "I was texting Maggie about you."

One single eyebrow lifts, and he says, "Were you now? What were you saying?"

"Nothing of your concern."

He leans in closer and presses a kiss to my neck. I really love those kisses, something that's surprised me. *Maybe it's because it's Hayes, and I like everything he does.*

"Seems like it's something that should concern me when you're smirking like that."

His lips move up to my mouth, and I settle in for his lips to control mine. He doesn't kiss me, just hovers right above me. He's within reach but not giving me what I want.

"Tell me," he says.

"No. It's embarrassing."

"Nothing to be embarrassed about when you're with me," he whispers. "Was it about last night?" I nod, and he smirks. "Tell her how you basically made me addicted to your body?"

"No, I told her how you made me addicted to you."

"Looks like we have a difference in opinion." He leans

down and presses a kiss to my lips. "I'll never be the same man after last night."

Butterflies take flight in my stomach as he stares down at me, his words so real. I know he means them because he never looks away. He's not one to blow me up with false rhetoric. He's true. He's real. He's raw, and I love all of it.

"When you say things like that, it makes me feel all gooey inside."

He chuckles. "Gooey, huh?" I nod. "That's cute, Hattie." He kisses my nose. "What else did you say?"

"Just about last night and how you showed me what it was like to be with a real man. I might have told her you have a huge penis."

He shakes his head and laughs while pulling me up so I'm sitting, and he's standing in front of me. "Not going to complain about that."

I snag my finger through his belt loop and pull him closer. His hand falls to my cheek as I stare up at him. "I said something about being your girlfriend, and she asked if that's what you called me. I said I didn't know because we haven't done any introductions. It seems so juvenile to have that conversation, don't you think?"

He shakes his head. "I don't think so. I think it's an honest conversation to have." His thumb rubs over my cheek. "And just to clear the air, because I'm not sure what you told Maggie, but you are my girlfriend, and there better not be any other fucker in the picture. Got it?"

My stupid, giddy smile stretches over my lips. "Got it."

"Good." He steps away. "Now put the phone down, we need to finish this room before your brother gets home, and you lying on his bed, looking sexy as shit in those shorts, isn't helping."

"As if you walking around with your shirt off is helping."

"It's not, but it's my choice to torture you. You don't have that option."

My mouth falls open as I stand up. "Pardon me?"

"You heard me." He slaps my ass, the sound echoing in the barely empty room. "Get to work, babe."

And then he walks out of the room, the dimples above his ass pulling my attention.

Damn him.

⸻

"I'M GOING TO PUKE," I say to Hayes as we stand in the living room. Ryland will be here any minute. Mac is with Aubree at the shop helping her make some cookies, so she's taken care of in case this surprise goes haywire.

We had a little extra time, so we cleaned up Mac's room, added a few of Cassidy's items, touched up the paint, hung new curtains, and Hayes even put together a mini bunk bed for Chewy Charles and his friends.

"It's going to be fine," Hayes says as he holds my hand.

"What if he's pissed, though? Like, what if he doesn't want to live in Cassidy's room? What if he wanted that room to live on forever?"

"We both know that's not healthy for anyone. You did this because Ryland needs a place to stay other than the couch, because there needs to be a new normal. And we even moved pictures and trinkets into Mac's room so she has more of her mom in her room. I promise you, this will be okay."

"I should have asked Ryland for permission. I mean, this is his house now, and I just went and renovated a room without asking."

"You painted it; you didn't renovate. And he's not going to be mad. He'll be grateful."

"I don't know," I say, starting to feel nauseous.

The telltale rumble of Ryland's large truck sounds. *Oh crap. Oh crap. Oh crap.*

He flies down the driveway and parks in front of the

house. We have the door open, but the screen door is closed. With a backpack over his shoulder, he walks up the porch and then stops when he opens the door and sees us standing in the living room.

"Uh, what's going on?" he asks. His eyes fall to our connected hands and then back up to us. "Are you here to tell me something?"

Oh God, I can see how this looks.

I quickly release Hayes's hand. "No. Nothing to announce. We're not announcing anything, just holding hands, but not like here to surprise you and be like a baby is on the way or anything like that." Ryland lifts his brow. "Not that we have done anything to make a baby." Hayes shifts uncomfortably next to me. "I mean . . . yes . . . we have. We've done the baby-making stuff, but with no intention of making a child."

"Jesus," Hayes mutters.

"But I'm on birth control, so no need to worry about that in case you were worried, but from the look on your face, you weren't worried, more horrified because I just told you, your little sister is having sex with your former best friend, turned ex-enemy, who is now your mere acquaintance." I look up at Hayes. "Is that what you are? Acquaintances?" When he doesn't answer, I continue. "So yeah, we're having sex, but you probably already knew that since Ethel heard us this morning. I completely forgot about The Almond Store below us, so that was a fun treat for everyone. Did Aubree tell you? I'm sure she told you. Ethel probably put out a newsletter about my screaming. Uhh, not that you need to know I was screaming—"

"For the love of God, Hattie," Hayes says next to me.

"I'm sorry. Jesus, what am I even saying to you?" I gesture toward Ryland as he just stands there, blinking.

"Uh . . . I have no fucking clue, but if you could stop talking about you having sex, I'd really appreciate it," Ryland says, looking slightly green.

Don't blame him. I'm a little sick myself.

"Yup. All done with that topic and moving on," I say, sweat forming on the back of my neck. "We're here for a reason, and it's to show you something."

Tentatively, Ryland sets his backpack down in the entryway. "Okay, what is it?"

"Well, you see, it all started back when——"

"Come upstairs," Hayes says, cutting me off from whatever tangent I was about to go on, and I'm grateful for it.

Hayes takes my hand in his, and he leads us up the stairs, Ryland trailing us. When we reach the room, Hayes steps to the side and pushes the door open, revealing the bedroom we set up for my brother.

A deep slate-gray paint coats the walls—Hayes picked out the color, and I love it—black curtains frame the windows, and a charcoal area rug covers the light-colored floor. A fake ficus is in the corner of the room, bringing a pop of color, and the hunter-green bedding almost looks black when the light isn't shining on it. The wood and iron nightstands we chose go great with the aesthetic, and the black and white pictures of a baseball field add that personal touch I know Ryland would appreciate.

Hayes wraps his arm around my front and holds me close as Ryland walks into the room with a look of shock on his face.

"Before you freak out or question what happened to Cassidy's things, I went through it all and put almost everything in storage. I put some items in Mac's room as well as dressed it up a bit for her in there. But we saved a good portion of her clothes that we knew would have sentimental value and donated the rest. All blankets have been saved, one placed on Mac's bed. And the pictures on her dresser have been placed around the house for everyone to enjoy."

Ryland glances around the room, still in shock, so I approach him and place my hand on his back.

"You deserve this, Ryland. You can't sleep on the couch forever, and I know you'd never have done this yourself. So Hayes and I did it for you. You're taking on a huge responsibility by raising Mac and giving her a loving home. You deserve a space where you can relax."

He drags his hand over his mouth. "I can't believe you did this."

"Is that a happy you can't believe we did this or a mad one?" I ask, fear prickling up my spine.

Ryland turns toward me. "A good one." And for the first time in my freaking life, I see tears fill his eyes. I didn't even see him cry when Cassidy died. He's always kept it together for us. He's always been our rock, but to see him get emotional over his new room? It . . . it brings tears to my eyes as well. "This is . . . wow." He shakes his head in disbelief and then glances at Hayes. "You helped?"

Hayes stands in the doorway, his hands stuffed in his jeans pockets. "I did."

Ryland nods. "Thanks, man. That means a lot." He then turns toward me and takes my hand in his. "I don't know if I'll ever be able to thank you enough for this because you're right; I never would have done it myself. I'd have slept on that couch until Mac turned eighteen." Then he pulls me into a hug and holds me tight. It's all I need to turn into a bumbling mess.

Because he deserves this so much. Ryland hasn't had the easiest life. Being the firstborn, with expectations of becoming a professional baseball player held over his head, he's never had any leeway. And when he quit baseball to become a teacher, our father harassed him constantly. But he made his way. He became head coach at Almond Bay High. He's built the program to where it is today, a hotbed for colleges to recruit from, and he's won Teacher of the Year twice. He's built his life around a community, he's been there for all of us, put his life to the side to help Cassidy when her husband passed, and when the unthinkable happened with Cassidy, he stepped up. He's always thinking of others, and it's about time someone thought about him.

When he releases me, I wipe at a few tears and say, "I'm so glad you love it."

"I do. I'm so grateful for you."

I look up into my big brother's eyes, the same color as mine, and I say, "No, Ryland, I'm the one who is grateful for you."

He smiles softly, and that's when Hayes says, "Want me to give you guys a moment?"

"No," Ryland says with a chuckle. "But I do want to know why there's a poster of you on the back of my door."

Hayes smirks. "Thought you might need to become reacquainted with me. It's been a while, after all. I've done some things you might not be aware of."

"Despite hating you for a better part of a decade, it's hard to escape the things you've done."

"Well, in case you wanted to listen, I left you two records next to your new record player. The song *Dark Liar* is about you."

"Is it?" Ryland asks, and I totally love this playful energy between them. "Looks like I need to hold the record case to my chest, stare up at the ceiling, and give it a listen."

"The only way to do it."

Ryland walks up to Hayes and holds his hand out. Hayes takes it right before Ryland pulls him into one of those one-armed bro hugs, and I swear to you, the moment they do it, this cloud that's been resting over Almond Bay lifts. A weight has been lifted from all of us. A friendship renewed. Sure, they have a way to go, but this is the start, the beginning. "Thanks, Hayes. I really appreciate this." Ryland pulls away. "After the way I treated you, I don't think I deserve your help."

"Water under the bridge, man."

They both turn to me, and tears stream down my face, which causes both of them to laugh.

I swipe at them. "Don't laugh at me. This is . . . this is a huge relief for me. I spent so much time worrying about you two getting along that it's a weight lifted off my chest to see you as best friends again."

"Whoa, hold up," Hayes says, holding up his hands. "Best friends is a bit of a stretch. The man did wrongfully accuse me for many years. I'd say we're categorized under friendlier acquaintances."

"I agree," Ryland says. "Don't be calling us best friends if we haven't even hung out alone yet. We'll see where we are after that happens. Maybe graduate to texting acquaintances."

"The obvious next step," Hayes adds with a nod.

"God, you're both annoying."

They laugh together as I leave the room . . . a pleased smile on my face.

Chapter Twenty-One

HAYES

"You promise she won't hate me?" Hattie asks as we make our way to Gran's apartment.

"No, she's going to be thrilled to meet you even though she technically knows who you are."

"How do you know? What if she thinks I'm some sort of fangirl trying to get pregnant so you're attached to me forever?"

"Honestly, she'd welcome the idea."

"Huh?" Hattie asks, the cutest crinkle to her nose.

"Gran has been a little nutty recently. She'll tell you she's dying in the next six months, but trust me when I say she's not. And she'll also most likely ask you if you're pregnant, but for her benefit because she wants a great-grandchild."

"Oh God, really?"

"Yes. She'll hammer home the idea of you getting pregnant. Just be prepared for that."

I pull into the parking spot for Gran's apartment and put the car in park.

"And if she says anything that offends you, I'm sorry in advance. Like I said, she's a little nutty. Just be mentally prepared for that."

"Nutty I can handle, but angry with me for having sex with her famous grandson? Not sure I can handle that one."

"There won't be any anger, I promise." I round the car and open her door for her.

Dressed in a pretty light green dress with her hair styled up into a high ponytail, she looks so damn beautiful that I keep telling myself how lucky I am to have her in my life. I take her hand in mine, and we walk up to Gran's apartment, wondering if I should start thinking about a single-floor place for her to stay. Although, she loves the second floor because she has a better view. Seems like I might need to look into one of those chairlifts for the stairs. That way she gets her view and doesn't have to worry about walking up and down the stairs.

When I reach her door, I squeeze Hattie's hand, and I offer a knock.

"Why do you always knock? Just come in," Gran shouts from her chair.

Turning to Hattie, I whisper, "Prepare yourself."

I open the door and step in first, Hattie trailing me. "There you are," Gran says. "But where is your lady friend?"

I tug Hattie forward who smiles and waves at Gran. "Hello, it's so nice to meet you," Hattie says.

Gran adjusts her glasses on her nose and gives Hattie the most thorough once-over I've ever witnessed. Slow and observant, Gran scans her from her feet all the way up to her face. And when she's finally done, she says, "Great hips for having a child."

Yup, I fucking knew it.

"Oh, uh, thank you," Hattie says awkwardly.

"Are you pregnant?" Gran asks.

"Can you please not start with that?" I ask her. "Maybe say hi and get to know Hattie before you start asking her about her uterus?"

Gran shakes her head. "We don't have time for pleasantries. I'm dying, and I need great-grandchildren. So, are you pregnant?"

Thankfully, Hattie handles Gran with grace. She walks into the room and sits across from her in the seat I normally occupy while visiting. "I'm not pregnant. I'm sorry."

"What a shame," Gran says. "You seem like you could handle a pregnancy well."

"You know, I've thought the same thing," Hattie says. "But your grandson doesn't want to get me pregnant. Told me to my face, can you believe that?"

What the hell?

"Hayes Richard Farrow!" Gran yells. "How dare you say you don't want her children when you know damn well she has the hips for it?"

"That's what I told him," Hattie says. "I pointed at my hips and said, 'these were made for your baby.'"

"Stand up," Gran says. Hattie stands in front of her, and to my horror, Gran grips Hattie's hips and gives them a good shake. "By God, they're sturdy." She looks up at Hattie. "Has he implanted his seed?"

"Okay, that's enough," I say, moving Hattie away from Gran. "Jesus. I didn't bring Hattie here so you can berate her about having my baby."

"Then why did you bring her here?" Gran asks as I take a seat on the chair across from her and pull Hattie down on my lap.

"Because I wanted to introduce you to my girlfriend."

Gran waves her hand dismissively. "Oh, I know who Hattie Rowley is. She dated that pipsqueak Matt for a while.

She leveled up if you ask me. Although she might be a little out of your league, Hayes. Have you thought about that?"

"Yeah, have you thought about that, Hayes?" Hattie asks, looking back at me.

Oh, is she going to pay for this later. "I have, and I'm just going to be grateful for every minute she gives me."

Gran shakes her head. "He says those kinds of things in his songs. Make sure you stay on your toes."

Hattie chuckles. "Oh, I will."

"Good." Gran takes a deep breath. "Well, I am glad to see that smile on my grandson's face. Not sure I've seen a genuine smile in a while. It means you're doing something right, Hattie Rowley."

"She is," I say, giving her a squeeze. "I like her a lot, Gran." I kiss Hattie's cheek, and that perfect blush of hers creeps out over her cheeks.

"Yes, I can see that. He's had quite the thing for you for a while now. Told me you were off limits a little bit ago, but it doesn't look like you were *that* off limits."

Hattie chuckles. "We had some complications to work through, but I'm glad we figured it out because as much as I don't like to inflate his ego, I've liked him for a while too."

"Then it's settled." Gran claps her hands together. "You're going to get pregnant."

Jesus.

Christic.

━━

"YOU GOOD, GRAN?" I ask as I sit her in a chair that overlooks the party at the inn.

"Yes, this is great. Just keep Ethel away from me, or else she'll find my cane up her butt."

"She's been properly warned," I say, which was an awkward conversation to have with Ethel. I just told her Gran was not in the mood for conversation, and unless she wanted to have an old lady go off during her event, just stay away. Ethel understood, thankfully.

"Can I get you anything to drink?"

She shakes her head as she holds her cane, staring out toward the ocean, and I can tell this is exactly what she needs. I wish she'd come out of her apartment more, and maybe that's on me. Perhaps I need to encourage her more. The moment I told her I was taking her to this event, she didn't put up much of a fight. I think the stairs are a challenge, though, and I'll look into a chair that will get her up and down the stairs without a problem. It's the least I can do.

"Okay, well, holler if you need anything, okay?"

"Hayes?" She reaches for my hand. I squat in front of her. "I like Hattie for you."

"I like her too, Gran."

Cupping my cheek, she says, "Are you okay? I know you can self-sabotage when things are good."

"I don't self-sabotage."

"You do, dear. When you got your first record deal, you started doing drugs. When you hit the Billboard, you decided to test your luck on your bike and got in a huge accident that could have ended your life. With your first stadium tour, you decided to drown your days in alcohol because your fame skyrocketed. You've found a way to drown, numb, and tamp down your success. Hattie is a success, and I don't want you to do the same thing."

Wow, from insane pregnancy to dying talk to this. Leave it to Gran to be able to bring in the serious tones when needed.

I roll my teeth over my bottom lip as I glance over at Hattie. She's twirling around with Mac out on the lawn, blowing bubbles. "In the back of my mind, I do fear I might fuck it up."

Gran forces me to look at her. "Don't put that fear in your head. You are right for her. You deserve her."

"Do I?" I ask softly. "The only love I've truly had in this world is yours. I was raised to think I wasn't important enough, good enough. You're the only one who has loved me."

"For good reason." She grips my cheek tighter. "Because you bring light to this world, Hayes. I don't care what your father said to you on his way out the door. I don't care what your mother said to you when you were seeking out her unnecessary approval. You deserve the world, Hayes. You deserve the good. You deserve the love. Hattie is everything I could ask for you. Recognize that and hold on to it."

I nod. "I'm going to, Gran."

She softly smiles and strokes my cheek. "She's so beautiful. Witty. She joked right along with me. And I can see the way you look at her. You love her, don't you?"

I don't even have to think about it as I say, "I do. It happened quick, but I love her."

"Have you told her?"

I shake my head. "No. It's too soon."

"It's never too soon to tell someone how you feel. It's something I should have done a lot sooner when I took you into my home." Her eyes soften. I swear I've never seen Gran like this. Not sure if it's the fresh air, or her seeing me with Hattie, but her demeanor has completely changed. "I'm so proud of you, Hayes. Everything you've done, everything you've gone through. I'm very proud of you."

Well . . . Jesus.

"Thanks, Gran," I say, feeling weird that we're having a heart-to-heart in the middle of a Five Six Seven Eight event.

"Now, go have fun. I want to sit here in silence as I contemplate the rest of my time on this earth."

Annnnd she's back.

I lean over and press a kiss to her cheek before standing and heading over to the bar for a drink.

I nod at the bartender. "Diet Coke, please."

"Not putting anything in that Diet Coke?" a voice says from the side of me. I glance to the right and find Abel and Ryland with drinks in their hands.

"Do you have something in your drinks?" I ask them.

They both nod and bring their glasses to their lips at the same time.

I turn back to the bartender and I don't have to say anything, he just nods and says, "I got you, man."

"Thanks." I reach into my wallet and pull out a twenty. I slip it across the bar as he hands me my drink, then I join the boys . . . something I didn't think I'd ever do . . . again.

"I didn't think you guys went to these events," I say as we step off to the side.

"Mac wanted to come," Ryland says. "I forced Aubree who forced Hattie, who I'm assuming forced you."

"Yup. But then I invited Gran because she needs fresh air."

"And I have serious FOMO, so that's why I'm here," Abel says.

"So basically, we can blame this all on Mac," Ryland adds. "Although, Ethel did corner us the other day and told her there would be cotton candy and carnival games. Of course Mac begged to come, so in reality, this is Ethel's fault."

"It's the whole Society's fault," Abel says. "Meredith, my nurse, overheard Dee Dee and Keesha talking about a friend they know who works at Lovemark."

"The romance channel?" I ask.

Abel nods. "They want to bring business to Almond Bay, have some movies made here. Apparently, a small town in Maine, Port something or other, has truly made a name for itself from some of the movies that have taken place there. And you know the Peach Society will do anything to make sure Almond Bay remains a popular tourist destination. So putting on more events like this is something they'll continue. And pressuring the community to join is part of it."

"Wow, and here we thought Ethel was just trying to bring the town together for a fun event," I say, shaking my head. "There's always motive behind everything."

"I don't know." Abel shrugs. "Could be kind of cool. Maybe we could be extras in some of those romance movies."

"Hayes Farrow as an extra in a Lovemark movie, now that's something I have to see," Ryland says.

"Why is that so funny to you?" I ask. "Don't I look like the Lovemark kind of guy? Maybe it's what I need for my acting career to launch. Jennifer Lopez had to start somewhere, so maybe this is where I start."

"Nah, you already started with those shirtless fragrance commercials," Ryland says with a teasing smirk.

"For someone who's hated me for the past decade, you sure know a lot about me."

He chuckles. "Hard to avoid you these days. If it's not your music on the radio, or my students talking about you, it's the fragrance commercials on the TV, or the mention of you in town. Pretty hard to avoid."

Abel rocks on his heels. "I think he's secretly been harboring feelings for you. Everyone says there's a thin line between love and hate."

"We're not even text acquaintances yet," Ryland says. "There's no fucking love."

"Not yet." I tip my glass toward him just as my phone buzzes in my pocket.

"He's easy to win over," Abel says. "Just bring him some donuts from The Sweet Lab, and he's sold," Abel adds as I pull my phone out of my pocket and see that it's a text from Hattie.

"I stopped eating the donuts," Ryland says as he pats his stomach. "Pants were starting to get tight."

"Says the guy with the eight-pack," Abel scoffs.

I glance at the text and read it just in case she was looking for anything.

Hattie: *You look so hot right now. I want your cock in my mouth.*

I nearly choke on my drink as I quickly turn my phone down, terrified that Abel or Ryland might have seen that.

"You okay?" Ryland asks as I cough out my rum and Diet Coke.

"Yup," I say in a high-pitched, *I'm actually not okay* tone.

"You sure?" Abel asks.

I nod as my phone buzzes again.

"All good. Just swallowed wrong."

"I once snorted Diet Coke, and I swear it stung for a week," Abel says.

"Why were you snorting Diet Coke?" Ryland asks.

"Not like . . . *snorting* snorting," Abel says as I glance down at my phone.

Hattie: *I want you to come down my throat . . . I'm thirsty.*

Jesus.

Fucking.

Christ.

I glance up at where she's sitting in a lawn chair watching Aubree and Mac play a bean bag tossing game. When her eyes catch mine, she mischievously smiles.

With one hand, I text her back.

Hayes: *Knock it off. Your brother is like two feet away.*

"You still like baseball, right?" Abel asks, elbowing me.

"Huh?" I look up. How did we go from snorting Diet Coke to baseball? "Oh, uh, yeah. Haven't been following it too much. Why?"

"Coach Disik from Brentwood is coming to one of Ryland's games. He's interested in a few of his players."

"Oh shit, really?" I ask. "That's the school Knox Gentry went to, right?"

My phone buzzes.

Mother of God.

"And Carson Stone," Ryland adds. "Yeah, I'm pretty excited. We've built the program to the point we're now gaining national attention. I have a left-hander on the mound that Disik really loves."

"Wow, that's amazing," I say, my phone buzzing again.

"Look at you two," Abel says, glancing between us. "It's like . . . we're family all over again. Just like old times."

"Only a few more wrinkles," Ryland says.

"Speak for yourself," Abel replies. "I have a solid skincare routine that keeps me young."

Buzz.

Christ.

I peek at my phone.

Hattie: *I'm wet just thinking about swirling my tongue around the tip of your cock. Uncomfortably wet.*

Hattie: *Meet me in the bathroom next to the registration desk. Knock three times so I know it's you.*

I glance up from my phone to where she was sitting, but she's no longer there.

Shit.

"Maybe we can have a sleepover sometime," Abel says, pulling my attention again.

"What?" I ask.

He shrugs. "A sleepover. Don't you think that would be fun?"

"We're in our fucking thirties," Ryland says. "Grown-ass men don't have sleepovers."

"If tents are involved, they sure do." Abel sips his drink. "You can't tell me a camping trip isn't just a grown man's version of having a sleepover."

"You want to go on a camping trip?" I ask.

"Wouldn't hurt for us to spend more time together now that you two are talking to each other. Also, it wouldn't hurt you two to buy me something. I'm looking for a new tent."

"Why the hell would we buy you something?" Ryland asks.

"Isn't it obvious?" Abel asks, my phone buzzing in my hand. "I've dealt with both of you for the past decade, and

I've handled it with grace. So yeah, you two owe me something. I like blue tents."

"Jesus," Ryland mutters as I glance at my phone. This time, it's a picture.

Holy.

Fuck.

I swallow hard as I stare at it for a second too long, Hattie's bare tits on full display.

Her small nipples are hard and pointed, her hand dragging down her cleavage, her tongue wetting her lips.

That's all it takes for me to go hard right in front of her goddamn brother.

"What are you looking at?" Abel asks, starting to lean over.

"Nothing!" I practically yell, sweat forming on my lower back as I slide my phone in my pocket. "Nothing." I nervously laugh as Abel and Ryland exchange confused glances.

Jesus, did Abel see her?

Can they see my bulge?

Can they tell that I'm sweating?

"You okay?" Abel asks.

"Fine, yeah, great." I take a huge gulp of my drink, trying to will my erection to fucking settle down, but it feels like an impossible feat with Hattie's tits branded in my brain.

"You don't look fine," Ryland says as my phone buzzes again. I have a feeling it'll keep buzzing until I show up in the bathroom.

"Actually, I, uh, I have to take a leak." I pat Abel on the shoulder. "Good luck with the tent and all; not sure you earned it."

"The fuck I didn't," he says.

Ryland asks, "When did you start camping?"

Perfect, I got them talking about something other than my awkward exit.

Fucking Hattie, she's going to be in so much trouble.

I set my drink down on the bar, and with a half hard-on, I make my way into the inn, past the registration desk, and straight to the single bathroom, where I knock three times.

I have no intention of getting my dick sucked at a town event where anyone could hear us, but I do intend to tell Hattie what she can and cannot text me while I'm talking to her brother.

The door opens, and I push through, only for the door to be slammed and locked behind me. When I glimpse Hattie naked except for a thin thong that wraps around her hips, my mouth goes dry.

Okay, uh, what was I going to say to her?

She pushes me up against the bathroom counter, and her hands fall to the zipper of my jeans.

"Hattie, what are you—"

"I was serious when I said I was thirsty."

And then she pushes my jeans and briefs down at the same time, releasing my cock. She kneels in front of me, and she has me in her hands, massaging me to my full length before I can blink.

You should stop her.

You were supposed to lecture her.

But Jesus . . . the way she's pumping me . . .

I grip the counter behind me and hold on as her mouth moves between my legs. She kisses my balls, lightly licking them, then sucking them into her mouth.

"Jesus, Hattie," I growl out. *No way I'm fucking stopping her now.*

Her hands run up my cock, move over the tip, and then back down again where she positions me at her mouth. Without giving me a second to catch my breath, she brings me all the way to the back of her throat and swallows. That's the moment when I lose all sense. She places both hands on my hips and moves her mouth over my length. Taking me all the way in, she then smoothes her lips over the tip when she gets to the end. It's such a delicious, toe-curling sensation. I'm quickly getting lost in the warmth of her mouth and forgetting everything else.

I stare down at her, her cheeks hollowing out as she sucks, her sexy tits bobbing with her movement, her puckered nipples needing my attention. I cup her cheek and watch as she takes me farther, gagging before she pulls away, and Jesus Christ, that feels so good.

"Again, baby," I say, and she does.

She takes me all the way back until she gags, and it sends a shiver of pleasure down my legs.

"Again."

She pulls me in tight, her tongue running along the bottom of my cock, and when she gags this time, I feel my balls tighten.

"Close," I mutter as my mind swirls with euphoria, my muscles contracting as my body prepares for what's to come.

Her mouth pulls to the tip, and her hand finds my length, where she starts pumping me hard, her lips only sucking the very end of my cock.

And she sucks hard, her lips pulling, tugging, fucking owning me.

"Fuck, baby," I groan as I hold on tightly to the counter.

She sucks.

She tugs.

She sucks . . .

And with her last tug, I still as a ferocious orgasm rips through me, buckling me forward as I hold back my moan, my chest and forearm muscles flexing as I try to control myself despite my dick convulsing in her mouth.

"Fucking hell," I say as I try to catch my breath while she licks me clean.

When done, she stands and presses a kiss to my jaw. "Thank you," she whispers before she picks up her dress hanging from a hook on the back of the door and slips it on.

"Wh-what are you doing?" I ask, feeling like she just sucked the life out of me.

"I told Mac I'd do the ping-pong toss with her. Trying to win her a fish Ryland will have to take care of as well." She has an evil grin on her lips as she attempts to move past me, but I stop her with a hand to her stomach.

"You said you were wet," I say.

"Yes, I took care of it before you got here."

"What?" I ask, my eyes flashing to hers.

"I was really horny, and you took too long. I came in seconds just thinking about how I'd suck you off."

My eyes narrow. "You touched yourself without me?"

She pats my chest. "Next time, don't take so long."

That doesn't fucking settle well with me.

Sure, I was hesitant, but I don't ever want her coming without me.

I don't let her move as I lower my lips to her ear. "I don't fucking like that," I growl.

Her eyes meet mine. "Well, I don't like that you took so long."

"You were sexting me when I was talking to your brother. What the hell was I supposed to do?"

Her fingers dance along my chest. "Forget my brother and fuck me."

Jesus, this woman.

In a deep, tortured voice, I say, "Don't do that again, you hear me?"

"What are you going to do about it?" she asks, testing me.

I lift her chin and say, "Punish you."

"Is that supposed to scare me?"

"When I tie you up and edge you all night, never letting you come, yeah, that should scare you." I move my hand between her legs and cup her. "This is my pussy. No one touches it, not even you. If you want to come, you ask me.

Don't ever take your pleasure without me again. Understood?"

Her heated eyes stay locked on mine as she says, "Understood."

She moves again, but I stop her. "And tonight, you'll come to my place and sit on my face until you scream my name. Got it?"

There's a hitch in her breath as she nods.

"Good." I lean down and kiss her gently on the lips. "Thank you for the orgasm, baby, but don't make me hard in front of your brother next time."

"But that was the fun part."

"You're evil," I say as she chuckles and exits the bathroom. I follow her, and when no one is around to see us walk out together, I link my hand with hers and bring her knuckles up to my lips. I press a light kiss to her hand, and she smiles up at me.

That smile.

Those eyes.

Fuck me . . . I'm so in love with this woman.

"You deserve the world, Hayes. You deserve the good. You deserve the love. Hattie is everything I could ask for you. Recognize that and hold on to it."

I hear you, Gran.

And I'll make sure I do everything in my power to keep her as mine.

Chapter Twenty-Two

HATTIE

Maggie: That's it. I'm taking a vacation.

Hattie: What happened now?

Maggie: The father of the bride kicked the mother of the bride in the actual crotch! Like shiny tuxedo shoe straight to the vag.

Hattie: What? Why?

Maggie: Oh, you know, rotten divorce. They were out on the dance floor, and he claimed kicking was how he danced, but he just happened to peg her between the legs, buckling her over. Bad move wearing a pantsuit. Men claim women don't have it bad when getting kicked in the crotch, but I beg to differ. I saw the pain on that woman's face, and it's now buried deep in my soul. The only way to release it is a vacation.

Hattie: Wow, that's quite the wedding. What happened after?

Maggie: I, of course, had to take care of father dearest and escort him away. Claimed he needed ice for his foot from the chastity belt the old hag wears—his words, not mine. I spent the rest of the night babysitting them so there wasn't any retaliation. The groom tipped me one thousand dollars for my troubles, and I'm investing that money into a vacation.

Hattie: *I think that's smart. You work so hard.*

Maggie: *I do. And you know what? I'm going to go somewhere warm. Somewhere where the men wear Speedos and maybe . . . maybe even a naked beach where I can hide behind a palm leaf and just stare at all the willies walking about. I can't tell you the last time I actually saw a penis in real life.*

Hattie: *A vacation fling doesn't sound like you.*

Maggie: *It doesn't, but I think I need a change. The business is thriving. I'm exhausted, and the beach is calling my name. Can you hear it? Maggie . . . Maggie . . . come to us.*

Hattie: *Have you gotten enough sleep lately?*

Maggie: *No, can you tell?*

Hattie: *Just a little.*

Maggie: *Soon, when I'm on vacation. I will get so much sleep. Have you gotten much sleep, or have you just been living it up with all the sex?*

Hattie: *LOL. I've gotten sleep.*

Maggie: *Shocking!*

Hattie: *I have my period, so it's all been put on a break right now.*

Maggie: *You know, some people still do it while they're on their period.*

Hattie: *And more power to them if that's their thing, but I feel so gross and bloated that the last thing I need right now is for Hayes to strip me down to nothing.*

Maggie: *I'd let him strip me down if I was suffering from food poisoning. Nothing would stop me.*

Hattie: *What did I say about your creepy narrative about my boyfriend?*

Maggie: *I'm a lost soul. There's no fixing me.*

Hattie: *You know, your vacation could always consist of visiting me.*

Maggie: *And watch you be all lovey-dovey with your hot-as-shit, famous boyfriend who has the voice of a god? Yeah, I think I'll pass. Let me have my island fling, and then I'll come visit you. Can't promise if I visit you first, I won't accidentally have my boob fall out* *right into Hayes's hand, and I think that would be uncomfortable for all of us.*

Hattie: *Fine, but after you have your fling, you come visit.*

Maggie: *Deal. So have you figured out what you're doing with your job and everything?*

Hattie: *Not really. Aubree and Ryland want to talk with me soon, though. They want to go over some things.*

Maggie: *Are you still working for Hayes?*

Hattie: *Yes, sort of. The last two days since I've had my period have been very productive. I've cleaned up all of my piles, and I've been able to get through a lot and even straighten up his office. But obviously, I don't want to do this forever.*

Maggie: *I wouldn't be mad if you came back to San Francisco in the fall.*

Hattie: *I know, but I just don't want to do it, Mags. I think going for my master's was a mistake. I should have just stayed in Almond Bay with Cassidy. I keep wondering what my life would be like if I hadn't gone on to earn my master's degree.*

Maggie: *You wouldn't be with Hayes, that's for sure. You'd probably still be with Matt. Yuck.*

Hattie: *He wasn't THAT bad.*

Maggie: *All I have to say is clit. He didn't know where your clit was.*

Hattie: *Hayes sure does.*

Maggie: *Ugh, I hate you. Think he would know where my clit is?*

Hattie: *MAGGIE!*

Maggie: *I know, sorry. Jesus, I really need to book that trip.*

Hattie: *Please! For the sake of both of us.*

Maggie: *On it. Let me know what Aubree and Ryland want. I want to hear all about it.*

Hattie: *Okay. Talk to you later.*

⊏⊐

"YOU OKAY?" Hayes asks as I'm curled on his couch.

He's been in his studio all day, finessing one of the songs he wrote about me. It's called *Electric Sunshine*. He played a little for me, and let's just say, it ended with me on his lap, naked. It was so good. Heartfelt, sexy, edgy. Everything a Hayes Farrow song is.

I have no doubt it'll be a number-one hit for him, especially the chorus with the rasp in his voice. Ugh, it's so good.

I grip one of his throw pillows and say, "Just breathing through some cramps. I'll be fine shortly."

His brow creases. "How long have you been like this?"

"Twenty minutes? The Ibuprofen should kick in soon."

"Hattie," he says softly as he comes up behind me and curls his chest to my back, pulling me in tight. "You need to tell me when you're hurting."

"I wasn't going to bother you over cramps. You're making such good progress."

"That wouldn't bother me," he says as his hand finds my lower abdomen, and he holds me gently. "I want to take care of you."

"Seriously, it's not a big deal."

"It is to me," he says, kissing my cheek. "Everything that happens to you matters to me."

The past few weeks since we've been together have made me realize one big thing. The difference between dating a man older than me rather than a man my age is astounding. Whereas Matt was more about having fun, Hayes is deeply intimate in every aspect of our relationship, not just the bedroom. And sure, there are probably men my age who are more mature than, let's say, someone like Matt, but Hayes is so different.

He's attentive.

He listens.

He cares more about what's going on in my life than what video game level he's on.

He's mature, sexy, skilled . . .

And moments like this, when he treats me with such care, solidify the thought I've been harboring for a while now.

I love him.

There's no question about it. I love him, and I'm waiting for a moment to say it. When I think he'll be ready. I don't want to come off clingy and scare him.

"Can I get you anything?" he asks.

I shake my head. "No. Just stay here with me."

"That's not a problem," he whispers as his head snuggles into my hair.

We stay there for a while, his hand holding me gently, helping with my cramps, and when they finally start to abate, I say, "I don't know if you know this, but my birthday is this week."

I feel him stiffen behind me and then lift. "It is?"

"It is. I wasn't sure if Ryland or Aubree told you, but I didn't want you not to know and then be upset about it."

"I would have been livid if you didn't tell me." He lifts me up and gently brings me to his lap. He rests a pillow behind me, and I lean against that for support while he strokes my thigh with his thumb.

"I know. And don't think you have to do anything special—"

"I already know what I'm going to do."

"Really?" I ask, stunned.

He nods. "I've been planning a special day for us for a while, and I've been trying to think of a good time to do it. This gives me the perfect opportunity."

"That's really sweet," I say as I curl in closer.

"You deserve it."

I look up dreamily at him. "You were such an asshole to me when I first came up to your house, and look at you now, spoiling me."

He lets out a deep chuckle. "Denial will make you do stupid things."

426

"Well, I'm glad you're no longer in denial."

"Me too," he says as he leans down and presses a kiss to my forehead.

MAGGIE: *HAPPY BIRTHDAY! I wish I was there to celebrate. I'm going to call later when I'm not in the church, listening to a priest tell the bride and groom about what it means to be bonded for life.*

Hattie: *Are you texting while in church?*

Maggie: *Never claimed to be a saint.*

Hattie: *More like a sinner.*

Maggie: *Listen, I wish I was a sinner at this point. What I wouldn't give for a little romp in the confessional. I would easily confess my sins for an orgasm.*

Hattie: *LOL. We need to find you a man.*

Maggie: *Vacation fling, it's happening. Me and Mr. Speedo. I'm going to enjoy snapping that fabric against his thick man thigh.*

Hattie: *I'm frothing in anticipation.*

Maggie: *I bet you are! So what are you doing today? I sent you a package. It should get to you today or tomorrow.*

Hattie: *Actually, I'm finishing up my makeup. Going to Hayes's place today. He said he has something special planned.*

Maggie: *Why didn't you stay at his place?*

Hattie: *We had a mini celebration last night for my birthday with Mac. I just stayed at my place last night, but Hayes wasn't happy about it.*

Maggie: *I bet. The man is possessive. So you headed to his place soon?*

Hattie: *Yup. No idea what he has planned, but he said it would be epic. We shall see.*

Maggie: *Keep me posted. I want to know every fine detail.*

Hattie: *I will.*

Maggie: *And happy birthday, my bestest friend. I love you and can't wait to see you again.*

Hattie: *Love you, too.*

———

I PULL up to the front of Hayes's house and spot him sitting in one of the Adirondack chairs on his porch. I smile to myself, remembering the first time I saw him in that chair. He startled me to my very core. This time, though, seeing him there just makes me exit my car quicker.

Not sure what he has planned for the day, so I chose a simple pair of jean shorts and a navy-blue sleeveless blouse that's super comfortable but also very flattering. I left my hair wavy and pinned it half up so it was out of my face.

As I approach, Hayes stands, wearing a pair of worn black jeans and one of his signature gray V-neck T-shirts. He skipped the hat today, opting to style his hair. He looks so incredible that I hope whatever he has planned for today includes me pulling his clothes off him.

"Happy birthday," he says softly as he pulls me in by the waist and places a kiss on the top of my head. "How are you, baby?"

I inwardly smile and rest my head against his chest as he holds me tight. "Better now."

"I wish you'd stayed here last night."

"I know, but it was late."

"As if I'd care. I didn't sleep anyway with you gone." He kisses the top of my head again and then loops his hand with mine, tugging me toward his house.

When I walk in, I immediately smell the bacon he's been cooking as well as the eggs. Then my eyes spot the bakery box from The Sweet Lab. Next to the box is a vase of flowers and a card.

"Is that for me?" I ask, knowing very well that it is.

"What do you think?" he asks, leading me to the island, where he has me sit on one of the stools. Hands on my shoulders, he leans down and presses a kiss to my neck. "Open the card."

He moves around to the other side of the island while I take the card in hand and slide my finger under the sealed flap. I pop it open and pull out a simple card with an almond on the front. I chuckle knowing he got this from The Almond Store.

I open the card, and on the inside, he's taken up nearly the whole page with a note to me. I look up at him, and he leans down on the counter, hands in front of him, and nods for me to read it.

Hattie,

I can remember the moments before you walked into my life.

Dark.

Dreary.

I was lost.

I was stuck in a rut, going from city to city but never feeling anything. I'd spend hours in my dressing rooms, staring up at the ceiling, not a thought running through my mind, barely a pulse to keep me moving. I felt so . . . numb.

And then I came home to Almond Bay where you stepped into my life, replacing that numbness with light. Hope. As you know, at first, I didn't respond well to your light, to how your presence in my home resurrected something deeply lacking within me. But you brought humor. You brought joy back into my very mundane life.

Your electric sunshine . . . it consumed me, and now that I can call you mine, I know I'll never be able to go back to a world where you're not in it.

Look up at me because I have something to say to you . . .

Tears welling in my eyes, I lower the card and look at Hayes. His eyes are so sincere, his expression soft and handsome, those steely eyes making me feel weak.

"I love you, baby," he says, stealing the breath right from my lungs.

I slowly lower the card to the island, my heart hammering.

I wasn't sure he was there yet. I wasn't even sure he'd say those three little words anytime soon.

"And I don't expect you to say anything in return," he continues, "but I couldn't go another day without telling you how much I care for you, how much you mean to me, and I figured today would be the best way to do that."

"Hayes," I barely say above a whisper, my throat choked up from the elation, the surprise, the relief flying through me. I reach for his hand, and he offers it to me. "I love you, too." A smile breaks out over my lips, and I repeat, "I love you so much."

His shoulders relax, and the sexiest smirk passes over his lips. "Christ, that feels good to hear that." He sighs. "And this is exactly why I put an island between us because I desperately want to show you just how much I love you." His eyes are full of innuendo.

"Show me," I say.

He shakes his head. "Not now, baby. Tonight." But he rounds the island and comes up to me. He grips my face, and his thumb presses under my chin, angling my head up for him. He leans down and places a soft kiss on my lips. "Fuck, I love you."

My fingers lace through his belt loop, holding him close. "I love you, too."

He sighs and rubs his nose against mine. "Hearing you say that is like a sin ricocheting through me, like I shouldn't be hearing such sweet words from your lips, but fuck will I hold on to them."

"You deserve them, Hayes. You deserve everything we can give to each other."

I slip my hands under his shirt, and he freezes.

"Hattie . . ."

"What?" I ask, my fingers brushing over his abs.

"I said tonight."

"And it's my birthday, so I say now." I lift my hands, taking his shirt with them, and he groans while letting me take it off. I toss it to the side and lean in, pressing soft kisses to his chest.

"Breakfast is going to be cold."

"It's in a warmer," I say as I move my hands up to his thick pecs. "I want to feel you, Hayes. I want you to . . . make love to me."

Groaning, he lifts me up by the ass. I wrap my legs around his waist, and together, he walks us down the hallway to his bedroom, where he places me gently on his bed. Eyes on me the entire time, he undoes his pants and pushes them down along with his boxer briefs. His delicious cock springs forward, and I feel my mouth water from the sight of him. Brawny biceps flex as he grips his cock for a moment, slowly gliding his fist up and down his length while his eyes stay trained on me and his teeth pull on his bottom lip.

While he slowly strokes himself, I lift and peel my shirt off and push my shorts down, leaving me in just my thong and bra. That's when he leans down on the bed, hovering over me, and grips my cheek before pressing his lips to mine.

Soft and sure, there's no question this man wants me and loves me. I can see it in his eyes, in the way he touches me, holds me . . . kisses me.

He gently tugs my bra strap down my arm right before trailing kisses along my chest, all the way to the other strap. He tugs that down as well, the thin fabric and the feel of his fingers sending chills up my arms.

"You're so beautiful," he whispers while he brings his mouth back to mine. His large hand wraps behind my neck, and he lifts me to unsnap the clasp of my bra with one hand. Gently, he removes it from my body and drops it to the ground, then laces his fingers through the waistline of my thong and pulls it down my legs, leaving me bare.

His eyes work over my body, taking in every inch of it. He drags his hand over his mouth. "I'm so lucky."

"I'm the lucky one," I reply as he scoops me up and brings

me to the head of the bed, where I rest on a pillow, and he moves over me.

He drags his hand down my body between my legs and runs a finger along my slit, finding that I'm already wet for him.

"My baby is ready," he says as he spreads my legs.

"So ready," I say as he lowers and captures my mouth in a kiss. There isn't any urgency behind his kisses, just desire. Like he can't get enough of my mouth, my tongue, of our connection. And I'm the same way. I can't get enough of him, and I don't ever want to be satisfied when it comes to him. I want to always yearn for him. *I can't think of a better feeling.*

His hand moves down between us to grip his cock. He gently rubs the tip along my clit for a few passes before bringing himself to my entrance, where he deliciously enters me at such a slow pace that I have to pull away from his mouth to catch my breath.

When he's fully inserted, he doesn't move. He stares down at me, his light eyes a shade darker as he says, "I love you, Hattie."

I bring my arms around his neck. "I love you, too."

And then he starts pulsing inside me.

It's slow.

It's thought out.

It's everything I want to hold on to and never let go.

His forehead connects with mine as his hips start to pick up slightly.

"Nothing will ever feel this good," he says, his hips thrusting into mine. "I want this with you, always."

I grip his cheek. "Only with you."

"You're mine," he whispers, his nose touching mine.

"All yours," I say as his hand falls to my breast, and he kneads my nipple, tweaking it just enough for my back to arch off the mattress and my orgasm to build higher. "Oh God, Hayes."

"Mmm," he growls into my ear and then lifts to push at my legs, bringing them to my chest. "Hold your knees and keep your legs wide."

I grip my knees, and the next time he thrusts into me, I feel all of him, every last inch of him.

"So . . . full," I say as he picks up his pace even more, his hips now flying, his abs flexing with every pulse.

"Jesus, this pussy. Fucking love it."

He brings his hand to my nipple again, and when he pinches the nub, I feel a jolt of pleasure rock through me, causing my pussy to clench around him.

"Fuck," he mumbles as he does it again, but this time, he times it with his thrust so when he buries into me, my pussy clenches around him. "Baby, I'm close."

I can't respond because, with the next thrust and pinch of my nipple, my body goes numb, the room darkens, and my orgasm rips through me faster than I expected.

"Hayes . . . oh fuck!" I yell as my body convulses and my pussy constricts around him.

"Jesus fuck," he roars as his neck muscles strain, and he stills, his orgasm hitting him just as hard.

I can feel him come inside me, the way his cock twitches against my pussy, and it's the most delicious feeling ever.

After a few moments of letting our bodies settle from our orgasms, he releases himself from me and lowers my legs to the bed, but he stays close, leaning over me, cupping my cheek and staring into my eyes.

"We were supposed to do that tonight."

"What did you expect to happen when you told me you love me?"

He smirks. "I don't know, a hug and a kiss and then breakfast?"

I chuckle. "Yeah, you miscalculated that by a long shot." I drag my finger over his bare chest. "Maybe for my birthday, we can just stay here all day."

"As much as that appeals to me . . ." He squeezes my hip. "I have plans for us."

"Better than all day in bed?" I wiggle my brows.

In a pained voice, he says, "You can't really compare the two."

"Then let's stay here." I drag my hands down his stomach to his waistline, where he captures my wrist.

"Baby," he says, heaving a deep sigh. "I promise you, when we get back from our plans for today, we'll spend the rest of our time right here. But I have some things I want to do with you first." He places a kiss on my nose and then rises from the bed. He scoops me in his arms and carries me to the bathroom, something I've become quite used to at this point.

After taking care of business, he helps me get dressed, which is very sad, and he puts his briefs and jeans back on before taking my hand and leading me back into the kitchen, where he retrieves his shirt and puts that back on as well.

Yup, all very sad.

I sit at the island like I always do and cross my legs.

"Don't look at me like that," he says.

"Like what?" I ask.

"Like I just took your favorite toy away."

"But you did. I love your penis, and I want to play with it."

He chuckles. "Trust me, you'll get plenty of time with it today, but first . . ." He pushes the pink Sweet Lab box in front of me. "This is for you."

I pop open the lid, and a wave of maple wafts in the air as I glance down at two large maple donuts.

"Oh my God, I love these," I say just as he pushes a plate of eggs and bacon toward me as well. "Do you know who used to love these?"

"Cassidy," he says.

"Yes. And with eggs and bacon," I say, chuckling at the coincidence. "And she used to pair it with chocolate milk too."

Hayes walks over to the fridge, opens the door, and pulls out two Nesquik bottles of chocolate milk.

He sets it down in front of me, grips the counter, and looks me in the eyes as I feel my heart beat faster.

"How did you know that?" I ask.

"Because I listen to you."

I glance at the plate, the donuts, the milk . . .

"This . . . this is the breakfast I described when I talked about what I'd do for my last day with Cassidy if I had one."

He slowly nods and takes my hand in his, squeezing it. He then grabs a wrapped present on the opposite counter and hands it to me.

"What is this?" I ask.

"Something I thought you could wear," he says.

Pulse beating rapidly, my heart in my throat, I open the present, and Cassidy's old cardigan that has now been patched up rests in my hands. "But this is—"

"Aubree said you could borrow it for the day."

I look at the old cardigan, the large embroidered flowers colorful against the beige of the fabric. "Who fixed it?"

"I found someone who could help bring it back to life. Like I said, Aubree expects it back, but for today, she said it's all yours."

Tears flood my eyes as I look up at Hayes. "What are we doing today?"

"If it's all right with you, I thought we'd eat breakfast here and then go to some antique stores to look for some stained and damaged vintage tablecloths." Tears stream down my cheeks. "From there, I thought we could go to Pieces and Pages to pick out a puzzle, bring it back here, and then watch these." He pulls out two Blu-ray discs from the drawer in front of him.

Sixteen Candles and *Can't Buy Me Love.*

My hand rises to my mouth. *More tears.*

"Hayes," I say softly.

"It's your first birthday without her," he says quietly. "I can't bring her back, but I can bring back her memory."

Reaching for him, I pull him in and wrap my arms around his neck, clutching him tightly. He runs his hand up and down my back as I squeeze him.

I know for a fact Matt would have never done something like this for me. He wasn't ever really thoughtful and didn't express a deep interest in my life on this level. And that's probably one of many reasons why I wasn't broken when Matt broke up with me. Thinking back to it now, I'm free to do what I want with my life without feeling like I was being held back.

Hayes would never hold me back.

He'd never make me feel less than I am.

He'd never cruelly tell me I was boring or not entertaining.

He doesn't have a compassionless heart.

And that's exactly why I love him, because even though he might be closed off and quiet when it comes to his personal life, when he wants to open up, he gives you every last inch of him, and that's what he's giving me now.

I release him and press my hand to his chest. "This is the best gift I could have ever asked for. Thank you."

"Anything for you," he says before pressing a chaste kiss to my lips. "Now let's eat breakfast so we can start our day."

"Donut first, then protein." I smirk.

"You lead the way, baby."

———

"WHAT ABOUT THIS ONE?" Hayes asks, holding up a white tablecloth with strawberries along the edge. "It looks like it has a mustard stain on it."

I walk over to him, and he holds out the tablecloth,

showing a yellow stain right near the corner, distorting the color of one of the strawberries.

He's been so adorable while going from antique store to antique store. He's been invested in the search, offering to buy every tablecloth we've come across, but I've been very picky. Just like Cassidy. It can't just be any tablecloth. It has to have a printed design, it needs to be vintage, and it needs to be marred in some way. We've come across some gorgeous ones, but that's what the problem is—they've been beautiful, and we don't want beautiful. We want the rejects.

I examine the strawberry. "I don't know. It doesn't look that bad, like someone could hide this edge."

"Could they hide the giant brown mark in the middle?" he asks, showing off a stain that makes me question what ended up on this tablecloth. I'm going to say it's pudding.

"Wow, look at that. It's huge."

"Exactly what you said to me this morning," Hayes jokes. I give him an exasperated look that makes him laugh out loud. "You walked into it, babe."

"And I thought you were better than that."

"I might be more mature than others, but I'm still a man."

"That much is true." I continue to examine the large brown stain. "You know, I think this might be a winner. Not sure anyone could get out that stain."

"Would you try?"

I shake my head. "That's part of the game—loving the tablecloth for what it's worth. I mean, would you look at an old person and say, the wrinkle between your eyes makes you hideous, and therefore, I won't dare associate with you?"

His brow cocks up. "I'm not sure anyone would say that to an old person."

"You never know," I say as I gather the tablecloth and fold it neatly. "People have real problems with wrinkles."

"I don't mind wrinkles."

"I gathered that, given the wrinkles by your eyes, old man."

His brows raise as shock passes over his features, causing me to smirk. "Excuse fucking me?"

I'm laughing as he wraps his arm around my waist and pulls my back into his chest. Speaking closely to my ear, he says, "If I were an old man, I wouldn't have been able to fuck you the way I have the past few weeks."

"Call it late-term adrenaline."

"Guess I won't be able to deliver tonight then, won't want to wear out my geriatric hips."

"I'm surprised you can walk without your cane right now," I say just as he bites down on my neck, causing me to squeal.

"Watch it," he mutters into my ear. "You won't want to see me prove my vitality."

"Oh no," I deadpan. "That would be horrible."

He chuckles and kisses my cheek. "Come on, smart-ass. Let's purchase that tablecloth. We have one more store to hit up."

"Okay, but if you need your afternoon nap, just let me know."

He wraps his arm around my shoulders and pulls me into his side. Kissing the top of my head, he whispers, "You're in so much fucking trouble tonight."

"WHAT ABOUT THIS ONE?" Hayes asks, holding up a garden landscape puzzle.

My nose cringes at his suggestion.

Well, at every suggestion he's made.

"What's wrong with this one?" he asks, visibly insulted that I don't like his puzzle choice.

"Nothing about it is interesting," I say.

"What do you mean nothing about it is interesting?" He

glances at the picture and then shows it to me again. "The flowers are vibrant. There's grass, a blue sky, and look . . . a pigeon."

"Ew, who likes pigeons?"

"People like pigeons," Hayes counters.

"No one likes pigeons. And if someone likes a pigeon, they might need to rethink their choices. I'd never associate myself with a pigeon lover."

"Jesus, that's harsh," he says as he sets down the puzzle. "What's with the hate on pigeons?"

"I lived in San Francisco for many years, and the pigeons there are out of control. And get this, there's a pigeon rescue where people actually donate money to save them. Who's deranged enough to do that? The homeless people need food, water, and shelter, and billionaires donate to save the pigeons. Honestly, what is the world coming to?"

He picks up another puzzle. "Making a mental note never to bring up pigeons again." He shows me the box. "What about this one?"

It's a picture of a library, but all the books are the same color, making it one of those impossible puzzles that a crazy aunt or mother-in-law would purchase for you for Christmas, thinking you'd like it. However, it was made purely to make the novice puzzler lose their mind.

I prop one hand on my hip. "Hayes, I love you. You know that, right?"

"As I found out today, yes."

"Okay, then you need to know that your puzzle choices are atrocious, and I truly hope you never buy me a puzzle."

He sets the puzzle down and sighs. "Then tell me what you look for in a puzzle that would appease you."

"Well, I'm glad you asked." I turn toward him. "Cassidy and I have always loved a puzzle we could do in a few hours. We never wanted something that would take us longer than one night. It needs to be easy but also be slightly challenging.

We like color blocking, so when you separate the edge pieces from the middle, you could also separate by color. Landscapes are okay, but there can't be too much of one thing, like . . . too much grass is stressful. Too much sky, etc. And the picture has to be clear, none of this pixilated bullshit. And bonus points for a wooden mosaic puzzle. Those are our favorite."

"Okay." He nods and looks around. "Well, I think I'm going to sit this one out and let you make the choice."

"Smart." I pat him on the shoulder. "Give me twenty, and I'll find us the perfect puzzle."

———

"YOU UNDERSTAND the irony in all of this, right?" Hayes asks as he pulls the puzzle he bought me out of the bag.

"I told you, we're not talking about it."

He sets the puzzle on the counter, letting me stare at the picture.

"It's pigeons."

"I know," I groan. "We don't need to keep talking about it. I told you I understood the relevance of my choice, and I'm not happy with myself, but the portraits of pigeons got to me, and the one with a piece of bread around its torso made me chuckle, and I know it would have made Cassidy chuckle. So let's just move on and be happy we found a puzzle."

"Makes me wonder if we should donate to the pigeons in honor of your birthday."

I point my finger at him. "You watch your mouth. It's bad enough I had to eat my words on my birthday. I refuse to give in to the absurdity of saving the pigeons."

I carry the puzzle to his large dining room table that can easily accommodate two adult bodies without a problem. I know this from experience.

Hayes grabs something from the fridge while I open up the puzzle box, where I'm pleased to see the pieces in a paper bag rather than plastic. Ugh, stupid pigeon puzzle hitting all the marks for me. It was also made of recycled materials.

"Thought you might want a snack," Hayes says as he sets a jar of pickles in front of me. But not just any pickles . . . THE pickles.

I look up at him, then back down at the pickles . . . and back up at him. "Wow, you realize I'm a pretty easy bet when it comes to sex, right? You don't need to be breaking down every wall I've ever erected."

He chuckles and presses a kiss to my cheek. "Not looking to get in your pants, baby, just looking to show you how much I love you."

"And it seems like a lot." I grip the pickles and softly say, "Thank you. This means a lot to me."

"Once again, anything for you." He pulls a chair close to me, takes a seat, and drapes one arm over the back of mine. "Now, what are we doing?"

"Well, we need to put a movie on first, then start sorting the pieces."

"Right." He gets up and grabs the Blu-rays from the island. "Which one first?"

"Well, Cassidy would make us watch *Sixteen Candles* first, but I'm thinking we do *Can't Buy Me Love*."

"Saving Jake Ryan for last, I get it." He winks at me as I scoff.

"No, starting the movies off with a bang! Patrick Dempsey sets the standard."

"I'll be the judge of that." He puts the movie in and presses play as he walks back over to the table. The open-concept living, dining, and kitchen combo makes puzzling and watching movies ideal. He drapes his arm over the back of my chair again, and I hand him a pile of pieces.

"Don't miss any. We're in no rush. Nothing makes me angrier than missing an edge piece."

441

"Why does this seem like a sport for you even though you claim it's a casual hobby?"

"I just know what I like. You're lucky I'm even letting you help me."

"This is a side of you I've never seen before. I'm not sure how I feel about it."

I sort a few edge pieces into the edge pile. "When you love me, you have to love all of me, which means loving this side of me. I never claimed to be perfect."

"You're far from perfect, babe, but that's one of the reasons I can't get enough of you." He leans in and kisses my neck, dragging his tongue along the column, and I swat at him.

"Stop that. We're puzzling, and this is serious business. None of that tongue stuff."

He chuckles. "Wow . . . okay."

⸺

"HATTIE," Hayes says as he leans back in his chair, letting me put together the last few pieces of the puzzle . . . after I slapped his hand away, telling him I could handle it from here. "I hate to tell you this, but your sister was right. Jake Ryan is superior."

I pause and turn toward him. "Why would you say that on my birthday?"

He chuckles. "I'm not going to lie to you. It's the truth. Something about him just . . . makes you fall in love with him."

"Oh please, you just like his car."

"Yes, true, but that sweater vest also calls to me. And the beret Patrick was wearing was very off-putting."

"It was in back then!" I throw my arms up. "Honestly, how many times do I have to tell you that?" I pick up the last puzzle piece and place it in the center, adding a finished bow tie to a stoic picture of a pigeon. For God's sake, whoever made this puzzle needs help. "Done," I say as I run my hand over the finished puzzle, loving the smooth feel of it under my palm. "Isn't it beautiful?"

"I could think of something more beautiful," Hayes says, bringing his lips to my cheek.

"Cheesy much?" I ask.

He growls in my ear. "You're spicy today. I'm not sure I like it."

"You'll like it later," I say as I slip onto his lap and place my hands on his chest, as *Sixteen Candles* plays in the background.

His hands fall to my hips, and he lazily smiles up at me. "Why wait?"

"Because our pizza is about to be here," I say. "And I'm starving."

"Are you thirsty? Because I could give you something to suck on until the pizza arrives."

"What is wrong with you?"

He chuckles. "I don't know. I think this is what happens to me when I'm happy."

"Yeah?" I ask, playing with the collar of his shirt. "You're happy?"

"Insanely happy," he says, his hands smoothing over my thighs.

"Well, I might have something that'll make you even happier."

"What's that?" he asks.

"I'm not going to go back to school."

He frowns, his brow knitting together. "Why would that make me happier?"

"Because that means I'm staying here . . . with you."

"Babe, don't stay here because of me. Whatever happens with school, we can make it work. It's just one semester."

"That's the thing," I say. "I don't want to go back. Not

because of you but just because I don't see the purpose. It's not what I want."

"What do you want?" he asks, the playfulness vanished from his expression as he listens intently.

"I want to be here in Almond Bay. I want to be close to my family. I want to grow those relationships. I want to help at the store . . . be closer to you."

"You know I want to be near you, Hattie. But I thought you couldn't help with the store."

"I know, but I want to see if there's a workaround. I mean . . . how can it truly be enforced?"

"Not sure. I have a lawyer if you want her to look at the will. See what can be done." He pauses for a moment and then says, "But I want you to know that if you went back to school, we would make it work." His eyes meet mine. "I don't want you staying here because you're worried, if that's the case."

"I'm not worried," I say as I play with his shirt.

"Are you lying to me?" he asks.

I look up at him and sigh. "I don't think I am. I know for sure that I don't want to go back to school. Maggie was the only reason I've been able to make it as far as I did, but she's not even in school anymore. She's thriving and doing her own thing. My family is here, doing their own thing, and I just feel like I'm doing something that doesn't matter to me. Why finish it if it doesn't matter?" I take a deep breath. "And then there's you. We could make it all work, but I don't want to leave this space. I'm comfortable here, and I've found myself here. I feel like I know what I want for the first time in a while. And I want you, Hayes. I want to be here with family. I want to be closer to Cassidy, and I'm closer here."

"Have you told Ryland and Aubree yet?"

I shake my head. "Not yet. I'm afraid of what they might say. I don't want them to tell me to go back to school. I feel like we're in a position where we're building back our relationship, and if they tell me to return to school, that could ruin everything we've built."

"But you have to talk to them about it, babe. Especially if you want to work at the shop. Unless you want to continue working with me." He rubs my thighs. "I wouldn't mind that at all."

"I think you and I both know that can't happen. I've barely done anything since we started dating."

"You barely did anything when we weren't dating," he says in a teasing tone.

"Hey!" I poke his stomach, causing him to laugh. "It was a process. You can't hate on the process."

"There was no process. It was just you trying to make me crazy with all of your piles. And all I have to say is good job. You made me crazy."

"It was not that—"

Ding

The doorbell sounds, and Hayes glances over at the door. "That's the pizza."

"Thank God, because I'm starving."

He lifts me off his lap and stands from the couch, tugging on my hand.

"Grab plates."

"Or . . . we can just sit on the island and eat pizza from the box."

He shakes his head as he moves toward the door. "You realize you're the only person I know who forgoes the island chairs and chooses the counter as their seat."

"Good. I wouldn't want anyone else sitting on your counter. I've marked my territory."

"We marked it the other night," he says with a wiggle of his eyebrows.

We did, and it was one of the best orgasms ever.

While I take out some napkins, Hayes opens the door to

grab the pizza. I'm situating the napkins on the counter when I hear him say, "What the hell are you doing here?"

From the kitchen, I find him standing stiffly in the entryway, his hand gripping the door handle while he stares at an older woman wearing a pair of worn jeans and a faded long-sleeved T-shirt. Her hair is a mixture of gray and brown, peppered heavier along her hairline. Deep wrinkles cover her face, especially around her mouth and her eyes . . . steely-gray eyes.

"Is that how you greet your mother?" the woman says as my jaw falls open.

This is Pam Farrow?

Wow.

I've never seen her. I'm not sure I was even born when she left Hayes to be with his grandma, and he sure as hell doesn't have any pictures of her around, but now that I'm looking at her, I can see the slight resemblance.

Very slight.

"What do you want?" he asks, standing taller now. From where I'm standing, I can see the tension in his shoulders, and I know deep down that I need to be there for him. So I move away from the counter and walk up to him.

When I come into view, I see the change of look on her face, the surprise and almost . . . shock.

"Well, who do we have here?" she asks as I put my hand on Hayes's back. He stiffens to my touch and pulls away.

"No one you need to be concerned with," he answers.

"Is she your girlfriend or just another girl you've brought back to fuck?" She makes eye contact with me. "You'd be one of thousands."

Hayes steps in front of me, blocking me from the view of his horrible mother. "Is there a purpose as to why you're here?"

"As a matter of fact, there is," she says. "It would be nice if you let me in."

"Whatever you have to say, you can say to me right here."

She winces. "You know, that might not be what you want." From her back pocket, she pulls out an envelope and smacks it against her palm. "This isn't a front porch kind of conversation."

I feel him tense even more before he steps to the side, pulling me with him. He lets her inside the house, and she walks in as if she owns it, chest puffed, a sadistic smile on her face. While she heads into the living room, Hayes pulls me to the side while shutting the door.

"You need to go home," he says quietly so only I can hear him.

"What?" I ask. "Hayes, I'm not going to—"

"It's not up for discussion," he says in a deep, commanding tone. "Go home, Hattie."

Caught off guard, I say, "But my birthday—"

"Hattie," he says, his patience growing thin. "I said, go home. Don't fucking argue with me."

I wet my lips, my heart starting to crack. "But, what about our plans?"

He leans closer and says, "I'll come to you when she leaves. Okay?"

That puts me at ease—only slightly—and I nod. "Okay." I step in for a kiss, but he moves away from me and to my keys and purse. He hands them to me and says, "Put your shoes on outside."

And before I even have a chance to respond, he shoves me out the front door to his porch and places my shoes on the pavement in front of me. I turn around to at least offer him an encouraging smile, but before I can, he shuts the door in my face.

What the hell just happened?

I slip my shoes on and walk out to my car, where I open the door and sit in the driver's seat. Hands gripping the steering wheel, I stare out the front windshield. My pulse races, and my mind swirls.

Should I really leave?

I know he asked me to, but he also tensed up to the point that I felt like he could snap the door in half. Shouldn't I be there to support him?

I don't want him to face his mother alone, not after what I know about her.

Then again, I don't want to step in when he clearly doesn't want me near her.

I bite down on my bottom lip, and I feel my hand itch to open my car door back up. *No, Hattie. Trust him. He knows what he wants right now.* If I walked through that door, he'd be pissed. Even if I thought I'd be doing what's best for him, trying to support him, he wouldn't be happy.

He made me leave for a reason, and I think I need to respect that.

So with a heavy heart, I start my car and drive away from Hayes's house. He gave me the best birthday today, the most thoughtful, and the most loving.

This is about *her. A woman who has only ever done him wrong.*

He said he'd come get me when he's done, so I just need to trust that he will. Because if there's one thing I know for sure, it's that I trust Hayes Farrow with every fiber of my heart.

Chapter Twenty-Three

HAYES

"How much do you want from me?" I step into the living room but remain standing as I fold my arms across my chest and stare down at the woman who, unfortunately, is my mother.

And fuck does she look even worse than the last time I saw her.

That's what greed will do to you. It will pull your soul from your body, leaving you a useless sack and a drain on society. Nothing about my mother is worthy. She doesn't offer any value to this world, and right now, as I stare down at her, I know that whatever she's about to say will take a toll on me.

Because she always does. *And I refuse to let Hattie see that.*

"Who says I want any money from you?" she asks, mildly insulted.

"The only fucking reason you ever come see me is because you want something. So just tell me what you fucking want so I can get you out of here," I reply, raising my voice.

449

I can feel my skin start to itch from standing in the same room as her. This intense, guttural pain occurs in my stomach, like feeling homesick but on steroids. A dread falls over me, and the little boy inside me, the one who watched her drive away without a worry that she was leaving me behind, begging her to stay, is replaced with the man I've tried to become since then.

Deep breaths, Hayes.

Don't let her get to you.

Don't let her take you back to a dark place.

"Do you want me out of here so you can fuck your girl-friend more?"

My molars grind together. "She's not my girlfriend," I answer, knowing that's a bald-faced lie. The last thing I need is for her to hold that over my head. The less she knows about me, the better.

If she knew I had a girlfriend, someone I actually cared about, she'd find a way to use it against me. And then torture me.

Torture her.

It's best she thinks we're nothing.

"She seemed pretty intimate with you."

"She's delusional," I say. "Just a good fuck."

"Your father used to say things like that, you know? Look where that got him."

"Wouldn't know," I say. "He drove away before I could get to know him."

"Lucky you," she says. "At least I had the common decency to find you a home before I left."

"Common decency?" I ask. "You treated me like a discarded pet. How is that decent?"

"Could have taken you with me," she says. "Not sure you'd have gotten where you are today if you'd come with me. I saved you from a life of drugs and alcohol abuse."

"Is that what you tell yourself at night so you can sleep?" I nod. "Okay."

Her eyes fall flat, anger simmering in her facial expressions. "You might think I was a terrible mother, but I was selfless by deciding to leave you with your grandma."

"How is that selfless? If you were any bit of a good mother, you would have stayed here and raised me. You had a good job. You had friends and a support system. You left because you were selfish. Not selfless."

"You have no idea what I was going through when I made that decision."

"Yeah, an early midlife crisis, where you thought your life could change if you just got rid of me."

She dramatically rolls her eyes. "Here we go, playing the victim card again."

"I'm not playing any card," I shout, losing what thin-veiled cool I had. I pat my chest. "I am the victim."

She shakes her head. "Sorry you see it that way, but from where I'm sitting, I see you in a beautiful, large house, your wallet full, and everything you could possibly want at your fingertips. You would not have had that if it wasn't for me."

"And I'd trade it all fucking in to have one ounce of a parents' love. Do you realize the trauma I've gone through, the abandonment issues I have because of you?" I say before I can stop myself. It's almost as if seeing her, knowing she's here to ask for something, has unleashed a part of me that I've suppressed for many years.

"Well, then, your grandma has filled your mind with delusions." She stands from the couch and holds out the envelope to me.

"What's that?" I ask, not taking it.

"Something Ray came across. Thought you might want to see it."

Fucking Ray, my mom's husband. He's just as much of a

drain on society as my mom. They met one weekend when she was still around, and he was one of the main reasons she moved away. Because she'd rather be with him. *Period.*

I take the envelope from my mom and open up the back. There are pictures inside . . . *fuck me.*

Blackmail? She's here to blackmail me now?

Fucking Christ.

I slip the pictures out, and it's of me from when I was on tour this past year. Couldn't tell you the night, but there's an empty bottle of tequila in my hand, a naked woman on my lap, and a dead expression on my face. You can't see anything but her butt crack, but she's naked, that's for damn sure.

"They're screenshots from a video that was taken."

"Wait, what?" I ask.

She nods. "A sex tape."

I drag my hand over my face, the realization hitting me.

"And that's the mayor of Nashville's daughter on your lap."

"What?" I ask.

She nods, her smile all the reason I hate this woman. A parent should be supportive, not thrilled that she's about to blackmail her own son.

"It was brought to our attention that it will be released in the next week if the demands are not met."

I grip the photo tightly in my fist and meet my mom's eyes. "What demands?"

"Seems like Ray has a way to stop this all from happening, but you know . . . it's going to cost something."

Of course.

"How. Much?" I ask through a clenched jaw.

"Three quarters of a million."

Jesus fuck.

I tear away from her and push my hand through my hair. Sure, do I have the money? Of course. That's a drop in the bucket from what I have at this point, but the fact that I'm going to have to just hand this over because of my careless actions, because I thought drowning my sorrow and pain in a bottle and between random legs was the way to go, makes me feel physically ill.

"How do I know it won't be put out there?" I ask.

"Because I have the only file of it, and I'll hand it over to you."

"How can I trust you?" I ask. "How could I possibly believe that this won't get out to anyone else? And how do you even have a copy?"

"Because only one was taken, and it's from a trusted source."

"How fucking trusted? And how did you fucking get it?"

"They came to us, knowing we could reason with you."

"They came to you?" I ask. "How would they even gain access to my dressing room? The only people who were allowed back there were Ruben and my—"

And that's when it hits me.

Matt.

No fucking way.

I know it couldn't be Ruben. He'd never betray me like that because he's practically a brother. But Matt took everything he could get—shirts, albums, signed paraphernalia, empty bottles. There's no doubt in my mind that he'd take a video of me to use it against me.

But why now?

Why not when I fired him?

Why did he wait this long? Probably to try to keep his name out of it, but he must be hurting if he's using it now. *And how the hell did he find my mother?*

Trying to keep my expression neutral—because this is a huge invasion of privacy and a legal battle waiting to happen —I take a deep breath and say, "Why not a million?"

My mom's eyes light up. "You'd be willing to pay that much?"

"I would, to guarantee there's no slip of this anywhere, and there'd have to be a confidentiality agreement signed as well as an NDA, but yes, I'd pay one million to make sure this never sees the light of day."

"Well." She stands taller, pure pride surging through her, probably assuming that she has me in a chokehold when, in reality, I'm about to make her, Ray, and Matt's lives a living hell. "I think I could go back to my source and make sure we guarantee this never reaches anyone else."

"Good," I say. "Do it. Let me draw up the contract with my lawyer, and I'll get back to you."

"How long will that take?" she asks, looking impatient.

"Given this is time sensitive, not long."

"Good to hear," she says. And there it is again—*that smile.* How do I share DNA with this woman? I'm no angel. I've never pretended to be either. But this? Blackmailing her own son for her own gain? *She's despicable.*

What person, let alone a mother, takes joy from causing her child harm? How could she honestly live with herself if I wasn't willing to pay her off? To know what the tabloids would say—how they'd smear her own son's name—for money?

I fucking hate her. Gran's right. I do *not* need her approval. She's not worth shit.

"Well, Ray is waiting for me. We're headed up the coast but made a pit stop here. You have my number, right?"

Unfortunately.

"Yes," I answer.

"Great, call me when your lawyers draft everything up, and we can go from there." She pats my arm. "Always great seeing you, Hayes."

And then she walks toward the door, ending the business transaction she came to make, not the visit she should have been making with her son. And as she gets into her car and pulls away, I stand there, lifeless in the middle of my living room, crumpled photo in my hand, feeling so . . . *so fucking broken. How can she still do that? How does she still have the power to shatter my heart?*

Robotically, I move toward the kitchen table where my phone is and pick it up. I dial Ruben's name before crumpling to the floor, where I pull my legs up to my chest and lean against the kitchen island.

The phone rings twice before he picks up.

"Hey, I was just going to call you. I heard back from the lawyers, and the loophole I thought we could use to get out of your contract actually is going to work. So I didn't send them *Electric Sunshine*. I want to keep that close to our chests in case you want to go a different route. I think producing it yourself is the best idea at this point. You have the popularity and the fanbase—"

"Ruben," I choke out, my emotions taking over, that little boy inside me fucking breaking with every breath I take.

"Hayes . . . are you okay?"

"No, man," I say, the flash of my mom's smile vivid in my mind.

"What's going on?" he asks, his voice growing more intense.

"She came back."

"Who?" he asks. "Hattie?"

"No." I shake my head even though he can't see me. "My mom, she came back."

"Fuck," he breathes into the phone. "I'm in LA right now, so I can be up to you in an hour."

"No," I say as I press my head against the cabinet. "I don't . . . I don't want you here."

"Hayes, you don't sound good. I don't want you doing anything stupid. I'm packing my things right now."

"Please don't," I say. "I just need you to work on something for me."

"What is it?" he asks. "I'll do anything."

"She has a sex tape of me, a sex tape I'm pretty sure Matt took. I need security footage from the nights we were in Nashville. I need to see if there was anyone else in that dressing room besides me and . . . the mayor's daughter."

"Jesus," he mutters. "Okay, I'm on it."

"And if Matt was in there, I want you to handle it with the lawyers. They're extorting money from me, and I want everyone brought to justice."

"Understood." He clears his throat. "Is Hattie there with you?"

"No," I say, my throat growing tighter. "I sent . . . I sent her home." Her sad expression finally comes to the forefront of my mind, and it nearly breaks me.

"Do you want me to text her, contact her, get her back to your place?"

"No," I say, just above a whisper. "I don't want her involved."

"She might be able to help—"

"No," I snap. "She can't help."

After a moment of silence, Ruben says, "Hayes, I know you, don't let this make you spiral. We'll get it figured out, but don't spiral. That's the last thing you need to do right now. Go find Hattie." *Not a chance.*

"Just figure out how to pin them for this," I say. "We're working on days, not weeks."

"Hayes—"

He doesn't get to finish as I hang up and drop the phone next to me. I push my hands through my hair, my eyes squeezed shut as I attempt to take deep breaths and even my skipping pulse.

Nausea rolls through me.

Memories of my mom leaving me behind flood my mind so rapidly that I can't control my thoughts or emotions.

I recall the smell of her perfume that clung to me

throughout the night when I wondered why she'd leave me with my grandma.

I could feel the stiff pat on my shoulder she gave me before she left, not even a parting hug.

And I could taste the stale pretzels she left me with as a snack, a parting present.

This woman who I was supposed to trust, who was supposed to be there for me every step of the way, she just . . . left.

My dad left, not even taking one look back.

Ryland left without hearing my side of the story.

It feels like everyone leaves, everyone who's supposed to love me, supposed to be there for me. They extinguish any trust I might form, and they leave me.

They leave me with a broken heart, a damaged soul, and a mind so fucked. I'm reliving every moment I've ever been hurt, scared, or obliterated by the few people who should always love me for me.

But they don't love me, and that realization fucks with my head.

I stand from the floor, my stomach roiling, and before I can lose all contents on the concrete beneath my feet, I run to the trash can, where I throw up, just as the doorbell rings.

<hr>

HATTIE: *Are you okay? I'm worried. Please let me know you're okay. I love you.*

I stare down at the text, feeling the physical pain of reading those words from her.

She loves me.

I had a feeling that she might, that there might be something there with her. And this morning, when I told her I loved her, when I admitted to my true feelings, nothing had ever felt more freeing.

But what a couple of hours will do to a person.

I open my car door and step out onto the dark pavement behind The Almond Store. Hattie's car is parked in one of the spaces, and thanks to one singular street lamp, I don't trip along the way to the back of her door, where I plug in the code to get in.

With my chest feeling heavy, I move up the stairs to her apartment. She must hear me approach because before I can knock on the door, she whips it open, a relieved look on her face.

"Hayes, oh my God," she says as she wraps her arms around me. "Are you okay?"

My body goes stiff from her touch.

My breath becomes labored as I stare down at her.

And dread fills my stomach as I realize what I have to do.

What needs to be done.

"Hey," she says, running her hand over my chest. "I asked are you okay? You're very stiff, and I know today must have been—"

"I can't do this," I say.

Her nose scrunches up in confusion. "What?"

It's her goddamn birthday.

We just said we love each other.

And yes, as I stand here on her doorstep, staring into her mesmerizing eyes, I know for a fact that she has the potential not only to hurt me but to obliterate me. I don't think I've ever trusted anyone the way I've put trust in Hattie.

I've let her into my home.

I've counted on the fact that even though she was my enemy's sister—for a moment—she wasn't going to sabotage me in any way, especially after my former assistant betrayed my trust.

I've told her about my past. I've invited her into my inse-curities.

She knows more about me than anyone else on this planet,

and I know, with one word, with one slip-up, she can be the one person who takes me down.

Not my mom.

Not my dad.

Not an old feud or an assistant who seems to use my fame for his benefit.

Her.

And as much as I love her, I can't . . . I just fucking can't.

"Us," I say. "I can't do us."

Panic sets into her eyes.

"What do you mean you can't do us?" she asks.

"I mean, this is all too much for me, and I don't think we should do this anymore."

Her lip quivers, and she asks, "Are you breaking up with me?"

I can't look her in the eyes as I nod.

"No," she says, pushing at my chest. "You look me in the eyes and tell me you're breaking up with me."

Caught off guard by her forcefulness, I slowly look up at her and say, "I'm breaking up with you, Hattie."

She rubs her lips together, folds her arms at her chest, and then she says, "You fucking coward. You just told me you loved me. Was that all a show?"

"No," I say. "I do love you."

"No, you don't," she says, her voice rising. "If you loved me, Hayes, you wouldn't be standing at my doorstep, attempting to break my heart because you're too scared to put yourself out there."

"I'm not scared to put myself out there," I say. "I'm scared to trust anyone. Every person I've ever trusted has ripped that trust right out of my chest."

"So you're assuming I'm going to do that?"

"I can't stick around to find out."

"Wow." She shakes her head. "So just like that, your mom shows up, and we're done?"

I stuff my hands in my pockets, and I sigh. "I wish I was stronger, Hattie." I lift my eyes to meet hers, and seeing the tears well in them nearly breaks me. "I told you I wasn't good for you. I warned you."

A tear cascades down her cheek. "Don't, Hayes. This is about you."

"This is about trust," I say. "Look at Ryland. The moment something went awry, he walked away. My mother walked away, you . . . you walked away."

"I didn't—"

"You did," I say. "When Ryland found out about us, you left."

"I was confused," she defends, wiping her tear.

"Didn't hurt any less."

"So . . . you're just going to give up, just like that?" she asks.

"I'm not giving up, Hattie. I'm just . . ." I look away. "Fuck, I'm trying to stay afloat here. I don't think I could take one more cut to my heart. It's already bleeding."

"I'm not going to stomp on your heart, Hayes. I want to heal it. I want to be there for you. I want to show you what true love really is."

I nod slowly, and then after a second, I say, "And I want to believe you . . . but I can't."

I take a step down, that small distance causing her to take a short intake of breath.

"Hayes, don't do this," she says, and I take another step down. "Hayes, please." Her hand reaches out, but I take another step down, the steel armor I've resurrected around my heart to keep it beating protecting me from the tears streaming down her face and the reach of her hand.

You need to leave.

You need to get out of here.

And that's just what I do. Without another word, I turn

around and head down the rest of the stairs, just as I hear Hattie say, "Please don't do this, Hayes."

But I ignore her and move forward.

I put her behind me.

I hold on to what little sanity I have left.

What little life I have simmering deep within me because the light keeping me running is burning out.

Chapter Twenty-Four

HATTIE

Hattie: *I don't understand why you're doing this to us. Please, Hayes, please come back so we can work through this.*

I stare down at my last text to him, hoping and praying he'll have a change of heart, but with every minute that goes by without an answer, I fear this might be the end.

But I don't understand why it has to be the end. How am I associated with whatever's going on with his mom? He didn't even tell me what was going on. How can I help him if I don't know what's happening?

I pace the small space of my room and consider what I should do.

I could crawl into my bed, pull the covers up to my chin, and cry myself to sleep.

Or I can drive over to Hayes's house, where he's isolating himself, and be with him, even though he doesn't want me. Even though he's convinced himself that he doesn't need me.

He's wrong.

We need each other.

Equally.

Not wanting him to walk out of my life so easily, I slip on a sweatshirt, throw my hair up in a bun, and grab my keys. When I reach my car and pull open the door, a few fat raindrops pelt the hood of my car, the windshield, the trunk.

Great.

I pull out onto Almond Ave, flip my windshield wipers on, and drive to Hayes's house. The entire time, I'm trying to keep my emotions in check so I don't get in an accident.

What is normally a fifteen-minute trip feels like a monotonous hour of me running his conversation over and over in my head, driving myself mad.

When I reach his place, I slip out of my car, the rain really coming down now, and I run up his sidewalk, only to be startled, just like I initially was, when I find him sitting in the Adirondack chair, staring out in front of him.

"Hayes," I say breathlessly, but he doesn't look at me. He doesn't even move. He keeps his head and body still, like he's frozen in place.

Gently, I walk up to him and squat in front of his chair, placing my hands on his knees.

"What are you doing here, Hattie?" he asks, his voice distant.

"I'm not going to give you the chance to break up with me, not after today, not after everything we've been through. You're not allowed to. That's the easy way out. You need to fight these feelings, fight the demons, and let me help you do that."

He shakes his head. "It's not like that."

"What do you mean it's not like that?" I ask as water streams down my face.

"You can't help. No one can help. And I don't want your help. I want . . . I want you to leave." I try not to let his words affect me as I stay put. He's hurting, he's distancing, he's spiraling, and I won't let him.

"What did she want?" I ask, referring to his mom.

"It's none of your business." He won't even look at me. Not even a glance in my direction. He just keeps his eyes straight ahead.

"It is my business. You're my person, Hayes." I press my hand to his, but he pulls away. "We've been nothing but truthful and honest with each other. So why stop now?"

"You want the truth?" he asks. "You really want to know how fucked up my life is?"

"I want to be a part of your life."

He shakes his head. "You don't, trust me." He stands from the chair but doesn't head into the house. I try to capture his hand, but he pulls away, another wound to my already battered heart.

Just hours ago, he was dependent on holding my hand and touching me. How could it possibly change that quickly? What did she say to him to make him flip a switch and be a completely different man?

"Hayes—"

"What don't you understand about me not wanting to be around you?" he shouts, startling me back. When I meet his eyes with mine, I'm greeted with emptiness. A shell of a man I was with a few hours ago. His pupils look soulless, like he's lost every ounce of life and is just going through the motions. "I said we're done, Hattie. Accept it and move on."

His words feel like sharp knives, stabbing me directly in the soul, nearly bringing me to my knees. And if it weren't for the earlier half of the day, I probably would have crumpled to the ground by now, where I'd have wept until someone found me. But he's saying these things to push me away because, for some reason, he has it in his head that his life would be better alone than with the person he loves.

"You don't mean it," I say. "You're trying to push me away because of what your mom said to you. Don't you realize—"

"It's because I can't trust you," he shouts. "Jesus Christ, do I have to spell it out for you?"

I feel my lip tremble, but I take a deep breath before I answer. "Hayes—"

"Your own sister didn't even fucking trust you."

I pause.

The air in my lungs seizing as I meet his soulless gaze.

"What did you just say?" I ask, my body shaking from the chill of the rain and the pain ricocheting through me.

"Cassidy, she didn't even trust you. She didn't leave you the shop; she didn't leave you Mac. She left you nothing."

"Don't." I shake my head. "Don't bring her into this just to be cruel."

"It's not cruel when it's the facts." He places his hands in his pockets and stares down at me. "If your own sister can't trust you, how the fuck am I supposed to trust you?"

For the life of me, I can't think of a response because I'm so stunned, so shocked that he'd throw *those* words out there, bringing up one of my biggest insecurities. Not even an insecurity but a question that has been resting heavily on my chest ever since we lost Cassidy, a question that's haunted me to the point I couldn't even concentrate during school.

"You know I'm right," he says. "I was fucked over by my dad, fucked over by my mom, by my assistant, by my label . . . how the hell do you think I can just sit here and think I won't be fucked over by you . . . when the person you were closest with didn't think you were worthy enough to hold a piece of her life."

My lip trembles.

Tears fill my eyes.

He didn't just say that.

But when I meet his gaze, when I see the hurt in them that

he's trying to impose on me, I know that he did. That he uttered those words without a second thought, without even considering how deep it would cut me. Because someone who truly loves, who would *do anything for you*, would not hurl such painful knives at an open wound. *That's not love. That's not fucking love.*

And that's what makes me back away.

It's what makes me stare him dead in the eyes.

And it's what causes me to utter, "Fuck you, Hayes."

I turn on my heel and take off, not bothering to glance over my shoulder.

MAGGIE: *Okay, it's been two days since I've heard from you. Now, I know you're in a dreamlike state of Hayes Farrow and his delicious penis, but if you get a chance, please text me back, you know, just so I know you're alive.*

Maggie: *Hattie, you can't possibly have had Hayes inside you for three hours straight. That's right, I texted you three hours ago. There is NO WAY! Unless . . . God, I need to find my Speedo man. Is this what good sex is now? Three hours straight of penis inside vagina? Wondering minds want to know.*

Maggie: *Six Hours!! Six freaking hours. Now I'm calling bullshit. I would have given you three hours, you know, with all of the cuddling and light caresses after a mind-blowing orgasm, not that I would know, haven't experienced one in what feels like a century, but there's no way you could go six hours with ten inches deep inside you.*

Maggie: *Okay . . . okay . . . I've heard of sex-a-thons. I get it, the dude wanted to carry your birthday through the weekend. And if I was getting fucked the way you are, I'd set my phone to the side as well and forget about everyone around me, but a thumbs-up to let me know you're still breathing from all of the sex would be great.*

Maggie: *Well, this is irritating. I didn't think death by sex was possible, but . . . I'm considering it now. Are you alive? What's happening? Please don't make me text Aubree. She scares me!*

Maggie: *Now, you see, I'm starting to really worry because I called you three times, and sure, is that a little stalkerish? Maybe, but I'm worried now that perhaps his dick got stuck in you, and you're in some emergency room situation. Please call back. Text back. Send me a picture of the stuck penis, whatever works.*

Maggie: *Goddammit, Hattie! You made me text Aubree. And I will have you know that when I pressed send, my boobs shriveled to the size of an apricot, and you know I have grapefruits over here.*

Maggie: *And . . . now Aubree is checking on you. I hope you're happy because she said if she walks in on you naked with Hayes, she's going to come for me. The apricots are now prunes!*

KNOCK. *Knock.*

"Hattie, you in there?" Aubree's voice comes from the other side of my door. "Maggie texted me to check on you and since your car is out front, I'm assuming you're in here."

I curl into my pillow some more, my eyes burning from all the crying I've done over the past two days.

When I don't answer, I think she's going to leave until she opens the door. I must not have locked it when I returned here after being at Hayes's house.

"Hattie?" she says as she steps into the apartment. "Are you—" She stops when she sees me curled on the bed, the covers pulled up to my neck, probably my tear-stained face in full view. "Oh my God, are you okay?" she asks as she approaches me and sits on the bed.

And because she asked if I was okay, what Hayes said to me comes back to me—*again*—which brings on a whole new fresh set of tears.

"Hey." She places her hand on my back. "What's going on?"

With a tight throat and through my tears, I manage to say, "Hayes broke up with me."

467

"What?" she asks, her tone harsh. "He broke up with you? For what reason?"

I wipe my eyes, but it's no use. "I don't . . . I don't want to talk about it."

"Oh, we're talking about it." She pushes my hair out of my face, something Cassidy would have done if she was here. "When did he break up with you?"

"On my birthday," I say just as a sob passes my lips.

"That motherfucker," Aubree says, rising from the bed and heading toward the door.

"Wait, Aubree," I call out before she can leave. "Don't."

"You don't even know what I'm going to do."

"I know you're going to do something to him, and I don't want you to."

"Damn right I'm going to do something to him. If Ryland doesn't take care of this, then I fucking will."

"Please don't," I say. "Please."

"Hattie, he broke up with you on your birthday. How can I just sit by and allow that to happen?"

"It's not worth our time." I wipe my eyes. "He's not worth our time."

She grumbles something under her breath and then comes back to the bed. "Well, here's the deal. Either tell me what happened or I'll find out from him."

I love how protective Aubree is, but her bedside manner is a little rough. Cassidy would have been softer, probably would have climbed under the covers with me and held me. Aubree is ready to draw the kitchen knives from the drawer and take care of business.

Knowing I don't want her over there, and she will go over there if I don't tell her what's going on, I sit up in bed and prop my pillow against the headboard. "We were having a good day." I wipe my eyes. "He, uh . . . he told me he loved me."

"Wait." Aubree squeezes her eyes shut as she tries to make

sense of what I just told her. "He told you he loved you, but then broke up with you? How does that make sense?"

"I believed him that he loves me. I still believe that's the truth, but then, when we thought our dinner arrived, it was actually his mom at the front door."

"Oh shit," Aubree says as if she already knows.

"He made me leave because he didn't want me to hear what she had to say. I went back to my place, and he said he'd come and get me. I waited and waited, and when he finally arrived, I knew something was off. That's when he said he was breaking up with me, that he couldn't trust anyone in his life not to break him. And he took off."

Aubree slowly nods, and I can tell by her dampened anger that this is making all the sense in the world to her. Too bad for me, I'm still confused.

"I didn't want him to be alone because I felt like he was spiraling from his visit with his mom, so I went to his place, and that's where I found him sitting outside in the rain. I could tell he was hurting, and I tried my best to get through to him, but then . . ." I feel my throat grow tight again, and my lips tremble. "That's when he told me that he couldn't possibly trust me if my own sister didn't trust me to take care of her responsibilities."

Aubree winces. "Shit, Hattie. I'm sorry."

"I told him to fuck off, and I came back here. I haven't heard from him, and I haven't reached out." I glance away, and before she can reply, I say, "And the worst part of it is that he was right. My own sister couldn't trust me."

"Hattie, that's not true."

"It isn't?" My voice rises. "How can you say that when she gave you the store, the most important thing we had together? How come she gave you all letters and wrote me nothing? You know I searched her room from top to bottom, wondering if it was lost? It wasn't. She just didn't leave anything for me. Which means what Hayes said is true. She didn't trust me."

469

"He's not right," Aubree says while placing her hand on my knee. "Honestly, I don't know why she didn't leave you a letter. I asked the lawyer when he gave us ours. He said he never received one." A lonely tear cascades down my cheek. "But the shop, that's because you were still in college."

"Fuck college," I yell, more tears coming. "I'm so over college. I should have never attempted to earn my master's in the first place. It was stupid. I was trying to be impressive and learn more about business to help Cassidy, but I should have stayed home and learned through real-life experience. I would have been able to spend more time with Cassidy, and I would have been able to convince her that I was trustworthy enough."

"You are trustworthy, Hattie."

I shake my head. "Clearly, I'm not. The man who loves me can't trust me. My sister can't trust me. I don't even think I trust myself at this point." I wipe at my eyes. "And all of this has just made me realize how lost I am. Like what was I thinking? Moving from one relationship to the next while I'm still trying to mourn my sister? I'm making shitty choices, Aubree, and it's showing because this?" I gesture to the small apartment. "This is rock bottom. The only reason you're even listening to me is probably because you feel like you can't leave out of common decency, but I know that being here, watching me cry is your worst nightmare."

"Enough," she says.

"You wouldn't even have dinner with me."

"I said enough," Aubree says louder, startling me to shut my mouth. She takes a deep breath and looks me in the eyes. "The reason I haven't hung out with you too much is because you're the spitting image of Cassidy, and it's startling. Sometimes when I see you, I feel like she's back, and yes, that's on me, but it's hard. I shouldn't have associated you with Cassidy like that, and I'm sorry. But don't you ever, and I mean ever, think that I'd never be there for you. You are my sister, Hattie, my blood, and no matter what, you are a priority to me. This conversation right here, it's a priority."

And just like that, I feel more tears rise to the surface and crest over my eyelids.

"And of course you're going to feel lost, Hattie. That's a natural reaction to losing a big part of your life. It won't be fixed overnight. It will take time, but just because it takes time doesn't mean you need to put your life on hold. Working with Hayes and finding a bond with him was good for you. It gave you an escape, someone to rely on other than me and Ryland, a separation from the family so you didn't get even more lost."

"But he crushed me."

"I know," she says on a sigh. "And I'm not going to sit here and defend him because what he said to you is inexcusable and false. She trusted you, Hattie. She loved you dearly, so much that she didn't want to distract you from what you were trying to accomplish."

"I don't even want that anymore," I say. "I don't want to go back to school. I don't want to live in San Francisco for another semester away from you, Ryland, and Mac. I want to be here. I want to help with the store and be a family unit. I just wish . . . I just wish that was an option. I wish Cassidy thought I was good enough."

"You are good enough." Aubree grips my chin, forcing me to look at her. "You are good enough, Hattie."

I shake my head and scoot down on the bed. "I'm not. Hayes made that quite clear."

Aubree goes to answer, but from the bottom of the stairs, someone yells, "Anyone here in the store?"

"Shit," Aubree mutters as she stands. "I'll be back. Let me handle this customer and close down the store."

"Don't come back, Aubree," I say, turning my back on her. "Thank you for wanting to, but I just . . . I just can't talk about it anymore." She loves me, I know that. But right now . . . I just feel so bereft.

And then I block her out and close my eyes, leaving me to stew in my own sadness.

———

MAGGIE: *Aubree told me what happened. Two things: I hate him now, and I hope his music is found in hell with his body. And I plan on coming to visit you. I have a few things I need to wrap up here first, and then I will be there. I love you.*

Maggie: *PS. We can have a music-deleting party if you want. My clicky finger is ready to remove all Hayes Farrow songs from my playlists.*

Maggie: *PPS. If you could just respond so I know you've read these, I'd appreciate it. And in case you were wondering, my boobs have returned to normal grapefruit size. Aubree thanked me for being vigilant. If anything, I got a little wet from her response.*

Hattie: *Please don't ever say that again.*

Maggie: *Ha, I knew that would do it. Love you, Hattie. I'm here for you.*

———

KNOCK. *Knock.*

I turn on my bed to face the door just as I catch Ryland walking into my small apartment. Yup, I saw this coming.

"Hey, sis," he says, shutting the door behind him.

"Let me guess, you spoke to Aubree."

He nods and walks farther into the apartment, where he sticks his hands in his pockets, just like Hayes. Fresh from practice, still wearing his shorts, Almond Bay Baseball shirt, and his baseball hat, he feels like the brother I grew up with, but just . . . bigger.

"I did, and I came to collect you."

"What do you mean you came to collect me?"

"You're not staying here alone. You have two choices, you

can come sleep in my room or you can sleep on the couch, but this apartment is not an option."

"Ryland—"

"Two options." He holds up two fingers to me. "That's it, that's all you get. So while you decide, do you want me to pack for you?" He walks over to the corner where my suitcase is and he opens it up next to the dresser. "I don't want to touch your underwear, but I will if I have to."

He opens the top drawer and cringes.

"Do you have some tongs I can pick these up with?"

"For God's sake," I say while getting out of bed and walking over to him, shoving him to the side so I can pack myself.

"Smart choice." He goes to my bed and sits while I shove my suitcase full of clothes. "He does this, you know," Ryland says, causing the hairs on the back of my neck to stand to attention. "He lets his past take over his present to guard himself from anyone hurting him. He's done it to Abel and me. He's masked his pain with drugs, with alcohol, with sex . . . anything to get his mind off the abandonment he feels deep within him."

"Looks like I was just one of those masks." I toss my shirts in the suitcase.

"That's the thing . . . you weren't. You were anything but a mask. If you were a mask, he wouldn't have waited so long to make a move on you. He would have made it right away. He cares about you deeply."

"If that were the case, he never would have said the things he said."

"He was pushing you away on purpose," Ryland says.

"Well, job well done, he did it." I turn toward Ryland and ask, "And why the hell are you defending him right now? You realize he broke me, right? Absolutely broke me."

"I'm telling you about him, not defending him, because I don't want you to be broken. I want you to know it's him, not you. There's nothing wrong with you. You did everything right, Hattie. He's the one to blame, he's the one who needs to work out his feelings, the demons chasing him down."

"Then why . . ." My breath catches in my throat. "Then why does this feel so awful?" I let out a sob, and Ryland is quickly at my side, hugging me as he pulls me into his chest and wraps his arms around me.

"Because you love him, that's why. Because you've suffered through a lot of loss, and this just adds to the pile of helplessness you're feeling. But this time, we're going to be here for you. We're going to get you through this."

I press my face into my brother's chest, feeling so overwhelmed, yet so grateful for him. For Aubree. For Maggie. For the people in my life who've filled a void in my heart that Cassidy left. Without them, I'm not sure where I'd be.

"HOW DID you sleep on that couch for over two months?" I ask Ryland as I stagger into the kitchen, searching out coffee.

"I don't have any feeling in my back anymore." He leans against the counter, drinking a cup of coffee.

It's been three days of staying on the couch, and at this point, I'm convincing myself I'm not heartbroken just so I can get back to my apartment. Still, every night, when Mac goes to sleep and I'm hanging out with Ryland and Aubree, I always burst into tears, rendering me another night here, on the couch, because they refuse to let me go back to the apartment still sobbing.

And I don't want to be upset anymore. I don't want to have these feelings bouncing through me constantly. I don't want to see his handsome, distraught face when I close my eyes or hear his darkly intense voice while sitting silently in the dark. I don't want to have this need to see him, to tell him that I'm someone he can trust, I'm someone who'd never hurt him.

I want to be able to hold on to the last thing I told him . . . fuck you. I want to hold that pain, that anger so I don't have this need to be near him.

Because I miss him.

It's hard not to when he commanded my heart so quickly.

With Matt, I felt relieved.

With Hayes, I feel like the air has been stolen from my lungs.

I grab a mug from the cabinet and the creamer from the fridge, filling up the bottom portion of my mug.

"I still don't think that's the right way to do it," Ryland says as the early morning light peeks through the windows. Mac is still sleeping and probably won't be up for another half hour. Ryland gets up early to work out, shower, and make sure Mac is set for the day. Like I said, not sure how he's doing all of this.

"This is the right way to make coffee," I say, remembering the same conversation I had with Hayes. "No mess, no spoon."

"Whatever you say, sis." He sets his cup down and asks, "Want some eggs?"

"I'm good."

"Are you?" he asks. "Because it seems like you keep skipping meals, and I think you know how I feel about that."

"I'm eating, Ryland."

"Yeah, what did you have for dinner?" When I can't answer, he says, "And for lunch? What about breakfast? I think the only thing I've seen you eat is some Cracklin' Oat Bran. I know you're sad, but that doesn't mean you get to let your body starve."

"Let me guess, you're making me some eggs this morning."

"Yeah, I'm making eggs."

Not surprised. I sit on the counter and bring my already

mixed coffee to my lips as Ryland moves around the kitchen, starting breakfast.

While I watch him, I ask, "Do you think Cassidy trusted me?"

"Yes," he says immediately. The automatic response should make me happy, but it doesn't settle well.

"You're just saying that to appease me. I want to know if you really believe those words."

"I do," he says, placing a pan on the stove. He turns toward me and says, "She considered giving you custody of Mac but didn't want to tie you down. She didn't want to give you a responsibility that took over your life before you could even start it."

"She was going to give me Mac?"

He nods. "But we both knew it wouldn't be fair. So do I think Cassidy trusted you? I do."

"But what about the shop?"

"We went over this. She wanted you to graduate." He cracks a few eggs into a large white and blue bowl and tosses the eggshells into a bowl of water to rinse before he composts. "I know what Hayes said to you has hit you hard, but when I say he was saying anything and everything to push you away, I'm not kidding. The relationship you had with Cassidy was strong. She wanted you to reach a position in your life where you decided what you wanted, not have it decided for you." He meets my eyes with his. "You need to remember that. She wasn't going to let her illness dictate your future; she wanted you to be able to do that yourself."

"But—"

"But nothing. That's what she wanted."

"Then why force me to go to school? I don't want to go back, Ryland. I want to be here. I feel comfortable here. I feel like this is home. I feel like this is where I'm supposed to be."

"Then don't finish school. Stay here."

"It's not that easy."

"It's pretty damn easy if you think about it. It's your choice. We can make it all work."

"But won't you be upset if I don't finish school? I only have one semester left."

"I'll be upset if you don't do something with your life. I'll be upset if you let a man ruin the confidence you have in yourself. I'll be upset if you don't want to be a part of Mac's life. Everything else, that's just inconsequential. I think we learned quickly after losing Cassidy that family is more important than anything. I want you close too, Hattie. I like having you around, even if you make your coffee weird." He smirks at me, which pulls a smile from me as well.

"I kind of like being around you guys too."

"Good." He nods toward the pantry. "Now make yourself useful and toast some bread. You know that Mac will demand an egg sandwich."

"On it." I hop off the counter, and for the first time since Hayes pushed me out of his life, I actually have a feeling that maybe . . . maybe everything will be okay.

477

Chapter Twenty-Five

HATTIE

Maggie: *Are you excited to see me? I bought some fresh donuts this morning.*

Hattie: *I am excited to see you, but I told you, I'm feeling better.*

Maggie: *Doesn't matter, I still want to see you, and I picked some things up from your apartment for you—mail and those sleep masks you've been begging for. I'm a good friend like that.*

Hattie: *I appreciate it. And you. But . . . where are you sleeping?*

Maggie: *We're investing in a blowup mattress, and I'll sleep next to you and hold your hand while you sleep. Why? Because no man will ever take the spirit from my girl.*

Hattie: *I told you, I'm doing better. Still sad, but better.*

Maggie: *I'd appreciate it if you could at least conjure up a little bit more sadness so I have an excuse to eat three donuts in a row with you.*

Hattie: *Oh right . . . I'm sobbing right now. The only thing that will fix it is donuts.*

Maggie: *Much better. (Yells in a Mrs. Doubtfire voice) HELP IS ON THE WAY, DEAR!*

MAGGIE'S CAR pulls up in the driveway, and she puts it in park. I walk out on the porch, wearing a holey shirt and a pair of cotton shorts, while my hair is pulled into a high ponytail that feels more like a side pony than anything.

And of course Maggie looks like perfection in a matching set of leggings and crop top from Lululemon. Her hair is in elegant waves, while her mascara makes her beautiful eyes stand out.

"You look like you've been sleeping in a dumpster," she says as she pulls me into a hug. "Ahh, but you smell good, so I guess that's all that matters." She grips my shoulders and puts a foot of distance between us. "How are you?"

"Doing okay."

"Do we still hate him?"

"I want to be mature and say no, but yeah, we hate him."

She nods. "Do we still love him?"

"Unfortunately."

"Okay, just trying to gauge where we're at. This is good information. Still upset, which gives us all the right to eat all the donuts, but doing well enough to walk off said donuts later. Am I correct?"

I chuckle, loving her so much. "Yes, you are correct."

"Good." She pulls me into a hug again and says, "I love you. You are perfect, and he's an absolute moron for letting you out of his sight."

"Thank you." I hug her back.

"Now, help me with my things. I got one of those blowup mattresses that's a double. I won't be on that floor anytime soon with the height I'll get with this baby."

She leads me toward her car and opens her trunk, then pulls out her suitcase and a laundry basket of mail and personal items from the apartment. "This is for you," she says. She places a box of donuts on top of my personal things.

"These are for us. The maple frosted is mine, so don't even think about it. I've been smelling that son of a bitch for this entire drive." She grabs the handle of the air mattress and says, "And this is my new lover, Winston. We might make a lot of noise together, but just know, he's keeping me comfortable."

"You have issues."

She shuts her trunk and picks up her suitcase as well. "I was not risking some small bed to share with you or a couch cushion on the floor as a bed. You know I demand the finest of things."

"Believe me, I know."

We make our way up the porch and into the house, the squeaky screen door slamming behind us. I carry the laundry basket to the table while she sets down her suitcase and . . . new lover. She then grabs the box of donuts, takes a seat at the kitchen table, picks up her maple frosted, and takes a huge bite.

With a full mouth, she says, "Sorry, not going to wait for you. My taste buds have been salivating for over two hours. It's time I reward them."

I glance at the box. "Dibs on the Boston cream."

"Why do you think I got it?" She wiggles her eyebrows as I grab some of the mail, only to find a box at the bottom.

"What's this?" I pull it out and turn it around to look at the return address, which is my apartment address in San Francisco.

Maggie shrugs. "Not sure."

Confused, I grab a box cutter from the kitchen junk drawer and split open the tape on the box. When I open it, I'm met with bubble wrap and tissue paper.

Maggie stretches to see what's inside. "What is it?"

"I don't know," I answer while I pull back the bubble wrap and tissue paper. "I didn't order—"

My words immediately fall flat the moment I see a card on the top, written in Cassidy's handwriting.

"Oh my God," I say, tears immediately forming in my eyes. "Oh my God."

"What?" Maggie stands now, setting her donut down, and when she sees the card too, I hear the lightest of gasps. "Is that from . . . Cassidy?"

I nod, my hand clutched over my mouth as I pick up the card. Underneath are individually wrapped items in pink birthday wrapping paper.

"She . . . she sent me a birthday gift." I shakily open the letter, gulping back the sob forming in my throat. *She didn't forget me. She didn't forget me.* I pull out the card, which is a picture of The Almond Store with a taped, cut-out picture of me and her when we were younger. She placed us right next to the door.

Swiping at my tears, I open the card, and I read it to myself.

My dearest, sweetest, favoritest Hattie,

God, it's taken me so long to even try to start this card because how the hell am I supposed to say goodbye to you? The one person who helped make my dreams come true. The one person who made me feel like a mom before I truly was one. And the one person who was my backbone.

Which means I'm not going to say goodbye to you. I can't, but what I can do is tell you this . . .

First of all, happy birthday, Hattie Hoo. I'm so sorry I couldn't be there, holding your hand while I sang happy birthday, tackling you to the ground with hugs, and giving you these presents in person. But knowing I won't be there, I decided to give you one last special birthday from me.

Second, I want to tell you how proud I am of you. I'm not sure I said that enough, but I am. We grew up in a home where love was scarce, drama was high, and self-preservation was the name of the game, but you . . . you're the one who made me realize if we don't come together as siblings to help one another, we'd never make it out of that house.

I know you'll believe I'm the reason you're full of love, of understanding, of resilience, but in reality, I'm the one who fed off you. When you were young, you filled me with love. When I was struggling to find peace and not be bitter from the cards that were drawn for me, you were the one who helped me find understanding. And resilience. Hattie, without you, I would have none.

You are my rock.

You are my person.

You are the sole reason I was convinced I could be a mom when my husband was constantly away . . . and when I lost him.

And when I was diagnosed with breast cancer, you were there for me every step of the way. I know this isn't what we'd hoped, but you know what? Hattie Hoo, I'd do this life all over again if it meant you were at my side, cheering for me, guiding me, and filling me with joy.

I know this is hard, and I know losing me won't be easy on you, but I have all the confidence in the world that if anyone is going to keep my spirit alive and show my daughter the kind of mother I'd have been for her, it will be you.

As you know, Ryland has custody of Mac, but I need you to teach her our ways. She needs to know how to make the almond cherry cookies the right way. She needs to know how to pick out the perfect tablecloth. She needs to know where to find the best sea glass, and how to look up at the stars. I need you to teach her everything, everything I taught you . . . including Jake Ryan. I will haunt you if you tell her Patrick is better.

And finally, I want you to live your life to its fullest. Spread your joy. Impart your smile on the grumpiest of people. Drive Aubree nuts with your constant chattering. Scare Ryland whenever you get the chance just to remind him he's alive. Fall in love. Fall out of love. And fall in love again.

Make mistakes.

Laugh about the tribulations.

Celebrate the triumphs.

And above all else, know that you are the most genuine, loving, intelligent human I know. You will do great things in this life, Hattie. And I promise to watch over you every step of the way.

I love you.

Your sis,
Cassidy

I set the card down and then bury my head in my hands as I sob uncontrollably. Maggie is immediately at my side, her hand on my back, rubbing soothing circles.

And I'm not sure how long we stay like that, but it takes me a while to pull myself together.

"Are you okay?" Maggie finally asks as I lift my head. She hands me a napkin from the table, and I dab at my eyes.

"I . . . I wasn't expecting that." I shake my head. "I thought she forgot about me."

"Cassidy would never," Maggie says.

"But . . . everyone got a card, everyone but me, I just assumed." I let out another sob. "God, I can't believe I thought that about her. That she would forget me. Instead, she tried to make my birthday special."

Maggie turns me to face her and meets my eyes with hers. "You listen to me, and you listen to me good. This package is not to make you feel bad or to second-guess everything that you thought or said. This package should bring you the closure you've been looking for. Do you understand me?"

I nod because she's right. I have been looking for this. Searching for it, actually. When everyone else got letters from Cassidy, I was the one who was waiting, begging for something from her, and it's finally here. I'm not going to dampen that gift by questioning my actions.

I sit taller and nod. "Yes, I understand you."

"Good." She picks up one of the presents and hands it to me. "Then let's enjoy what she picked out for you."

On a deep breath, and with Maggie sitting next to me, I open the first present. Just by feeling it, I know what it is.

A jar of our favorite pickles.

There's a pink note attached to it, so I read it out loud. "'I made Dee Dee Coleman swear to me that she'll always have these in stock. She gave me her word. Chow down.'"

Maggie hands me the next gift, and I open it. A shirt that says *I Love Jake Ryan*. A snort pops out of me before I can stop myself. I read the attached note. "'I require you to wear this at least once a month, and you better wear it with pride because you know I'm right.'"

"She's right." Maggie nudges my arm.

"I beg to differ."

Maggie hands me another package. I open it and find a vintage tablecloth with a giant coffee stain front and center. I laugh and wipe my nose with the back of my hand. "'Found this at Days Gone By and held it for your birthday. The brown spot made me think of the brown spots you used to leave in your diaper when I changed you.'" I laugh even harder. "Oh my God, what is wrong with her?"

"That's my favorite gift so far." Maggie reaches into the box. "Two left."

I open up the next one, and it's an autographed Hayes Farrow album.

"Oh Jesus, if she only knew," Maggie whispers as I read the letter.

"'Don't act like you never liked his music. I'm calling you out on it. Just don't let Ryland catch you with this. And yes . . . I got it signed for you. You're welcome.'"

I stare down at the picture of Hayes on the front, his leather necklace strung around his neck and gliding down his thick pecs. The scruff on his jaw that I've felt between my thighs, and those gray eyes that still haunt my dreams.

"Okay, enough of that," Maggie says, taking the album. "We might still be a little raw from this situation. Actually, I think I might just keep this for myself. As a best friend, I think that's my duty."

I take the album from her, laughing. "Nice try. I might hate love him, but this is from Cassidy, so I'll be keeping it."

"Okay, but you know, I'd take on that burden if you want me to."

"Sure." I roll my eyes.

"Okay, last one." Maggie hands me a flat box and rests her head on my shoulder as I unwrap it.

I pop the lid off the box, push back the tissue paper, and find a folded-up piece of paper.

"What is it?" Maggie asks.

"I don't know," I answer as I unfold it. It's a document, and it takes me a few seconds to read it, but when I do, I gasp out loud.

"What is it?" Maggie asks, sitting tall and holding half of the document to get a better look at it.

"It's . . ." My throat is clogged with emotions as I whisper, "It's the ownership of The Almond Store. She gave it to me."

"What?" Maggie asks, her voice rising as she takes it from me. That's when I see the letter at the bottom of the box. While Maggie looks over the document, I read the note.

I'm sure you questioned every one of my choices, but I truly wanted to give you a moment to breathe after my death. I wanted to make sure you could focus on yourself before you focus on preserving me, and I know that's what you would have done if I gave this to you right away. Hopefully, you've had some time to figure things out, to at least gather your feelings together, because Hattie Hoo, your journey is about to start.

This shop is yours.

It might have been my idea, but it was your execution that made it come to life.

I don't want anyone else in charge of it besides you. Aubree has been holding it together, but she belongs on the farm, and you belong in this safe space we created. I know you'll carry on my legacy within these walls. All I ask is that when Mac is old enough, you give her the chance to work here, you teach her the things I taught you, and when the time comes, you pass it on to her.

I love you.

Do great things, Hattie Hoo.

Love hard.

Live freely.

And for me . . . laugh often.

I tilt my head back, closing my eyes as I take deep breaths, silently thanking Cassidy.

I promise I'll make sure Mac knows and loves you deeply, Cassidy.

That she knows all of our ways.

I promise she'll love The Almond Store. That if she wishes, it will be her legacy as well.

I promise I'll make you proud, Cassidy.

I promise.

"WOW," Ryland says, shaking his head and looking over the letters Cassidy left, his eyes misty. "I wish she'd have told us. It would have saved a lot of heartache." He passes the letters back to me.

Maggie is sitting with Mac in the living room, playing with Chewy Charles on the air mattress that Mac has claimed to be hers while I sit at the table with Aubree and Ryland, showing them everything Cassidy left me.

"I'm just relieved I no longer have to worry about the shop. I love that store for what it is, but running it . . . no, thank you."

"I wonder if this is why her lawyer called me the other day," Ryland says. "We've been playing phone tag, but I'm assuming it has to do with this."

"He reached out to you?" I ask.

Ryland nods and strokes his jaw. "Yeah, I'll be honest, it took me a second to call him back because I was worried he had another piece of information that was going to rock us, and I wasn't sure I was ready for it, but this . . . this could not have come at a better time."

"Do you think it's okay that I didn't finish school?"

"She gave you the deed," Aubree says. "I don't think it matters. It might have been a technicality in the will to make sure you tried to finish, but . . . it says effective June 1, you're the owner. Which means . . . we're going to have to work hand in hand to make sure the shop's needs are met."

I smile at her. "I don't mind that . . . do you?"

She shakes her head. "As long as you don't chatter my ear off and make me have awkward dinners."

"That dinner was awkward because of you, not me."

Mac comes running into the kitchen, holding her stomach. "I'm hungry. What are we havin' for dinner?"

"I'm going to go pick up some sandwiches," Ryland says as he lifts from the table.

"Maggie and I will go get them," I say, standing as well. "I need some fresh air anyway."

"That works. I'll get Mac into a bath, and then we can have dinner together."

"And then have a jumping party," Mac says, raising her arms to the sky.

"Or . . . we can watch some *SuperKitties* while the adults process the heavy day we had," Ryland says.

"Yay!" Mac sprints away and up the stairs.

"I'll text you my order," Ryland says as he jogs after Mac.

"I'll text you too," Aubree says as she leans back in her chair, relief set in her shoulders. I can't imagine what she must be feeling right now.

So I walk over to her and tug on her hand, forcing her to stand. When she does, I wrap my arms around her.

"I love you, Aubree."

She's stiff for a moment, but then she relaxes into my embrace and squeezes me hard.

She doesn't say anything but doesn't need to. *I know.* Her heavy breaths and the feel of her arms around me show me that her bottled-up stress has been alleviated.

When I pull away, I look her in her glassy eyes and hold out my hand to her. "Business partner?"

A watery smile passes over her lips as she shakes my hand. "Business partner."

I offer her a smile. "I still expect you to help in the shop, especially with Ethel."

She shakes her head. "In your dreams."

⊏⊐

HAYES

"SO YOU'RE NOT GOING to talk?" Abel asks as he sits across from me.

"What did you expect me to do?" I ask. "Gab about how shitty my life is?"

"Yeah."

I push back in my chair and twist my beer on the table in front of me. "Not happening."

"Okay, then why did you agree to meet me for dinner?"

"It was either that or you were coming to my house. Since kicking you out of my house is a lot harder than just standing and leaving a restaurant, I chose meeting you."

"Sound logic." He takes a bite of the pickle on his plate. "But I did buy you dinner. Therefore, it's a requirement for you to talk to me. Out of courtesy."

"What the hell do you want me to say?" I ask, tossing my hand up. "Hattie and I are no longer together. My mom extorted me for money. And I'm pretty sure I'm out of a label contract that could have distracted me from the rest of the bullshit in my life."

"Yeah, I hear you. But don't you think it's good you can't rely on the kind of distraction you used to?" he asks.

"What does that mean?"

He dabs his mouth with a napkin. "Anytime anything has

triggered you, you've resorted to past behaviors. Getting lost in sex, alcohol, or drugs."

"I don't do drugs anymore."

"Which I'm happy to hear," he says. "What about sex . . ."

"What's the point?" I ask, tipping back my beer. "No one will compare to Hattie."

And that's the fucking truth. She . . . I got so lost in everything about that woman, and then I went and blew it. I said the shittiest things to her during a low point in my life, and I fucked up. Does she deserve better? Of course. Should she be as far away from me as possible? Fuck yes, she should. Doesn't mean it doesn't hurt, though. Doesn't mean I don't miss her.

Doesn't mean I don't think about her every second of every goddamn day.

"From the sag in your shoulders and your avoidance of eye contact, I'm going to presume you believe you messed up when you pushed Hattie away."

I shake my head. "No, I did the right thing."

"For who exactly?" Abel asks. "Because from what I know, Hattie is hurting, you're hurting, and nothing good has come from this breakup."

"Hattie's hurting?" I ask, sitting a little taller.

"Last I spoke to Ryland, he had to force her to move in with him because she was just crying in her bed in her apartment day in and day out. No one knew you broke up with her until her best friend asked Aubree to check on her because she hadn't heard from her."

"Shit," I mutter.

"Yeah, exactly. So remind me how this is helping anyone?"

"It's not that easy," I say. "I know I messed up, Abel, but I also . . . I'm broken, man. I'm not in a position to be able to be there for someone. To be there for Hattie, who needs someone strong in her life right now." *And the real crux of the problem? As much as I do love her . . . she's human.* "Not to mention, how do I know she won't turn her back on me one day?"

"Oh, like you turned your back on her? Pretty sure she's learning from experience right now." I turn away, and because he's Abel, he won't let me sit here and stew, so he adds, "How's everything going with the extortion?"

I brush my hand across the top of my thigh, pushing off an imaginary piece of lint. "Ruben located the security camera, and it was Matt. So my lawyers are drawing up the paperwork to scare the shit out of him, and my mother for that matter. Ruben is also drawing up a restraining order for my mother so I won't be bothered by her anymore."

"Wow, okay, so that's pretty much taken care of."

"Yeah," I mutter.

"So then why are you sitting across from me like you're still waiting for the worst to happen?"

"The worst has happened," I say as I stand from the table.

"Let me guess, I've annoyed you to the point that now you're going to leave."

"Yup," I say while I push my chair in. I pick up my bottle, drain the rest of it, and then start toward the door as Abel stops me by grabbing my wrist.

When I look down at him, he says, "You're better than this, Hayes. You've grown. You've evolved. Just because it's scary doesn't mean you need to avoid it. Hattie belongs with you. We all see it. You just need to see it."

He lets go of my wrist, and instead of responding—because frankly, I have nothing to say—I make my way toward the door. I only had one beer, but just to be sure, I feel like a walk around the beach will help me clear my mind and make sure that I'm good to drive my bike.

I nod toward the cashier and then push open the door to The Hot Pickle, turn the corner toward the beach, and run smack into Hattie on the sidewalk.

Fuck.

She tumbles into my chest, Maggie right next to her, and a slew of apologies come out of her mouth as I right her by the shoulders and put about a foot of distance between us. When she finally looks up at me, another apology about to fall from her lips, her eyes widen.

"H-Hayes," she says, looking just as stunned as I feel.

I take another step back and stick my hands in my pockets, preventing myself from feeling her again. "Sorry, didn't see you there."

"I . . . I didn't see you either."

That much is evident. Nor were either of us expecting to run into each other.

Awkwardly, I shift as I say, "I'll, uh, I'll get out of your way."

But I don't move.

Not even a fucking inch because seeing her has stunned as me, renders me useless in this moment as my heart thumps against my ribcage, begging to reach out to her.

Hold her.

Take her into my arms and never let her go. Instead, I stare at her.

I notice the faintest darkness under her eyes, indicating countless nights of lost sleep. Mine rival hers with depths of regret and hatred for myself. Her hair is pulled back into a high ponytail but is slightly askew, making her look so fucking adorable that it's painful to have her here in front of me.

Yet I still don't move.

I can't.

Not when . . . not when I never stopped loving her.

Not when—

"You're an asshole." Startled by the harsh words, I glance over Hattie's shoulder to a fuming Maggie. A fuming, protective, ready to pounce Maggie. "Did you hear me?" she repeats. "I said you're an asshole."

"Maggie," Hattie whispers, looking embarrassed. "I think everyone on Almond Ave heard you."

"I hope they did." Maggie props her hands on her hips

defensively. "I can't believe I touched your face and said you were handsome. I mean . . . sure you're still handsome, and this added scruff to your jaw doesn't help our case over here of hating you, but how could you be so cruel to my friend Hattie?"

"Maggie, it's fine."

"It's not fine," Maggie says, her eyes on me. "You hurt her and for no reason. She's a good person, a trustworthy person, and you're lucky you even had a chance with her."

"Maggie——"

"She's right," I say, head tilted down, barely looking up at Hattie. "Maggie is right. I was lucky."

Hattie's eyes lift to mine in surprise. Those beautiful, soulful eyes I've spent many nights staring into, they split me in half, crushing my heart between my ribs.

Fuck, I am such a moron for pushing her away.

"See, at least he's intelligent enough to know that he was lucky." Maggie loops her arm through Hattie's. "Let's get out of here, we have sandwiches to purchase, enough time has been wasted letting him stare at you and feel his regrets."

Maggie tugs Hattie away and immediately I feel my heart leap out of my chest, begging me to stop them, trying to knock some sense into my head.

Blame it on my desperation, but before I can stop myself, my fingers reach out and drag over the back of her hand and over her knuckles as she walks by.

A gasp escapes her lips just in time for her to look up and match my gaze with hers.

In that moment, with her looking up at me, I feel time slow down and the memories of us flash through my mind. Fond memories that pumped life into my lungs, jump-started my heart again . . .

Memories like when she first showed up on my porch with her box of stolen possessions, revenge on her mind.

Her in the middle of my living room, listening to the Mamas and the Papas with letters scattered around her.

Her sitting on my counter, showing me how to make cookies.

Sitting under the stars with her, staring up at the sky that grounded us throughout our lives.

Our first kiss . . .

It strikes me like a tornado, spiraling through my body, hitting me left and right with what should have been . . . what could be.

"Hattie . . ." my voice croaks in near silence, my throat tight, my apology on the tip of my tongue.

But I don't get a chance to say anything else as Maggie tugs her toward the sandwich shop, Hattie turning away, offering me her very cold, very distant shoulder.

Fuck.

My heart sinks.

What could have been . . .

Probably for the better. I pushed her away for a reason, but that knowledge doesn't refrain me from squeezing my hands into fists with the feel of her skin on my fingertips as frustration trips through me.

I fucked up and I'm paying for it now.

⌈▭⌉

HATTIE

"WHY WOULD HE DO THAT?" I ask as I shove another donut in my mouth.

After dinner, we set Maggie up with pillows, blankets, and sheets for her air mattress. This of course was done after Mac was put to bed for the night because if she was still around, the blankets and sheets would have been used for a fort, and we never would've gotten her up to her room.

Maggie dabs at her mouth with a napkin and says, "Explain it to me again?"

I roll my eyes. "How many times do we have to go over this?"

"At least one more. I'm sorry, I'm still reeling over the fact that I told Hayes Farrow he's an asshole. Positively shaking over here, so excuse me for my lack of comprehension."

"Yeah, I'm still a little shook from your brazenness as well," I reply. Maggie is loyal to her core, would defend me to the moon and back, but never in my wildest imagination would I have pictured Maggie telling Hayes off in front of a sandwich shop. I was equally stunned and proud . . . and grateful.

"Don't treat my friend like shit and I won't call you an asshole, simple as that." She shrugs, trying to play it cool, but I know damn well, she was shaking just as much as me in that moment.

"You called Hayes an asshole?" Ryland asks, walking into the living room with a beer in hand. He takes a seat on the couch, shoving my blanket toward me and letting himself get comfortable.

"I did," Maggie says, puffing her chest with pride. "I said it right to his face."

"Ah, to his face. So not to his elbow?" Ryland jokes.

Maggie smirks. "I thought about his elbow, but I didn't think it would be as effective or as menacing. Conversations to the elbow although a novelty of enjoyment, not the impact I wanted. Face was the way to go."

"Smart choice." Ryland nods. "Although, elbow might have confused him, which would have been entertaining."

"We weren't looking for entertaining, Ryland," Maggie says, making a fist. She slams it on the air mattress, before saying, "We were looking for intimidation. We wanted to make him weak in the knees and not in a good way. We wanted to set the tone that we weren't falling for his handsome, scruffy face defense and now when he sees us walking the mean streets of Almond Bay, he'll have pure, nut-shriveling fear race up his spine."

"Nut-shriveling fear, huh? How come I can feel that all the way to my scrotum?"

"Because that's the kind of power us ladies have." She raises her fist to the air. "We are the Nutcrackers of Almond Bay." She nudges me with her foot as an idea passes over her eyes. "We need to make T-shirts with that saying on them. Possible merch for The Almond Store, something to consider."

"Can I buy one?" Ryland smirks.

"Women only."

"Hey, I'll crack any nuts that bring harm to the women in my life."

"Is that so?" Maggie folds her arms over her chest. "Then please regale me with the reason as to why Hayes still had full intact nuts in his pants."

"Did you look inside his pants?" Ryland raises a brow at her. "Or have do you have X-ray vision I don't know about?"

"I don't need to feel around between a man's legs to know if his nuts are attached or not. It's all in the walk, and he was walking around like his scrotum was still hanging pretty. And I only say pretty because even though I hate him, there is no way in hell that man doesn't have a pretty package."

"Um," I clear my throat. "Can we please bring it back to what I was talking about? The moment?"

"Oh, right." Maggie waves at me to continue. "You were saying . . ."

"Well, we started with the fact that he agreed with you."

"Right," Maggie says.

"What did he agree with?" Ryland asks.

"Maggie said he was lucky I even gave him a chance and then . . ." In a low whisper, I say, "He agreed with her."

"Oh wow, it's almost as if he scandalously showed off his

ankle." Ryland sips his beer, finding far too much joy in this which is different for him. I love my brother, but it's not very often that he relaxes and right now, in this moment, he's relaxed.

Wait, is that his fourth beer? Is he a little . . . drunk?

Maybe he is loosening up.

"Are you drunk?" I ask him.

"What?" He shakes his head. "No. Are you?"

"No, I haven't had anything to drink, but you have. You're drunk. When was the last time you were drunk?"

He shrugs. "I don't know, but Aubree is home, you're here, and Maggie is here, which means I have three people who can take care of Mac if I get a little tipsy." He brings his bottle to his lips and takes a long pull before sinking further into the couch, a small smile playing on his lips.

Huh, never thought about that aspect of his life. Ryland has always enjoyed having a few beers, nothing crazy, but he probably doesn't drink much now because he's in charge of Mac, and if anything were to happen, he'd want to be cognizant to take care of her. Just another thing I never considered about how Ryland's life has been turned upside down.

"Not sure many men use the word tipsy," Maggie teases him.

"Not sure many men use the word potty either," Ryland counters. "But Jesus Christ, the other day while hanging out with Abel, I told him—as a grown ass man with a few grey hairs near his temple—I had to go potty. The fucker hasn't let me live it down." He drags his hand over his face. "Hell, I've spent so much time with Mac that I'm surprised I didn't announce I had to go potty, grip my crotch, and then waddle off to the bathroom, putting fear into Abel's heart if I was going to make it in time or not." Ryland sighs as Maggie and I both chuckle, the image so vivid in my mind. "So," he brings the bottle to his lips again, "he showed off his ankle, then what happened?"

"He didn't really show off his ankle," I say. "But he said that he was lucky that he was with me. And then, Maggie wasn't having any of it."

"Because he's an asshole who broke our girl's heart."

"Cheers to that." Ryland holds up his beer and takes a sip.

"Are you cheering to Hayes being an asshole, or are you cheering to Hattie's heart being broken?" Maggie asks.

"The asshole thing, obviously," he says.

"Good." Maggie fluffs up her pillow.

"Anyway . . ." I carry on in an annoyed tone, because these two . . . "When I was walking away with Maggie . . ." I pause and lean forward for dramatic effect. "His finger grazed my hand." When Maggie and Ryland don't say anything, I nod, confirming what they heard. "Yup, he grazed my hand."

"And there it is." Maggie lays down on her bed with a plop. "The love."

"You think that's what it is?" I ask.

"What else could it be?"

"Maybe he twitched, and his hand accidentally brushed yours," Ryland says, not being helpful.

"That is the worst explanation you could have offered. Way to be a dud," Maggie says.

"How is that being a dud? Do you even want him brushing his hand against yours?" Ryland looks over at me, his inquisition making me feel unsure. So, I offer him a I shrug.

He eyes me with that big brother gaze he's given me many, many times.

"No, I guess I don't want him brushing against me." I feel my shoulders sag. "He hurt me, and it's the kind of hurt that I don't think is easily erasable. Not to mention, he pushed me away for a reason, because he didn't want me—"

"Bullshit, we've been over this." Ryland sets his bottle on the empty coffee table. "He pushed you away on purpose.

Was it smart? No. But trust me, when Hayes is hurt and spiraling, he does nothing better than self-sabotaging . . . also known to him as self-preservation. He broke up with you because, in his mind, it was easier to push you away than suffer the blow if you ever pushed him away." Ryland rests his head on his propped-up arm. "You can blame his parents for that and probably me. I'm sure me abandoning him was the cherry on top of his abandonment issues."

"But he said he couldn't trust me," I say.

"Yeah, he can't trust you not to leave him. Think about it, Hattie. If you were in his position, where your parents left you on purpose because, in your eyes, you weren't good enough for them to stick around, you'd have a very hard time dealing with that as well. Add on top of that your best friend believing you're the scum of the earth and deleting you from their life as well as everyone in the world wanting something from you because of your fame and not because of you as a person, you'd be jaded too."

"So . . . are you on his side?" Maggie asks.

"No, I'm on Hattie's side. I think what he did to her was shit. The only difference is, I understand why he did what he did. Not saying it's right, just saying I understand why. And to bring this full circle, the hand brushing . . . it probably was because he misses you."

"Oh no, you don't." Maggie sits up, waggling her finger at Ryland. "Don't you dare put those thoughts in her head. We don't need her thinking this man who broke her heart is out there pining for her."

"Yeah, I don't think I could handle that," I say, my voice softer. "Between losing Hayes and receiving Cassidy's package, I honestly don't think I can take much more."

"Well, let me ask you this. If he came and apologized, if he asked for you back . . ." Ryland pauses. "Would you take him back?"

498

"Would you?" Maggie asks, whipping her head around to look at me.

My heart immediately screams yes because I love him. I miss him. I want to hold him and help him through his pain.

But my head . . . that's a different story. My head is protecting my heart, telling me I shouldn't give him a second chance because he hurt me so bad the first time.

"I don't know," I say, biting on the corner of my lip. "I really don't know."

HAYES

RUBEN: *It's been taken care of.*

Hayes: *Everything?*

Ruben: *Everything. Including the restraining order.*

I stare up at the ceiling where I've been looking for what feels like the past hour.

Everything is done.

I don't need to worry about my mom coming back, about Matt extorting me . . . yet I feel nothing.

I don't feel relief.

I don't feel satisfaction.

I just feel . . . empty.

But that's what happens, right? Pushing the one good thing out of your life tends to make you feel absolutely nothing. You just turn numb.

That's where I'm at.

Numb.

Not a fucking thought, emotion, or pinch of life passing through me.

I set my phone down on the coffee table and consider

reaching for my guitar, but there's no use. I know I'll just strum the same chords over and over again, the chords that remind me of Hattie, of the song I wrote about her.

And it's not like I'm on a deadline anymore.

Not like I need to come up with something new to appease others.

I can really do what's best for me . . .

So how come I'm not doing that?

How come I'm not figuring out a way to make me feel again?

Because the one thing, the one person that made me feel, I broke her.

She doesn't want me back. I know that to be the truth.

The sound of a car pulling into the driveway attracts my attention. I lift on the couch just in time to see Ryland walk up to the house, his head bent down, a purposeful stride to his every step.

What the hell is he doing here?

A strong knock echoes through the more than empty home, and I make my way from the couch to the front door.

When I open it, he doesn't bother saying hi. He just welcomes himself in and heads right to the couch where he takes a seat.

Okay.

I shut the door behind him and follow him into the living room, where I say, "Uh . . . want a drink or something?"

"No." He presses his hands to his legs, looking jittery. "Take a seat."

Confused, I sit, and when his eyes level with mine, he says, "I'm sorry."

Okay, was not expecting that.

Could I see him gearing up to punch my face in? Yup.

Maybe lecture me on how I'm such a dick for hurting his sister? Absolutely.

But an apology? No, not even for a second would I have believed that coming out of his mouth.

"For what?" I ask.

"For treating you the way your parents treated you."

Oh . . . fuck . . .

"Ryland, that's not—"

"Don't give me any excuses," he says, looking more serious than ever. "I owe you this." He takes a deep breath and says, "You deserved so much more than my accusations. You deserved more than *my* betrayal. I abandoned you. You deserved my trust, my friendship, and yet, I turned my back on you. That was shitty of me, and the more I think about it, the more I know . . . you wouldn't have done that to me. You would never have betrayed me because your loyalty is one of your best qualities. It's why we became friends in the first place . . . when you defended me on the playground from Lyonel Redbach. You stuck by my side ever since, and the minute I thought you wronged me, I pushed you to the side." He shakes his head. "It's inexcusable, and I'm sorry."

"You were in a shit headspace," I say.

"Don't excuse me."

"But it's true." I don't let up. "I should have followed up with you, I should have talked to you when you cooled down, but I acted like a stubborn ass—"

"You acted like someone who'd already lost his trust in the people supposed to love you and be there for you. There's no excuse, Hayes. I fucked up and I'm sorry."

Uncomfortable, I smooth down my jeans with my palms and say, "Well, water under the bridge."

"No, it's not."

"What do you mean?" I ask.

"It means that we need to fix this."

"What more is there to fix?" I pull on my hat. "You want to be texting friends now?"

He chuckles and shakes his head. "I mean with Hattie."

Oh.

Should have known he was here for that.

"Listen—"

"No, you listen," Ryland says, his voice turning darker. "I told you not to fucking hurt her, didn't I?" I nod. "And you did."

"I'm—"

"I'm not finished," he says. "The only reason you're not tasting my fist right now is because I know you actually didn't want to push Hattie away, but you did it as a defense mechanism."

"She could do so much better," I say, dropping my shoulders.

"That's where you're wrong." His eyes ring sincere as he says, "I've seen her at her happiest and I've seen her at her worst, and when I say she was extremely happy with you, I mean it. There was pure joy in her eyes during a dark time. This past week, watching that darkness creep back in, it's killed me, because I know this could be avoided. This heart-break, Hayes, it could be avoided."

I shake my head. "I'm . . . I'm not the kind of man who's strong enough for her." I grip the back of my neck and whisper, "I'm scared."

"I know you are. Your actions wreak of being scared. But pushing the people away who matter most to you, that will only bring you loneliness and fuck, Hayes, don't you want to be happy? Don't you want to get over this fucking hill you've been climbing for how many goddamn years? Isn't it time to stop running from the hurt of the past, accept that it happened, and move on? You're better than this, you deserve better than this, and you should really give yourself the chance to actually be happy."

I sigh, leaning back on the couch. "She hates me."

"She doesn't," he replies. "She might be hurt, but trust me when I say, she doesn't hate you. She actually loves you."

"She does?" I ask. "After everything I said?"

Ryland nods. "She does. And I'm going to tell you right now, if you don't go after her and make this right, you're going to have to deal with me. I might have let you slide the first time, not the second."

I glance to the side. The thought of going up to Hattie and telling her how much I love her, how fucking sorry I am is very overwhelming.

"I'm . . . I'm not in the right headspace."

"Because you won't allow yourself to be in the right head-space." Ryland leans closer, and he knocks my knee with his hand. "You're worth it, dude. And I'm not just saying that because I don't want to see my sister hurting. If I thought you'd fuck her over in the long run, I wouldn't be here right now. I'd be helping her move on. But seeing you two together, it's special. And look at me." He pauses for our eyes to meet. "Don't you want to be happy? After all of the shit you've been through, don't you want to sit in this life surrounded by joy? Tell me the last time you felt that before Hattie?"

I give it some deep thought because I wasn't happy even at the highest points of my career. I had no one to share it with besides Gran and Abel, but even at that, I didn't share that much. I didn't come home, knowing Ryland was here. I didn't talk with my mom, knowing what she'd ask of me. So I isolated myself, even on the biggest days of my life . . . I isolated. So the last time I was truly happy . . .

"When it was you, me, and Abel hanging out," I say. "A band of brothers. Those were my best days. Those were the days that mattered to me."

Ryland slowly nods. "Then let's make it happen."

"What do you mean?"

Ryland pulls out his phone and hands it to me. "Add yourself. I think we're texting friends now."

A large laugh pops out of me as I shake my head. "Don't be a douche."

He laughs too. "I'm serious, man. I want things the way they were too. I miss talking to you. I miss our friendship. I have for a long time, but I was just too fucking stubborn to admit it."

"And you're admitting it now because you've been listening to those records I left you, haven't you?"

He smirks. "*The Reason,* man, that song . . . fuck, it's catchy."

I smile. "So I've been told." I sigh and push my hand through my hair. "She really loves me?"

"She does."

"After everything I did?"

"Yup." He must see me waver because he adds, "And honestly, dude, fuck your dad, fuck your mom, fuck the Ryland who didn't trust you. That shit is in the past. Let it stay there, and let yourself be happy."

I want to be happy.

Fuck do I want that more than anything, and the happiest I've ever been was with Hattie in my life. Am I scared? More than ever.

I've been fucked over far too many times to ever really trust someone again, but is that how I want to live my life? No. I realized that quickly the moment I pushed Hattie away. I lost stability in my life. I lost love. I lost the ability to just feel something, anything. Returning to a numb state isn't how I want to live this life I've been granted. I want to feel something deep in my bones. I've been living in this immobilized state for so long that the moment Hattie entered, I actually felt like she kickstarted my heart again. I felt warm, like my blood was pumping for the first time in years.

And I want that.

Don't you want to get over this fucking hill you've been climbing for how many goddamn years? Isn't it time to stop running from the hurt of the past, accept that it happened, and move on?

I want that. I want all of that.

504

Forever.

"I want to be happy," I say.

"Good." He stands. "Then let's go make you happy." I lift a brow at him, and he rolls his eyes. "I mean, let's go get Hattie."

"Right now?"

He tugs on my arm, making me stand. "Right now." He pushes me toward the door. "I might have had patience with you about hurting my sister, but I'm not going to let you make her wait any longer. Let's go."

⊏⊐

HATTIE

"WE SHOULDN'T HAVE EATEN three donuts yesterday," Maggie says as we rock on the farmhouse's porch. "Because then we could have at least had some today."

"You should have gotten two dozen, knowing that we'd each have three, Mac would have one, and Ryland and Aubree would have demolished the rest."

"It was really just poor judgment on my end."

"It was."

She tilts her head to the side. "Are you feeling better?"

"Sort of," I answer. "I mean, I'm not crying into a pillow, so that's progress."

"But you still ache for him?"

"Unfortunately."

"What if you went over to his place and maybe tried to talk to him?" Maggie asks.

"And risk getting hurt again?" I shake my head. "He doesn't want me."

"The finger graze tells me differently."

MEGHAN QUINN

I pull my legs into my chest. "I thought you were thinking he was an asshole, and we weren't supposed to like him at all."

In all seriousness, she looks at me and says, "I want you happy. I could go either way. I can love him because you love him, or I can hate him because he hurt you. I'm here for you, so you take the lead, and I'll follow."

I rest my chin on my arms and say, "You're a really good friend, Maggie. I don't know what I'd do without you."

"Remember that when I'm knee-deep in Speedos on my vacation."

"For your sake, I hope that you are."

From a distance, Ryland's truck heads down the driveway earlier than usual. Although I know that Mac is with Aubree at the store today for her after-preschool activity, something we all agreed would be good for her since she spent so much time there with Cassidy. Technically, I tried to go to the store today, but Aubree told me I needed to get my head on straight first, which I understood. I don't need to take over the store and fill my emptiness with work. It's not healthy. She's learned from experience.

And *I've* learned a lot too over the last few days. I've thought about Cassidy's words, read over her letters many times.

Fall in love. Fall out of love. And fall in love again.
Make mistakes.
Laugh about the tribulations.
Celebrate the triumphs.
And above all else, know that you are the most genuine, loving, intelligent human I know. You will do great things in this life, Hattie.

I have to believe her, because she knew me like no one else in this world. So I'm going to trust in those words. *I was her rock. Her person.*

And I'm going to do great things in this life.

Ryland's truck pulls in front of the house, and the minute I notice he's not alone, I feel all the hairs on the back of my neck stand to attention.

"What the hell is he doing?" I whisper just as Hayes steps out of the car.

"Oh dear God," Maggie says. "It's so hard to hate him when he looks like that."

"Maggie," I whisper yell at her.

"What?" she shrugs as if she didn't say the wrong thing. "It's true."

"Hey, Hattie," Hayes says, stepping up on the porch, his hands classically stuffed in his pockets. It's his signature position. "Think we could talk?"

I glance over at Ryland, who gently nods his head. What did my brother do?

"Uh . . . sure," I say.

Hayes nods toward the potato fields. "Come take a walk with me."

I stand from my chair and then look down at my feet. "I need shoes."

"I can wait."

"Okay, yeah," I say while robotically turning and heading toward the house. Thankfully, Maggie follows me inside.

We huddle toward the side where my shoes are located, and I whisper, "What the hell is he doing here?"

Whispering back, she says, "I think he's here to confess his undying love for you."

"You don't know that," I say as I pick up a shoe, but Maggie swipes it from my hand and gets down on her knees to put it on for me. "I can put my shoe on."

She shakes her head. "Not in this sort of distress. And why else would he be here?"

"I don't know," I say as I slip my foot in, and she ties it. "To fire me . . . we never really finalized job things. And I haven't reported to work in a while, so it could be a firing."

Maggie pauses and raises her brow at me in disagreement.

"Please, would your brother bring Hayes here so he could fire you?"

"Maybe . . ."

She swats at my leg. "Stop it. You know he wants to tell you sorry and that he loves you."

"What if he does? What if he says he wants me back? What do I say?"

She slips on my other shoe. "You have two choices. You can either kick him in the crotch and leave him in the potato fields, seeking vengeance for the way he hurt you. Or you could listen, understand, and give him another try." She stands after tying my shoe. "Kicking him in the crotch is a gut reaction to seek temporary satisfaction, but I think that forgiving him is a way to guarantee an amazing life. If he's your person, and he's come to make sure you end up together, take it. If you trust him, leap."

When I glance to the side, unsure, she grips my shoulders and forces me to look at her.

"You want him. Be happy. You have everything lining up. You have the shop, you have the closure, now get the guy."

I nibble on the corner of my lip as I wince. "I really love him."

"Then let him grovel to get you back." She kisses my cheek and then slaps me on the ass. "Go get him."

God, I love her.

I push through the screen door and walk up to Hayes.

"Ready?" he asks.

"Yeah," I answer, glancing at Ryland quickly who offers me a smile.

Together, Hayes and I walk out toward the potato fields, a weird place to have a conversation, but probably better than sending Ryland and Maggie away somewhere so I can have some privacy with Hayes.

We walk along the dirt, getting far enough away from the

house so we have a lot of privacy. After a few seconds of silence, Hayes says, "I fucked up, Hattie."

Hope springs in my chest because there's a distinct possibility he's about to apologize. I truly hope that's where he's going with this.

"What do you mean?" I ask.

"With you," he says, turning toward me. I turn as well, and I'm immediately captivated by his light, pleading eyes. "I pushed you away when I should have clung to you for support. I said horrible things to you when I should have been saying the opposite. And I displaced my horrible past on you when you deserved nothing but a happy future with me."

He reaches out and takes my hand. I let him link our fingers together. "Your birthday was perfect. Everything about it and then . . . my past came knocking on my door. It's not an excuse, but I want to be honest. My mom and Matt were trying to blackmail me, and it brought back all of these ugly feelings. It made me fall into a dark headspace, and instead of talking to you, I pushed you away so you didn't end up hurting me as well."

"I would never, Hayes."

"I know that. Fuck do I know that, Hattie. And I'm so sorry. I'm so fucking sorry that I said those things to you. That I pushed you away, that I made you feel any less than what you are. Because you're so fucking special. You breathed oxygen back into my lungs and made me feel when my entire body was living in a numb state. Because of you, I learned to love; I learned to fucking feel. My soul was woken up and nurtured . . . by you." Tears well up in my eyes, and he takes a step closer. "I love you, Hattie. You're the very reason I wake up in the morning with a smile on my face. You're the reason I'm able to strum a guitar with an outpouring of love flowing through me. You're the reason the colors around us are so vivid. You're the reason that when I look up at the stars, I feel more than grounded, I feel at peace. And you're the reason I'll spend the rest of my life making sure I make you just as happy as you make me."

"Hayes," I say softly, one single tear falling.

"I love you, baby. And I'm sorry. I'm so fucking sorry, and if you can't forgive me now, then I'll let you take as much time as you need, but I won't stop loving you. I never have, and I never will."

I swipe at my tear and grip his hand tighter. "I never stopped loving you. It's impossible. You have my heart, Hayes."

He wets his lips, taking another step forward. "Tell me you want to be with me. Please tell me you forgive me."

My hand lands on his chest, and I say, "I forgive you, Hayes, and I want to be with you."

Relief washes over his face, and he bends forward to kiss me, but I stop him with my hand to his mouth, confusing him.

When he pulls away, I point at him. "But if you ever, and I mean ever, treat me like that again, we're done. Got it?"

"It will never happen again. I swear. You're my life, Hattie." He presses his forehead to mine. "You're my every-thing. I need you more than I need air. I'm sorry, baby. I'm so fucking sorry."

I bring my hands up his chest to his shoulders as he grips me at the waist. "Thank you," I whisper just as I stand on my toes and press my lips to his. It's soft at first, our lips just brushing together, but then he grips me tighter, and the urgency to be closer takes over. His hand floats up to the back of my head, keeping me in place as his mouth rotates one way and then another.

"Fuck," he mutters between kisses. "I've missed you."

I wrap my arms around his neck, bringing him in tighter. "I've missed you."

Heart racing, I let my body feel his. I fall into his kiss, into his touch, into his desperation, and I soak up every second of it because this is what I want. This is what I need as well.

Him.

Hayes.

I need him in my life. And despite the loss of Cassidy, failing out of my semester, needing a job and finding it in the darkest of places, I truly believe there was a reason I hated this man, because deep down . . . I was supposed to love him.

Epilogue

HAYES

"Why do I feel like I could throw up?" Hattie asks as she walks into the kitchen wearing a pair of blue shorts and a white T-shirt with a small pocket on the breast. Her hair is pinned back so it's half up and half down, and she's wearing more mascara than usual. She looks so fucking good.

And she's all mine.

"I don't know, babe. It's not like you haven't worked there before."

"I know." She shakes her arms out by her side. "This is different, though. It will officially be mine."

"Which is a good thing." I walk up to her and pull her into my chest, tilting her chin up with my finger.

"I just want to make Cassidy proud."

"You will," I say as I press a kiss to her lips. "Now go get your shoes on. You don't want to be late for your first day. A minute late counts."

She rolls her eyes. "At least this time, I don't have to bring a demanding boss coffee in the morning."

I smirk as she takes off to grab her shoes.

After I begged for her forgiveness in the potato fields, I asked her to move in with me. It took her about three days to say yes, but once she did, I was there with my SUV, packing up her apartment and making sure there was no way she'd go back to that small apartment. She's mine now.

We've spent the past few days reconnecting, and when I say reconnecting, I mean spending every waking moment naked and talking . . . and fucking.

Maggie went back to San Francisco, but not before going into detail about how she was going to meet an island hottie who would bring her to—in her words—O town.

In a surprising and awkward moment, I asked Ryland if *he'd* ever consider dating Maggie. *She is attractive, and he thinks she's amusing.* It was an immediate no from him. And from Hattie. Maggie has a thriving business in San Francisco, and she's not going to give that up to move to a small town and be a stepmom. Not that that's a bad thing, but it's not in the cards with her. So . . . here's hoping she finds her island hottie.

Abel, Ryland, and I went out for burgers the other night at Provisions. We drank beer, talked about the good old days, and also talked about what was happening in our lives now. Currently, I'm the only one dating someone. Abel has no interest, and Ryland claimed he has no interest either, but I got the impression he'd be open to a grown-up to talk to other than his siblings and Abel. I could see him opening up to someone else, but it would have to be the right person.

Aubree . . . well, she's as grumpy as always, although with the store switching over to Hattie, I actually saw her smile for a moment. When I pointed it out, Hattie swatted at me, telling me never to point out an Aubree smile or else it might never return. I made that mental note, but seeing her relax for a moment was good.

And as for me and my music, well . . . I'm stockpiling some songs. I wrote one the other day with Mac in mind that I sang to Hattie. She was in tears by the end. But told me it was beautiful and that I needed to finish it as there was so much meaning behind a little girl still feeling her mother's spirit. I promised her I'd finish it, just needed to find the right special touches to make it perfect. I'm out of my label's contract, I just have to do a Christmas album for them to fulfill the contract needs, but any new music will be produced through me. And my mom, well, she's been served, and I won't be seeing her anytime soon unless she wants to go to jail. Matt was also told that he should remove his experience with me from his résumé because he wouldn't be getting any glowing reviews. Haven't heard from him and probably never will.

"Ready," Hattie says.

I smile at her, grab my keys from the side table, and then I help her into my SUV once we're in the garage. Since I don't have any schedule, I told her I'd drive her and pick her up for now, giving us that extra time together in the car.

I pull out of the garage with one hand on the steering wheel and the other on her leg as she adjusts the music to Blondie's *Heart of Glass*.

Together, we sing while we make our way to town.

Hattie has a terrible voice, but it's so fucking cute, listening to her try to hit the high notes and not giving a fuck that she's singing next to someone who makes millions a year singing for a living. One of the many reasons I love her.

When we reach the shop, I pull in front, only for her to see Aubree, Ryland, and Mac standing by the front door.

"What's this?" Hattie asks.

"They wanted to wish you good luck on your first day being the official shop owner."

"Oh my God, they're going to make me cry."

I squeeze her leg. "Don't worry, babe. I have tissues in my pocket."

I help her out of the car, holding her hand as we walk up toward the door.

Aubree holds out a key to her. "This belongs to you."

With a wobbly lip, Hattie takes the key and holds it to her chest. "Thank you."

Ryland steps up and hands her a box of donuts. "Cassidy would have brought these to you to celebrate, so I figured we could all have a donut in her honor this morning."

"I'd love that."

Mac steps up now and hands her a handmade card. "This is for you, Aunt Hattie." I take the box of donuts from her so she can open the card. Inside the folded paper is a stick figure drawing of a woman with wings and a halo over her head. "That's Mommy watching over you."

"Oh, MacKenzie." Hattie squats down to her level and pulls Mac into a hug, tears falling. "Thank you. This means so much to me."

She squeezes her hard and then lifts up.

She holds the picture out and says, "I'm going to frame this and put it next to the card that your mom made me for my birthday. I'll hang them by the register."

"Will you really?" Mac asks as Ryland pulls her into his side.

"Of course." She stands taller, glancing between her siblings. "Thank you for putting up with me as I navigated through all of this."

"No need to thank us. We're here for each other. We're in this together," Ryland says.

"And you'll do great things with the store," Aubree says.

"And *you'll* do great things with the farm."

She smiles softly. "Now that I can focus my attention on it, I know it will be better than ever."

On a deep breath, Hattie turns toward the store, and with her key in one hand and a picture of Cassidy in the other, she opens the door to The Almond Store.

I know this woman loves me and will always love me. But this place is her heart, her passion, and an equally important part of her future. Something grown from love. Something that brings joy to others. She's going to do great things with her life, and I'm going to walk beside her every step of the way. Because that's what love does. It stays. It protects. It fortifies.

Made in the USA
Monee, IL
01 August 2023

40296239R00292